A Bard's Folktale: Roaming Cadenza

Aramis Barron

To Mrs. Madeline Thompson, and every teacher whose lessons do not end at the classroom.

Table of Contents

Introduction

Remember the glory days? Back when you used to get all nervous when that special someone came rollin' around? Or when all eyes were on you 'cause you were just that awesome? Hell, remember the first time you ever fell in love? Just curious.

Anyway, hey, how's it going? Name's G. That's what the people I like call me, anyway. Figure if you're listening to me, must mean you've got some interest in a tale or two, huh? Or at least found yourself a little lost along the way. But it's all good; I think I can whip up a pretty good story for ya, but I'm telling you right now I ain't makin' any promises on a happy ending. This is a pretty long story, so I don't think I'll be able to get through all of it in one go. Let's call this the first part.

Anyway, this is a story that always comes to mind for me. It's the one about a few friends of mine who went on a road trip a while back, right after graduation. Seemed simple enough for sure. They were just out messing around trying to have some fun, but damn those dudes didn't have the slightest clue of the mess they'd be getting themselves into. Other than the usual sex, drugs, and rock & roll, anyway.

Well, don't let me ruin it for you. Let's get started.

1. Ace Deuce

"They always say, 'Today is the beginning of the rest of your life,' but I guess that doesn't really say much for everything I've done up until now, does it?"

– The Diary of Alma Grey

Ann Arbor, Michigan

Ann Arbor. Full of trees, as the name might suggest. A fine mix of city and nature, yet not wholly one or the other. The sun shone bright and cheery on the early June day, with its sky an ever-expanding blue. Only a few clouds drifted through the troposphere. Birds sang and chirped their choruses throughout the schoolyard, without much care or attention. The place itself was an average sort of school, made of red brick and a severe lack of parking for its students, though they always somehow managed to make room.

The arrival of the first buses indicated seven twenty in the morning, and only some of the students had started to arrive. Among them were Charisma Roberts and Alma Grey, the latter cruising elegantly in the passenger side of her best friend's ride. It was early for them to be there, but Charisma, more commonly referred to as Cris, was excited. They had already graduated, but many of the seniors still had work to finish up before their transcripts were complete. Cris had come to catch up and say goodbye to her friends.

She parked her car and waited for their friends to arrive as she looked over to Alma. Her best friend and partner in crime, Alma was only slightly shorter than Cris, but more bubbly with fuller curves and less inhibition. Alma was the older of the two, having just passed her eighteenth birthday. Her mid-length disarray of sun-warmed hair contrasted her naturally tanned skin—a testament to her fiery nature. Her luminous hazel eyes found no trouble in lighting up an entire room. Breaking out of her trance, Cris returned Alma's smile as they got out of the car.

Some of their friends walked by, and the two casually worked their way into the group. Unfortunately, there weren't a whole lot of places to walk to, and they would hardly want to be seen wandering around school this early in the day. They loitered about idly, but after a short while, headed into the building to find more entertaining things to do. Eventually the first bell of the day rang.

It was at about this same time that Konrad Lehane, stuck in traffic and enjoying the ska punk ballads of We Are the Union, was finally en route to school. Dirty blond hair with jaded green eyes, Kody's boyish figure may have done him justice for a man only seventeen years of age. He wore his medium build and average height like a snuggly fit suit.

He rested his head against the window and sighed, looking at the long stream of cars lined up on the bridge. He knew he wouldn't make it to his first class on time, but he was proud he could at least say he'd tried.

Even so, it made little difference since he still didn't have much hope of arriving before the end of his first class. The perfect excuse he'd been saving up all semester would go to waste if he didn't hurry. Whether it would be his fault, or a result of the parking situation, was another story. His train of thought moved along with the realization there's always second hour.

Reaching the school, he drove through the parking lot searching in vain for an open spot. His rusty station wagon eventually ended up down the road in a nearby townhouse community. He dragged his feet on his way back to school, still in no particular hurry.

With no real desire to get to class, He spent a good fifteen minutes enjoying the warm summer sun baking his skin as he strolled along. A well of regret rose in his stomach, knowing he'd soon be rid of a lovely morning in exchange for a bland, only mildly entertaining classroom. The injustices of the educational system were too great, denying children the simple beauty and freedoms of nature and youth so soon after spring blossomed.

He considered whether his opinion might be swayed by his hatred for sitting around in class when he could be outside with a notebook.

He arrived at the school building and trudged into his second hour only a few minutes late. Cris's expression caught his gaze. He did his best to avoid it. Her amber eyes called out to him, emitting a charismatic warmth, indicating for him to join her. Her smile drew him in. She brushed mahogany tresses aside as she waited for him, revealing light freckles decorating her lean, athletic frame. Though it was impossible to tell if she was aware of it, she always reminded him of textbook jailbait.

Kody knew if he took a seat next to her a scolding would be in order. With no other seat open, however, he began the march of shame. The cold stare of his classmates penetrated from all sides as their teacher stopped the lesson, watching him pretend he was invisible as he slinked over to his seat. He saw Mrs. T. pick up the phone on her desk, and all the students knew what was coming next.

"Hold the phone, Kody! Before we continue with the lesson, please share with us what delightful story you have for today." The teacher's voice caught him off guard.

"My mom didn't want me going to school today. I know, I know…I couldn't believe it either. I tried to convince her I needed to go, but it was no use. She was like, 'You need to quit being so mature and responsible all the time!' So I ended up having to wait until she left the house so I could sneak out. If you could do me a huge favor, Mrs. T., please don't tell her I snuck out to go to school today, on skip day of all days. She'd be very disappointed with me," he replied, smug and pleased he'd got a chance to use his excuse after all.

His teacher grinned.

"I won't say anything about it, Kody. Now if you could take a seat and get out your textbook, we're on page 273," she finished.

Kody relaxed in his seat and pulled out some books to appease his teacher.

"Busted," Cris whispered, smirking.

"Hey, you know how it works. Mr. Sunshine says good morning, I say good night," he quietly replied.

"Maybe if someone would actually wake up when his alarm went off, it wouldn't be such a problem," she chided him. "Today's the big day, and you still get up late? What, were you up all night messing around or something? You should've had your stuff packed days ago!"

"I'm not a girl, Cris; I don't have lots of bags of useless crap. I just didn't feel like getting up. I like my sleep, really."

"I didn't think guys needed beauty rest," she countered. "Did you at least call Glenn?"

"I haven't even had breakfast; I had to rush just to get out the door in time."

"How'd that work out for you?" she cut in, sarcastically.

"Oh, hey, look, we're learning! I'm gonna pay attention now, to someone that's glad I'm here!"

"Oh, really? Where?" He shot Cris a dirty look.

"I'm just messing with you. I'll call him after class and find you third hour, okay?" she teased as she turned back to the front.

Kody opened his notebook, leaning it against the desk to make it appear as though he were taking notes. Although Kody paying attention in class seemed suspicious, he appeared so diligent in his task even Cris gave him the benefit of a doubt. As the lecture drifted on, so did Kody's imagination as he jotted down the various verses that traversed his head.

"What should I write about today?" Kody thought aloud, trying to narrow his focus into something a little more cohesive. He began drawing in the margin of the page, hoping he might sketch out some kind of inspiration.

"Guess I'll just let it flow."

He began to write. He thought of the flowers he had seen on his walk to the school, and drew one in the margin. He kept staring.

The flowers, their shimmering leaves share the joyful dance of the green throughout the field, careless to the fact they are bound in chains of sand and stone. They drink bountifully of the water that hails them, and shudder; sharing anticipation as their oppressors flee. They remain undercover in their bed of soil, thick as thieves and grateful for their reprieve, swaying ever so gleefully in the moistened plot, enjoying their sweet refreshment under a light morning haze.

He continued to write.

Raining mist abash, crimson embers alight, their retreat no longer a safe haven. That which was no longer is, thus it feeds off the dispassionate green for a chance to breathe. The ash is unsettled and time has no place. As the flame burns away, the flight of its last waning wisp...

He finished.

"It always comes out so depressing—even now," he muttered to himself.

Cris overheard him. "Hm? Kody, are you okay? You seem a little down," she whispered.

"What?" Kody looked up. "Are you watching me?" He had a smug grin.

"Why, should I be?" Cris challenged him.

"You know, it's amazing. I'm hearing voices and yet I'm not Joan of Arc!" All eyes were drawn back to the front of the class, to the teacher who was now waiting politely for Cris.

"Sorry, we're good, Mrs. T.!" Cris's cheeks turned red.

"I hope so," Mrs. T. said. "I realize you all have taken your finals already, but there is still plenty to learn. Life in itself is a lesson." Mrs. T. continued on, shooting a kind but authoritative glance in Cris's direction.

"You got it!"

Cris put on her award-winning smile to ensure the incident was quickly forgotten. Kody shuffled through his notebook, pretending to find some reference materials.

"Oh, no, mister. You aren't getting out of it that easy." Cris was onto him.

"What? I just don't really get all these literary devices," he responded, trying to sound convincing.

"You seem to have a lot of notes for someone who doesn't understand them," she glanced at his notebook.

"There's a difference between taking notes and understanding them."

"Really? Can I see them then? Maybe I can help you out."

"I don't think you'd want to, it's just a bunch of scribbling. Mostly bored doodles, really."

"Then you wouldn't mind, right?" she pressed on.

"I guess not."

He reluctantly slid the notebook to the side of the desk, watching her pick it up. He managed to control his nerves enough to keep pretending to focus on the lecture. That is, until he caught a glimpse of Alma looking over Cris's shoulder.

As he not so subtly watched them, he could see the look of surprise on Cris's face as Alma whispered to her, but was relieved by the sound of the bell ringing out his reprieve.

"Hey, look at that! Class went by fast today! Gotta hurry to third hour! Trying out this new thing where I get to class early, by which I mean on time, so let me know how it goes with Glenn!" Kody rushed out of the room.

"He's a little stranger than usual today, don'tcha think?" Alma inquired.

Cris nodded, still holding his notebook as they both headed out of the classroom.

"Goodbye, Charisma! Goodbye, Alma! Both of you have a wonderful day!" Mrs. T. called out to them as they left.

"Bye, Mrs. T."

"See ya later!"

Mrs. T. watched them go as she prepared for her next class. They continued down the hall.

"So, it's really over between you two, huh?" Cris turned her head to Alma as they walked.

"Yeah, let's just say it wasn't working for me," Alma said.

"How come? It seemed like you two were doing pretty well."

"Eh…I don't really want to talk about it. Hey, that Kody's notebook?" Alma noticed Cris was carrying it.

"Yeah, he rushed off so fast I didn't have a chance to give it back to him."

"Huh…hey, can I see it?"

"Sure."

Cris handed her the notebook. Alma looked it over, seemingly unaware Cris had stopped to wait for her.

"Hey, I gotta get off to class, but I'll make sure I get this back to him!" Alma called out as she headed off down the hallway.

"Alm, wait! We have the same third hour!" Cris shouted, trying to stop her, but she was already gone.

Cris continued down the adjoining hallway, debating whether she should attend her third hour, considering her grades were already set. Most of the seniors who were there attended only because their parents made them go, or because they honestly had nothing better to do. For her, all she wanted was to see her friends one last time before summer. The more she thought about it, though, the more she found she had already seen the few people she really wanted to.

She headed out to the practice building, behind the main body of the school. She sometimes passed her mornings there since classes weren't held in the building until after lunch. She checked the back door, knowing it would be open because the lock was busted and the school faculty was simply too lazy or cheap to fix it. As she entered, she found the normally occupied auditorium empty. Usually there was at least a slacker or two catching a good nap. She had also walked in on couples on more than one occasion.

She pulled the door shut behind her as she wandered around backstage. She loved playing around behind the curtains, pretending that maybe she could be an actress, or a rare well-behaved teen idol of some sort. Once, she had imagined herself a princess, and that she was wandering through a dark maze looking for her prince. Unfortunately, all she had found was two girls getting high, which quickly brought her back to reality.

Still, she loved hanging out on the stage. She had grown accustomed to it when she tried acting in the theater club, even though the club itself didn't suit her. Singing for her own personal amusement was more her style.

Cris made her way through the heavy curtains, coming up to the front of the stage looking out into an empty auditorium. She paced back and forth, trying to determine where the center was, and found what she thought to be a good approximation of it. She looked down to see a black X marked by electrical tape and remembered that this was the spot. She prepared herself by clearing her throat as she tried to think of a song to sing. She had a select few she always hummed to herself, but this was a golden opportunity and she didn't want to waste it.

She pulled out her small mp3 player and shuffled through some songs until she found one she could work with. She grabbed a small bottle of water out of her bag and took a sip. She did a little curtsey and took a deep breath into her diaphragm as she prepared to perform.

She started out slowly, singing the first few lines from the Magnetic Fields' "Book of Love" until the sound of clapping from the balcony of the auditorium startled her.

"Lovely performance, pet, truly inspiring." Cris heard a confident, somewhat accented male voice as she noticed a man applauding from the balcony.

"Who's up there?" Cris was more embarrassed than alarmed.

"Just me. A bit surprising, I must say; I never would've expected something like that from you. I suppose it makes sense, though. The little sister of Emma Roberts has a voice on her after all."

"Daron?"

8

"Of course."

"What're you doing here?"

"Waitin' on me, probably."

Cris recognized Geroge as he walked out from behind the curtain, guitar case slung across his back. He stood larger, both wider and taller than her, scruffy dark hair covering his scruffy dark face.

"Geroge? Oh, are the Bards rehearsing?"

"Nah. Well, sorta. But since dickhead and Tits McGee are MIA, we're just chillin'. Keep goin', though, sounds like you're puttin' on a better show than we do."

"You weren't supposed to hear that." Cris blushed.

"Damn. Guess we should consider ourselves lucky, eh, D?"

"Suppose we should, G." Daron made himself comfortable on the balcony.

"Guess I'm not gonna convince you to join the band anytime soon, huh princess? We could definitely use a female lead. The Bards could work a whole new sound."

"Sorry, I'm not really interested. What about Jence though?"

"Jeany? Girl can rock a keyboard in ways I can't even understand, I'll give her that. But she's a bit lacking in the vocal talent department."

"Plus…she isn't exactly eye candy," Daron contributed.

"Hey, D., a little respect. Besides, that girl has far more impressive skills than you could ever dream of." Geroge, now redirecting his attention to Cris, said, "Anyway, can I interest you in some tickets to tonight's show?"

"I actually have other plans. Thanks for offering, though."

Cris slowly started making her way offstage as she decided she had worn out her unanticipated welcome.

"Gotcha. Well, if you change your mind, let us know. We're puttin' on a special show tonight. You're more than welcome. We'll hook you up Bard style." Geroge threw on his heart-melting smile as Cris made her way out.

"Thanks, I'll remember that. See you guys and good luck with the show!" Cris grabbed her bag and slipped out the back, the same way she came in.

"Damn, man, that's one hot *chica*, no?" Geroge took center stage, positioning himself in various places, getting a feel for the environment while he waited for Daron to make his way down.

"I wouldn't say no."

"Dude, you wouldn't say no to her cardboard cutout."

"No, I wouldn't. But neither would you."

"I'd consider it. If nothing else, a man should at least pretend to have principles in the absence of actual character. Might help him develop one someday, ya' know?"

"Could be. Although I do have standards. I just wouldn't say no to Charisma Roberts."

"Not many men alive would, my friend, not many men would." Geroge patted Daron on the back as he finally arrived on the stage, chuckling to himself and heading back outside to haul in some more equipment.

* * *

Alma had hit the jackpot and wasn't going to squander such a rich opportunity. She wasn't interested in what Kody was doing—much—but as long she had his notebook she may as well take a glimpse of what was going on inside. Her conscience tingled just a little, but such opportunities were rare. It'd be a shame to let it go to waste. She found her way inside a nearby bathroom and camped out in one of the stalls.

She thumbed through the notebook, finding a lot of unimpressive doodles and drawings. Various quotes and quirky expressions lay sprawled across the pages. She found a sketch of some kind of small animal, and couldn't figure out what it was supposed to be. There was a caption that read Combustible Duck, but maybe she'd be better off not trying to figure it out.

"Let's see, what do we have here? 'He gave us light first and the sun two days later. God: the bad play-write – J. Joyce.' What is this?"

Alma wasn't sure what kind of stuff Kody was writing down or why, but at the very least she was determined to find out if he wrote anything about her. After all, it wasn't snooping since she was trying to understand him better, doing him a favor, really. Leafing through the pages, she eventually found something of interest. She thumbed across a passage entitled "My Fox". "I'm tired of paying for yesterday," it read.

So I'll tell you what. Meet me by the pier tonight. If you're still interested, then we'll work it out. Tonight, I'm gonna swim away. The only question remaining is will I find you on that distant shore when I arrive? Don't come just to compliment me, or to see if I made it. Come only if you plan on staying. This will be my new home. If you are not my fox, then you are my snake. Though both do a bit of mercy.

As she finished reading, a small tightness grew in Alma's chest. Was it anger or compassion? It didn't matter. She figured he'd been fine; after all, he seemed okay in class. "So do I…" she thought as she closed the book. She sat for a moment, playing with the hem of her dress. Blowing hair out of her face, she needed to figure out a good way to blow off some steam. She stuffed the notebook in her bag and pulled out her phone, sending a text message to a friend as she started heading toward the gym.

She opened the stall door and looked herself over in the mirror. She had only a light coat of makeup on and wore a black floral dress with a button-up top that was a little tight around the chest. Her blue jeans showed just underneath the hemline. She unbuttoned the top two buttons of her dress, giving herself a little more to work with without exposing too much. She took her time walking to the gym, knowing that her "friend" would already be waiting.

She arrived at the gym with no one in sight. She stopped for a moment to watch a basketball game that looked like it had just started, debating whether she should stay for that instead. She checked out some of the guys practicing, recognizing a few, and licked her lips. This could be a worthwhile endeavor, with very lucrative prospects. She started getting into the game and was ready to walk in when she heard her name coming from one of the empty side hallways. She decided to check it out.

"Hey, Alms. How's it goin', sweet thing?" She instantly realized who it was.

"Hey, Thad, how've you been?"

"Busy as always. Sam's been riding my ass hard the last few days."

"That literally?" she smirked.

"I wish. She wants to make summer plans and all this shit, but I ain't tryin' to hear that. I just wanna chill for a bit."

"Yeah, I know what you mean. So you and Sam still together?"

"Man, I don't even know anymore."

Alma tilted her head, about as convinced as Thad was convincing.

"Huh, I hope that works out for you."

"What about you and that weird emo poet kid?"

"Kody? He's not weird or anything. We just weren't really seeing eye to eye, I guess."

"Huh, that's a shame. I know how hard that can be."

"Do you now?" Alma's lips perched back.

"I surely do."

"Funny, 'cause you don't seem to be looking at my eyes." She called him out.

"So? Can I help it if a hot young thing is standing right in front of me, looking all luscious?"

"I'm luscious now, huh?"

"Like an apple."

"Did you just call me an apple?" She cocked an eyebrow.

Thaddeus leaned in to kiss her. She didn't expect it, but she wasn't all together surprised.

"Hey, what about Sam?" she said, stopping him.

"What about Sam?"

He leaned in once again, this time pinning her against the wall. She didn't resist. He kissed her, and she found herself kissed—a small amount of comfort and relief in it. She broke it off.

"Thaddeus, I don't know about this…"

"What's there to know? Nothing we ain't done before."

"I know, but still. . . I just. . ."

"Oh. . . I gotcha. Don't like a crowd."

Thaddeus grabbed her hand and led her down the hall into one of the open offices as they made their way inside.

"Thad, this isn't what I meant."

"Funny, 'cause you texted me. And we both know what that means. 'Sides, I don't see you lookin' to leave. Or maybe you wish it was your little poet boy?"

She looked away.

"Don't worry, sweet cheeks, it's just like ridin' a bike. A very fine, well-tuned bike."

She took a deep breath. There might be more than a little truth in his words. But she had left *him*, and decided to be here now. The awkward combination of shame and comforting familiarity both came creeping back along her spine. She couldn't tell which was the stronger. Thad paid little attention to her as his hands roamed freely. The tension built as she searched for an answer. Her body took over.

"Close the door." She kept quiet.

She thought briefly that maybe she should do something different, but it was her choices that had brought her this far, and she had always made it through. She was abandoned to circumstance, a victim of fate. Whatever happened to her wasn't her fault—it was just another page in the story of her days. She was just along for the ride.

2. Ill-Lit

"Even when he smiled, Glenn always seemed sad. They say there just isn't any pleasing some people, but I honestly don't believe that. I think everyone is capable of happiness, and I aim to prove it."

– The Journal of Charisma Roberts

"Y-yet another dream; will I ever be rid of t-these?" Glenn Redcliffe lay there for a moment, staring at the ceiling. It was only when he sat up in his bed that he realized he was covered in sweat.

"This c-certainly can't be good…"

He pondered his options before crawling out of bed and looking out the window. The light hurt his eyes. He stepped away from the curtains, letting them conceal the window and shroud the room in darkness once more. He could barely make out the shapes of the quietly messy room as he stumbled about. He found his way into the living room and stood there for a moment, scratching his head. He glanced around: shirts lying on the floor, nearly all long sleeves; the sink filled with dishes; and his small kitchen table cluttered with books and other assorted papers. He shrugged.

Every window remained draped with heavy curtains, preventing any more than small rays of light from shining through. He lived alone in a small apartment, leaving ample room for his large bookshelves and scattered notes. A dingy t-shirt hung off his lanky frame, barely concealing the patches decorating his old cargo pants. His shaggy, mud colored hair resembled the dim echoes reverberating behind his glasses as he brushed loose strands aside. Today was his twenty-third birthday and he sat at home, alone as usual.

He flicked on a dim light in the ill-lit living room. There was a bowl on the counter, filled with half-eaten dry cereal. Glenn opened the refrigerator and pulled out a cold gallon of milk only slightly past its expiration date. He looked it over and took a strong whiff. He poured it into the bowl anyway and placed the nearly empty carton back into its specifically designated location within the even emptier fridge.

The apartment was silent, a place so bereft of sound he could hear the distinct fizz of milk interacting with cereal. He sat down at the disorganized table, brushing aside a spot for his breakfast, carelessly knocking several objects onto the floor. Maybe he should've been careful–perhaps there might've been something important amid all of that clutter, but he doubted it. He ate, ignoring insomnia's weary grasp on his body. He adjusted his glasses and cleaned the crusties from his eyes.

"If this k-keeps up, I'm never g-going to get any better." He leaned back in his chair, tilting it off the ground as his thoughts drifted to more relevant matters.

"What am I d-doing getting involved with a bunch of c-children?" he mumbled aloud.

He began to doze off as he ate. His head bobbed forward, the momentum bringing his chair back down to ground as he caught himself just before hitting the table. An annoying ringing sound chirped out from amid the mess. Half-startled and half-asleep, he regained his posture and began searching for the phone. He found his way to the floor and scrambled through the various medication bottles and papers until he finally found the receiver. He pressed a few different buttons until he heard it connect.

"Mm…h-hello?" he spoke into the phone, holding back a yawn.

"Glenn? Hey. How are you?" a female voice replied, leaving him mystified until he recognized who it was.

"Oh…Charisma! What's the matter?" he woke up a little.

"Nothing, I'm fine. Just checking up on you."

"Me? I'm the same, f-fine, just a bit t-tired is all." Glenn's stutter became more pronounced.

"Are you sure?"

"Yes…so what did you n-need?"

"I wanted to see if you needed help packing. I got all my stuff done earlier, so I figured maybe you could use some help."

"Yes…I've, uh…b-been working on that." The uncertain wavering in his voice betrayed him.

"I figured as much." Cris's dry sarcasm came through clearly. "So once Kody and I get our stuff together, we'll come over and help you pack. Just sort out what you need, and we'll take care of the rest, okay?"

"Are you sure? S-seems like a lot of work for both of you to d-do on my behalf."

"Yeah, it's fine."

"All right…thank you, C-Charisma."

"Glenn, relax. And I've told you a hundred times already…call me Cris, okay? Cris."

"R-right. Sorry, I've some business to attend to before you both arrive. B-besides, aren't you in school? You'll be late for class."

"Heh…it's no big deal. It's just math."

"If you insist. In any case, I'll talk to you later Charisma—Er…C-Cris. Goodbye."

"Bye Gle—"

He hung up before she had a chance to finish.

Glenn set the phone down and remained on the floor a while longer. The world started feeling lighter, less connected. He clutched his head as he felt like the room was beginning to spin. Unwelcomed as this sensation was, it was not unfamiliar. He doubled over in pain. He started taking slow, deep breaths, trying to calm himself.

He held his sides, gradually recovering, though not fully recomposing himself. Reality seemed less…real; he stared blankly at the phone, almost as if he expected it to ring again with pleasant news, or at least something that interested him. He was convinced it was bound to happen, though he knew this to be a lie. It was always a lie.

He remained focused on the phone when he got that funny all-too-familiar feeling in his belly right before he passed gas. He jumped, scaring himself, though he scarcely even noticed.

He sighed, deceived by the phone yet again. He staggered, making his way back to the table and eating a few bites of his cereal. Having lost his appetite, he stood there in place, noticing little, with even less passing through his mind.

He felt a small gag in his throat and doubled over once again, now hunched over on the ground as the contents of his stomach liberated and revealed themselves. He was no longer bothered by this and continued to heave, waiting for this session to end. Eventually, there was nothing left, and he was able to breathe.

He looked down in wonder at the unamusing creation he had brought forth. He recognized small bits of cereal and little else. The wretched stench began to foul the stagnant air, and only the light breeze of a fan behind him recirculating the vile odor in the background made any difference.

He grabbed some of the papers resting on the ground next to him and used them to clean up what he could of his mess. He trashed the papers and scrubbed the carpet with a washcloth, making sure to spray plenty of air freshener and being grateful for the fact that his landlord's horrible taste in rug colors actually happened to coincide with the former contents of his stomach's. Though he tried for several minutes, his best effort proved useless, and he wandered back toward his bedroom.

He searched in the dark for his nightstand and reached for some pills. It didn't matter to him which they were, though he knew by shape and texture exactly which ones he had grabbed. He fumbled around a bit more and found a glass of water from the night before. He swallowed the pills half-heartedly while taking another sip from the glass, before collapsing onto his bed.

He hated staring at the ceiling. It was too dark to accurately define anything, yet he was certain he could always make out the image of the monsters lining it. He could make out an eye here, claws there, and of course, always the teeth. Always the teeth. He could barely tell if he was watching them, or if they were watching him.

He sometimes imagined that he was in the ceiling, observing a pitiable man feigning his way through life, toward death. He wondered why he dragged on, either indecisive or watching this grotesque display; why he didn't take initiative and expedite the process or end it altogether he had no idea. He had no respect for such a false character in either case.

His thoughts became less coherent while his rationale depreciated into simple amusements and pleasures at any inane notion still cogent within him. The medication began to kick in. Drowsiness overcame him, and he finally began falling into what he was sure would be a restless sleep.

3. Cinematic Buffet

"You only live once, right? Guess there's no way to know that for sure, but it's a good excuse to do whatever the hell I want before I get too old to do it."

– The Notebook of Kody Lehane

Cris sat in the bleachers outside, enjoying the sunny pre-afternoon. She still had a bit of time to kill until nightfall. The longer she sat there, watching geese roam around on the soccer field, the more agitated she became; something was off, and she couldn't let it go. She was certain that something greater was going on, that both Kody and Glenn were keeping something from her. They didn't seem like themselves, and she was determined to find out what was going on.

Despite that, it was too pretty a day to let petty issues distract her from what she needed to accomplish. She got up, watching the wayward birds waddle off as she left and made her way toward the parking lot. She strode across the paved blacktop of the road when she recognized her partner in crime waiting by their getaway mobile.

"So...what'cha thinkin' about?" Alma asked, donning unfashionably large shades.

"Other than how much those look like my missing pair of sunglasses?" Alma made her innocent pouty face. "Nothing..." Cris looked away.

"Cris."

"Just not really up for talking about it right now."

"Mm, I can understand that. Well, how about Italia's? We haven't had pasta for lunch in a while!"

"That's kinda pricy for lunch, isn't it?"

"This is the last time we'll get to go out to lunch instead of going to fourth hour, and you're worried about something like that?"

"Good point."

They both got into Cris's convertible and put the car's top down.

"No matter how many times I'm in this car, I never get tired of this! Even if it is a little messy," Alma explained, brushing her hair back.

"Yeah, but what about when it starts raining?" Cris replied.

"Pessimist! It's still cool, even then! It's like a free roaming shower!" Alma retorted.

"Complete with environmentally friendly sewage water."

"Pessimist!"

They left the school, and headed downtown. Unfortunately, they left at the wrong time of day and got stuck in the lunch-rush traffic.

"Great timing, Cris," Alma complained.

"Now who's the bitter one?"

"Tantalizing me with thoughts of special non-school lunch, only to make me sit around and wait all day," Alma pouted.

"You were the one who was waiting outside before I even thought of going.

Alma smirked as she turned up the radio, catching part of Third Eye Blind's "Bonfire."

"I love this song! Kody and I used to listen to it all the time!"

"That reminds me," Cris started in, "did you give Kody his notebook back?"

Alma hesitated, dancing along with the song before she replied. "It's taken care of."

"Good. The last thing we need is for that to go missing. Have you noticed Kody acting…I don't know…weird at all lately?"

"Not really, but we don't talk or hang out all that much anymore."

"What's the deal with you two anyway? You didn't even tell me you two broke up. I thought it was just a fight."

Alma stopped dancing as the song ended. She gazed along the side of the road, taking a moment before she turned back to Cris. She shrugged.

"You have to give me more than that Alm. Was he one of those needy guys who couldn't stand being away from his girlfriend for more than five minutes or something?"

"Something like that, I guess."

"Hm. Do you think it was one of those relationships where he cared about you more than you cared about him?"

Alma raised an eyebrow as she glanced at Cris.

"Cris, don't tell me what I think it is…you like him, don'tcha?" Alma turned a devious grin as she cornered Cris.

"Kody? Not so much. I'm just curious. I mean, you two had such a good thing going and all, and then out of nowhere it just kind of stopped. It doesn't really add up."

"Uh huh." Alma giggled, sticking her tongue out. "He probably did care more about me than I did him. Don't get me wrong: I really liked him and all, but I could go more than twenty minutes without seeing him, ya know? I dunno if he could've done the same."

"Yeah. Sounds horrible…" Cris trailed off.

"This again? Sweetie, you'll get a decent boyfriend someday. Promise!" Alma patted her on the shoulder.

"I know. It's just the only reason guys ever like me is because of how I look."

Alma cocked an eyebrow. "What's wrong with that? It just means you have your pick of the guys! I mean damn, look at you! If I had your body— oooh the things I could do!"

Cris chuckled to herself.

"Umm…thanks, I think. But it'd be nice to meet a decent guy who actually cared about me for who I am—because I'm me. Like someone who thinks looks are just an extra perk or something. Do you think there's a guy like that?"

"Probably, somewhere. Like in a monastery or something. I hear monks are very devout."

"I'm serious, Alm!"

"I know, I know…you'll find your prince charming soon enough. Until then, we're both single! I say we live it up and make the best of it." Alma wore a huge grin as blonde tresses fell over her sunglasses.

"Maybe you're right."

"Of course I'm right! But forget about that, it's food time!" Alma started getting excited.

Almost as if the vehicles were attuned to Alma's whim, the road cleared up, and they made it to Italia's, home of the legendary Super Pasta Bowl. Rumor had it that if a customer could finish an entire bowl, they'd win a fantastic prize. No one knew what this prize was, but that only added a sense of mystery to an already great legend. Cris and Alma had been no match for this challenge before, but it didn't mean they couldn't try.

Cris parked the car while Alma took off her sunglasses, and they headed into the restaurant, catching the faint aroma of garlic bread sticks in the air as they passed through the door.

As soon as they entered, they noticed the vast array of seats available. They figured the place being mildly empty was due to it being the middle of the day and not the lack of excellent food choices.

"Ooh, let's get the booth in the back! I really like that one." Alma chimed in.

They asked the waiter to seat them in the back, and he was more than happy to oblige.

"Oh, crap…what do I want?" Alma became wide-eyed at all the food options that lie before her. Cris looked up at her, and they locked eyes.

"Shall we?" Cris's lips contorted into a devilish smile.

"I don't think we dare…do we?" Alma grinned her mischievous grin, following Cris's lead.

"Oh, we dare!"

Alma's quickly growing fervor alarmed a nearby waiter, who immediately brought her a glass of water and some bread sticks.

"Are you alrigh—" the waiter tried to be attentive.

"We want the legendary Super Pasta Bowl!" Alma exclaimed, slamming her fists on the table and shaking some of the silverware.

"You know that the promotion doesn't count if you girls split it right?"

"Screw the promotion, we just want the pasta!" Alma ordered.

"Gotcha. I'll go put in the order now."

With that, the waiter headed to the kitchen. He stopped for a moment, glancing back, before continuing.

The girls chowed down on bread sticks while looking around the restaurant. There were many miscellaneous decorations, mostly of European origin. Most of them appeared to be Italian, but there were things that hinted of having either a French or Germanic origin. Cris noted that their waiter's name was Luigi—as it had read on his nametag—and watched as Alma couldn't help but giggle.

"So, what do you think of Luigi?" Alma asked.

"What? Alm, you're kidding, right?" Cris partially turned her head to look him over before quickly looking back.

"He was totally checking you out!"

"Me? I thought he was looking at you."

"He probably was. I bet he was looking at both of us! We are yummy treats, after all." Cris couldn't help but smile. "And besides, he's a waiter you know…probably all about sampling each dish, if you know what I mean."

Alma winked at Cris, arching her back to show a little cleavage. Cris lowered her head as Alma offered Luigi a little something for his trouble.

"Alma!"

Cris picked up the straw next to her water and ripped the tip of the wrapper off, rolling it into a little ball. She stuck the small piece of paper in her mouth and moistened it to prepare for battle. She took aim after carefully placing the straw in her mouth and readied her miniature cannon.

"Cris, you better no—!" Alma squealed as she felt the soggy missile hit her face, right below her eye.

"Oh, it's on!" Alma readied her miniature plastic cannon and retaliated.

Their spitball fight was cut short by dirty glances from other guests, and more importantly, the arrival of their mythic dish. They called a truce in honor of being in the presence of a true legend.

"Mmm! This looks amazing, but it's so big!" Cris said, as she started assaulting her half.

"It smells even better!" Alma said as she began ravishing the plate.

"This was such a good idea, we should do this more often," Cris said between bites.

"Well, if today wasn't your last day of school, we would!"

"It's okay; we'll go out all the time once I get back."

"You're starting that trip today, right?"

"Yeah," Cris managed between mouthfuls.

"With Kody?"

"And another friend of ours."

"Who?"

Alma looked up after hearing Cris mention someone she hadn't met before; there wasn't much the pair didn't know about each other.

"You wouldn't know him. He was my neighbor until he went off to college. He invited Kody, and then Kody called me up."

"Kody knows him too?"

"Yeah, I think they used to work together downtown or something."

"How long are you guys gonna be gone?"

"I'm not sure. As far as I know there isn't much of a plan, we all just wanted to get out of town for a while."

"How are you going to pay for all that?"

"My dad is covering all my expenses. He encourages social development and fostering a worldly perspective. Perk of having straight As all of high school instead of a social life."

"Heh…well, hope you guys have fun." Alma did her best to hide her disappointment.

"I'm sorry you can't come with us."

"It's all right. Someone has to stay and take care of Maria—er…Mom."

"Don't worry; I'll bring you back some souvenirs."

"You better!" Alma stated as she finished her dish. "Almost ready?"

"Definitely. I'm so full."

Cris, ceding victory to Alma for the mighty spitball fight, paid the bill. She and Alma left unfulfilled, having marginally lost to the legendary Super Pasta Bowl. Alma ran ahead of her and jumped behind the steering wheel.

"Ready, lady? Let's get this show on the road!" Alma was nearly cackling.

"And who said you could drive my car, missy?" Cris said, maintaining her authoritative demeanor.

"To the victor go the spoils."

"Crazy…" Cris muttered to herself as she got into the passenger seat.

Alma caught wind of it. "What was that?"

"I said you're crazy!" Cris laughed, screaming at her.

"Don't yell at me! So full…I shouldn't have run." Alma rubbed her belly as she put the key in the ignition.

Cris just smiled at Alma as they pulled out of the parking lot and headed back to school. Alma played around with the buttons on the dashboard as they drove back. She caught a glimpse of Cris relaxing on the passenger side as she pulled out and put on a hidden pair of sunglasses.

"Cheater! Hiding a second pair."

"Nyaa!" Cris stuck her tongue out, teasing Alma.

The two continued down the road, basking in the light breeze and warm sun on their skin.

"My, my, my," Alma sighed to herself.

"What is it?"

"You don't know?"

"Know what?" Cris looked up, trying to read Alma's face.

"It's a shame, you know. You're gonna miss the show tonight."

"Show? Oh, you mean the Bards?"

"Hell yeah, I mean the Bards! They're debuting their new single tonight! Daron told me that he and Geroge co-wrote it."

"Really? I'm surprised. Daron doesn't really seem like the creative type."

"Maybe not, but he's wicked hot."

"Alm, is there anyone you don't think is hot?"

"Yeah, probably. But I haven't met him yet. C'mon, girly! It's all about looking at the bright side! Everyone's got something neat about them, right? I mean we're kinda obvious, but even your scrungy, everyday book nerd has something cool about him." As she listened on, Cris couldn't help but see Glenn come to mind. "I think for you it's just that you don't really get to know people all that well. For someone so popular, you're pretty much a recluse."

"Opposed to your getting to know everyone?"

"Hey, different strokes." Alma's grin returned. "Promise me this: you won't leave town before taking me to that show."

"Alm, you know I already have plans."

"So? I'm pulling the best friend card." She could see the reluctance in Cris's face. "C'mon! It's your last night in town for God knows how long! Kick it off with a bang!"

I'm sure you will, Cris thought.

"Besides, if I have to go all by my lonesome, who knows where I'll end up? Maybe one of the Bards will try to whisk me away and I'll have no one to protect me."

"All right, all right. Fine. Geroge offered to hook me up earlier anyway. I'll get some tickets from him later."

"Sweeeet! I love you, Crissy!"

Cris reminded Alma that she was still on the road and driving *her* car as Alma swerved to avoid debris on the road. They continued the ride back listening to the Bards homemade EP, psyched for the night ahead.

4. Blue Skies

"I never understood the self-righteousness of teenagers. They entitle themselves to everything including knowledge of the world, with the one exception of not having been a part of it."

– The Chronicles of Glenn Redcliffe

Kody lay daydreaming underneath a tree on the school campus. He stretched out beneath the leaves, covered in shade, on a hill overlooking the main building. It was still lunch—or at least the extended lunch period that all the seniors seemed to be taking—and he didn't have any kind of plans. He stared at the clouds, through them, beyond imagining, into the inverted deep-blue ravine of the sky.

He thought of how he lay on the grass, looking up past the leaves, through the atmosphere, into a large black abyss of nothingness in space: he could almost see the darkness beyond the cloud animals drifting along the azure skyline. Protected by a layer of gases that surround the sphere on which he lay, he could breathe and live peacefully if he so chose.

There was a massive rock—its origin unknown to him—which circled the mighty sphere as if to watch over it as an older brother might watch his younger sibling. Or perhaps it only waited, until it's time came to perform a more sinister act. It held no shame, for it did not hide itself from view, even in the presence of its brilliant antithesis and archaic counterpart. The night was its domain. Now, in the day, it held no place but to watch, even if it remained unwelcome. Kody let loose a small sigh.

Such idle ideas wasted the day away, and his thoughts shifted to more relevant matters: Alma. He thought of her face. He remembered her shimmering eyes, her cheery smile, her rambunctious spirit.

"What did I do wrong?" he wondered aloud. "I did everything I thought she'd want...everything I could for her; it still wasn't enough. Am I not a good enough man for her? Am I ugly? Am I a bad person?" He ran through the list of all the things he could think of that could've possibly gone wrong.

"Maybe she found someone else...maybe she found someone that's all tall, athletic, funny, rich, charming, and all that other crap girls want," he said as he sat up, his voice rising. "Sure, maybe he's a funny guy—just ignore the fact that he's about as intelligent as Sunday Morning Football. So what if he's as sensitive as a cabbage, he's ripped! He's got abs of steel! Abs! That's all that matters anyway, right?"

"It's always what they see, they don't take the time to find out what's there on the inside... just window shop and move on through. They even rub the glass, just to see it stain. Curiosity...why the hell is it that the only person I care about doesn't even notice how much I suffer for her! Because of her!" Kody took to his feet, feeling the passion of his rant coming full swing.

"It's not like I wanted these feelings, and I can't exactly get rid of them, so what do I do? I try to be a nice guy, I try to do everything I can for her, and what do I get? Squashed like a little tiny bug in the heel of her shoe, and she doesn't even realize I'm there!" he realized he was shouting now, and furthermore, several students were staring at him, including Cris and Alma, who had just returned from lunch.

It was about this point Kody noticed them standing there, speechless. He stared at Alma for a moment, looking her over and inspecting every inch of her. He had hoped maybe he'd just become so desperate that he was imagining her, but the look on her face told him otherwise. He broke out of his trance and rushed to the parking lot.

Alma and Cris were hesitant to pursue him, unsure of what to say or what they could do. Alma still had a small stomachache and nudged Cris, who began to chase after him. Kody managed to keep ahead of her for a short while, but ran out of places to run when he noticed a small truck, tinted blue, pulling out of a parking space. He recognized it immediately and hopped in the back. The rear window slid open to a smiling, rugged face decked out with aviator sunglasses. The man inside was as amused as he was surprised to see a kid riding in the back.

26

"Hey, Kod, what's up buddy?"

"Nothin' much, G. Mind getting me outta here?"

"You got it, chief."

With that, the truck left the parking lot and made its way away from the school. Kody could see Cris watching him in the distance, disappointed, but quickly averted his gaze. He climbed into the cab from the rear window and took a seat next to his friend.

"So, that was pretty bad ass, I gotta say. Great escape and all. What's the deal, man? Runnin' from the law?"

"Sorry about that, Geroge. Thanks for saving my ass again, as always."

"Hey, that's what friends are for."

"Yeah." Kody gazed off, distracted.

"You eat yet?"

"Not yet," Kody replied.

"Good deal, I got the perfect place in mind."

"The usual?"

"Oh, yeah."

They rode on, Kody once again being forced to listen to his buddy's improv of the Arcade Fire's "The Suburbs" as he watched people pass by on the sidewalk, oblivious to everything around them. He saw people walking with one another, people walking their pets, and even people rocking out to music that he felt, based on the way they were dancing, really didn't seem to fit the time of day. Still, he couldn't help but chuckle.

"Seriously, pretty cool getaway, man, but uh…I don't think I've ever seen a dude actually run away from Cris like that…did'ja piss her off?"

"Nah…and it wasn't about her, anyway."

"Ah, the Alm'ster then. Got it. You two still hashing it out?"

"Not really. Just did that thing where words come out of my mouth."

"Oh…the mouth. The part of the body we so seldom control, but so quickly gets our asses inta' deeper shit than we can handle. But what can ya' do?" Geroge shrugged.

Kody nodded as Geroge pulled into their favorite fast food restaurant of all time.

"Dude, just so ya' know, this is so about to happen."

Kody let out a small laugh before turning to Geroge. He canted his head as Geroge pulled around to the Drive-thru.

"We're not going in?"

"Nah, rehearsal and sound check in a few. We'll hang after, though, if you want."

"Can't."

"No? What's up with that—oh, riiiight, you got that trip thing or whatever. That tonight?" Geroge asked as he pulled up to the end of the Drive-thru line.

"Supposed to be. Dunno if I should even go now."

"Dude, you should totally go. Fuck it, man! Go. You deserve it. Live it up, get over the girl, and have some damn good times! I promise you won't regret it. Am I right?"

Kody couldn't keep back his smile.

"Besides, no way I'm lettin' ya' back out of a trip with a girl like Cris, man. You two alone, in a car going cross-country for what could end up being weeks, maybe even months? We're talkin' long hours, close quarters, man. Tell me ya' don't want a shot at that!" Geroge sported a huge grin now as he watched the thought cross Kody's mind.

"It isn't like that. We're just friends. Plus she and Alma are thick as thieves; Alm would kill me in so many different ways. 'Sides, another friend of ours is going anyway."

"Kod, do you know how many guys would fuckin' kill to be *just friends* with Charisma Roberts? I mean straight homicide. We're talkin' full on premeditated murder man. I'm not so worried about it, both being a musician and having a chick like Jeany and all, but in any other life? I'm just sayin', bud, think about it. And fuck your *mutual friend*, you're way cooler."

Kody kicked back and relaxed as the line in the Drive-thru started to wind down.

A voice came through the speaker as Geroge pulled around. "Welcome to Burrito Bell, what can I get for you today?"

"Hey, lemme get that big meal thing that comes with the ten tacos or whatever."

"Anything else?" the speaker responded without any of the implied enthusiasm.

"Hey, Kod, you want anything?"

"Uh, yeah…get me a few quesadillas and a Lemon-Lime Splash."

"Oh, shit, right. Hey, can I get some quesadillas and two extra-large Lemon-Lime Splashes?"

"Sure, gimme one second for your total."

"No ice!"

As the clerk was calculating the total, Kody noticed Geroge watching him from the mirror. His comrade wore the expression of an old mentor watching his star pupil tackle the material on his own for the first time. For no reason he could explain, Kody became more of aware of the blood flowing fiercely through his veins. He clenched his fist. They pulled around and picked up their food before heading back.

"Sorry to bail on you so early, man, but I gotta get this thing started. You parked in the Palisades?"

"Yeah."

"Gotcha. We'll definitely hang when you get back. Hell, maybe we'll even book a gig and meet you on the road!"

Kody gave him a thumbs up as he started eating his quesadilla.

They rode back in a quiet ambiance, allowing it to pervade the air as they ate their food. Geroge shook his soda back and forth as he sipped it, tiny little clinking sounds clacking together as they reached a stoplight. He pulled the lid off and scowled, showing it to Kody, who stared at him, expressionless.

"This look like 'no ice' to you?"

"You knew they'd forget."

"They always forget, except for that fine momma Sharita, but I keep on hoping one day..."

Kody reassured him as the light turned green and they continued until they reached their destination. Geroge pulled up next to Kody's car to let him out.

"Hey man, I've been thinkin'," Geroge turned to him, "The Bards are puttin' on one hell of a show tonight. It'd be a shame for my best buddy to miss it."

"I'm sorry about that, G."

"Do me a solid, man. We're gonna need some help setting up tonight. I'm thinkin' that if I had someone who was willing to help out with that, I could accidentally sort of lose a few tickets."

"I'm listening..." Kody kept an attentive ear as he finished his quesadilla.

"Well, here's the thing. Even if someone had some big plans tonight, I'm sure he could find a little time—and I'm thinkin' a nice lady to bring along—to see all the awesome work he did setting up for the school's best band. I'm thinkin' that one would look pretty cool in the process, and it'd be a hell of a way to start off any summer vacation. The lady might even be grateful to him for it."

"She might, huh?"

"Oh, she might indeed."

Kody rubbed the back of his head. "Well, if I see any gentlemen in the area who are free, I'll be sure to send them your way."

"Kod, c'mon, once in a lifetime, man. You owe me, brother!" Geroge put his finger in Kody's face.

"Heh, all right, all right! Dunno when I'll be free, but I got you."

"That's what I'm talkin' about man. You're a fuckin' hero."

"See ya in a bit." Kody waved, opening the door.

"Right on. Top of the rock, brother."

"Top of the rock, man."

Kody climbed out of the truck as Geroge nodded and took off. Kody stood there for a minute thinking about where he wanted to go first. With no real plan in mind, he hopped into his car and began driving around aimlessly. He turned up the radio and scrambled through the stations when he instinctively headed toward his house. At about the midway point, while sipping on his soda, he realized that his mom was probably home and that it might not look too good if he came rolling in the door during what little was left of the school day.

He decided instead to take a little detour to gather his thoughts. He couldn't go to any of his other friends' houses since they'd all be at school, or at least not at home. At that point he realized that there was only one place he could go, a place from which he was certain he wouldn't be turned away.

He decided to save one of his quesadillas, and turned his crusty rust bucket around getting onto the expressway. Although his destination wasn't far, the embarrassment from earlier in the day hadn't quite left him. He turned the radio up until the dial refused to continue and sped down the highway. A firm mix of Billy Talent and Taking Back Sunday blared out the windows as he drove well over the speed limit—while keeping a keen eye out for cops—most of the way there.

His brief stint of pseudo-road rage didn't last long, leading him to his destination in record time. He took a few side roads and ended up at a nice apartment complex surrounded by woods.

The place had an almost regal feel to it, which seemed odd since it was so far off the beaten path. As Kody looked it over, he thought about the strange people who must like living in a far-out-of-the-way place like this, but then realized who he was here to see. It made a kind of sense.

Kody had been to the place only a few times before, but it already felt like a place he'd always known. It almost had a sort of homey quality, and he figured it was that exact quality that drew people in—like their own private reserve.

These apartments, unlike most others, were not connected by simple hallways, but rather by exterior walkways much like that of a cheap love motel. Kody walked along the bottom walkway—admittedly feeling a little dirty—until he reached a flight of stairs and proceeded to climb them.

When he reached the top, he came up to a door he recognized but still had little desire to knock on. He knocked only twice—he knew that's all it would take—and waited patiently for a response. About a minute later, he heard movement from behind the door, followed by a muffled "W…what?"

Kody dispiritedly replied, "It's me, Kody. Let me in." The door opened, and Kody stepped inside the ill-lit apartment.

5. The Mission – Step One

"Things are only as hard as you let them be. Think about it."

– Cris's Journal

Glenn stood at the door, still groggy, trying to figure out why Kody was standing before him. Particularly because Kody was a few hours early, and Kody was rarely on time, much less early.

"Uh, y-yes…well, I s-suppose I should offer you s-something to drink?" Glenn asked, trying to wake himself up, though his body refused to cooperate.

"Don't worry about it, I'm good. I saved some food for you, though; figured you haven't eaten anything halfway decent in a while."

"Th-thanks."

Glenn moved aside, allowing Kody entry. The two stood awkwardly, forcing Glenn to interact with his guest.

"So, um, rough d-day?" he said.

"Oh, yeah."

Kody took a seat on the couch, doing his best to ignore the rank smell Glenn had barely tried to cover up. "Kinda said some stuff I wish I hadn't." Kody lightly kicked the foot of the coffee table repeatedly, avoiding any form of eye contact.

"Alma? You n-needn't say anymore. B-breakups can be hard; s-sometimes people react in s-strange ways."

"I know, I know. It's just I can't think straight when it's about her…not that she'll talk to me ever again, but still."

"D-did something else happen?" Glenn's adjusted his glasses.

"Heh, I uh…kinda started shouting?"

"S-shouting?"

"I was thinking, then I was thinking out loud, and then I was thinking very out loud."

"J…just how 'out loud' were you thinking?"

"Loud enough for her and Cris to overhear, at least. So I figure I'm screwed. Royally boned. Thinking maybe I can find a very large rock, just kinda crawl under it for a while? Oh, say…maybe a decade or two?"

"Well, that c-certainly is a plan, though I'd qu-question the merits of it. You are aware C-cris is c-coming here after school, yes? This may not be the b-best hiding spot if that's what you intend t-to do."

"Yeah, I know…"

"Might I make a suggestion?"

Kody stopped fidgeting and looked up to Glenn.

"R-rather than run from the issue, c-confront it. If you step up and handle it before it c-comes to you, then you can take the advantage and address it on your own t-terms. Seems better than waiting it out and d-dreading it."

"Who knew you were so clever?"

"Oxford, e-evidently," Glenn retorted.

"Er…right. I think the thing for me though isn't the hiding so much as I just didn't want Alma to see me like that. It's hard enough trying to deal with this without her and Cris talking about it behind my back. 'Sides…this is my issue. It isn't for her. She doesn't need to know about it, me, or anything else for that matter."

"As a rule, K-kody, if you don't want someone to know something, you probably shouldn't think it 'very out loud' in his or her presence."

"Now you're pitying me? The world must really be ending."

Glenn pulled out a cloth and began cleaning his glasses. "In any case, I have something of a project that I need to get back to, so if you'll excuse me."

"What? How're you going to work on a project with us leaving in only a few hours?"

"It won't t-take long, but it is a matter of some urgency. C-cris said that you and she wouldn't mind helping me p-pack?"

"You aren't even packed yet?"

"P-project."

"Right. Sure. I owe you anyways."

"Th-thanks."

Glenn wandered off back into his room. He considered whether it'd be wise to leave Kody in his living room unattended, but too many other issues took priority over any outside considerations. He closed the bedroom door.

As Glenn meandered about trying to decide where to begin, he noticed a small ray of light shining in from his window. He gazed at it, mesmerized, until he realized that it was illuminating something: a cup. He slowly walked over and picked up the glass, cutting his finger on its now jagged, broken edge. He could feel the damp moisture of its previous contents on the carpet, wetting his socks. "It was on the nightstand, wasn't it?" he muttered to himself.

He tried to remember if he had perhaps gotten up at some point during the night and maybe dropped it, but nothing came to him. "Nightmares?" He noticed a small piece of it was chipped, lying on the ground, but gave up trying to discern the heart of the matter and returned the cup back to its rightful place.

He sat on the bed and let his eyes drift in and out of focus. Listening to noises outside his room as his thoughts came back to the issue at hand. He heard Kody shuffling through various things, presumably deciding on what may or may not be needed. Kody's actions were not important, however, and Glenn once again lay on the mattress in the poorly lit room.

He set his glasses on the nightstand, and dragged his hand across the smooth surface until he felt a small piece of paper: a photograph. He examined it, as he had many times before, and traced the outlines of the picture with his finger. Despite being unable to see the images, he knew quite well what they were and could imagine them with perfect clarity. They were two boys playing at the beach, and behind them a young girl, hiding behind one of the boys. The three looked like an inseparable trio.

As he continued to imagine the faces on the faded paper, his insides began to cringe. Moist beads trickled along his cheeks. His face became warm. Thin streams started seeping from his eyes, though he tried to hold them back. There was too much guilt for him to let it all in. He couldn't focus; if he didn't stop it now he would never be able to, and he needed to focus. For only a moment, he let his thoughts drift back to what happened that day. Having had his moment, he forced himself to set the picture down as he remembered the mission at hand. "One th-thing at a time."

He took two more pills, having forgotten his glass of water had spilled onto the carpet, but managed to swallow them with little difficulty. Taking a deep breath, he groped around for his cell phone until he accidentally knocked it onto the floor. He quickly found it, and tried to remember an old French adage as he returned a missed call.

Kody, having overheard Glenn's quiet ruckus—for it was indeed a quiet apartment—waited in the living room as he finished packing a bag. He heard indistinct murmurs of a conversation and waited for them to die down before taking his place on the couch. "Is this really okay? It's for his own good, I guess," Kody rationalized as he prepared for his own covert operation.

He shuffled up to Glenn's door and tried the handle to see if there was any reaction. He waited briefly and cracked the door just a little. There was nothing. He peeked around the door, seeing Glenn unconscious on his bed, and continued in. He crept around Glenn's room, trying to get a feel for it. Not knowing the layout or where to find what he was looking for, he moved slowly with a kind of alertness even a parliament of owls would envy.

First, he checked on the dresser, and then inside it. Nothing there. Still with no success, he tried the small bookshelf next to it, but there was nothing there either. He decided after some deliberation that they must be on the nightstand and slowly crept over to it. He could hear Glenn's labored breathing and reconsidered whether it was worth the risk. "It's for his own good, it's for his own good," Kody kept whispering to himself, trying to rebuild his courage. He quietly but quickly glided his fingers across the soft oak surface. There, he finally found what he had been looking for. He slowly reached for the item as Glenn's breathing began to soften and he started to stir.

Kody tried to contain the pounding in his chest as every part of him came to a complete standstill. He could feel every pulse of every fiber in his being. It crossed his mind that at this very moment he'd make an excellent statue, and he wished even more so that he was one. Glenn rolled over, now face to face with him, though his eyes were still closed.

Kody tried to calm down and breathed softly, deciding to exit the scene of his crime before any more complications could arise. Regaining his posture, Kody slowly inched his arm up to the nightstand and seized the pills. As he grabbed the bottle, however, a picture that had been resting on top of bottle fell to the ground. Kody quickly grabbed the picture and crawled back outside to the safety of the living room, quietly closing the door behind him.

6. Grey Skies

"Nothing calms me like getting a piece of nature. There just ain't anything in the world that can compare."

– Alma's Diary

Alma sat beside the tall oak Kody had rested under not long before and began to think. She recalled their past and debated if it had really been as bad as she kept saying. She thought she'd made the right call. She was sure of it! Still, she couldn't help but wonder what he was doing as she gazed off into the cerulean sky.

"Cris," Alma began, "why do you think he shouted like that?"

"I don't know," Cris patted her shoulder, taking a seat next to her best friend.

"Maybe he's just having a hard time with all of this? To be honest, I was a little surprised when he called me up with the idea for a trip so suddenly, but maybe he felt he needed to get away for a while."

"Kody brought it up?" She glanced at Cris, seeing her own unusual melancholy reflected in Cris's eyes.

"Yeah, I told you earlier. Remember?"

"Oh, right…I forgot. I wonder if Kody just wanted to get away from me that much." She stared at ants navigating through a forest of grassy blades.

"I don't think it's like that."

"Why not? He hates me so much he's already yelling at me! Why not just get the hell out of town?" She threw her hands up in the air, flustered.

"Almy, you don't mean that. Besides, it's really more of a summer vacation thing! I'm sure he just wants to see some place that isn't a school building for once. And I'm not trying to play devil's advocate, but I have to ask…weren't you the one that broke up with him?"

"I know that!" she burst out, taking Cris by surprise.

"I just…I don't know, damn it! I didn't think I'd care is all! Most guys I don't ever think twice about. It's like, there's him: Ooh, hey, Kody. A guy just like every other guy. And everything between us is okay, but I just wish he'd go away for a while, but he never does! So I figure, 'Gotcha, bucko, you don't wanna leave? I can fix that!' It wasn't like I was mad at him—I just needed my space! And just like that, he's completely gone! No more Kody around, like, ever! So all of a sudden, it's just me. Just Alma. Nothing special. I'm not special to anyone anymore. Just another girl, ya know? What makes me matter now?"

"Alm, it's not like that. You *are* special! And Kody realizes that, too. I mean, it was you he was talking about earlier, right? Guys don't just go off like that because they don't care. You still mean a lot to him." Alma looked up, teary eyed.

"I guess…but what do I do now? I can't just go back to him and tell him I was being dumb."

"Why not?" Cris ribbed her.

"I'd look like a total idiot, for one." Alma spoke through her sniffles. "But the thing is…I don't even know if I was wrong. What if, after all of this, it turns out he really does annoy the hell out of me, and I just can't stand him? What if I'm just feeling lonely and pathetic and sorry for myself because I want someone to hold me until I don't feel like shit anymore? What then? I just tell him, 'Hey sweetie, thanks for keeping me company. Now would you kindly get lost?'"

"Breathe. If you don't know, then that's okay! You don't have to have everything sorted out right now. Take some time to figure out how you really feel about this, and then do what you need to do."

"I don't have time, Cris! You guys are leaving kinda now!"

"Well, what if we—"

"Just stop, Cris, okay? I know you're trying to help, but I need to think."

Alma readjusted herself, sitting against the tree now and holding her legs close to her body, resting her chin on her knees. Cris sat quietly nearby, tapping her feet against the dirt. Her shoelaces combated each other as they danced on the wind.

The women sat in silence for some time under the tree, listening to the leaves blow around, watching students walk by, and staring at the clouds. The rustling wind rifted the scent of small flowers from the Earth, drifting it saliently along, catching Alma's hair on the breeze. She blew golden tresses out of her face time and again, but after a while remitted herself to the whims of nature, the mother. The fragrance of careless blossoms brought solemn relief, comfortable enough to rest her eyes. She let her spine slouch back, sinking further into her lap, letting consciousness drift away.

At some point the bell rang, though the two remained on the hill, unaffected by its marking the passage of time as sixth hour began.

"Alma," Cris finally spoke, "we can't just sit here all day."

Alma drew a deep breath, slowly opening her eyes as she turned to Cris. "Then go."

"What?"

"I wanna sit here. I need to think, and this place is quiet and peaceful. It's nice, breezy, pretty, boring. As long as I sit here, I feel like this moment can last forever. Quiet and peaceful—"

"Nothing can last forever, Alm." Cris patted her back.

"Maybe, maybe not, but even if all this changes, even if everything fades away, I can keep this memory. I can save this place in my mind and never let it go. Then, no matter what, I can come back to this instance and remember how clear everything was, even if only for this one brief moment."

"Alm, I'm really worried about you, the things you're saying…they don't sound like you at all."

"Maybe you just never knew me."

Cris looked up at her and Alma could tell it felt like her bestie was seeing her for the first time. There was no cheery smile or playful giddiness—just a quiet reserved girl, shrouded in a pensive fog that seemed to consume her. Little more than someone who always remained alone even with people nearby.

"All this time we've been friends, but I don't think you knew me much more than anyone else. Always smiling, always laughing…yeah, that's me all right. But have you ever seen the real me? Do you even know who she is? Who I am? When have you really seen me sad? Have you ever seen me cry? I can't show these things to anyone because I'm me. I'm supposed to be the strong one that holds everything together. If I don't, then it all falls apart. Ever since Jake…doesn't matter how I feel, just as long as I put on a shiny face. Maybe I'm more than just a stupid worthless doll," she said, as tears began to lightly stream down her face.

"Alm," Cris offered up her sleeve.

"No!" she pushed the sleeve away as she tried to hold back the tears.

Cris moved closer to her and put her arm around Alma, holding her. Alma resisted, but couldn't hold back the tide she knew was coming as her insides tightened. She buried herself in Cris's shoulder, the tears bursting out.

"Alma…" Cris said quietly as she held her friend close.

"I hate everything so much! Everything is so stupid! School, Kody, life, everyone! Even me…I just want to be left alone," she managed to say through the sobs.

"You don't mean that, Alm," Cris said.

"I do! I hate Kody so much! I just wish none of this had ever happened! It's all his fault! If he would have just stopped being so stupid and running away, everything would be fine!"

Cris sat there silently, holding her best friend as she worked her way through the sobs. She drew her fingers through Alma's hair, listening to the wind rustle through the leaves as the clouds passed before of the sun, slightly darkening the afternoon sky. As the sounds of Alma's sniveling began to die down, the cicadas in the nearby woods continued chirping rhythmically with the shifting of the branches.

"Almy, I'm gonna take you home, okay?"

"Ugh!" Alma punched the ground, to no avail.

"Honey, you can't sit out here like this. We'll take you home and let you get settled, okay? We'll get you into pj's and get cozy on the couch. We can even make some popcorn and watch a movie or something before I go."

Alma looked up, canting her eyebrow as she exhaled. With Cris meeting her gaze, she submitted. "Fine, I can't stand being here much longer anyway. But I don't want to watch the stupid movie."

Cris helped Alma wipe away her tears with some tissues she kept in her purse as they walked back to her car.

"Are you up for driving?" Cris asked.

"No, just let me know when we get there," Alma responded as she got in the passenger's seat, keeping her head down and avoiding eye contact.

Cris nodded as she took her seat and started the engine. She started the car, forgetting the radio had been turned up, blaring the White Stripes "Fell in Love with a Girl." Alma cringed at the noise, glaring at Cris until her bestie turned it down. They continued back to Alma's house, complete silence all the way. Cris pulled into the driveway.

"Just go home, Cris, I can take it from here. I need some me time right now."

"Alm—"

"I'll be fine…just need a good bath or something."

Cris stared at Alma in contemplating, biding her time until she finally spoke.

"Hey, tell you what. Why don't I let you borrow my car for a while, huh?"

"Hmm?" Alma raised her eyes only a little.

"I know you love it. It's the least I can do. Not like I can use it while I'm gone anyway."

"M'kay." she feigned a little interested.

"Please let me know if you need anything, all right?" Cris tried to appease her.

"Mm," she barely made a sound as she nodded and got out the car.

"I'll come back and check on you later; I'll drop it off then, okay? We still have the Bards concert tonight if you're up to it."

Alma nodded, turning to face the seemingly endless walk up her driveway. She trudged to her front door and then disappeared into the house, without ever looking back.

7. The Sisters Roberts

"The more I look at the state of the world, the more I come to feel that the value of family is completely underrated. Well, other than mine, at any rate."

– Glenn's Chronicles

Cris pulled into her driveway, right behind her father's car, as she turned down the radio and grabbed her bags. She headed inside and took off her shoes, carrying her bag upstairs to her room as she thought about what she'd do for the afternoon. She still had awhile before she was supposed to meet with Glenn, and wanted to give Alma some time to herself. She got to her room and set the bag down on the floor, lying back into the comfort of her luxuriously large bed.

Looking around her room, she found it to be a little bare, with most of her important things already packed. Still, her room was quite festive, even despite its unusual famine. There were numerous posters of different bands and a nice vanity, though it had only lotions, perfumes, hair ties, and brushes on it. She got changed out of her school clothes and put on a breezy summer shirt with casually comfortable pants.

She sat up on her bed, from which she could easily see the mirror on her wall, and began to fix her hair. She messed around with it, trying out some new hairstyles she thought might be fun for the Bards' concert, finally starting to look forward to it. Thinking of the Bards, she looked over to her acoustic guitar sitting on its stand in the corner.

"The Bards want a new vocalist, huh? I don't know about a band, though, I don't think I'm that good," she muttered to herself as she finished fixing up her hair. "Besides, I only sing for fun."

She got up and picked up her guitar, strumming the strings to get a feel for the sound. She played a full chord, cringing at the sound of the untuned instrument. She took some time to tune it, listening to each string as she plucked it, and felt the subtle reverberations as the strings wound down. Finally, when she was satisfied with the pitch, she decided to play around a bit. She practiced a few chords of "Free Bird," finally getting down some of the more complicated riffs as she sang along.

Although making good progress, she slowed down midway through the second verse. An unfamiliar sound was throwing off her rhythm. A flute was accompanying her melody in the background. She stopped playing and opened the door to see her bleached-blonde, twenty-two-year-old sister standing there continuing merrily.

"Hey, Emmy! I thought you weren't going to be back until next week!"

Emma lowered her flute. "And miss my little sister striking out on her own for the first time? Of course not! Have a seat, little Crissy, we need to talk!"

"About what?"

Emma walked Cris back into her bedroom, setting her flute down next to Cris's guitar. She sat Cris down on her bed as she pulled up one of her chairs.

"I want to make sure you stay safe." Emma said.

"Mom put you up to this, didn't she?"

"Dad, actually. But that's not the point. I wanted to do it."

"Seriously? I figured he'd want to do it himself."

"He did. But you know his biggest fear—"

"—A mysterious boy will convince me to worship the devil in his cult-o'-doom, while offering me special Kool-Aid and impregnating me with his satanic spawn?"

"Pretty much. I figured you'd want to hear it from me instead." Emma's lips pulled back, cracking a wry smile.

"Good call."

"Of course. That's what sisters are for."

"So, safety-brief me."

"Right. So who's going on this trip with you?"

"Kody and Glenn."

Emma leaned back, cocking an eyebrow. "*Glenn* Glenn? As in my ex-boyfriend Glenn?"

"Yup."

Emma hesitated before responding. "How is he?"

"Um…" Cris looked away, unable to find any answers written on the wall.

"Still a little out there?" Emma saved her.

"Just a little."

"And who's this Kody? Should I be making plans to meet my new brother-in-law soon?"

"Definitely not. He's one of Alma's exes."

"Geez, that chick goes through guys like she'll get a gold star for every one she snags. How'd Almy's latest end up on a trip with you?

"He's one of Glenn's friends."

"Huh. Small town."

Emma got up and took a seat on the bed next to her sister.

"Crissy, we both know how Dad is about guys and everything. We also both know that while Dad thinks his rules are steadfast and universal, we're women and we have urges that aren't exactly in line with his expectations."

"Em, I really—"

"Just listen. Things happen when you get away from home, okay? There aren't any rules or boundaries. If my first year at college taught me anything, it's that a woman can do pretty much whatever she wants.

"Now you were always the mature and responsible one, and maybe that's because Dad was a lot more protective of you than he was of me. I don't know. But because of that, you haven't been exposed to a lot of the stuff I have, specifically that there are a lot of weird and creepy guys out there that are going to try and take advantage of you. Especially 'cause we're so dang hot."

Cris held back a laugh.

"I'm not going to ask because it's none of my business, but please just promise me you'll be careful and responsible, okay? I don't want anything to happen to my baby sister. I love you, brat."

Emma gave her sister the sort of warm hug that can only come from a loving sibling. She then slipped something into Cris's pocket. Cris pulled it out and read the label.

"What? A glow-in-the-dark condom? Em!" Cris couldn't stop herself from blushing.

"Keep it down! It's a big world, Crissy, and you might find more than you're looking for while exploring it. And while this might not be Dad's preference, I'd prefer to keep you safe. Practicality first, trust me."

"But…glow in the dark?"

"They're handier than you might think."

"I don't want to know this about you!" Cris cringed.

"Then pretend you didn't hear it," Emma chuckled as she kissed her sister's forehead and got up.

"When you get a few minutes, come downstairs: Mom and Dad want to say goodbye, too."

Cris shoved the condom back into her pocket as she got up and followed Emma downstairs. They made their way into the kitchen, but found no sign of their parents.

"Huh, they were just here!"

A clanging sound echoed from the pantry, drawing the sisters in to investigate. Emma took the lead, opening the door to what could only be described as a gross parent make-out session. Having just received the lecture, the last thing Cris wanted was a live demo. She shuddered as she squirmed back, waiting until the scene was clear.

"Oh, hey! Um…surprise!" Elly called out, trying to save face.

"Elena, dear, I think they might be onto us."

Cris and Emma's father knew when to throw in the towel. Cameron turned around and grabbed a beautifully encased cake off the shelf of the pantry before coming back into the kitchen with the rest of his family.

"What is this?" Cris was confused and surprised.

"Uh, yeah. I feel like I should've been a part of this, too. Except for that whole last thing." Emma and Cris were on the same side, as usual.

"It's a surprise party! We wanted to make sure we sent you off the right way!" Their mother was chipper.

"How come you didn't tell me about this?" Emma scoffed at having been kept out of the loop.

"It's for both of you! You're going up north for a week, and your sister is going…um, where again?"

"We're still not sure, Mom." Cris answered.

"That doesn't sound like a very well-thought-out plan to me," Cameron cut in.

"I'll be fine, Dad. I'm going with Glenn Redcliffe, remember him? He used to live down the road?"

"Oh, yeah…the Redcliffes. Good people. A little off, but respectable."

"And I'll have my phone on me, too—promise. Everything will be fine."

"I still don't like this." Cris could always count on her dad the play the papa bear.

"Cameron, honey, she's practically an adult now. She's been more than responsible, and she deserves our full faith and trust."

"I know, dear."

Cameron shifted his glance toward his younger daughter.

"I'm sure you'll be fine, Charisma, and you'll do us proud. I just worry about my little girl sometimes."

"Right here, you know." Emma threw her arms up, defeated.

"We all know you can take care of yourself, Emma." Elly replied. "Now, we have plenty of cake. It's low fat with little frosting; I know how careful you girls are about watching your weight, so I made sure to get a good cake we can all enjoy!"

"Why do you think that, Mom? When have we ever said that?" Emma tried in vain to reason with her mother. Cameron pulled Cris aside, stepping into the hallway.

"I trust Glenn. He's a good kid. And I trust you. But there's a lot that can happen."

"Emma already gave me the speech, Dad."

"Yeah…I love Emma, but sometimes I think she could stand to learn a thing or two from you."

"I'll be fine, honest."

"I know, kid. It's a father's job to worry about his daughters, even if there's nothing to worry about."

"C'mon, we're missing the party."

Cris walked her father back into the kitchen, where it appeared that her mother and sister had reached some sort of compromise, though she couldn't begin to fathom what that might be. They all sat down and enjoyed some cake and ice cream as the warm summer day pressed on.

They listened to Emma's stories of what she had planned for the upcoming week, Cris trying to figure out which parts Emma was changing to avoid parental intervention. Elly scrutinized Emma's plans while all of them tried to figure out just what exactly the eldest Roberts lady was talking about. They then watched Emma's reaction to her mom's nonsense, which always seemed to end up in the two of them getting caught in yet another quarrel. Cris and her father just sat back and watched the two with amusement, priding themselves on the being the rational ones of the bunch.

Cris looked at the clock on the microwave as she realized that she still needed to help Glenn get all of his stuff together. She finished in a hurry and excused herself as she grabbed some last-minute stuff before carrying it downstairs.

"Hey, let me help you with that!"

Having established a temporary conciliation with their mother, Emma called after Cris. She walked Cris out to the car, carrying her other bag and helping her load them up.

"I meant what I said earlier, little sister. Be safe, okay?"

"I will, Emmy."

"You have my number. Call me if you need anything. Anything at all, got it? I don't care what time it is, where you're at, or what's going on. Understand?"

"I do."

"Even if it's just to gossip about boys or to tell me you found a fiver in your pocket that you totally forgot about. Because sometimes that happens and it's always awesome."

"I got it, Emmy. I will," Cris giggled.

She hugged her big sister and got into her car, taking one last glance at her home as she drove off, eager to meet up with her friends and bring on the night.

8. The Mission – Step Two

"Trips and adventures are pretty sweet. You can learn so much more about someone traveling with them for a few days than you might hanging out with them for years."

– Kody's Notebook

Kody took a breather on the couch, needing a minute to calm himself down.

"Man, I should totally go out for covert ops or something, I'd be a shoo-in," he chuckled to himself. He stopped to think for a moment about what that really meant.

"Shoe in? How can someone be a shoo-in or even a shoo-out? Eh, I don't get it." He let it go.

He reached into his pocket and pulled out the pill bottle, setting it on the table. He examined it closely, but the label was ripped off, removing any opportunity to get any kind of information from it. Kody opened the bottle and dumped out some of the pills, looking them over to see if there was anything useful he could recognize. He was unable to tell much about them and kicked the leg of Glenn's coffee table.

"Ugh, lame. All that ninja work for nothing."

He stopped and stared at the pills for a moment as a new, far more harebrained idea entered his head.

"So I don't know what they are or what they do. But…there's an easy way to find out."

He picked up one of the pills and looked it over closely to see if he could find something that would indicate danger or a hazard.

"Gotta figure, if these were dangerous or lethal or maybe mutant power causing, they'd have some kind of marking, right? Like skull and crossbones or kryptonite or something."

Kody considered the most adventurous route to determine the pill's usage.

"Hmm…much fun as it sounds, it's probably not the best idea. At least not right now," he put the pills back in the container.

He leaned back into the couch and looked around at how disorganized the apartment was, in spite of him packing the better half of it into two suitcases.

"Dude, even for a guy's place this is messy. Ugh, gotta find a way to kill some time."

He started picking up all the trash lying around, mostly small scraps of paper or rubbish, and tossed them into the trash can. He found a few more pill bottles somewhat hidden under the couch and underneath books lying about. He examined the bottles but had no better luck.

"More and more of these pill bottles…they look like they're prescription, but the labels are all scratched off. He knew we were coming today so why would he leave these out?" Kody wondered aloud as he scratched his head. He gathered all the bottles he could find and made a collection on the now clean table.

"At least they're all the same type of bottle, I just gotta figure out what was in one of them."

At that point, he remembered the picture he had taken from Glenn's room. He had shoved it in his back pocket when he snuck out of the bedroom and it had escaped his mind during his post-larceny excitement. He checked his pocket but couldn't find the picture.

"Damn it! Did I lose it?"

Kody started searching throughout the apartment, checking all the places he had just picked up. He looked the table over but didn't see the photograph anywhere.

"Heh, wouldn't it be the perfect cliché if it was under the couch?" Kody muttered to himself as he walked back over to the couch.

He kneeled down and looked under it but didn't see the picture. He stood up and looked at the table again, noticing the small picture sitting underneath it.

"I just checked here! Huh…figures. Always in the last place you look anyway. Why would you keep looking after that?"

He chuckled at his own bad joke. He picked up the picture and sat back down, getting comfortable on the couch as he examined it.

He recognized a boy in the picture who was obviously a much younger Glenn. There was another boy about the same age, but he was a total stranger. The girl behind the boy, however, seemed a little familiar, but he couldn't quite place her.

"Huh, she's kinda cute. For a kid, anyway. Why do I feel like I know her?"

He sat down on the couch and studied the picture more carefully. The boys didn't look like they could be older than twelve. He was sure he had seen this girl somewhere before. He brought the picture up to his face, squinting, but it was no use—he couldn't remember who she was or where he had seen her. Frustration started to sink in as he set the picture down on the table and leaned his head back to think.

"I don't even know any little kids, other than my dorky little sister. So who the hell—?"

Kody slapped his forehead as he realized how much younger Glenn looked in the picture.

"Right. If Glenn's that much younger, then so was the girl, which means she's not a kid anymore…"

All this thinking hurt his head. He looked down on the table again and saw the pill bottles. At this time, an old idea previously deemed bad suddenly crept back into his mind and developed a few points of merit.

"Eh, they're probably just some super Vitamin Ms or something. Can't be that bad if Glenn's taking them by the boatload."

Kody scratched his head for a moment, looking the pills over. They could be anything—they could make him crazy, or leave him in a coma. He hesitated, but before long curled his lips into his trademark grin, signaling game time. He grabbed a glass of water from the table along with half a pill and tossed it down the chute, chasing it vigorously with water.

"Welp, now time to wait and see. This should be interesting."

Kody waited a good five or ten minutes to see if the pill would have any effect, but found himself disappointed at the results.

"Heh, just regular vitamins, I guess. Why not go with the Flintstone kids or some…"

Kody felt relaxed, and stopped caring about what he had to say. The sentences drew on far too long, and the words felt quite heavy. He laughed at himself a little as his head fell to one side. He tried to lift it up with his arms, but it was to no avail; they too were heavy. Instead, they fell to his side, and his body slumped over along with them. Before long, Kody was sound asleep.

* * *

Kody's nose itched. It annoyed him, but it wasn't reason enough to get up. It was then he realized he had fallen asleep. He jumped up to meet the surprisingly stern expression of Glenn glaring down upon him.

"Uh…hey, buddy. What'cha doin'?"

Kody tried to cover his tracks, though it was of little use, evidence all around him.

"I shall ask you. Intriguing that a picture on my n-nightstand found its way out here," Glenn remarked, drawing both his own and Kody's eyes to the picture lying on the table.

"And that is, of course, ignoring the rather c-conspicuous arrangement of all of these bottles on the table, which I m-must assume there is good occasion for?"

"So much for spy school," Kody muttered to himself.

"Hm?" Glenn snorted.

"I said you could be a little grateful for me helping you clean your room. You were asleep, and I didn't want you to end up missing anything, so I helped clean up as I packed."

"C-clean my room?"

Glenn looked genuinely surprised, both at the fact that Kody would feign such consideration, as well as his ability to come up with a semi-legitimate alibi on the spot.

"Yeah, of course, buddy!" Kody sat up resting his arms on his legs, self-confidence rising.

"The picture fell down while I was cleaning, and I didn't know where to put it, or the rest of this stuff, so I brought it out and set it on the table for you to sort out."

"I see. Well, thank you for your c-consideration." Glenn adjusted his glasses as Kody leaned back into the couch, kicking his feet up.

"So who's the girl?"

"E-excuse me?"

"The girl in the picture; is she a friend of yours?"

"W-why do you ask?"

"I feel like I've seen her before."

"P-perhaps. This is an old p-picture, from many years ago as you m-might imagine."

Kody kept his eyes on Glenn, who paid little attention in return as his focus remained on the old photograph. "So, um…" Kody fumbled with his fingers as he stared at the medication bottles. Glenn eventually took notice.

"Sleep aids. They help sometimes when insomnia k-kicks in. On my more involved p-projects I sometimes have t-trouble establishing a good stopping point. These ensure that I find one."

"Must have a lot of projects. What's with the labels?"

Glenn squinted, looking Kody over. "I have a h-habit. Of peeling the labels off." Kody pointed a finger-gun at Glenn, nodding. Glenn sighed, shaking his head and taking a seat next to Kody. The men examined the picture together before setting it down.

"Must've been a good time. Don't think I've ever seen you so happy."

"It was. One of the b-best of my life."

Glenn stared at the ceiling. As Kody watched him, something felt off. It didn't seem so much that Glenn was simply looking at the ceiling as much as staring back at something watching him. The thought was too unusual to entertain. He shook it off.

"So forget the girl; who's the guy?"

"Oh, him? A very old friend of mine."

"He have a name?"

"Jake."

"Where's he at? Haven't seen him around lately."

"I should be alarmed if you did. I'm fairly c-certain he drowned."

"Oh man, Glenn, I—"

"It's of no c-consequence. It was a long t-time ago."

Kody tried to ignore the new sinking feeling in his gut, wishing he had just stayed quiet and packed up Glenn's things like he had planned to. Despite his curiosity, it wasn't worth stirring up even more painful memories for someone who already seemed so fragile.

Still a little groggy from the mystery pills, Kody's gaze languished on all of the empty bottles lying around the apartment. Even though half a pill had hit Kody like a brick-laden boxing glove, Glenn seemed fine…more or less. If he was still using them, Kody could see no indication.

Glenn sat next to Kody in quiet reflection, neither of them having any idea of what to say. Kody remained unsure of whether he even wanted to break the silence.

In this still and quiet surrounding, a sort of mutual understanding developed between them that words could not have found. They both sat in the poorly lit stillness, waiting for nothing, and understanding there was no need to understand it.

Though they were not ready for their session to part, a knock at the door disrupted whatever the moment had brought, and it was gone. Though they were both startled, it was Kody who was more surprised.

"Hey, it's me. May I come in?"

They could hear Cris through the door. It was time to go. Glenn got up to let her in while Kody slunk into the couch. Cris stood in the doorway, apparently awaiting an invitation but receiving none.

"Hey, Glenn, is Kody here?" Cris asked as she stepped inside. Glenn responded with a glance in Kody's direction.

"He—y, Cris," Kody spoke, slowly sliding up to meet Cris's gaze.

"So you were here the whole time? I spent a good half-hour looking for you, you know."

"Sorry, I should've called, but… no phone?" Kody shrugged, unable to feign a good excuse.

"You're right, you should've. But I understand. It's been a hard day for everyone."

"Everyone?" Kody cocked an eyebrow.

Cris turned to Glenn. "Ready to go?"

Glenn nodded, "We need to g-get going soon if we intend on m-making any real progress t-tonight. The van is p-parked outside, so o-once we load it up we can leave."

Kody grabbed the picture off the table as he and Cris carried the suitcases out to the red, rundown van. Glenn stayed behind to finish gathering up a few small effects in his room.

"Cris, I'm really sorry about earlier, for the whole outburst and everything."

"Don't worry about it. We've got other things to do."

"I found out what those bottles were, though."

"What? What were they?" Cris's turned her attention to Kody.

"Well, Glenn says they're sleep aids. They do make you sleepy, but I don't think that's what they are."

"What do you mean they make you sleepy? How could you…you took some?" Cris shoved him lightly.

"I figured it was safe! I had a headache, and if he's downing these things like candy corn then they can't be that bad for you!"

"Are you kidding me? Do you know how dangerous that was? I mean look at him! Half the time he looks like he's got the mental capacity of a banana!"

"I'm fine! And anyway, now we know."

"Yeah, I guess…wait, you said he told you what they were?"

"Yeah?"

"So you asked him about them then? The whole help-me-find-out-what's-up-with-Glenn-is-a-secret-mission-so-don't-tell-anyone-most-of-all-Glenn' part didn't really get through, did it?"

"Remember how I told you they make you sleepy? I fell asleep. I woke up, and he was just standing there like 'What the hell are all these p-pill bottles just s-sitting around like this for?'"

"Did he actually say that?" Cris snickered at his impersonation.

"Close enough. But you get the idea…oh, hey, check this out! I found this while I was cleaning up, too. He was acting all weird about it, so I figured we might as well take a closer look at it."

Kody pulled out the picture from before.

"And the stealing just keeps on…"

Cris stopped talking as she looked at the picture.

"What is it?" Kody was lost.

"That's Alma. Why does he have a picture of Alma?" Cris was baffled.

Kody dug his fingers through his hair as he realized why the girl in the picture had seemed so familiar. He couldn't even recognize an old photo of his ex. Cris began to notice his sudden withdrawal, however, and he realized he had to get back to the issue at hand. They reached the side of the van and found the door unlocked as they started loading up the bags. Kody spoke up.

"Huh, this is getting weirder and weirder. Glenn's popping sleep aids like the Super Mario brothers at a free mushroom convention and has an old picture of him and Alma."

Cris canted her head toward Kody, restraining a chuckle, before redirecting her attention to the picture in hand.

"He's in there, too?" Cris stopped to take another look at the picture. "Oh, huh! That *is* him. I didn't even recognize him at first. So who's the other guy then?"

"Oh, some old friend of his. Jake."

"Jake?" Cris gazed off into space.

"Dunno. Doesn't ring any bells. How about you?"

"What?" Cris was clearly lost in thought.

"I said, 'Doesn't ring any bells, how about you?'"

"Huh…sorry. Alma…I think she mentioned that name when she was crying earlier."

"Alma was crying?"

Cris's eyes widened as she covered her mouth.

"Um…yeah, she stubbed her toe. It was really bad. Blood everywhere. Huge mess. Horrible. Be glad you weren't there."

"Cris…"

"So! The mystery of Glenn and Jake, what's the big connection?"

Kody scoffed, taking a step back, but knew he wouldn't get anywhere picking fights with her at the moment.

"Well, he said that Jake had drowned a while back."

"So this guy died? When?"

"Who knows? Ten years ago? Last week?"

"So this might've happened a long time ago. What does that have to do with him and Alma, though?" Cris asked.

"Good question. And how come the two never talk about each other?"

Cris tried to come up with something. "Maybe they don't remember? It was a long time ago."

"Maybe not Alma, but if Glenn's keeping this picture so close…"

"This is a tough one."

"Yeah. Well, we got nothing for now, so we may as well finish up here."

"You're right. Let's do my stuff next." Cris lead him over to her car.

As the two continued to hash it out, Glenn stood in his room, checking his phone to make sure hadn't missed any calls during his brief nap. He checked his text messages and found one marked new.

He opened it immediately to find a brief message waiting for him.

"*En cours…J'ai besoin plus de temps.* M."

"M-more time? What d-does she need more time for?"

His heart stopped only for a moment, but he knew he couldn't let the matter distract him. He closed his phone and placed it in his breast pocket as he left his room. He walked out the door, locking it tightly behind him.

Back in the parking lot, the two continued loading the van. "So how do you figure he pays for all this stuff?" Cris asked, trying for a second attempt to redirect Kody.

"I dunno. Rich parents? Not that uncommon around here."

"His family is wealthy enough to pull that off. Seems strange they wouldn't come visit him, though. Especially after he got back from England. He dropped out of college so suddenly. Just left. He's always alone up there in that dank place. It isn't healthy…I'm afraid he's not—oh, here he comes!" Cris abruptly closed her mouth as she and Kody finished loading her bags into the van.

"There's a force on this Earth s-strong enough to not only stop you two from b-bickering, but to keep you quiet all together?" Glenn asked curiously, almost cheery.

"What?" Cris seemed flustered. "Oh, it's nothing. Kody's just telling me dirty jokes again, you know him. Pervert."

"Not my fault you don't have a sense of humor," Kody said, smiling.

"Hey! I do! I *so* do! I'm full of humor! I'm humorous!"

"Ah, it resumes. My hopes are d-d-dashed yet again. Well, let's prepare for C-charisma's…" Cris glared at Glenn "um…C-cris's things next."

"Actually, she's already good. Brought her stuff with her."

"G-guess that just leaves you then, K-kody," Glenn stated.

"Let's head over to my place then."

They closed up the van and started figuring out seating arrangements. "Oh, shit!" Kody exclaimed. He caught both of their attention.

"What?" Cris was the first to respond.

"What time is it?"

"I don't know, around seven?"

"Crap, crap, crap! I'm supposed to help Geroge set up for tonight's show!"

A mild glimmer of alarm and panic arose in Cris's eyes as well.

"I totally forgot about the show!" she exclaimed.

"You're going, too?"

"Yeah, of course! It's the last school show of the year!"

"I didn't know you went to those."

"I usually don't, but if not now, then when, right?"

"Hurry up then, let's go!" Kody began rushing.

"Hold on, we need to stop by Alma's first," Cris protested, watching Glenn for any kind of reaction to Alma's name.

"What? What for?"

Kody indulged his interest with anything Alma, but was also both crunched for time and doing his best to avoid her at the moment.

"I told her she could borrow my car while we're gone, and I promised to take her with me to tonight's show."

"You two were planning on going together?"

Kody dropped his head, defeated, since his only options for dates were both going together.

"Yeah, I owe her at least that much."

"As if lending her your car wasn't enough?"

"She's my best friend! And since when it is your business, anyway?"

"Since you won't let me touch it! I didn't think you'd let anyone touch that thing."

"Well, she's special, so get over it!"

Glenn sat this one out as the two settled the matter among themselves. He stared up into the sky, seemingly catching random parts of their conversation.

"When did you learn to share in the first place?" Kody wouldn't drop the subject.

"Look, I'll think about telling you all about it on the way, ok? But can we get going?"

"Fine. How do you guys wanna do this?" Kody asked, trying to sort everything out. They both just looked back at him.

"Seriously? Fine. I'll drive the car—"

"I'll drive my car," Cris interjected.

"Cris'll drive her car, and you follow behind us. Sound good, Glenn?"

"That's acceptable. Just try to stay within a r-reasonable speed limit."

"Don't worry, I don't drive like him." Cris smirked at Kody as she hopped in the front seat.

Kody jumped in next to her, fidgeting with the radio while Cris noticed an odd expression on Glenn's face.

"You seem happier today, why's that?" she asked him.

"It's been some t-time since I've been involved with anything. It's just nice to have a sense of p-purpose, I suppose."

"It's good to see you getting out more. It can't be healthy staying in that apartment all the time."

"Isn't that one of the objectives of th-this little adventure? To get out?"

"You know what I mean. There won't always be vacations. You can't just stay in there and hope another adventure will come find you."

"That may be, b-but then again, the less I go out, the more exciting each event should be, right?"

"I guess." Cris gave up.

"Quit picking fights with everyone, Cris, it's a bad habit!" Kody gleamed, finding his golden opportunity to scold her.

"Hey, you can always walk. For the entire trip. We'll just stop every few miles and wait for you," Cris countered. Kody ceded, unwilling to test Cris's determination.

Glenn shook his head watching the two of them fight. Cris started the car and headed off with Kody bickering beside her. Glenn climbed into the van, never bothering to look back, as he started the engine and followed them closely behind.

9. Bixby (Canyon Bridge)

"I can't overstate how important friends are. But people seem think the word 'friends' has gotta mean people. I just don't think that's always the case."

– Kody's Notebook

Kody flipped through different radio stations, much like a fidgety child, until he surrendered hope of finding anything decent.

"Nothing good? I thought I heard a good one a few back."

Cris glanced to the side, undecided on how she felt about Kody's antics.

"Well, usually there's this new rock-alternative station, but reception's really bad for some reason."

"Did you check Alma's CD book? It's under the seat."

"Oh, right!"

Kody reached under the seat and found a small book full of CDs that looked like it hadn't seen some use in a long while. He started flipping through the book.

"No, no, no…Paramore? Uh…no."

He continued to look through the book, but lost faith that he would find anything that could meet his satisfaction. He was disappointed at what Alma had kept on hand, knowing she had much better stuff.

"Just throw something in. They're all pretty good." Cris kept her eyes on the road.

"Pretty good? That's ok with you? Would you eat a sammich that was just pretty good?"

"Yeah, sure." Cris shrugged.

"Well… this isn't food! It's music! It can't just be *pretty good*, it's gotta be the best! It's like—hey! Rilo Kiley! Jackpot." Kody shuffled about, dropping some of the CDs out of the book as he put Rilo Kiley's *More Adventurous* in.

"Happy now, buster?" Cris chided him.

"Buster?" Kody cocked an eyebrow. "And yeah, this is much better."

"Great, now sit back and relax! We've got a long, exciting night ahead of us."

Cris smirked, taking her time getting used to Kody's abundant energy. It was at this time she noticed him making an observation.

"Hey Cris, when did you get so bossy? I don't remember you being so bossy."

"Newsflash, buddy, we haven't been friends that long, so you don't really know enough about me to be remembering things like that, now do you?" She stuck her tongue out.

"Ouch. Cris: the cold-blooded."

"Maybe I just like messing with you." Cris brushed her hair aside as she focused on driving.

"That's not very nice, ya know."

"So what're you going to do about it? Tell on me? I'd be surprised if Glenn cared."

"Is he even still behind us?"

"I think so." Cris checked her rearview mirror to see if Glenn was anywhere in sight.

There was no indication whether or not the vehicle behind them was Glenn's. She pulled over for a minute to let him catch up before continuing on.

"Aw, didja lose him?"

"No! I just…didn't keep good tabs on him."

"Wow. Very nice. Good tab keeping." Kody chuckled.

"You know what…?"

"What?"

"I don't know! I…I'll tickle you to death. I will tickle you to death if you keep messing around, buddy. You'll be very uncomfortable, and you might even pee yourself!"

Confused and unsure of how he felt about that threat, he contemplated it. Kody was almost tempted to risk it, just to see whether she'd follow through with it. Almost. He tried to figure out whether or not that'd be a good way to go when a seemingly unrelated thought passed through his head.

"So, about Alma earlier?" he started up again.

"Kody, please just let it go. Listen to the music, okay?" She was pretty patient, but the scowl on Cris's face made it evident she didn't want to discuss the topic again.

He sat quietly after that, watching the smallest cusp of the sun fade from view as the street lamps came on and the moon established its dominion. Two more songs played: one Kody liked quite a bit, and one he was barely familiar with—and happy to keep that way—as they came up to the side of Alma's house. Cris sighed, making peripheral eye contact with him.

"Look, I'm sorry… It's just been kind of a weird day for me, and I'm really worried about Alma. If you promise to behave and not talk so much, you can come up with me to check on her. Deal?"

Kody nodded as Cris turned off the engine. Both of them got out of the car and walked up to the door.

Glenn pulled up behind them, listening only to the hum of the engine as he placed the van in park and waited for them to do their thing. He sat there, mostly bored and distracted, without any real thoughts or concern to speak of. He had too much on his mind for it to focus on any one thing, and he decided to get a little fresh air while he waited. He got out of the van and wandered across the street as he found a comfortable curbside to sit on. He fell back onto the early-evening grass, smelling the green and gazing up at the stars.

"Q-quite the sight. I had f-forgotten how bright the evening sky c-could be. Or perhaps I never knew…I d-don't remember." His eye started to itch. He nudged his glasses out of the way. "To think, of all d-days, today would be my b-birthday." He bowed his head. "I n-need to make progress soon."

He sat up in pensive repose, without any real purpose or direction. He could see Cris and Kody still waiting at the door and wondered what could be taking so long.

"Mreow?"

He turned around to see a small, silvery-gray striped cat with white patches looking him square in the eye, curiously.

"H-hello! H-how are you, little friend? Are you l-lost?" Glenn's eyes lit up at this miniature discovery.

"Mreow?" The small cat stared at him, wondering what the strange man would do next.

"Huh…I b-bet you're hungry, aren't you? Hmm…h-hold on!" Glenn dug his hand into his pocket as he pulled out a bottle of water.

"I'm s-sorry, I haven't any food to offer you just n-now, but I do have s-some water if you'd like."

The cat tilted its head, eyes narrowing on the water bottle in his hand. Glenn unscrewed the top and poured a small portion of water into the cap, setting it down on the grass in front of him. The cat immediately ran up and began lapping at the lid, trying to get to the water.

"Oh, so you're t-thirsty! Well…g-give me a moment."

The cat watched as Glenn picked up the bottle while drawing a knife from his back pocket. He now had the cat's full attention, as it seemed the large kitten had never seen anything as wondrous as a big creature with a container full of delicious water. Glenn poured some water out onto the ground, the overgrown kitten eagerly making its way to water point to start lapping it off the grass.

"Not y-yet, little friend!" Glenn said, his countenance brimming with his rare, nearly satiated smile.

He cut the bottle in two, setting the full portion on the ground for the cat to drink. The kitten changed its mind about the murky ground water and immediately took interest in this new clean, contained water. It began to drink and quickly emptied the cup.

"You must b-be starved. It d-doesn't seem as though there's anyone taking c-care of you…on that we c-can relate. Though it may be a b-bit of an inconvenience to you, would you like to c-come live with me?" Glenn offered the cat, quite sincerely.

"Mreow?" the cat replied, rubbing itself against his leg.

"You accept my offer then? Wonderful. Hmm…c-come with me, I'll make you a comfortable little nesting spot in our van. I have some friends who I'm sure would like to meet you."

"Mreeeeooow."

The cat did not seem to object to this course of action, or to care about much of anything at all for that matter, and allowed Glenn to pick it up and bring it back to the van.

* * *

"What do you think is taking so long?" Kody asked Cris, both of them still waiting at the door.

"I don't know. Alma usually doesn't make me wait. She should've answered by now."

Cris opened the door and stepped inside.

"Almy? Are you home?"

"Are you crazy?"

Kody yelled after her while still standing outside, apparently very uncomfortable with the notion of any more spy games for the moment.

"What? I do this all the time. We practically live at each other's houses."

A withered but strong voice echoed from inside. "Cri—s?"

"Oh, Mrs. Grey, how are you? Is Alma home?" Cris asked as she moved into the den.

Kody stuck close behind. He stopped just short of the entryway, standing directly behind Cris. Looking passed her, he saw that Mrs. Grey was confined to a wheelchair. Most so, he was surprised to see she was Hispanic, as he hadn't noticed any particularly Hispanic traits in Alma. He set this thought aside as he continued to observe Mrs. Grey.

He noticed she looked a little sick, but he couldn't tell as to what. He tried to still his breathing in a vain attempt to avoid some sort of odor. The stink seemed to creep around the place, trying to impose itself upon his nostrils. In a brief moment of weakness, one such odor managed to sneak in, causing him to reel back as it hit. Catching Cris's elbow in his side, he remembered to maintain his composure. He tried to ignore the strong stench of alcohol.

"Cris, what're you doing here?"

Mrs. Grey's manner was not that of a welcoming mother, but rather of a harsh interrogator who simply forgot the difference between work and home.

"I came by to see Alma and let her borrow my keys. Is she here?"

"No, she hasn't been here most of the day. She left pretty much…right after she got back from school. Where're the keys?"

"They're right he—" Cris tried to tell her, but Mrs. Grey already had her hand outstretched, apparently disappointed Cris would waste her time with words instead of action. She placed the keys in Mrs. Grey's hand as she turned to make her way toward the door.

"If you see that girl, you tell her to get her ass back here. There's a mess of shit that still needs to get done, and I don't want her out after dark."

"Will do, Mrs. Grey!" Cris responded in her most appeasing voice as she gently grabbed Kody's wrist and pulled him out of the room. They quickly made their way for the door, escaping Alma's home and the odors it held. They sighed, taking slow deep breaths as they arrived back outdoors with the relatively fresh air.

"What the hell was that?" Kody leaned forward with his hands on his thighs, taking in the air.

"You've never met Alma's mother?" Cris looked to him.

"No... she never wanted to go back to her place, so we always went to mine. And Alma's mom is Mexican? Since when is Alma Mexican?"

"She's not. Mostly not, anyway. That's just her mom. But other than her strong sense of Latina pride, I don't think anyone would be able to tell that Alma has much Hispanic blood in her at all."

"Huh...so what's the deal with her mom?"

"I don't even know anymore. She had some kind of bad liver infection or something, I think, and it just got worse from there. She can't even work anymore, so she just collects disability and treats Alma like her live-in nurse."

Kody stood upright. "Was she drunk?"

"Probably a little bit. Not as bad as she usually is, though."

"How can you hang out here like this?"

"Alma's my best friend; how can I not? Besides, it isn't always like that. She's usually asleep most of the time, so it isn't so bad. But with Alma being out of the house and unaccounted for, I guess she's a little more restless than normal. I am a little surprised though: how could you have dated her for as long as you did and not known anything about this?"

"It never really came up. Alma never wanted to talk about her family, so we never did."

"I guess it makes sense: she was never big on bringing guys home, and it's not like you two were dating that long anyway."

"Hey!"

"Oh, um...I mean..." Cris tried to backtrack, but she stumbled over her words.

"Yeah, yeah, I know what you mean. Look, I don't wanna leave things with Alma like they are, but if she's not here then there isn't a whole lot we can do right now. We're already on a tight schedule and running late. The show's gonna start any minute now. We gotta go."

Kody tried to get out of there as soon as possible. They made their way back to the van before Mrs. Grey appeared, whom he figured was probably ready to start stoning them for standing on her lawn.

They reached the van, where they found Glenn standing in front of the sliding side door. Kody ran around to the driver's side and hopped in the seat before Glenn could say anything. It was only then that he noticed Glenn was distracted with an entirely different matter.

"Glenn…is that a cat?" Cris asked, seeing the kitten nearby on the back seat.

"Yes, I found him outside. Would you like to p-pet him?"

"Um…no? He might be feral or something."

"I assure you, he's q-quite safe."

"Well, just to be safe, I'm gonna stay up front for now. If you two become good friends, then we'll see," Cris said as she climbed into the seat next to Kody.

"Dude, are you seriously bringing a cat with us?"

"Yes, is that a problem?"

"Uh…how's he gonna…you know, crap and stuff?"

"We'll stop by a p-pet store. I'm sure we c-can manage one small addition, can't we?"

Everyone stopped to look at the cat, which was now nestled in one of Glenn's long-sleeved shirts on the seat next to him.

"Well, he is cute. I guess," Cris agreed.

"Hey, whatever. Just keep him out of trouble and we're good. So what's his name?"

"Name? He never told me," Glenn remarked with a completely straight face.

"Never told you?" Kody looked back at Glenn like he was crazy.

"Little one, what shall your n-name be?" Glenn spoke softly, almost as though he was whispering to the tiny cat.

The cat continued to stare at him, with the same puzzling look it had when Glenn first found him.

"Mereeow." The cat showed little interest.

"I suppose it's settled then."

"What's settled? He just meowed." Kody said.

"He has a name. It's Allister Th-theodore Bixby."

"Er…what? He agreed to that?"

Kody stopped trying to understand and turned back toward the front to start the van up.

"Where'd you come up with that?" Cris was curious.

"I d-didn't, he did. He says he'd like to be c-called Bixby, if you must call him something." Glenn seemed quite adamant on this point.

"It's very regal, important sounding. I like it."

She smiled at Bixby, who showed little regard for her presence.

Kody buckled up his seat belt with a wild smile, glad he was finally in charge of something, and started heading on down the road. Cris watched Glenn interact with his newfound friend. He petted Mr. Allister Theodore Bixby—"The Third, Esquire," he added later—gently with a reserved smile before lying back himself and resting his eyes. Cris then looked at Bixby, who only briefly glanced at her before yawning a little cat yawn and falling asleep.

10. The Spoony Bards

"Why do I love music so much? I guess because it takes me to a different place. I can let myself go just a little, and become a part of whatever world I choose."

– Alma's Diary

They arrived at the school only a few minutes before the show. Cris patted Kody on the back, applauding him for finally managing to arrive on time. They both looked back at Glenn, who seemed more interested in his newfound friend.

"Hey, Glenn, buddy. You comin' with us?" Kody asked.

"I'm f-fine, thanks. I w-would hate to leave this little one all alone. I have work I need to f-finish anyway."

"You sure?"

Glenn nodded.

"Alright, we'll try not to take too long."

Kody smirked as he turned to Cris, who was more than ready to go.

"So, you gonna be my date?"

"I don't know if you can handle me, Kody: I'm pretty high maintenance," she teased.

"Hey, I guess you could go stag to the last event of the year, but I wouldn't recommend it. Especially not with such a prize catch like me making this once-in-a-lifetime offer. I'd definitely act now."

"Well, when you put it like that," she nodded playfully.

He hopped out, running around to the other side of the van to open the door for her. Cris furrowed her brow, canting her head at his antics. She continued watching him, unable to stop the smile that crept along her cheeks as he extended his hand to her.

"My, quite the gentleman! I never would've expected."

"I don't think you've known me long enough to make those kinds of generalizations, hmm?" Kody smirked as he took her hand and helped her out.

"Fair enough." She stuck her tongue out at him as they headed for the door.

As they reached the door, Kody told Cris about the kid he recognized from art class who was always hanging out in the Photoshop lab, handling tickets at the door. He may have indicated that the guy was a total prick.

"Hey, man, what's going on?" Kody tried to be cordial.

"Hey, Kody. Tickets?"

"Uh...I'm here to help setup."

"Setup was a while ago. Hell, the show's about to start."

"I know, I overslept and totally forgot about it."

"That sucks. So do you have tickets or not?"

"G said he had us covered."

"I don't see G here. So unless you have tickets..."

Kody and Cris stood staring at each other, each trying to figure out what to do. Kody caught sight of a small commotion and gestured to Cris to turn her head, at which point they saw a grizzled face break through the crowd inside the auditorium to greet them at the door.

"Hey, buddy! Glad you could make it!"

Geroge wore a huge grin as he came rushing out, pushing passed the ticket kid and walking Kody and Cris inside. He quickly took notice of Cris, looking her over while navigating his way through the group of students loitering idly in the back hallway. He looked over at Kody and nodded approvingly as they found their way backstage.

"What was that guy's problem?" Cris asked.

"Dustin? Heh, my guess is our boy Kody," Geroge was more than happy to explain.

"What'd you do, Kody?" Cris turned to him.

"Me? I dunno. Nothing, I think."

"Riiiight. Remember his little digital paradise deal?" Geroge nudged him.

"Oh, yeah." Kody rubbed the back of his head.

"Yep."

"Heh, my bad."

"What happened?" Cris asked.

"There was a thing. Geroge and I were messing around in class one day. I tripped and hit the plug on his computer. Lost a project or something. He was pissed about it for a while, but I figured he would've gotten over that by now."

"No way, dude. He was totally obsessed. Guy was pretty plugged in to that thing. He's probably still steamed."

"Anyway, glad you guys could make it. Good timing, too: we're about to open. Jay's band is winding down, and its standing room only, kiddies!" Geroge could barely keep still, hopping around from spot to spot.

"Kody, take the lady and show her a good time. Remember my spot up in the cats?"

"Up in the catwalk?"

"Hell yeah, up on the catwalk. Take her up there. She'll love it."

Cris watched the two of them, amazed at how in sync they seemed to be, and wondered if people ever viewed her and Alma like that. It was at that time she started thinking about Alma and felt bad her best friend was going to miss this. She held a small hope that maybe Alma had made it to the show and was watching from somewhere in the crowd, but she doubted it.

"What's up?" Kody noticed Cris off in La-la Land.

"Just thinking about Alma. She's gonna be so bummed she missed this show."

Geroge threw his arms around both of them. "What? The Alm'ster couldn't make it? Man, she was stoked! We can't have our biggest fan missing out on tonight of all nights." Geroge stuffed one of his hands in his pocket, pulling out a camera. "Kod, take my camera, man. The cats are as good a place as any to record a live show." Geroge was a solutions man. They all turned towards back stage as they heard a band finishing up.

Back to feel this...

They could hear the applause as the set was finishing up.

"All right, kiddies, time to take your seats. The real show is about to begin!"

Geroge shuffled around backstage, gathering up the rest of the band as Kody and Cris headed back toward the stairs. Kody lead her up into the second level of the practice building that was normally closed off. She had never been up there before and almost hit her head on a set of lights while staring at all the equipment.

She saw the sound booth with the stoically calm and in-charge soundboard operator, as well as the tenaciously laid back lighting crew checking the lights to make sure everything was set right. Kody led her down to a row that sunk into the floor and opened out to a direct view of the stage below. Cris kept looking around, seeing no sign of the stage, until she realized that the dip in the ground was actually a built-in walkway for the lighting operators to manage the show lights from above. Looking down, she found that she could see the last band clearly as they were leaving the stage.

"This is amazing! Won't they need to use this for the show though?"

"Nah, G was never a big fan of pretty light shows. Always felt the music should speak for itself. Once the lights are set, they won't be changing them."

The two took their seats, viewing the stage from the rafters as the show began to open up. Kody pulled out G's camera and set it next to him, pushing the record button before kicking back and watching the show. As they sat there, they heard a familiar riff as the Bards started playing their opening song. The curtains cleared away, and the whole band emerged, amped and ready.

"Ooh, they chose their version of 'I'll Be Seein' You' as their opener?"

"Have you seen a Bards show before?" Kody asked.

"Um…not really. I like their music…Daron made me a copy of their EP once, but I've only caught a part of their show in passing."

"Gotcha. Well, if you're curious…"

"I am!" Cris nodded vigorously.

"Geroge almost always opens with this song because he feels it sets the pace, even despite its name. He likes to start slow, to give the audience a chance to feel the music before he picks it up and gets into it himself."

"Huh…I never knew there was so much behind running a show."

"Oh, yeah, takes a lot to get this stuff off the ground."

They quieted down as the set list continued. They watched the band members strut their stuff as Kody introduced each one for Cris.

"You already know G. He has to be the center of attention, of course, so he does vocals and lead guitar. The one on his left is Daron, the bassist. He's from somewhere in Europe—I wanna say Romania, maybe? His parents are American, though; they just happened to live there for a while. The Asian chick on the right is Jence, G's girlfriend and keyboardist. She's kind of quiet, but once you get to know her, she's a beast. A quiet riot. Almost scary. The tall Native American dude in back on drums is Thteve. He's a little reckless and doesn't say much, but it works for the Bards."

"How long have you known all of them?"

"I've known G forever. The Bards themselves…only the last year or so? G and I tried to start a band, but I have zero musical talent, so I ended up bailing and helping him write instead."

Cris looked up at him curiously. Her eyes lingered on him for just a moment.

"Oh hey, check this part out. I wrote the upcoming verse, right before the bridge."

They both stopped and listened:

If at the beginning and the end,
You were the best I'd ever dreamed,
Then I'd be blessed for all I'd seen,
And I'd never dream again.

"Classy."

"You like it?"

"It's original, for sure."

They continued listening on and watching the show, entranced as the next few songs played on. Cris casually glanced around, astonished at the size of the crowd below. She sat, grateful for their quality seating, and considered how jealous Alma would be when she found out about this. Maybe she wouldn't tell her. Her gaze found its way back to the stage as the music slowed down and Geroge stepped forward, preparing to make an announcement.

"All right, Bards fans, this is what you've been waiting for. We're gonna debut our newest song tonight! Before that, though, the Bards would like to give a special shout-out to my boy, Kody, and his girl, Cris! They got the special high-rise seats for tonight's show on account of being the guests of honor. Leaving town and the whole nine, much like the rest of us who can't afford to get into our local powerhouse of a university. All right, this one is for you two! Our new song, 'I Heard!'"

They both looked down as a number of faces in the crowd now looked back up at them. Many in the crowd only now realized there was a spot to watch the show from up above, and a few looked jealous they hadn't found it first. Cris latched onto Kody's arm, trying to hide her blushing. She kept her eyes on the stage, pretending the crowd had disappeared.

You tell me you hate me
You tell me I'm not the guy you like
But then I look over
And you're droolin' on a man that's just my clone.

Cris let out a sigh of relief, grateful that she hadn't chosen to wear a skirt. She looked up to Kody and asked him a question.

"Did you help him write this one, too?"

"Not so much. He did say I inspired it, but I think it was more about Alma than anything else."

"Alma, huh?"

Cris knew, of course, that being Kody's date for the evening was only a temporary situation. Even so, that made the evening hers.

Party last weekend
Saw me with a girl you used to know
Ya stormed right over
And you two went at it on the floor.

"So...that part...?" Cris inquired.

"No idea. All G. Maybe he was thinking of Jence?"

You're always pissed off, you're always mad,
But you're always at my door
We laugh, we smile, we kiss, we break up,
And still I beg for more.

Really does sound like Alma Cris thought to herself.

Cris shuddered as she caught a cold draft drifting through the rafters. She tried to ignore it and crossed her arms, but it started getting to her.

Tell me, baby, won't you now, if what I heard is true,
Even though it's always someone else, you want me like I want you.
Tell me baby can't you now, before the evening is through,
Do you really hate me, or is this your secret way of saying that you want me, too?

She heard the air conditioner kick on and realized it was the cause of the draft. It started blowing harder now and ruffled her hair a bit.

"Oh, hey, sorry about that. Should've warned you. The cats have a great view, but they do have some drawbacks."

"It's fine, I'm okay."

You come to our shows, standin' at the back behind the crowds
I wanna reach out to you, but you're always hangin' on someone else
You try to play tough, but you're in the same spot every night
This time I can't help you, it's up to you to make it right!

Yep, definitely about Alma crossed Cris's mind as she shifted around a little more, trying to get comfortable.

Kody stood, catching Cris off-guard, and moved to her other side, taking a seat next to her and blocking the draft. She looked up at him, receiving only a passing glance as he continued watching the show. She tried to focus on the stage but now found herself distracted. Now overly aware of it, she tried to keep her breathing normal. Her pulse quickening didn't help. He was right next to her. She could barely smell whatever lame cologne he was wearing and wasn't even sure if she even liked it. But she couldn't stop from fidgeting. It made no sense. It was just Kody.

Her body reflexively shifted closer to him before she realized what she was doing. She casually watched him to see if he reacted. No response. Her chin dropped just a little as she found herself wanting more. Feeling the music from the stage flowing through her, she took a deep breath. She leaned over and, slowly, rested her head on his shoulder. Whether it was nerves or she was actually shaking she couldn't tell, but she tried to contain herself as the show continued on. She felt the vibrations of Kody's voice as he spoke.

"Here it comes…c'mon G, big finish!"

73

Tell me, baby, won't you now, if what I heard is true,
Even though it's always someone else, you want me like I want you.
Tell me baby can't you now, before the evening is through,
Do you really hate me, or is this your secret way of saying you want me, too?

Tell me, baby, you have to now, if what I heard is true,
Even though it's always someone else, you still want me like I want you.
Tell me, baby, you gotta now, before the morning is through,
I know you want me so just be honest 'cause, baby, I want you, too!

The Bards closed their set, and the auditorium went wild. Thunderous applause rang out as G and the others wrapped up the instrumentals.

"Thanks for comin' out! If you guys liked the show then support us and the other local bands by buying our EPs! Just find one of us and we'll hook you up right!"

With that, the Bards cleared the stage, and except for a few diehard fans, people started herding out of the auditorium. Cris left her head in place, despite no longer having a reason to keep it there. She spoke as she watched the people file out of the building.

"That was amazing."

Kody leaned over, looking down to her. "Liked the show, huh?"

"Like it? I loved it! I can see what Alma was talking about now."

"Heh, yeah. Worthwhile to sit through a whole Bards show."

"Definitely. Best first concert ever."

"This was your first concert?"

"Yeah. Is that bad?"

"No, it's fine. I'm just surprised. Figured a girl like you would've been to all kinds of shows."

She canted her head as she looked up at him.

"What do you mean *a girl like me*?"

"Nothin'. Hey, wanna go catch up with the band?"

"I guess." Her enthusiasm began to wane as the scene started dying down. "Don't forget, we've got to get back quick. We left Glenn outside, you know."

"Oops. I totally forgot about him."

"I think most people do."

"Yeah, well, we aren't most people."

Kody turned off the camera and stuffed it back into his pocket as he got up and offered his hand to Cris, helping her up. They made their way back down the catwalk and back downstairs, finding themselves backstage. They got stuck in the crowd trying to find their way through until Kody saw a familiar face.

Kody sidled up next to Jence. "Hey Jeany."

"Don't call me that." She glared at him.

"Have you seen G around?"

"He's outside, living off the energy of his admirers. I'm sure he'll make his way back inside soon enough."

"Makes sense. Lemme help you with that."

Jence pushed him back. "No touching the board, Kody; you know better."

"But do I ever learn?"

Jence sighed casually as she kept pushing him away. "God I wish you would."

"It's her winning personality that I love the most." Geroge made his way back inside.

"Oh, look, it's the love of my life. Go talk to your boyfriend and then help me finish loading this stuff." Jence sighed, punching Geroge's shoulder as he sidled into the group.

"Such hostility!" Geroge rubbed his shoulder.

"You're an idiot."

"Aw, you're my favorite." He wrapped his arm around her.

"Only because you know I'd kick your ass if you said otherwise." Jence broke away from Geroge, heading outside.

"Fair enough! Kody man, what'dya think? No, no, wait. Our musician in training… Cris, milady, did our show meet your majestic expectations?"

"It was a really great show. Thanks for inviting me."

"Of course. 'A really great show'…I agree. We could put that on billboards across the nation! It's honest and straightforward while telling the people what we're all about. Hey, we just might do that." Geroge ribbed her, smiles all around. "And thanks for gracing us with your humble presence. Though it pains my heart to treat a lady so, might I ask you to step outside while I share a few words with our dear gentleman of the hour?"

Kody chuckled. It was clear G still had a strong post-performance rush going.

"Um...sure. I'm going to go check on Glenn. Don't be long?" Cris said, motioning to Kody, who nodded back as she headed outside. Geroge planted his hand firmly on Kody's shoulder.

"Buddy boy, yay or nay?"

"Good show."

"Fuck the show. My shows are always great. You know what I mean."

"Oh, heh...if I had to pick, I'd say yay."

"What the hell do you mean, 'If I had to pick?' Bro, she's a blessing! A genuine saint! I'm telling you, go for it or I will, man! Dude, I put a personal fucking endorsement in my show for you! It don't get no bigger than that!" Even now, Geroge was rocking his fashionable smile.

"Thanks."

"That's it? All right, all right...your heart's not in this, I get it. You're still swooning for your old chickadee. Well, if you aren't gonna make things right with this fine fox, then you damn well better make it right with her second best. Dunno if I could forgive you for lettin' both of them get away, ya know?" Geroge said, nudging him.

"Yeah, I gotcha, I gotcha."

"Good, brother boy, now it's time for you to get your ass in gear. You got all your huge plans, and I have one hell of an after party to go to. Just take my word for it that it's always so much better when Jeany is pissed. She's a hell of a lot more frisky, and I don't just mean with me."

"G, I don't need the details."

"Only 'cause you already know."

Geroge mussed Kody's hair, walking him outside. The duo narrowly avoided a dirty glance from Dustin, who was now cleaning up the trash and ticket stubs left outside. The boys stopped on the curb before the parking lot, Geroge taking Kody's hand.

"Hey, I'll see ya' when I see ya', brother. Stay cool and keep in touch. Let me know how it's goin', okay?"

"How *what's* going?" Kody said, catching the sly undertone in Geroge's voice.

"Whatever's goin' on that you might wanna let me know about." Geroge winked.

"Heh...uh huh. Top of the rock, man."

"Top of the rock, brother man."

Geroge flashed Kody his dirty smile once more with feeling before shaking his hand and heading back inside to finish packing. Kody made his way back to the van to find Cris warming up to Bixby, now petting him as Glenn click-clacked on his laptop.

"Hope we didn't keep you bored for too long."

"N-not at all. I had a n-number of th-things to occupy my time. I w-would like to recharge my laptop if p-possible, however."

"Sure."

Glenn passed the adaptor up front. Kody started the van and plugged it in as Cris turned back around to buckle up.

"Thanks for being my date tonight, Kody; I really enjoyed it."

"Hey, thanks for being mine. I hate going to these things alone. It's no fun, ya know?"

She nodded.

"And I even got it on camera for the Alm'ster! Er, I mean Alma!" Cris giggled.

Kody realized as he said it that he still had Geroge's camera in his pocket. Knowing what Geroge would probably use it for later that night, it occurred to Kody that he might actually be doing G a favor by keeping the camera on him for a while. Maybe his friend would learn to be a little modest for a change. Or at least not have as much incriminating evidence of himself, Jence, and whoever else is unfortunate enough to stumble into their private after party.

Kody started the van, heading off down the road. Sitting next to him, Cris took a deep breath and cleared her mind as the echoes and memories of the music still played clearly in her head. Though it was written for someone else, she had to admit that the song of the night was catchy, and couldn't stop herself from humming along as they got back on the road.

11. The Llama Lies in Wait

"I've always found myself with an affinity for the evening. It's quiet, secluded, and completely free of children. It's a world unmarred by appropriateness and censorship. It's the side of society that is far more accepting of man's darker nature."

– Glenn's Chronicles

As Kody drove on the expressway toward his house, he glanced in the rearview mirror. He turned the radio down despite his appreciation for the indie rock that reminded him so much of the Bards.

"Hey, what'd you do that for?" Cris asked, her humming of the Bards sauntering melodies now interrupted. "That was a good song, I was actually enjoying it."

"Okay, one: that was a great song. You should show some respect for Four Star Mary," Kody started. Cris looked at him as he continued: "Two: try to keep it down. Glenn's sleeping."

She looked back, seeing Glenn knocked out with his laptop still on his lap. Kody continued driving, humming along to the album in play and barely able to hear Bixby's rhythmic cat snores between verses.

Cris watched them sleep. "Those two are so cute. I'm really glad Glenn found a friend."

"Yeah, the guy could use one."

Kody took a deep breath, turning to Cris while keeping an eye on the road. "Hey, I have a question."

"Yes?"

"Does Alma ever…ever talk about me?"

Cris glanced toward Kody, trying to read his expression.

"I mean…I'm sorry to keep asking, it's just that…I dunno. I feel like it'd help if I knew."

"Um…she doesn't really say much," Cris offered.

"Huh."

Kody shifted back toward the road, turning the radio up slightly as he kept driving. Cris looked back toward Glenn again, who was just coming around. She watched as he groggily stared out the window, watching the road go by.

"Counting the white stripes?" she asked.

"Hmm? W-what? Oh, n-no. Just thinking." Glenn barely raised his head.

"About what?"

"A n-number of things."

"Such as?"

"W-where we should go first, what kind of things we'll see, how th-things will end up… all sorts of strange ideas." Glenn glanced at his laptop screen before turning it off and putting it away.

"What do you mean: how things will end up?"

"I really d-do wonder… Hmm, sorry. I'm r-rambling," Glenn said with a melancholy smile as he cast his eyes back toward the road.

"I wanna know! What do you mean?"

Glenn just continued to smile and watch the road.

"C'mon, Glenn, tell me! I hate secrets!"

"I w-wouldn't worry so much, it'll only c-cause wrinkles."

Cris shot him a dirty look, which he immediately shrugged off. Resigned, she took his advice and let the issue slide for the time being.

She grabbed one of her bags resting just in front of Glenn's seat. She pulled a pillow from it and set it on the armrest. She laid her head down and closed her eyes to get some rest before her turn to drive. Kody waited until she started elegantly snoring, to speak up.

"What was that all about?" Kody said, halfway talking to Glenn and halfway to himself.

"The whole how-t-things-will-end-up r-remark?" Glenn responded, no longer interested in the intricacies of the road.

"Yeah, know something you wanna tell me?"

"Not p-particularly. I just t-thought it'd be fun to mess with her a bit. She's been p-pressing me about everything lately. She q-questions every small thing I do or say like it has some sort of intrinsically h-hidden value. It's as though she suspects I'm some sort of c-cultist or something so macabre."

"She's just concerned about you. You're always cooped up in that backwoods apartment, cut off from the rest of the world. Gets her worried."

"I'm aware. I j-just find it… d-difficult to maintain my focus elsewhere. People, for the most part, only serve as a distraction. That's why I did so p-poorly in c-college."

"I have a hard time believing that. You're a pretty smart guy."

"Perhaps, but I lack m-motivation. "Glenn couldn't restrain a small, arrogant smirk.

"Is that why you got kicked out?" Kody caught a glance of Glenn in the rearview mirror.

Glenn raised an eyebrow. "A-am I often the subject of discussion amongst you and C-charisma? It's interesting; I should th-think you'd have more interesting t-topics of conversation with such a ch-charming young woman."

Kody chuckled to himself. It was the first time he'd heard Glenn talk about Cris in that way. He'd wondered if Glenn had any interest in people at all. He turned back to Glenn.

"Sorry, I should've thought that one through. It's none of my business. The only thing Cris and I really talk about is Alma, but she's been pretty quiet about that lately."

There was silence. Glenn watched Kody's face dimly reflected in the windshield—Kody himself could see it too. He knew he looked uneasy. His expression betrayed the question still lingering in his mind.

"You want to k-know why I n-never mentioned that I've met Alma before, d-don't you?" Glenn stated bluntly.

"What?" Kody had been caught off-guard. "Yeah, I thought it was a little strange you never said anything."

"You remember my friend, J-Jake? The one I had mentioned previously?"

Glenn caught Kody's nod in the reflection.

"He was Alma's brother. We were g-good friends once, but he d-drowned several years ago. On my birthday, c-coincidentally enough. I s-suppose that would make today the anniversary. Tenth? Or p-perhaps eeleventh…?" Glenn scratched his head. "I haven't really spoken to his family since then, and A-alma was so young that I doubt she'd even r-remember me."

"Alma had a brother…" Kody stopped to think the story over. "Whoa, shit! Today's your birthday? Happy birthday, man! Although…I guess for you maybe not, huh? Sorry, this is confusing as hell."

Kody was stuck deep in thought, trying to break out of his own internal loop of mysteries. It must've seemed obvious what his next questions were as his gaze met Glenn's in the rearview mirror. Glenn stopped him before he could speak up.

"Th-that's enough for now."

Glenn's subtle efforts to repress his melancholy revealed an entirely new aspect of him to Kody. An uneasy feeling welled up in his stomach at the thought of asking anything further.

"Sorry, I won't bring it up again."

Kody became laconic as he continued the drive to his house. They were only a few blocks away when he noticed the gas gauge was nearly on empty. *He's a freakin' genius, but he can't remember to fill up the tank,* Kody kept to himself. He considered whether it'd be better to get home and load up his bags, or stop and fill up the van first. He stomach rumbling, the path became clear.

"You two want anything?" Kody asked as he pulled into the gas station.

"I'll have a Splash soda, if it isn't t-too much. Could you check for some c-cat food for B-bixby, too, please? I'm sure they have a c-can or something," Glenn responded.

Kody nodded as he looked down to Cris, who was drooling on the armrest of her chair. He grinned, counting the ways he'd never let her live it down. He got out refill the van.

With the nozzle filling up the tank, he stood around awkwardly without much to do. He looked at the various posters strung about, the warning on the pump from the local sheriff about driving off without paying, and looked back into the van to watch Bixby roll over uncomfortably. He waited until he heard a loud clicking sound, seeing Bixby jump a little at the thump of the pump, before removing it and heading inside to pay.

He noticed that they had a two-Splash-Cola-products-for-two-dollars special going on, and so he picked up two. One of them was a shiny new flavor he wasn't too sure about, but he decided he'd give it a shot and try something new. Worst case, it would turn out horrible and he'd just give it to Glenn. He thought about Cris drooling all over the van's armrest, and figured she'd probably at least have dry mouth by the time she woke up. He picked up some flavored tea and some water for her, and some candy bars for later. He walked up to the counter and immediately—and unintentionally—caught a whiff of the clerk, who wore way too much of the gas station's own cheap cologne.

"That everything?" the clerk asked him.

"Yeah," Kody said, trying not to breathe as much as possible. His nostrils had been assaulted enough for one night. He suddenly realized he'd forgotten the cat food.

"Oh, wait, hold up."

He ran to look at the small stock of cat food and tried to decide the difference among them. He wanted to get the one Bixby would like the best. He looked at the differences between the dry food and the moist stuff, between turkey, chicken, and shrimp.

"Wait, what the hell…it's a damn cat!"

He grabbed the cheapest can off the shelf and ran back to the front, paying for everything. Kody shuffled everything around, trying to carry it all in one arm as he stepped out of the store and walked back to the van. A warm breeze blew by as he got nearer to the door. He stopped to take it in. He was finally going to get away from the town—to do something on his own. He didn't feel much like a kid, not like he used to.

He got to the van and opened his door, setting the stuff in his seat. He divvied it up between them—handing Glenn his soda and cat food, while setting Cris's stuff next to him in the cup holder and on the floor, stealing a glance at her before setting his eyes back on the way home.

G was right…she's a hell of a girl. Guess maybe I am kinda lucky to have her as a friend, he thought, smiling to himself and starting up the engine.. He felt a small, private satisfaction as he watched the gas gauge needle raise to *F*, and pulled out of the gas station, finally ready to head home.

12. Home (Chocolate with Marshmallows)

"If love and hate are opposite ends of the spectrum, where does jealousy fit in?"

– Cris's Journal

Kody told Glenn to wait in the van as he pulled into the driveway. His mom's car sat in front of them, so he figured she and his sister probably stayed in to have one of their girl's nights, to which he was seldom invited, and even less frequently attended. He climbed out of the van and walked up to the porch. As he approached, he noticed a light on in his room. He tried peering through his bedroom window without looking like a creeper, but the curtain prevented him from seeing the full figure of the trespasser.

"It better not be Kara," Kody thought aloud, "she knows she's not allowed in my room when I'm not home! Ugh, I hope mom's still up."

Kody put on his devilish big-brother grin as he made his way for the house. He got up to the porch and unlocked the front door. He made his way inside and tried to stay quiet since he wasn't sure if his mom was actually awake. Besides, he wanted to surprise the intruder. He crept down the hallway to his room and slowly opened the door. Kody stopped short as he walked in, realizing who was in his room. She must've been waiting for him for a while, because she had fallen asleep on his bed.

* * *

Glenn unwrapped a candy bar and began eating it when he noticed Cris trying to sit up.

"Arm fall asleep?" Glenn looked as smug as ever, enjoying the crunchy peanuts in his candy and listening to Bixby devour his cheap tuna.

"Where are we?" she asked, still groggy.

"We're at K-kody's; he just went inside to get his stuff."

"Oh, we're here already? How long was I out?" She rubbed her eyes.

"Only about h-half an hour or so."

"Huh. Felt longer."

"Maybe it w-was."

"Hey…are you messing with me again? Hasn't anyone taught you that it's not nice to mess with the sleepy girl? Might end badly for you."

Cris tried to scowl, but wasn't very effective while she was still yawning.

"Hey, let me ask you a question."

"And thus, the c-courtesy was granted." Glenn snickered at his own bad joke.

"I'm serious! How come you take so many sleeping pills?"

"H-how do you know about those?" he arched an eyebrow.

"I saw all the bottles on the table; Kody told me what they were."

"Ah, of c-course. I have trouble sleeping."

"A lot of people do. Insomnia isn't exactly uncommon, but the amount you take…it's way too much! It can't be healthy for you, and there's no way you need that many, so what's really going on?"

"Don't worry about it, C-cris."

"I'm not just going to ignore all that, Glenn; I'm really worried about you!"

"What about K-kody?"

Cris was taken aback. "Huh? What about Kody?"

"I'd bet it's h-him you're more concerned with than anyone, am I right?"

"What are you talking about? He's just a friend."

"Does that d-disappoint you?"

Cris stared at him, mouth agape. Shaking her head, she quickly recomposed herself and watched Glenn, trying to figure out where he was coming from. Normally she would assume it was just Glenn being Glenn, but the unusual nature of his comment made her second guess that notion. Bixby let out a satisfied meeerow as he finished his can of tuna and nuzzled it, knocking it to the ground. He scratched his claws against Glenn's leg before turning around and crawling back to his little nest.

"I apologize, I didn't mean to r-read so much into it, but for someone who so adamantly denies such a claim, you certainly do seem…c-concerned with that boy."

Cris maintained a restricted interested. "How so?"

"You've taken more than just a p-personal fascination in his and Alma's little quarrel."

"Of course! I'm worried about them! He's a good friend, and Alma's my best friend!"

"That may b-be, but you forget that while I may not kn-know you as well as they d-do, I've known you for much l-longer. You haven't changed that much from the little girl who used to ask for my help b-baking cookies."

"Thanks for that, by the way. You bake some mean cookies."

Glenn was caught in a rare opportunity that forced him to reveal his oppressed smile.

"Of course. I'm j-just saying…though he c-can't see it, you wear your h-heart on your sleeve."

"I'm just concerned about my friends, okay?"

Glenn nodded, ceding his point.

Seeing Cris's rising agitation, he changed the subject.

"Hungry at all? Kody picked up some snacks from the g-gas station. We have some candy bars and your choice of either tea, a Splash soda, or water."

"Is it bubble tea?"

"I don't think so."

"I'll take the Splash cola, thanks."

"Good choice."

Cris stared out the window, watching the stars in the night sky above. She twisted the top off her soda, enjoying the crack and fizz of a freshly opened beverage. The Splash cola burned with sweetness as it washed its way down her throat. Whether Glenn was onto something, or simply rambling his nonsensical ramblings didn't matter much—it was a good night, and nothing would take that away from her.

* * *

"I was pretty surprised when I saw her at the door."

Kody jumped as he heard his mother's voice behind him.

"She came by an hour or two ago. I told her you hadn't come by to pick up your things yet, so she asked if she could wait. I didn't think you'd mind."

"Mom, you're still awake?"

"Of course. I wanted to say goodbye to my baby boy before he went on his trip. Who knows when I'll see you again? I made some hot chocolate: the marshmallow-y kind. Want some?"

Kody nodded.

"I'll go get you a cup," she said as she walked off toward the kitchen.

Kody, not wanting to disturb the girl on the bed, gathered his bags and set them in a pile near the door. He sat on the foot of his bed, anxious and watching her sleep for a minute, as his mom came back into the room.

"Here you go, honey," she said as she handed him the hot chocolate. "I made some for Alma, too; I'll just leave it on the dresser."

"Thanks, Mom." He sipped some of his hot chocolate.

"You're welcome, sweetie." She began to walk away, but she stopped and looked back toward him.

"She seemed pretty upset when she got here. What happened between you two?"

"We kinda got into a fight. Didn't mean to. She kinda…walked into the wrong place at the wrong time?"

"Wrong place at the wrong time, huh? Believe me, we've all been there. Well, don't worry too much about it. You two will work it out, I'm sure. She knows how you feel about her. After all, she's your first love."

"Yuh huh."

Kody cringed as his mother playfully mussed up his hair before giving him a hug. He tried to resist, but found his efforts futile and quickly returned the sentiment.

"I love you, Konrad; be careful and safe, all right? You better come back in one piece. Kara needs her big brother. Promise me you'll call."

"I will."

"Okay. Have a nice trip," she told him as she left the room.

Kody's heart started to race at the thought of whether or not to wake Alma up or let her rest. He sat for a minute, watching her sleep. He eventually realized she would never forgive him if he didn't say goodbye, and prepared to defend himself against whatever flurry of violence Alma was sure to inflict upon awakening. He moved next to her, reaching out to her before pulling his hand back, trembling. He took a deep breath, steadied his hand, and gently reached out again, this time shaking her shoulder. Her skin was as soft as he remembered.

"Alm, you awake?"

She rolled over and looked up, slowly becoming aware that Kody was back. She sat up.

"Hey…" she said in a sleepy haze.

"Morning, sleepyhead," he said, breathing a sigh of relief and flashing her a coy smile. "Want some hot chocolate?"

"What?"

"My mom made some. It's cooled off a bit, but it's still warm."

"Oh, yeah. Sure."

Kody got up to get the cup off the dresser and handed it to Alma, who started blowing carefully on it to make sure it was cool enough.

"What time is it?" she asked him.

"A little after ten."

"Geez! I didn't mean to fall asleep for that long!"

"How long did you mean to fall asleep for?"

"Ugh, you dork!"

She nudged him playfully, releasing some of the tension. She was careful not to spill her hot chocolate as she took a sip.

"I was just gonna rest my eyes for a minute. Didn't think it'd take you this long to get back."

Kody stopped carefully to consider how he should proceed, without trying to offend her.

"Okay, so…I'm back. Why were you waiting for me to come home?"

"To say goodbye? I wanted to talk to you before you left goofus."

"It's not like I'm not coming back. I'll only be gone a few weeks. It's no big, really."

"I couldn't leave things the way they were. I didn't want my last memory of you to be you yelling at me about how much you hated me. Even if you'll only be gone for a few weeks."

Kody rubbed the back of his head. "I don't hate you, Alm, and I didn't mean to yell at you either. I didn't even know you were there!" He groaned as he rested his forehead in his palm, trying to think. Alma watching him with bright, expectant eyes only added to the pressure.

"It was just...I don't know...it's hard sometimes. I see you every day, but I can't say anything 'cause of the stupid break-up rules or whatever. 'Cause then I'm *that guy* that just can't let go. That, or you would've just ignored me."

"Kody, you *are* that guy. But that's okay, that's who you are. I actually kinda like that about you. You find something and you stick with it, even if it doesn't work the greatest. And you could've said something to me. I wouldn't have ignored you."

Kody looked up, regaining his focus.

"The last time I talked to you, you broke up with me. Not exactly strong incentive for a second go-around. It hurts too much to be near you and not be with you. I can't even... ugh, damnit. I can't even think straight when it comes to you, okay? I try to do what I think is right, but it always comes out wrong and dumb and I just end up making things worse."

Alma took his hand. Feeling the smoothness of her fingers on his own once again calmed him down. His heart slowed enough for him to breathe. The odd mixture of sweetness and alcohol that he so often smelt on her reminded him of their finest moments. She felt like home.

"It hurts me, too, you know! It's not like I don't like you, or don't care about you. It's just that there was too much going on with me then. School, putting up with my mom, trying to find a college: I couldn't handle all of that and having a boyfriend!"

"I'm sorry about all that. Hopefully now it's a little better for you."

"Hardly. I mean school's over, but everyone's got their summer plans, and I'm stuck here with no college, no boyfriend, nothing but Maria...er, Mom."

"I'm sorry, Alm," Kody hesitated before continuing, "a lot of that's on you."

"I know." Alma let him go, dropping her head in her hands. "I'm not perfect, okay? Sometimes I'm stupid and I don't know what I want, ya know? I mess up."

Kody sat up, putting his arm around her shoulder. "Hey, forget about it. You've got me."

"No, I don't. Kody, you're a sweetie, but I don't *have you*. You aren't even going to be here in the morning. You're leaving, remember? You were so desperate to get away from me?"

"Alm, this whole thing has nothing to do with getting away from you; it's about getting away from *here*."

Kody saw a small glimmer of hope in her eyes as she raised her head.

"Wait…so you really aren't mad at me?"

He shook his head.

"You're not trying to get as far away as possible?"

"Of course not." He had a brilliant idea. "In fact…you should come with us."

"What? On your road trip?" Alma looked at him, disbelief filling her henna eyes.

"Yeah, we have room. Looks like the policy is everyone's invited. Even cats, apparently."

She gave him a funny look, but he continued.

"I'm sure Cris wouldn't mind sharing some of her stuff until we can pick up some things for you, and between us we should have enough money to cover you."

"Are you sure about this? Do you really want me to come?"

"Definitely."

Alma nurtured a reluctant smile, seemingly unsure of whether or not she should give in to Kody's flights of fancy. She looked away from Kody, standing up and pacing around his room. Her line of sight followed the pattern of the faded yellow wallpaper along the wall to the window, and she walked up to it. She brushed the curtains aside, looking out at the van running and rumbling under the evening starlit sky. She stopped and turned back to look at Kody's face. Seeing the energy flowing from it, it was enough to cause her dimples to crease just a little more. She nodded.

"All right, I'll go. I'll call my mom tomorrow. I don't really feel like talking to her tonight."

"Okay, but we gotta get my stuff out to the van; Glenn and Cris have been waiting out there for a while now."

"'Kay," Alma said as her small smile grew into a gleaming one.

They each grabbed a bag and started heading for the door.

"Hey, wait up a sec." Alma stopped him.

He stood and turned to look at her as she set his bag down. She walked over to him and paused just short of him, looking up into his eyes.

"Hmm, what's up?"

"Nothing," she trailed off as she leaned into him, raising her head up to kiss him. As their lips connected, she leaned her body in closer, knocking Kody off balance and causing both of them to fall onto the door, pushing the knob into the wall.

"Just wanted you to know where I stand," she told him quietly as she pulled back, helping him regain his balance.

"Alm…" Kody was breathless.

"Knocked you off your feet." She winked at him.

"Aww, you two were smoochin'! I'm *so* telling Mom!" a little girl yelled from the opposite side of the doorway.

"Kara! You brat!"

Alma backed up as Kody gave chase after his little sister, watching her run right into their mother.

"Ow, Ooh…Mommy, guess what Kody was doing!"

"Kara, sweetie? You don't need to worry about what your brother was doing. I think it's time for you to go to bed," their mom replied.

"But Moooom!"

"Now, sweetie."

"Damn it…!" Kara accidentally let it slip out.

"What was that?" Kody's mother feigned fury.

"Shit! Oh no, I meant crap!"

Kara started to cry as she ran off to her room, her mother smiling at both Kody and Alma as she started after her daughter.

"This is what you choose to teach your little sister?" Kody's mom shook her head. "Have a safe trip," she told them as she went to go attend to Kara.

"Thanks, Ms. Lehane."

"Tabby!" she heard called out from Kara's room.

"Right. Thanks, Tabby!" Alma corrected herself.

"Thanks, Mom!" Kody shouted back as he and Alma headed out the door.

Kody slid the side door open as they got back to the van, managing to get the attention of both Cris and Glenn, who were now fighting over the radio.

"Took you long enou—Alma!" Cris stated, shocked.

"Hey, Cris."

They exchanged glances, Cris seeing the joy brimming from her best friend's face. Alma reached forward and made her best attempt at hugging Cris from behind the seat. Glenn hadn't noticed Alma at first, as he had won control of the radio, and resumed his position by the window in the middle row seats. He just now noticed her and couldn't help but stare.

"Aa-a-alma…" he spoke in complete disbelief.

"You must be Glenn; nice to meet you!"

She introduced herself politely, taking his hand and pulling him into a friend hug.

"L-likewise," he said in a distracted tone, before forcing his attention on Bixby.

"Glenn, could you move your stuff to the back row of seats?" Kody asked.

"Y-yes. W-wait, why?" he replied as he broke out of his odd trance and helped Kody move both of their bags to the back seat, packing them down so they would fit.

"She's coming with us," Kody stated firmly.

"As in *with us* with us?" Cris couldn't contain her surprise.

"Yup, yup. I'm with you guys all the way! Speaking of...I might need to mooch off you ju—st a little until we can get my stuff together. That okay?" Alma was chipper as ever.

"Yeah Alm, that's fine..."

Distracted, Cris looked to Kody, hoping for some kind of explanation, but he was too busy helping Alma get situated to notice anything else. Her attention was redirected to her best friend.

"Um...Cris?" Alma stared at the passenger seat.

"Huh?" Cris just looked at her, expectant, until she realized what Alma wanted.

"Oh, right." Cris got out and took her place next to Glenn and Bixby.

"Is everyone ready?" Kody asked as he made his way back to his seat.

"Y-yes," Glenn responded. Cris, now next to him, nodded.

"Mhmm," Alma replied, climbing into her new spot next to Kody.

Glenn looked at Cris, who turned away and set her attention on the sidewalk just on the other side of the window. He nudged Bixby toward her, but Bixby only bit his hand and climbed into the far back seat, upon his new throne of bags. Glenn gave up his efforts for the time being and continued to plan his plans and scheme his schemes.

Alma put her hand on Kody's knee and smiled at him, as he reciprocated the effort and placed his hand on top of hers. They pulled out of the driveway and started heading for the city limits, ready to finally hit the road.

13. Dusty, Starry Darkly Clouded Sky Night

"Too much time is spent worrying about the past and the future; it's the present that'll kill you."

– The Memoirs of Alexandria Matier

Somewhere near the Mojave Desert

The stars gleamed brightly over the warm desert sand. Brush and ash covered the scenery, only a few near-dead trees standing. A man, a rough, rugged man, with sandy blonde hair covering his stubbled face, locked the doors of the bar for the night. He was probably in his early twenties—though even he didn't know for sure—and wore a long, brown leather duster, much like the cowboys of old. He glanced at the sky, searching for the constellations he still remembered."Waste of time," he muttered under his breath as he turned from the bar.

He stepped down from the curb to cross the street, though his footing was a bit off. He caught the curb instead as he reached the other side, causing him to stumble onto the sidewalk. He moved on down the causeway with little grace, oblivious to what had just transpired. He continued further along the sidewalk until he reached the only twenty-four-hour convenience store in town. He stared at it for a moment, shielding his eyes from the bright of the sign. He pondered it had too many damn lights, but in the end it didn't matter. Somehow he was still alive. He went inside.

"Hey, how's it going? Haven't seen you in here for a few days," the clerk called to him.

The man pulled out a small list of items he needed to pick up."Been busy," he replied, disinterested in petty conversation.

"We're out of cinnamon right now; we should get some more in a few days."

"All right," the man said as he grabbed a gallon of milk from the freezer. "Any oatmeal left?"

"Let me check the overstock cart in back."

The modestly overweight clerk proceeded to enter a door behind him that looked like it led to some sort of office. While the clerk was in the back, the man moved over to the cooler and grabbed a 40-ounce bottle of beer and some assorted liquor. He waited at the counter as the clerk returned with a box of oatmeal that looked as though it was never intended to leave the stockroom.

"That gonna be all for you, bud?" the clerk asked him.

"Yeah, just put it on my tab. I'll get it on Friday," the man responded as the clerk bagged his items.

"See you on Friday then. Take it easy until then, chief," the clerk called out to the man as he left the store.

The man continued down the road, accompanied only by the dim glow of the street lamps. He passed by a few dilapidated houses with fenced-in front yards and no fencing on the sides. He recognized one with an old swing set and a large rubber ball being blown around by the less-than-forceful wind. He kept going until he reached a small building that looked more like a shady motel than an actual apartment complex. He wasn't too eager to head back inside yet. He found a dusty patch of what passed for grass in the town and took a seat as he fished around in his pocket for some smokes.

"Fuckin'—where are they?"

He kept searching until he finally remembered he had left them in his coat. He reached in and found them hiding out in his upper breast pocket. He pulled his Zippo out along with them and lit one up as his gaze wandered toward the stars nestled in the dark cloudy sky.

"All of 'em shinin'… fer what? Don't mean a damn thing."

He inhaled and embraced the exhilaration as the smoke filled his lungs. He let it take him over, the slow burn searing his throat as the smoke gradually seeped out through his mouth and nose. He tasted of ecstasy of decay; he bones sought it more than he could ever express. The nicotine invigorated his otherwise lifeless body. He reluctantly exhaled.

"I'm gettin' too old fer this shit."

He didn't mind smoking in his apartment, he just didn't want to be back inside. The cold dank held nothing for him. He was a child of the wind and of the earth. Dirt felt more natural beneath his torn up feet than carpets.

He cast a secret prayer into the dark, clouded sky. Didn't matter if anyone was listening. No harm in stacking the odds. And maybe, just once, things would play out for him. Cigarette ash fell to ground, scuffing his boot.

"Damn, done already? Figures."

He left the butt on the ground and went up the flight of stairs, proceeding to unlock the first door he came across. He realized it was already open, but he was just going through the motions. He entered the apartment and locked the door behind him. He always left the lights on, and could hardly seem surprised to see a woman passed out on his couch. Despite her uncouth appearance, the woman was stunningly dressed and physically maintained. She just wasn't what one might call pretty. He went into the kitchen to put the groceries away.

"Didja bring back anything for me?" the rather unattractive woman asked as she sat up to see what he had brought home.

"Didn't think ya'd still be here," he stated coldly.

"Should've figured I'd come back at some point…or at least think about what you'd do if I did," she responded, more sly than seductive.

"How 'bout this: they were sold out or I didn't have the money. Take your pick. Rent's late; I left my half on the table, so take care of it tomorrow," he told her as he went into his room, sternly slamming the door shut behind him.

"Ass!" she scoffed. "Fine, I'll cover it, but that means I get half of everything!" she shouted toward his room as she pulled herself off the couch.

She checked around to make sure he wasn't coming out. With the site secure, she checked her phone to see if she had missed any messages. She put her phone away and stumbled over to the fridge, taking his beer and a small bag of popcorn, and aloofly staggered back onto the couch. She began drinking, her eyes glazing over as she became mesmerized by the television once again.

14. Cold Summer Mornings

"The more I try to figure something out, the less I understand it. I think the lesson here is some things should just be appreciated as they are."

– Kody's Notebook

Near the Southern Border of Ohio

It was dark and serene, with only the quiet sound of the engine humming to complement the chorus of snores. Kody was still on deck for driving, but that didn't bother him much. He didn't feel like sleeping; he had far too many things on his mind to even try. Cris had fallen asleep, resting her head on Glenn's shoulder, with his head resting softly upon hers. Kody listened to the radio, trying to keep it as low as possible so he wouldn't wake the others.

His mind drifted, thinking about what had happened only a few hours before. The concert was still fresh in his mind, and he had not forgotten Geroge's song—or his words. He glanced over at Alma, who was now sleeping peacefully in the seat next to him. He couldn't help but smile.

He hadn't hoped, let alone imagined, things would go this well for him. It had been a long time since he felt content, and he didn't want to risk letting that feeling get away by falling asleep.

He reached over, grabbing his bottle of Splash soda from the cup holder. He twisted the cap, waiting for but never hearing the satisfying crunch and then hiss of a freshly opened soda. He inspected the bottle and discovered that someone had drank about half of it before putting the cap back on and replacing it to its rightful spot in the cup holder.

He went through the list of suspects. Alma had been with him the whole time; it wasn't her. Glenn had his own soda between his legs, which Kody observed teetering with the motion of the van. This left only one suspect who wasn't a conceited cat. She happened to be resting on Glenn's shoulder. He decided on account of his exceptionally good mood that he would dismiss her crime and treachery, just this once.

He started humming along to the music and kept on driving down the highway. He became absorbed in the melodies and lost track of the time. As the album neared its end, he heard some rustling in the back seat. He checked the rearview mirror and noticed that Glenn was now sleeping with his head leaning against the window. Cris was sitting upright, groggy but conscious. *The bandit stirs* was the first thought to cross his mind.

"Morning," Kody said quietly, as not to wake the others.

"Hey." she smiled.

"So, was it good for you?" Kody smirked.

"What?" Cris blew a mess of hair out of her face, still rubbing her eyes.

"Snagging my Splash cola. I bet it was pretty tasty, huh?"

"Oh, that was yours? Glenn said you got it for me."

Kody could see the surprise plastering her face, condemning the sneaky prodigy resting next to her. "Did he now?" Kody looked over to Glenn, certain that he had just seen him flash a subtle smirk in his sleep.

Cris looked out the window before turning back to Kody. "Sorry."

"Don't worry about it. Went to a good place."

"Sure did." Cris patted her stomach. "Hey, what time is it?"

"Dunno. Sometime around four?"

"Wow, I was out that long? And you're still driving? You've got to be crazy tired by now!" She started raising her voice but quickly caught herself.

"Maybe a bit. But I've still got a little Splash cola left to keep me going." Kody waved away her concerns.

"You should get some sleep. Get off at the next exit and let me drive for a while."

"You sure? I'm really not that tired."

"Yeah, I need to use the bathroom, anyway."

Kody nodded. He was fighting it, but his fatigue showed.

"I don't know how you can listen to Death Cab for more than half an hour and not fall asleep," Cris said, noticing he had the CD on repeat.

"What, you don't like Death Cab now?"

"It's not that, it's just that the music is so slow. If I was listening to Ben Gibbard for any period of time while I was tired, I'd definitely pass out. I mean maybe if it was The Postal Service or something, but not Death Cab."

"You know about The Postal Service?" Kody looked back, genuinely surprised.

"Hey, I'm not just another pretty face you know. Just because I don't have a freaky obsession with music like some of us doesn't mean I don't know a thing or two. Besides, chicks dig musicians." She winked at him. "Didn't you know?"

Kody thought about how much she sounded like G as he laughed off his small embarrassment by changing the subject.

"So…caffeine. It's great."

He took another swig of his soda. She grinned as she pointed out the upcoming off-ramp. Kody made his way off the highway and crossed the lanes, pulling into a rustic gas station sitting just off the side of the road.

"Alma, Glenn: you two want anything?" Kody asked them. Glenn barely grunted before falling back asleep.

"Hmm?"

Alma rubbed her eyes as she woke up a bit, the dim lights of the gas station still being too bright for her.

"We're at a gas station. Want anything?"

"Um, a blanket and a pillow would be nice."

Alma made her request, barely conscious and slipping, before she shifted around and completely fell back asleep.

"I'll get the van while you use the little ladies' room," Kody said, mocking Cris as usual.

"Nah, I'll wait." She barely even noticed.

"I thought you had to go." He gave her a strange look.

"I'm not going into that creepy gas station by myself! There might guys even more perverted than you in there!"

"Really? Guess that means I should start recruiting for my creepers club then! We could have meetings where we just stand around and creep girls out all day. Hmm, we'd need a treasurer though…" Kody pulled his fingers across his chin, stroking his non-existent beard.

"Wait, you guys have meetings now? And wouldn't you have to take a little break before you officially started? Otherwise we might not realize that you've all organized." she smirked.

"Ouch, Cris, ouch."

"Hey, you set me up for a twofer. Had to take it. Now hurry up, I got to go!" she stuck her tongue out at him.

Kody remained baffled by the insane girl logic as they both got out of the van. Cris stood outside crossing her arms while she waited for Kody to refill the van. He continued to observe the craziness that was Cris during the warm, early summer morning.

"Are you cold?" he asked her, half-joking as he began to refuel the van.

"What do you think? This shirt isn't nearly as warm as you might think," she remarked. She wore a thin, dark-green, low-cut, button-up t-shirt with the picture of a pink lion on it. He just stared.

"What?" She furrowed her brow.

"It's summer, Cris. June. It's like 70 degrees outside in the shade, in the morning!"

"It's still four a.m., and it's colder than it usually is!"

"So it's 65?"

Kody noticed that despite her irrational protests, her shirt was protruding a bit more than it normally did; apparently her body didn't disagree. The pump made its thump sound, drawing Kody's attention back to matters at hand.

"Oh, thank God." Cris rushed Kody, trying to get inside.

"Seriously! You can't be that cold! The stores all have air conditioning on for Pete's sake!"

"Ugh! Look, Kody, you aren't a girl so you'll never understand, okay?"

"Guess I should be grateful for small favors." He chuckled.

She hit him less than playfully, and suddenly it wasn't so funny. They started heading inside as Kody took off his light spring jacket and brushed it off a bit. He placed it around Cris's shoulders as they reached the doors.

"Hmm, it looks like you really might be a gentleman after all... since when?" she said, looking at him with an unusually soft eye.

"Since there's no way you'll be less crazy in Air Conditioning Land than you were outside," he smirked. "Not saying my shoulder hurts, but I'd like to avoid getting punched again, if at all possible. You hit surprisingly hard."

"Hey, I know how to throw down."

"I'm sure." He smiled wryly.

"Oh really?" She caught him. "And Mr. Konrad Lehane, who was until a minute ago too good to give up his favorite jacket, has something to say on the matter?"

"How do you know my first name? I've never told anyone. Only my mom calls me that."

"I got ways."

He couldn't tell what kind of look he saw in her eyes, but his curiosity drew him in.

"Go pee!" he scolded her as he looked around for some food.

"Hmph!" She snubbed him as she went to go find the bathroom.

"Crazy, crazy woman," he muttered to himself.

He grabbed some snacks from the shelf and then made his way around to find something for their furrier counterpart. After carefully examining their selection—for Cris was a woman who liked to take her time—he found that they had the usual, or what he imagined to be the usual, for cat food.

There was turkey, beef, tuna, chicken…he continued to look. He found a turkey–chicken hybrid that sounded so appetizing that Kody thought he might just make Bixby share (he may have been more tired than he realized). Deciding his odds against the apparently strong cat weren't all that great, he snagged a second can for just in case.

He meandered about the soda aisle for bit, not finding anything in particular, and made his way back up front, starting up a conversation with the clerk as he paid. The guy was about as tired as Kody, and while no potential for meaningful dialogue was present, some interesting discourse regarding upcoming video games brought a brief surge of life and amusement back into Kody.

In what seemed like a lifetime later, Cris emerged from the bathroom, and the two made their way back to the van. Kody crawled into the back seat and dug out some blankets and pillows while Cris made her way into the driver's seat. He tossed blankets over Glenn and Alma and gently placed pillows underneath each of their heads before getting comfortable himself.

"Where are the keys?" Cris asked.

"They're not up there?"

He checked his pocket and felt a small surge of panic course through him as they were nowhere to be found.

"I don't see them!"

"Crap, that ain't right!" he said as he checked his pockets again. He was sure he put them in there!

"Got 'em!" Cris found them in his jacket pocket.

"Don't scare me like that, geez!" Kody started to calm down.

"Sorry." She glanced back, waiting for him to look up. She caught his gaze.

"And thanks. Now get some sleep, all right?" Cris politely commanded as she passed his jacket back. He wrapped himself up with it and nodded. She changed the CD, putting Death Cab away and putting in Paramore.

"Oh, Kody, one more thing. Do you mind if I finish this off?" she asked, holding up his Splash cola with the cap already off.

"Not that I mind, but we were just in a store. Why didn't you get one then?"

"Trying to cut back on sugary soda."

"So…" he stared at her, to which she simply stared back expectantly. He shrugged. "Yeah, sure, whatever. Go for it."

"Crazy girl logic…crazy ferret logic," he muttered, barely still awake.

Cris drank the rest of his Splash soda before starting the engine. She drove out of the gas station and headed back toward the highway. She noticed that Alma was covered up now, the blanket carefully placed around her so she was both insulated and warm, as Kody now knew how cold those warm summer mornings could be.

She noticed a pillow cautiously placed right behind Alma's neck to keep her comfortable without waking her up. *He cares about her so much,* she thought to herself as she got back on the freeway. It started to drizzle, though she found the sound relaxing and a welcome distraction. She noticed Bixby wander up near her leg.

"Aw, you can't be down there, little guy; it's dangerous. Come up here with me."

She picked him up and found it odd that he offered no resistance. She set him on her lap, and he snuggled up between the warmth of her thighs as he lay quietly, purring. She petted him gently and couldn't help but wonder if this was the best she'd ever do.

15. Once Upon a Danny's

"Personally, I'm not one to set out without a plan. But it turns out you find some of the coolest stuff that way."

– Cris's Journal

The sun began to rise when Cris made the call that they needed to have an actual destination. While she enjoyed driving and being with her friends, she realized that they weren't actually going anywhere. She thought about places they could go when her stomach began roaring with bestial fury. She realized they hadn't stopped for food since the last gas station. She kept driving until she finally saw the shiny yellow placard posted on the side of the highway. Switching lanes, she set a new course and got off at the next exit.

"Where are we going, Kody?" Alma asked, awakened by the van's sudden change in speed. She rubbed the sleep from her eyes, looking around in a groggy haze.

"Just the best place ever...Danny's!" Cris responded, excited at the prospect of getting solid food in her stomach.

"Cris? Oh, hey! Mm, that sounds really good. Are we close?"

"I think it's only a few minutes from here. That's what the last sign said anyway."

"Okay, just wake me up when we get there," Alma said as she drifted back to sleep.

Cris started thinking about where she wanted to go, what could be fun for all of them, and places she'd never been able to see but had always wanted to. She went through a list of places in her head and kept the ones she'd like to visit most in a neat and tidy order in her mind, so she could discuss them at breakfast.

"We also need to find a place to shower and change around here," she considered, catching a whiff of the van's collective stench. The thought had crossed her mind that there may even be a faint scent of cat pee, but her seat felt dry and she let the notion pass. She tried to think of where the closest motel might be, but realized that she wasn't familiar with the area or even the county they were in. "Hmm…hope Kody or Glenn know their way around here."

She looked around a bit as she was driving, realizing that the plants and trees seemed somehow different. It occurred to her then that she didn't know how far Kody had driven and hadn't paid much attention to the road signs; she had just decided to keep on the same road after she took over. She would have to figure out where they were before she could figure out where they were going.

She saw Danny's coming up on the right hand side of the road and pulled into the parking lot. She parked the van and paused for a minute, considering the best way to wake everyone up. She let out a rather boisterous "Good morning!" in hopes of waking everyone at once. However, only Alma stirred, starting to shift her body a little bit before she sat up.

"Morning," Alma replied, still visibly tired. Cris's face contorted into a devious smile, which Alma recognized with unfortunate familiarity. She had no idea what Cris was about to do, but she knew it couldn't be any good.

"Alma, plug your ears."

"What? Why?" Alma looked at her, plainly confused.

"Plug your ears," Cris insisted.

Alma cringed as she covered her head with a pillow. Cris turned the radio on quietly to search for some hard rock station. She found one playing Rage Against the Machine's "Sleep Now in the Fire" and cranked it up all the way.

Cris snickered at her genius until Bixby hissed and clawed his way out of her lap. He started running up her stomach, claws sticking to the thin cotton and tearing up her shirt in the process. He continued climbing along the side of her face before getting tangled in her hair. She became rather

102

cross with him when she realized urine was slowly trickling down her forehead, some of which was getting into her mouth.

"Ew, gross!" Cris was furious, but quickly closed her mouth as she wiped her face off with part of her sleeve.

"Oh my God, honey. Are you okay?" Alma quickly reached across the center console and turned the radio back down.

"Gah! What the hell, Cris? Turn it down!" Kody shouted, flailing about wildly, overwhelmed with anger and confusion.

Alma carefully pulled Bixby out of Cris's hair, trying not to tangle it too much. He continued peeing as Alma got him out, and she opened her door to take him outside. She set him down in the grass, just on the other side of the parking lot curb, and stayed with him.

Glenn looked surprised more than anything, but also with a less-than-subtle hint of irritation covering his face. He got out, checking on Bixby and readjusting himself, having near had an incident akin to his little friend's. Stepping outside of the van, he shielded his eyes as they adjusted to the bright light of day.

Kody's initial confusion having worn off, he calmed down and started to piece together what had happened. Seeing Cris, the aftermath of Bixby's mangling, he couldn't help but burst into laughter.

"Dude, that cat is awesome!"

She glared back at him as she looked in the mirror to survey the damage. Her face was a little bloody from light cat scratches, and she was covered in cat piss. She took her shirt off, using its remains to wipe the blood and piss off her face, before realizing that Kody was still in the back, cackling.

"It's not funny, Kody!" Cris could barely contain her rage.

"You're right. It's poetic justice!"

He started to calm himself down as his eyes traced the curves of Cris's body, her sitting there adorned in only her bra and a tight pair of jeans. Once she finished cleaning herself off as best she could, she realized Kody was still in the back, checking her out.

"Hey, quit staring, you perv! Get out!"

Kody scrambled out of the van to see Alma coddling Bixby, who was surprisingly inviting of Alma's touch. Glenn, while concerned for his kitten, could see he was in good hands as he noticed Kody walk up behind him.

"Heh…qu-quite the awakening, huh?" Glenn was still a bit frazzled.

"Seriously…having second thoughts about her coming with us?"

"C-charisma? Sh-she's a bit inquisitive, but otherwise livens things up. I imagine you might be having such doubts, however."

"Nah, she's usually pretty cool. Besides, it was totally worth it to see Bixby put her in line!"

"That's not—" Glenn let it go.

The men watched Alma as she babied the small fur ball. She nuzzled his tiny kitty whiskers, rubbing her nose against his own. Bixby did not appear averse to the course of action, and even returned the gesture.

"You were just so scared, weren'tcha? You're a feisty one, you are!"

She gently rubbed behind his ears, forcing a soft purr to reverberate through his tiny kitty throat. Kody and Glenn conversed idly while waiting for Cris. Alma found herself completely infatuated with Bixby, who had since grown weary of such affections and was now pawing around in the grass. The kitten spotted what looked like a duck off in the distance, and slunk low to the ground, creeping along the grass with predatory awareness.

Alma couldn't help but think about how cute he looked as she reached into her pocket to pull out her phone. She couldn't find it, and kept feeling around until she realized she had forgotten it at home. Calling her mom would have to wait. She turned back, seeing the little whiskers now taking a little squat and moved away to give him some privacy.

"Good morning, boys, where's Cris?" Alma asked sweetly, rejoining them.

"Getting herself cleaned up." Kody replied.

"Bixby sure got her good, huh? Crazy girl." Alma rolled her eyes as she shook her head.

"I'll say," Kody barely let out aloud.

"I'm gonna go see if she needs any help. C'mon Bixby!"

She went to grab the kitty when Glenn stopped her.

"Huh?"

"I might think she may not w-want to see him right at this very moment..."

"Oh, right...he can't just stay out here though." Alma tried to think of a plan for him.

"I'll tend to him."

Glenn knelt to the once-again disconcerted Bixby, who no longer displayed an interest in much of anything.

"Well I'm starving, and conveniently enough, there's a Danny's right here! I'm gonna head inside and get us a table," Kody informed them as he waited for Alma to walk back to the van. Kody always enjoyed watching Alma walk away as she had nice assets—particularly when she wore her short lime-green skirt. As she got to the van, a slight warm breeze drifted by and ruffled her skirt, briefly exposing the hint of red polka dots.

"Jackpot!" he exclaimed, grateful for the fortunate gust of air. Looking around, he realized both she and Glenn were now staring at him. He quickly averted his gaze and coyly headed inside. Alma giggled at his antics and turned back to check on her friend.

"Hey, how's the weather in there?"

"Stormy. And gross. And nasty." Cris made no effort to conceal her pouting.

"Aw, it's okay, sweetie. It happens."

"Cats tearing up your favorite shirt and peeing all over you happens?"

"Um…apparently. I mean, not usually *that*…you just have bad luck with pranks, I guess. You should really leave that to me." Alma smirked.

Cris sighed with resignation. "Seems like it… how do I look?"

"Like a bear just tried to eat you."

"Ugh!" Cris frowned.

"Kidding! You look fine. The little guy didn't do anything that can't be fixed."

"God, I need a shower!"

"And we'll get you one after breakfast, 'kay? Now c'mere and let me fix your hair."

Alma took a seat in the middle row, sitting Cris down in front of her.

"I smell horrible, don't I?"

"It's nothing we can't cover up with some good body spray. Or maybe Febreze."

"Alm!"

"I'm just kidding! Kinda."

Alma kept playing with Cris's hair. She quickly brushed it out before trying to braid it, despite it still being a little damp. Not having much luck, she put Cris's hair up in a ponytail instead.

"Are you sure about this? I hate wearing it in a ponytail."

"It'll work for now. We'll get you fixed up right after we eat. Now put a shirt on; I'm hungry!"

"Okay, okay, hold on."

Cris got up and started digging through one of her bags as Alma got out and blocked the door to obscure Cris from view.

"Why'd you take it off anyway?"

"Um…it was covered in cat pee?"

"Oh, yeah…"

Cris dug through her bag to find something decent she could throw on for the time being.

"Ugh, stupid Kody."

"Hm?"

"Oh, he wouldn't stop staring at me. I didn't know he could be such a perv sometimes," Cris remarked absentmindedly.

"Yeah, well that's just part of his…"

Alma realized what Cris had just said. She turned around to look at her, forgetting Cris was getting dressed, before quickly turning back around. She suspected Cris realized what she had said, although a bit too late.

"Not like that, Alm: he was laughing at me because of the pee," eventually came out of the van.

Alma shrugged it off as she waited. Cris finished changing and got out of the van.

"So what's the verdict? Am I presentable?"

"Even better than presentable: you're shiny!" Alma remarked in a manner that only she could pull off. Finally ready, the two of them hopped out of the van and headed toward the restaurant. They passed Glenn on the way, Bixby rolling in the grass next to him.

"You've won this time, cat." Cris scowled as they passed. Alma gave her a funny look while Glenn picked up the innocent little devil.

"Hey, you keep that tiny demon away from me! He's already marked me!"

"I was just g-going to put him back in the van. I don't think they'd very much like us bringing a c-cat into the restaurant, wouldn't you say?"

Cris rolled her eyes as she and Alma continued. Glenn rubbed Bixby's furry little head as he went back to the van.

"D-don't worry, friend, I'd n-never let anyone hurt you."

Bixby looked at Glenn intently as he was set upon the seat, as if perhaps he was searching for something in Glenn's earnest eyes. Being but a young kitten, he surely forgot whatever interesting cat thoughts he might have had as he began to wander around aimlessly. Glenn closed up the van and made his way back to the restaurant, rejoining the rest of the group at a smallish corner booth. He took the only available seat next to Cris.

"So…" Kody started.

"Let's just stick to the menu." Cris was terse.

"I haven't had Danny's in forever! Good call, Cris!" Alma took a strong whiff of the waffle scent emanating from the kitchen.

"It does smell good. I figured we could all use a break from gas station food." Cris was affirmed in her decision.

"And disappoint the gods of starchy goodness so?" Kody, while grateful for Danny's, was fine with anything.

"Uh, sweetie? Look around. Still plenty of starchy goodness."

Alma brought Kody back down to earth.

"Y-yes, besides…being as we're the only non-senior citizens here, perhaps we might be able to opt for the discount."

Glenn snickered to himself as the others looked on.

"Who knows, maybe."

Cris assumed it had been his bad attempt at a joke, but there was no way to be certain. She noticed at this point that Kody and Alma were sitting rather close to each other. This forced her to recognize that in contrast Glenn was unusually distant from her, despite the close quarters the booth provided.

Though she hadn't noticed it much before, she found herself unused to not having attention in general, male or otherwise. She rarely found that people were trying to get away from her, but rather much more often trying to get closer.

"Glenn, there's plenty of space here, buddy. Why're you on the edge of the seat? Scared?" she asked.

"Oh, me? Uh…not so much as th-that, it's…just…well…"

"He thinks you're a little…pissy."

Kody couldn't hold it back any longer. He started laughing again and showed little indication he might ever stop. His outburst had caught the attention of the few other patrons. A sharp pain in his shin, caused by a well-designed yet cute and affordable shoe, however, is what caused him to yelp with pain and shut him up for good. Recovering from the sudden attack, he was assaulted yet again, this time by a soft but firm hand to the back of the head.

"Quit being a jerk, Kody. I bet we could get Bixby to pee all over you."

Alma was less tolerant of his games when they insulted her best friend. At that same moment, she and Cris caught each other's eye line, and it appeared Kody realized how much trouble he could be in if those two didn't quickly change their train of thought.

"Wh-where are we?" Glenn asked.

"Um…did you hit your head? We're at Danny's." Cris was regaining her composure.

"No, I mean *where* are we? Danny's wh-where?"

They all looked at him with the sudden understanding that they had no idea where they actually were. They all turned to Kody.

"What?"

"I just followed the road you were on. Where're we headed?" Cris had never thought to ask.

"Wait, you guys don't even know where you're going?"

Alma appeared surprised at the lack of planning on Cris's part; something like this was expected from Kody.

"Good question; I don't know." Kody resigned himself.

"I'm thinking by now we shouldn't be too far from Cincinnati. That's probably not where we we're headed, so…anyone have any ideas?"

Alma raised her hand.

"Ooh, how about we eat first? Before I become so hungry I start gnawing on you?"

"Gnawing, really?" Kody just looked at her.

"Only if you don't behave," Alma teased.

The waitress, having seen Alma wave her hand, made her way over to their table just as Alma was finishing her remark.

"I'm so sorry; I thought someone had already taken care of you guys. My name is Annie, and I'll be your server this morning. Can I start you all off with something to drink?"

They all looked at each other before deciding. They were all a bit surprised at her appearance; their waitress had a punk-rock feel they couldn't really decipher, though it resonated of early 20s independence and a lack of direction they could respect.

Glenn ordered first. "I'd like a c-coffee, please."

"Can I get two orange juices please? One for myself and one for the lady." Alma cordially motioned toward Cris.

"I'll have a hot chocolate, thanks."

Cris retaliated, not having a strong desire to drink anything yellow at the moment. Alma glared at her playfully.

"I'll take the lady's juice, please," said Kody, ever the smart ass.

"So let's see…a coffee, an orange juice, a hot chocolate, and a lady juice?" Annie smirked, revealing some rather impressive pearly yellows.

"Sounds good."

"For the hot chocolate, do you want some whipped cream on that?"

"Ooh, please!" Cris's eyes grew wide at the thought, smiling eagerly in an attempt to contain her excitement.

"Gotcha. I'll be back with that stuff in just a minute."

Annie winked at Glenn as she turned and left.

"Ooh, hey! Didja see that? Somebody likes you!" Alma teased Glenn.

"Wh-what? You're j-joking! A rather bad q-quip at that! I-I-I...she doesn't even know who I am! There's little here th-that could interest a woman like her," He said, trying to defend himself.

"Sounds like somebody's got a crush on our wait—ress!" Cris nudged him.

"I must insist all of you d-desist."

Glenn directed this at Alma, though it appeared Cris was the most severe offender.

"All right, all right...so, we need to figure out where we're going, and find a place to stay. Are we all agreed there?" Kody took charge.

"Ooh, Mr. Serious! Me likely...yeah, sounds good." Alma supported him.

Kody opened up the floor. "Is there anywhere anyone wants to go in particular?"

They all stopped to take a few minutes to deliberate. They looked around at each other to see if they could discern a glimpse of what the others were thinking, but no one really had any ideas. They glanced through their menus, deciding what to order instead.

Annie returned with the drinks, placing them in front of the respective person, Kody's having a little daiquiri umbrella in it.

"Err...are you serious?" He was half-joking.

"What, you don't like it? It's our lady drink special."

Annie appeared unconcerned with Kody as she took out her notepad and prepared to take their orders. Cris sipped on her hot chocolate, reverting to her inner child and enjoying the whipped cream most of all.

Having gotten the rest of their orders, Annie, as well as everyone else, redirected her attention to Glenn. The man in question couldn't stop fidgeting and was clearly a bit nervous. He appeared unsure of what to order.

"What can I get for you, sugar?"

"Um...d-do you have...well, that is...well, not you, p...perhaps, but your establishment, rather..."

"Uh huh?" she nodded, waiting.

"O-omelets?" he felt foolish for even suggesting it.

"Of course. We'll make yours extra special."

She smiled for Glenn, more kind than provocative, but a strong taste of both as she went back into the kitchen. The girls looked at each other without saying a word, while Kody was still messing with his umbrella.

"Not sure what you wanted?" Cris asked.

"I-it's not so much that, I just wasn't s-sure..."

"Of what?" Alma followed up close behind.

"I-I just didn't know if they had o-omelets."

"How do you not know if they have omelets? Is there anywhere that doesn't have 'em?" Kody tried to clarify.

"I-I've never been to a Danny's before."

They all looked at him, astonished. He lowered his head with shame. The group immediately came to his defense, trying to comfort him.

"Oh, hey, don't worry about it, buddy. They aren't all that popular anyway!" Kody reassured him.

"I...I just d-don't get out much."

"Well, that's why we're here, right? We'll make sure you get to check out all sorts of cool places. And you can show us some places we've never been, too!"

Cris was determined to make him feel better.

"S-sure."

"And hey, now you know that Danny's serves omelets. And for your courage, you shall be rewarded with a nice tasty breakfast!"

Even Glenn found Alma's sudden enthusiasm infectious. She slid to the side and got out of the booth, standing up.

"I'll be right back."

Cris knew where she was going and opted to go with her. She scooched passed Glenn as she got up. The girls headed toward the bathroom as Kody and Glenn sat at the table, Kody still messing with his drink and Glenn sipping on his. Glenn grabbed his coffee and got up to take Alma's seat, moving her drink to his former spot.

"Oh, hey, hi. Uh...what'cha doin' there, buddy?"

"I apologize, b-but, um...well, C-cris..."

"Ohhh, yeah, gotcha. Normally I wouldn't be complaining about sitting next to her, but this morning?"

"You n-noticed, too?" Kody nodded while Glenn took a deep breath of clean air.

"So, that Annie..." Kody had his usual inappropriate grin primed.

"P-please don't."

"Huh?"

"She d-doesn't like me, despite what those two might think. People tend to t-take pity on me. They see me as a helpless puppy or s-something to be protected and taken care of. It's c-condescending, more than anything."

"Huh. Well, don't worry about it. Whether she likes you or not, you're a cool guy. I'll vouch for that any day."

Kody's grin changed from something mischievous to more welcoming.

"Th-thanks. I apologize for taking Alma's seat. I d-don't mean to get between you two."

"Nah, it's all good. She can sit just as cozy over there."

Glenn gazed out the window, back toward the van. The kitten Bixby was rolling around on the dashboard, apparently sunning himself. Glenn redirected his attention back to Kody.

"You t-two seem to be doing better."

"Yeah? I don't know...I mean, I feel like we are, but it's still not the same, ya know?"

"Not r-really, but these things tend to take time, don't they?"

"I guess. I figure we probably just need some one-on-one time. We haven't really been alone since we patched things up. Need to finish patching is my guess." The devious grin returned.

Annie brought the food out, more attentive to what looked like a preferable change in seating. "Your girlfriends leave?" she asked.

"G-girlfriends?"

"Yeah. The cute brunette. She's not with you?" She directed at Glenn.

"N-no. I mean she's w-with us, but not *with us.*"

"Goof ball. You're kinda cute, ya' know that?"

Glenn blushed.

"Ya' from around here?"

Glenn shook his head.

"Huh, that's too bad."

"Thanks," Kody cut in, signaling her time to leave. She looked over to him, apparently sizing him up.

"Hmph. Let me know if I can get you guys anything else."

Glenn could see Annie was a little annoyed by such overt disrespect, and begrudgingly readjusted his glasses as the mutual sentiment began to settle in.

"You s-scared her away!"

"I thought you said she was bothering you! What with the pity and all!"

"I-it isn't all bad."

"Seriously?"

Seeing his knavish side, Kody was beginning to wonder if Glenn was a little more deceptive than his countenance let on, or if he just liked the sympathy more than he said.

"J-just as well."

Glenn sipped his coffee, the caffeine now kicking in and raising his spirits a little. The girls returned from their extended bathroom break to find the table rearranged into an unusual assortment.

"Aw, Cris, you shouldn't have! You went through all this trouble just to get Kody to rearrange the table so we could sit together? But, sweetie, I would've sat next to you! All you had to do was ask."

Alma playfully took Cris's hand in her own.

"Yeah...or hey, I didn't do it."

Cris looked at Glenn, her eyes demanding an explanation.

"Wh-what?" he just stared at her.

"Aw, you mean you don't wanna be my date anymore?" Alma asked her, taking her hand back away from Cris.

"Sorry, you're an expensive date." Cris wasn't playing along.

"What? Am not! You're just cheap!" Alma placed her hand over her chest, aghast.

"Oh, really? We'll see who buys you lunch next time."

Cris started getting into it, smiling evilly.

"Hmph. My Kodykins will, won't you, hun?"

Cris looked at him and mouthed "Kodykins?" with her obnoxious smile growing even wider, to which he simply shrugged, unable to provide an explanation.

"Hey, can I not be dragged into this?" He tried to play the peacekeeper.

"Fine, don't buy me lunch then. Meanie. But I'm not talking to you for the rest of the day."

Alma did her best to feign a temper tantrum, stomping her foot and snubbing him to show she would not easily be appeased.

"G-glad to have her back?" Glenn whispered into his ear. Kody chuckled.

"Whoa, hey! What was that? You two aren't allowed to keep secrets. Only we're allowed to do that!" Cris wasn't prepared to let this go.

"When did you two become such good friends anyway?" Even Alma was intrigued by this turn of events.

"Like she said," Kody began.

"It's a s-secret."

The fighting finally died down, and the ladies took their seats as they all began to eat. Alma somewhat violently devoured her Grand Slam will little effort. Cris took a little more time and consideration while eating her breakfast (she managed to keep most of it on her plate). She started with the hash browns and worked her way around the plate, finding special enjoyment in the melted cheddar on her scrambled eggs.

Kody tried to enjoy his pigs in a blanket, but he kept thinking about Annie and her lady drink remark. He wasn't going to let it stop him, but he was uncomfortable about it. Glenn unabashedly enjoyed his omelet, the caffeine finally starting to take its full effect. They started cleaning up their own table, finding it odd that Annie hadn't stopped by in a while to check up on them.

Kody restarted the discussion. "Okay, so we need to figure out where we're going…and find a place to stay."

"Anyone come up with anything yet?"

There was only a brief silence.

"California," came from Glenn.

"Cali, huh? Never figured you for a sun and beach man." Kody floated the idea.

"I've always wanted to go. I've never seen the P-pacific. I may well never get another chance, so this d-does seem like an opportune time."

"Eh, works for me," Kody agreed.

"I like it, I'm in." Cris had no objections.

"Hey, I'm just tagging along; this is your guys' trip."

"Alm, you aren't tagging. You're a part of this," Kody reminded her.

"Well, I do like pretty beaches," she hinted. "Crap, I don't have a swimsuit, though! Guess that wouldn't be too much of a problem…"

"Alma!" Cris could already see where Alma's mind was headed.

"Or we could buy one, whatever! I do need to get some stuff anyway."

"Yes, and B-bixby needs some things as well."

"Furry little devil…" Cris was still upset with the cat.

"Good, I like this. So, Cali it is. We'll go find a place to get cleaned up, get some rest, and then head out." Kody took charge.

"Don't forget about my clothes!"

"Right. You still need to call your mom, too, right?"

"Err…yeah."

Annie came back around to pick up some empty plates and dropped off the check. Kody passed it to Glenn, who got up to go pay it.

"Hold on, I still have a question for you since you failed to answer it earlier."

Cris eyed Glenn intently.

"Why'd you move?"

Glenn made no response.

"Um…are you going to give me an answer?"

She was getting impatient. Kody took another sip of his lady drink, watching how this would play out. Glenn leaned in, getting closer to her face. He was feeling bold now with the caffeine waking him up. She followed his lead, leaning in closer, expecting him to whisper his response. Alma watched on, in suspense.

"Mereeeooow," Glenn uttered.

An ocean of orange came flooding from Kody's nose and mouth, splashing the unfortunate Cris and the remainder of her food once again. Kody immediately pulled back his laughter, but it was too late: the damage was done.

"You've gotta be kidding me!" Cris was utterly defeated.

"Kody!" Alma reprimanded him, but there was no point; Cris pushed her aside, got up, and left.

"Look what you did!"

"I couldn't help it! Are you kidding me? You've gotta admit…that was pretty damn funny!"

"Maybe, but Cris has already had enough for one morning! And Glenn, what's gotten into you?"

"An interesting q-question, indeed."

They both looked at him, no idea what to make of him or his antics. They cleaned up before getting up and heading toward the exit.

"Hey, sorry about the mess," Kody explained to Annie on the way out.

"Blue skies, man," was all she said, indifferent as she went to clean up the table. Glenn looked back at her just once, but she was busy cleaning up his mess. He covered the bill and followed the rest of them outside.

"I'm driving," Alma insisted as they walked back to the van. "And both of your mouths stay shut. Hopefully I can convince Cris not to outright kill the both of you."

They got back to the van, with Cris already seated and waiting in the passenger seat, her new clean shirt covered in sticky orange. Alma climbed into the driver's seat.

"I'm not sitting in back with that little devil. Or the two bigger dumbasses," Cris remarked flatly, handing Alma the keys.

"It's okay, honey, we'll teach those meanies a thing or two. Let's go find a place to get you washed up, 'kay?"

Kody and Glenn both got into the back of the van rather sullenly, like two despondent children awaiting the verdict of an angry parent. Neither dared to speak or even make a gesture out of place for fear of the wrath of Cris—or Alma's reprisal. Alma checked her mirrors to make sure everything was set properly. She noticed Glenn had seemed despondent once again, and was now sitting somber, eyes cast toward the road. He was too erratic for her to predict. She could see the sorrow reflected in his eyes, and couldn't help but pity him. She wondered just what it was that he thought about when he stared out the window as she got the van back on the road.

16. Wishing on Welkin

"I must admit, though I appreciate the rationality and maturity that often comes with growing older, I do at times find it difficult not to envy the impetus of youth."

– Glenn's Chronicles

Alma drove in search of a motel or some kind of cheap accommodation so Cris could get cleaned up and find some decent rest. She found it odd that she couldn't find any places along the highway. Slowly noticing how rural the area was, she accepted it and continued with hope it would soon change.

"You've been quiet for a while now, sweetie; you okay?" Alma wasn't sure if Cris was still mad and decided to test the waters.

"Yeah…just tired of things consistently going wrong. I'll feel better after I get a good warm shower, if we ever find one." Cris replied.

"Don't worry, I'll keep looking."

Alma tried her best to maintain her cheery demeanor, hoping it would pass along to her friend. The longer she waited, however, the grimmer the outlook appeared. She decided to change the subject.

"So…California, huh? Gonna be fuuun."

"I hope so. I've heard nothing but good things. I wish I had known we'd be going to an ocean, but we'll make it work."

"That's the spirit! Besides, it's not like it would matter anyway. When aren't you ready for beach season?"

"Eh…" Cris looked down at herself, growing accustomed to the smell of orange and urine.

"Me, on the other hand…" Alma sighed.

"Alm, you look fine."

"She's not wrong!" Alma heard her boy from the rear.

She looked back to see a wide grin smiling straight ahead. She pursed her lips out, gesturing a kiss right back at him. Kody laughed and nodded as he returned to writing in a new sketchbook.

"Oh, I'm not saying I don't look good. And don't think I don't know it, either! I'm just saying… you, you're like naturally fit. Me? I gotta work my ass off for it and even then I still can't manage whatever it is you do."

"Alm, really…"

"Hey, you know what we should do after we hit the sunny white sands? We should go to Mexico!"

All eyes turned to her.

"What? My aunt and cousin live down there. I'm sure they'd be psyched to see us!"

"Oh, you mean little Lauren?" Cris tried to remember.

"She's not that little, you know. She's actually only a little younger than us."

"Seriously? I guess it's been so long since I've seen her…when was the last time they came up to visit?"

"I don't even remember, I haven't heard from them in so long…I think it must've been when Maria first got sick." Alma's brow furrowed as she sorted out her thoughts.

"Well, anyway, it's just an idea…just something to think about after California, if you guys want."

She let the topic die down as she checked the rearview mirror. She glanced a bit to the side when she noticed a small but alert fur ball perched atop Glenn's already shaggy head.

"Glenn, what're you…?"

"Hmm?" He saw the reflection of a puzzled look in her eyes. "Oh, him? He's d-decided that he's rather fond of the view f-from on high. I'd try to convince him to come down, but…"

They both knew there was no way to finish that sentence without reminding Cris of her earlier episode, which was something neither of them wanted to do. It was at this time that Alma noticed Cris starting to nod off.

"Hey, sweetie?" Kody looked up, summoned by Alma.

"Can you clear off that back seat for me?"

"Sure. What for?"

"Cris needs to get some more rest. I dunno how long it'll take us to find a place."

"'kay." He started clearing the seat. Overhearing them, Cris began coming around.

"What? Alm, I'm fine."

"You're still tired. We all are, but you more than anyone since you did most of the driving this morning. Besides, wouldn't you rather sleep than smell OJ?"

Cris took a moment to contemplate this.

"Those hash browns were pretty tasty," she rubbed her belly.

"Go get some sleep, girly girl."

"Fine, fine. In the name of Sister Alma I shall abide."

"Damn right! Dork," Alma teased her and stuck her tongue out before quickly returning her attention to the road, narrowly dodging a small car in front of them. "Oops."

Cris made her way to the middle row of seats, keeping a wary eye on Bixby as she passed Glenn. She awkwardly shuffled around Kody as she got to the back row of seats to lie down.

"There, made it all nice and comfy for ya. Get some rest." Kody nodded to her as he made his way up front.

Cris dozed off on the seat after a few minutes, her head resting on a small pillow. The sun kept getting in her eyes, however, and it wouldn't let her sleep. She tried to ignore it, but as she kept nodding off, the drifting of the clouds brought the brilliant rays back onto her eyelids, seemingly to shine directly in her eyes. This round of the world against Cris was enough, and she decided to do something about it.

"Hey, does anyone have something I can cover my face with?"

"I thought you'd never ask!" She could hear Kody chuckling up front.

"Funny, smart ass. The sun keeps getting in my eye."

She looked around a bit when suddenly she found it became dark and musky. She felt around as she realized there was now a familiar jacket on her face.

"Hey! Who threw that?"

She shouted, half-jokingly as the jacket muffled her voice.

"What? Mmphmphmphmph?" Kody taunted her yet again as she pulled the jacket off. "Just kidding. No idea."

"I suppose the only p-possible option then would be me," Glenn said, volunteering himself as the culprit.

"Glenn, please. As if you're even capable of mischief, much less pranks. I'd believe your cat did it before you did."

"B-by all means I resent th-that! Of course I c-could very well have b-been the one to have thrown the jacket at you."

Glenn tried to be convincing, but he wasn't fooling anyone. Finding the entire course of events to be out of the scope of his interests, and still feeling rather funny from earlier, he pulled out his laptop in an effort to distract himself and continued work on his project.

"If you say so. Anyway, Kody, try to be less of an ass next time?"

"Of course, Highness."

She sighed as she pulled the jacket back over her face, now trying to figure out its unusual scent. It was a peculiar smell; it wasn't an attractive or even particularly pleasant, yet the more she inhaled it, the more she found it oddly calming. She held the jacket close as she drifted off to sleep.

* * *

This was definitely a good call, Alma thought, reinforcing her decision as she continued to drive. *Cris has had a pretty rough day. Might be the first one of her life, though.* Alma hated thinking such things about her best friend, but she was all too aware of how drastically different their lives were, even if they always pretended otherwise.

"Kody, Kody, Kody…" she muttered to herself, seeing him caught up in his writing and knowing anything would serve as little distraction for him.

"Hey, baby, what'cha writing?"

"Huh?" he raised his head, vaguely aware anyone was speaking.

"What're you writing?"

"Nothing really. Just different ideas and stuff."

"Like what?"

She knew he hated it when she prodded about his writing; he was usually sensitive and insecure about such things, but she was always curious to know what was going on in that strange head of his.

"Um…just about life in general, mostly."

"Read me something?"

"Like what?"

"I don't care. You can read me anything."

"Hmm...'kay... gimme a second." He flipped through his notebook, looking for an appropriate poem or short story to read to her.

"Oh, here we go. Got it." She tensed up and quieted down as she prepared to listen to his story.

Friends, dear friends. Glistening like the sun, hair flows twixt the glimmer and shine, rapt 'tween sky ever the night. Show me your fire and I'll show you the stars.

Everything for her. Eyes. Those starry eyes—eyes like the stars forgotten by time, light escapes. Brings sweet peace to twilight lovers.

She sees me. Solace. One less than lost to the last. My boyish dreams for you. Childhood forsaken, steadfast and valiant, I stand ready at your guard. Until tomorrow. Nevermore.

She didn't know what to say. She wasn't sure she understood all of it, or even most of it, but she felt the passion behind it.

"Sorry, I know it sounds a little goofy. It's been giving me a lot of trouble," Kody said, "but I'm hoping I can get it right." He appeared apologetic, though knowing him like she did, she felt he was being modest.

"It was great, hun; I loved it!" She wanted to clasp her arms around him but had to restrain herself; she kept her hands on the wheel.

"Hey...do you ever write anything about me? Anything like that?"

"Uh...this is a new book, so there really isn't much in it." She let it go.

She knew better than to embarrass him like that, but she was enamored. She drove on for a little while longer before speaking up.

"I'm sorry I ever hurt you, baby."

"Huh?" Kody was wide-eyed now. "Hey, uh...don't worry about all that. It's in the past."

"It really is." she couldn't wait to show him how much she really cared for him.

He returned to his writing, and she returned to her memories. Thoughts of an ill mother and negligent father. She could call her mother, perhaps, but should she? Her family had fallen apart long ago. Cris was the only one who had been there for her all these years, and even she didn't know; she couldn't relate. Now she had *him*. Could he save her? Was she worth saving? Did she need to be saved? She couldn't tell.

She was strong—she knew this. She endured the end of her world with a weak smile. She rebuilt after the chaos and calamity, after her life had been washed away. This boy was the first one to stir the painful echoes of that past, and the fear was searing. She was once again a little girl, and there was nowhere left to run. If she let him in, if she lost herself in someone else, she might disappear completely. She wasn't ready to risk that. Not yet.

* * *

A funny, wet sandpaper sensation grazed against the tip of Cris's nose as she realized the jacket no longer covered her. She opened her eyes to a furry blur, and couldn't make out what was right in front of her. Though his visage had not yet come into focus, the cat made his presence known. Bixby continued licking her face.

"Oh, you…stealing my boogers now?" Cris scrunched her face at the whiskered prince.

"H-he means to make amends. He's remorseful of the events that t-took place earlier—th-though he still feels he acted in his b-best interests."

She heard Glenn's voice over the seat. She looked at the hairy face of her betrayer, who appeared to be making a genuine effort at reparation.

"So, you're sorry, huh?"

He cocked his head as he looked at her. He sat back on his haunches in an almost regal manner and began licking his paws. He pawed her gently, this time without claws.

"You're lucky you're so adorable."

"Hey, who's talking about me?" Kody's voice came echoing back.

"And also that you ended up with Glenn instead of that clown."

She pulled the little prince closer and gave him a little kiss on his furry little head. He pawed his ear before jumping down and disappearing under the seats.

"Is she awake?" she heard coming from the front.

"Yeah, sounds like."

"Hey, Cris!" Alma called to her.

"Good news, we found a place! It's just a few miles down the road, so we should be there in a few minutes!"

"Thank you, Saint Alma, my friend and savior! I shall not forget your act of charity here!"

"Not that I'd let you anyway!" Cris could hear the smile in Alma's voice.

She turned her head to the side in a weak effort to find the jacket. She stayed quiet and kept a low profile as she reached over to feel for it on the ground. She found it after a moment and lay back down, covering her face once again. She continued to rest her eyes until they got to their next destination. Several minutes later, she felt the van slow down and stop. She waited until the humming of the engine quieted and ceased reverberating to get up.

"Are we there?"

"Yup yup," Alma nodded.

"All right, hang out for a minute while I go grab us some rooms."

Kody got out and headed inside the main office of the rundown wrap-around motel.

"Oh, sweet, sweet, merciful shower waters, I hear your call," Cris recited to herself, almost in the form of a neo-pagan ritual. Alma giggled.

"Ah, did you hear that Mr. B-bixby? You'll get to go inside and rest comfortably on a bed!"

Mr. Bixby rolled around on the ground, pawing at his tail. Glenn put his laptop away as they waited for Kody to come back out. A few minutes later he returned to the van, keys dangling in hand.

"Good news and bad news; which do you guys want first?"

"Who cares? Just give me my room key, I need a shower!"

Cris grabbed one of her bags from behind the seat, impulsively grabbing the jacket and stuffing it into one of the side pockets. She quickly navigated her way around the seat and jumped out of the van. Stumbling only slightly, she ran up to Kody, snatching a set of keys from his hand. She ran off to look for the corresponding room. Taking a minute to figure out how the number assignments were set up, she soon found the room she was looking for near the end of the building. Entering the second to last room, she burst through the door, jumping onto the freshly made bed.

She enjoyed the comfort of the rather uncomfortable mattress for only a moment. She stared at the ceiling, glad to be lying down, but unable to stand the smell of orange a moment longer. She rolled over and pulled out a small shower kit from her bag, allowing miscellaneous clutter to fall out onto the bed. She bounced back up off the springy mattress and ran over to close the motel door, having trouble getting it to lock. She finally got it shut as she stripped herself of her orangey confinement. She joyfully frolicked to the bathroom with shower bag in hand. She started a stream of warm water from the faucet and locking the door behind her as she sang herself a little song. She was finally ready to be clean!

* * *

"So, what's the news?" Alma asked as she stepped out of the van.

"I was gonna say that we got the best set of rooms here."

"That s-sounds wonderful." Glenn carried Bixby out of the van.

"The bad?"

"This place is still a crap hole, so having the best rooms amounts to having free cable and one room with A/C."

"Which room?" Alma inquired.

"Ours."

"Lucky us," she smirked.

"By 'ours,' of course, I mean me and Glenn."

"Huh? Wait, what about us?" Alma raised an eyebrow as she crossed her arms.

"We have two rooms. You gonna pair Cris with Glenn?"

"Why not? They're good friends and all, right? She'll be okay."

"I m-must object," he said hesitantly.

"Likewise. Sorry, Alm, but that isn't fair to Glenn or Cris."

Alma, seeing that she was losing—and not being one to lose—leaned in close to whisper into Kody's ear.

"Believe me; it's plenty fair to Glenn."

She nudged him.

"Alm…"

"Fine, whatever. But what about us? When do we get our *us* time?"

"Don't worry, we'll get that. I'm sure Glenn has stuff to do," Kody spoke up, "right Glenn?"

"What? Oh, almost c-certainly the opposite of w-whatever it is you're saying."

"See? C'mon! I could owe you favors." Alma put on her seductive tone.

"Aw, don't do this to me, Alm. I gotta make the right call here. Besides, Cris wouldn't stand for it anyway."

"Since when are you so worried about what Cris thinks?" Alma's tone shifted slightly.

"Since I've pissed her off in more ways I can count in the last six hours."

"Fine, fine. Just give me my room key," Alma said, submitting with marginal disdain.

"Actually…"

"What?"

"Cris took both of yours."

Alma awarded him a dry, cold stare.

"Just means you get to come hang out with us for a bit after all!"

"Yay me," she said sardonically, carrying one of Glenn's bags.

They made their way into the room on the very end, Kody taking the far bed. Alma dropped Glenn's bag next to Kody, and moved Kody's stuff to the bed nearest the door. He looked at her, confusion on his face.

"Planning ahead," she winked as she sat down in his bed.

Glenn came in behind them, placing Bixby on the floor and setting up a small food and water dish for him on the ground, which he quickly made out of the motel's disposable cups left sitting on the counter.

"So, once Cris finishes showering, why don't we go to the store so I can pick up some things? I don't have any clothes or shower stuff," Alma remarked.

"Actually, I c-concur. Bixby still needs some things as well."

"Why don't you guys go on ahead? I'm still pretty wiped from last night. I could use a quick nap in an actual bed."

Though she hadn't noticed them before, the heavy bags under Kody's eyes strongly reinforced his suggestion.

"Maybe I should just stay here with you then?" Alma was shameless.

"I mean an actual nap. Besides, you need stuff, right?"

Alma leaned in to whisper, "It's not that I don't like him or whatever, but...he's kinda weird..."

"Who? Glenn?" Kody asked, trying to keep his voice down.

"Yeah! Haven't you seen the way he looks at me? He just kind of stares, like he's looking *through* me or something."

"You'll be fine. He's a good guy. You should get to know him. Besides, someone should stay here and keep an eye on Bixby anyway, so he doesn't tear up the place."

"Hmph, fine, fine. Have it your way. I'm going. Have a good nap!" She reached in to kiss him as she waited for Glenn.

"Ready?"

"J-just u-us?"

"Yep, you and me, bubby. Don't worry, I won't bite."

"Of c-course." Glenn followed quietly behind her as they headed out to the van.

Kody could hear the engine start as he got up to look out the window and watch them drive off. He tried to pet Bixby, but the tiny demon hissed violently as Kody neared his food dish. Kody decided to back off, still unwilling to challenge the undefeated fur ball champion, but noticing how much he seemed to enjoy his turkey–chicken hybrid meal.

Kody stepped outside and leaned against the railing, staring off into the late afternoon sky. He knew he was tired, but it was the sort of tired that would not allow him to find sleep. He was anxious, as his nervous fidgeting showed; mild apprehension kept fluttering around in his stomach like butterflies, but he was unable to figure out why. He looked again to the clouds, though there were few in the sky. They seemed a little darker than usual, but he had no real concern. They were floating away.

His life had changed so much in so little time. He had gone from being alone with only a handful of people he could barely talk to, to having some close friends he could truly rely on. He and Glenn were finally starting to understand each other a bit, he and Cris were getting along better than ever (when he wasn't antagonizing her), and things were just as he had always hoped they would be with Alma. Life was good.

He wanted to talk about these things, to share them with someone. The only person that came to mind was Geroge, but Kody didn't have a phone, and the others had already left. He thought about Cris. She was a great girl and a good listener. If there was anyone he could talk to about this stuff it was her. He persuaded himself otherwise. He thought about how tired she must be, having had even less rest than him. Besides, she was probably still mad at him.

He thought about her situation in general. She didn't really have anyone to talk to. Before, she could've talked to him or Alma, but they had been so wrapped up in each other that she really had no one. He started to feel bad for having let her down like that, especially since at least for the last few months she had been there for him, even if they hadn't known each other that well. He felt the need to make it up to her. He had an idea in mind, but he was too tired to do it now. It'd have to wait until after he'd rested. And found some beads.

He turned to go back into his room when he thought about how Cris would react to coming out and seeing the van gone. She didn't know where he was staying and she might assume they just left her. He figured he should at least let her know what was going on and see how she was doing before going to bed. He went up to her door and knocked.

"Hey, Cris?"

No response. He tried the door and found it locked, but it felt…loose.

"Cris?"

Again, no response. He recalled his brief time as a ninja in Glenn's apartment. The importance of his current mission made it worthwhile to go for round two. He might even level up! Kody hesitated a moment, trying to muster the courage to enter the girl's room. He took a deep breath, steeled himself, and braved the unknown. He jingled the doorknob a few more times until the latch popped loose and the door opened.

He walked into the room, noticing it was a mirror image of his own. The sound of running shower echoed throughout the room. Cris's orange juice-stained clothes lay strewn out in a pile on the floor. He hadn't realized how much his accidental outburst had bothered her, but seeing how quickly she must've rushed in the shower was a sure indication. *I should be a little nicer to her,* crossed his mind. He'd find a way make up for his past indiscretions and not leave her hanging again. After all, what was he if not a man of honor—complete with a criminal skill set?

He looked around for some paper and pen, finding some on the little table near the door. He started writing out a note. As he finished the note, he realized the faucet in the bathroom was no longer running. He took the little Post-It and placed it on her bag as he started walking toward the door. Heading out onto the breezeway, he heard the sound of the bathroom door open. He turned back to let Cris know about the note.

"Hey Cris, I left a note on your—" He went silent as she walked out wrapped in a short towel.

They stared at each other in awkward silence for only a second before Cris's eyes grew wide with indignation.

"Get out!" was all he heard as he scrambled out of the room and made it back to his, latching the door behind him as if fleeing from a fury.

"That didn't just happen, that didn't just happen," he kept telling himself, as he took a seat trying to catch his breath.

* * *

"That didn't just happen, that didn't just happen," Cris kept telling herself as she furiously put on some clothes and tried to contain her embarrassment.

She saw the note on her bag, noticing Kody's jacket sitting just underneath it. She figured the jacket must have fallen out in her haste to get into the shower. She didn't even understand why she took it, but she definitely didn't want him knowing about it.

"Oh, God, did he see it…?"

She stopped panicking and read the Post-It, trying to figure out both how he got in and why he was there in the first place. She soon figured out he was only trying to help, and not spy on her or anything else, though he had managed to accomplish that as well. She tried her doorknob again, finding that it was pretty old, and decided that using the dead-bolt might be a better option.

She debated what she was going to do on the matter as she dried her hair. Completely exhausted and planning to get some rest, she took off the random assortment of clothes she had thrown on in her panicky haste and put on some pajama pants with a comfy t-shirt. She pulled a light hoodie over her outfit, since her body was still trying to convince her she was cold.

She lay in bed for a few minutes, deliberating whether she should try and clear the air with Kody, or just ignore him and hope it went away. She found that if life had taught her anything, however, it was that issues don't just go away; they grow bigger and larger until you're forced to confront them like the giant elephant they are. She got back up and slipped on some sandals before going outside. She stepped outside and headed next door. She knocked on his door and waited for a response.

"*Occupado*!" was all she heard. She had an idea.

"Housekeeping!" Cris iterated in her shrillest voice as she waited. After a minute, her patience wore thin. "Oh my God, Kody, quit being dumb and come out here."

She waited another minute before the door opened and he stepped outside, dressed in lounge pants and a wife beater. She took a moment to look him over, finding that despite the fact he wasn't muscular, he wasn't unattractive. She quickly put this thought on hold to address the issue at hand.

"Hey…" He leaned against the railing, avoiding eye contact.

"Hey. Look, we're pretty much adults, so let's just be grown-ups about this, okay?" She played his game, leaning on the railing next to him, both of them examining the darkening evening sky.

"Sure, okay."

"You walked in on me half-naked. No big deal. It didn't mean anything and it was just an accident. I mean, we're traveling on the road and these kinds of things happen, right?"

"Yeah, I guess they do."

"Particularly when you break into my room. But…I know you were just trying to help. So we're cool?"

"Yeah, we're good."

"Good. Normally I'd charge you a viewing fee, but I don't think Alma would be too happy about that. And besides, I think there's been enough public nudity for one day."

"Viewing fee?" Kody looked up.

"Tit for tat," she smirked.

"Oh geez!" He couldn't help but laugh it off.

"Like I said, you get off free this time, mister. Not many men can claim that. Actually, you'd be the only one… Besides, it's not like I want to see that anyway."

"Not like I'd show you! It'd be a hell of treat, and personally, I just don't think you're ready for it." Kody was as bold and courageous as ever.

"Hmph." She had clever retorts but none that she felt would be appropriate.

Though there was nothing left to say at that point, they both stood there, waiting for something. She didn't know what, or even if he felt the same way, but it just felt right. The warm evening breeze started drifting in as she noticed Kody's body finally started giving way. His head bobbed forward.

"Hey, you're falling asleep, you know."

"Yeah, yeah…I'm heading inside in a minute."

"Hmm…" her voice was softer now, more than she had ever been with Kody.

"I'm glad you guys let me come."

"Hey, I'm glad you came. I don't know I could manage Alma on my own."

"Yeah…"

She tried to think of something to say, though she actually enjoyed the silence between them. There was no need to break it, and if she had any real words they would find their way on their own.

"My world ends with you…"

"What?" she looked up at him.

"Just thinking… So, I think I got this whole thing figured out."

"What whole thing?" She cracked an awkward smile as she tried to read his face.

"This thing with you and Glenn."

"There's a thing with me and Glenn?" she chuckled, turning toward him.

"I dunno, maybe…I got this theory…you're all worried about him, right? And then he dated your sister, so that makes him like a close friend of the family or something."

"I guess." She cocked her eyebrow.

"So, I'm thinking that you like him, and that's just your funny way of showing it. The whole investigating-him angle, I mean."

"That's your theory?" she chuckled.

"Pretty much."

"Needs some work. I've known Glenn for I don't even know how long. He's far more like a brother to me than anything else. I've just been worried about him because I don't like the way he's living his life. He wasn't always like this."

"Uh huh…"

"Since when did you become so interested in my love life anyway?"

"I dunno, I guess I haven't. I just figure you must be pretty lonely sometimes. I mean, I know we weren't really the closest of friends or whatever, but we've hung out a few times, and you've always been cool with me. And I guess I just kinda bailed on you, especially now with me and Alma back together all the time, I can't imagine Glenn's doing the greatest job filling our shoes. Not with his little buddy to keep him busy."

"Heh, yeah that little guy isn't the best of company, is he…but he grows on you. Kind of like a furry wart or something."

"Gross imagery. Thanks for that."

"Of course." her small dimples pulled back to reveal a sincere smile.

"Anyway, I guess I'm saying if you need someone to talk to, I'm around. I know I might not always be the most available person, but I don't want you to feel like you're alone; you're not."

"I know."

"Just making sure."

They rested quietly for a moment as the warm evening breeze came rolling through.

"Looking out for me now, huh?" She looked over at him, seeing a calm strength in his eyes.

"Yeah, I guess so."

"Guess that means I'll be safe then." A small warmth coursed through her as she cherished the thought.

Watching Kody suddenly flinch, she saw Bixby run up the back of his leg, and then up his spine until he reached the top of Kody's head and perched himself there.

"Err…hi, big guy." Kody winced at the cat scratches that woke him up.

"And here I was thinking I was special. Two-timing cat." Cris put on a playfully jealous smile.

"Nah, he's just making the rounds. I'm pretty sure it's you he has at heart."

She couldn't help but read a deeper meaning in his words.

"C'mon, trouble maker. Time to get some sleep."

Kody tried to pull the furry demon off his head, but it was rooted in place. He resigned himself as he turned to head back to his room.

"Hey, Kody?"

He turned. "Yeah?"

"Thanks."

"Uh huh."

He smiled and extended his hand; she watched him, unsure of what he intended. She hesitantly began to open her arms before she realized he meant to shake her hand. He shifted his gesture and moved closer to give her a hug. She held him awkwardly at first, but soon comfortably and rested her head on his shoulder, for a moment, just as she had done the night of the show. She breathed in as the snug felicity of that evening came rushing back.

He held her, glad he was able to support her and make her feel better. As he did, she felt soft and warm. She had a light, airy scent he couldn't place. It reminded him only of the warmth of summer and calm yet ferociously beautiful wild rains that came with it, replenishing the fortitude and bloom of the land. He found the fragrance immediately endearing and casually started to lose himself before he began to feel guilty, though he was unable to explain why.

He let her go, and they traded coy glances as each made their way back to their respective doors. They both felt a part of something they needed, if only for a moment, and felt the sting of letting it go. Neither knew for sure if the other had been there with them, but they couldn't allow themselves to become lost in it. It felt forbidden—like it wasn't meant for them.

Bixby, apparently deciding he no longer liked his new roost, jumped off Kody's head and landed on the ground, rubbing himself against Cris's leg.

"Guess he wants to stay with you. See? It was about you all along."

"Yeah, I guess so."

She couldn't let the memory fade so quickly, even though she tried.

"Good luck with him. 'Night."

"Goodnight," she told him as he went inside, though it was clearly still late in the afternoon.

She made her way back inside with her new narrow-eyed benefactor. She cleared everything off her bed and curled up on the edge of it under the blanket trying not to think too much. Bixby climbed up the side of the bed, sitting inches from her face and bathing her in stinky cat breath as he found a comfortable spot to lie down next to her.

She lay there for a minute, listening to the rhythmic purring of her feline friend, and tried her hardest to fall asleep. She found trying only made it more difficult, and no matter the effort, she couldn't perish the thoughts of the moments that preceded her. Unable to think of anything else, she recalled something that had worked for her before and reached over the edge of the bed to find the jacket habitually lying on the ground.

She picked it up and drew it close, nestling it into her chest. She found she didn't mind Bixby's chicken-flavored breath much, as the faint scent of the jacket just barely overpowered it. She held the jacket close to her heart as she felt a calm wave of serenity wash over her. Before she knew it, her eyelids met and she was fast asleep.

17. Remnants Remain (Happy Birthday)

"Despite the greatest plans, despite the best intentions, despite everything that tells you otherwise... sometimes you just gotta let go."

– Alma's Diary

Glenn managed to get ahead of Alma as they reached the van, taking the lead and the driver's seat.

"Whoa, hey there, bucko. I'm driving." Alma was insistent.

"You might find that s-somewhat difficult with me being in the d-driver's seat. Unless, th-that is, you intend to sit on my lap. In such a skirt, however, I could h-hardly recommend it." Alma snorted, stomping her foot. The two standing in a stalemate, she eventually handed over the keys.

"Okay, you can drive, peaches, but you keep your hands to yourself, got it?"

Glenn pulled out a CD from his personal collection and popped it in the CD player before starting the van and heading out. Alma listened along, surprised by Glenn's taste in music. In a strange sort of way it fitted him. She loosened up, becoming more comfortable with Glenn, who was himself still a little on edge. She tried some light conversation.

"So...who is this?"

"The band?"

"Yeah."

"Darling Violetta. *B-Bath Water Flowers.*"

"Huh. They're kind of interesting."

"Th-they are."

She sighed, unable to pull much from Glenn. She listened along to Darling Violetta's "Blue Sun," watching as the evening clouds rolled in.

"D-do you like it?" he asked her.

"A little." She kept her gaze focused on the clouds.

"You've had a p-peculiar look on your face since it c-came on."

"Been watching me long?" She asked his reflection in the window.

"P-perhaps. Little else t-to see around here."

She lifted her head. "Huh…w-well, it's just a strange song is all." She stuttered, surprised by his frankness. For the first time, she found herself stumbling over her own words. Her thoughts began drifting to a place beyond her, becoming something unlike her own. The clouds circling above seemed far off, yet a part of her own mind—unusually deep and temperamental. She didn't like the feeling; it made it harder for her to be herself. She had to focus to maintain her own concept of self-image. As the lines began to blur, she cared less about context and conformity. She knew who was responsible—asking her such odd questions. She confronted him.

"Why are you always watching me?"

"I d-don't know. M-maybe you remind me of someone."

"Who?"

"I really c-couldn't say."

"Bullshit."

He shrugged her off. Her pensiveness grew deeper as did her intrigue. She returned her gaze toward the window, watching the grass and trees that seemed to rush pass them. She wondered if they had always hated being stuck in the same place. She didn't know what she was thinking, or why. She watched as the ground slowly became darker, and noticed ominous clouds looming overhead. She clenched her hands together, tensing up.

"What is it?" Glenn cast an eye in her direction.

"It's gonna storm!" she tried to calm herself, clutching the armrest in an attempt to control her anxiety.

"K-keraunophobia? Interesting."

"Keno-what?"

"F-fear of storms."

"Yeah, I'm afraid of storms, so what?"

"Nothing. I s-suppose it's to be expected. And j-just so you know, there's no s-storm forecasted. Those seem to be c-cumulus clouds, which indicate a s-storm isn't likely at this point. There's no c-characteristic shift of atmospheric p-pressure or humidity, nor any in-indicative olfactory sensations." He remarked, taking in a deep breath of the cooling warm air coming in his rolled-down window.

"What the hell are you? A human barometer?"

"C-close enough, apparently. D-don't worry about any storms, we're almost there."

They arrived at a local Wally World. Glenn parked the van as he looked toward Alma.

"Sh-shall we?"

"We shall." Alma dared to open her door and venture out into the world despite the threat of a storm.

"See? D-does it feel like stormy weather?"

"No. Just shut up about storms, and I'll be fine."

"Fair enough."

They walked inside and looked around, observing the cultural differences between the local store and home before they began shopping. They wandered around until they got a feel for the layout of the store. Once they oriented themselves, the first thing they found were the litter boxes. Glenn examined a few of them, observing the variances, but they were so subtle that he made no progress. Alma recommended the most aesthetically pleasing one she could find. Glenn questioned her, wondering how a litter box could be described as "pretty," but Alma's resolve left him with little choice.

They next found themselves in the swimsuit aisle. Alma wasn't proud to be buying a swimsuit from Wally World, but with few options she made due. She figured that regardless of what she chose, she'd probably look all right anyway, so it'd be okay. She went through the suits repeatedly, evaluating each pattern, design, and color scheme, as well as the sizes for each.

"Damn it!" she exclaimed, scaring a small boy walking by with his mother.

"W-what is it?"

"They don't have it in my size...this one either! They have a half-size down, but that's not gonna work."

She shuffled impatiently through swimsuits, hoping in vain to find something that would please her.

"Th-that one should be c-close enough, I would think."

"No, Glenn. I guess you haven't had much experience with women, so let me break it down for you," she said, oblivious to her own condescending remarks.

"A half-size *might* work, but do I really want to be popping out of my swimsuit? Maaaybe, if the circumstances were right; but if that were the case, why would I wear one? On the other hand, if I went down a whole size it might work in some ways—and oh, how I could make it work—but it'd make me look too big in others. Got it?"

"I s-see." Glenn scratched his nose. "Why d-don't you go w-with the one you're h-holding? It s-seems that would fit nicely."

"Well, it's ugly as hell for one."

"You j-just said that you 'love that pattern.'"

"I do. Just not on me. And not as much as the other two. The whole time I'd be wearing it, I'd just be thinking about how much I hated it because it wasn't one of the other two."

"P-perhaps a c-compromise then?"

"Hmm?"

"Wh-what if you got this one only t-temporarily, so you have a suit, and p-perhaps we'll look for another one later at a more fitting place?"

Alma stopped to contemplate his suggestion.

"Hmm…ooh, that could work… that's a great idea, Glenn! You're a genius!" She hugged him as she grabbed the suit off the rack to go try it on.

He adjusted himself, unused to affection of any kind, least of all from Alma. He tried to brush the thought off and instead began thinking of other, more pertinent thoughts. Other than his project, however, he couldn't think of much. His mind lingered and drifted back to Alma. *She's become quite strong. He'd be proud.* His thoughts casually became somber once more. He waited around, idly looking at shorts and briefs, thinking of how he loathed both and could never understand why someone would choose to wear either.

"Hey, how do I look?" Alma returned, decked out in a skimpy lime-green bikini with tiny

pastel-pink polka dots. Glenn was left stunned, speechless. He stammered before finally getting something out.

"It's q-q-quite fitting."

"Fitting?" She scrunched her face. "Not exactly what I was going for…but this suit *is* a little weird…it's a little loose in the chest but it barely covers my butt." She modeled it as she examined the suit and stopped to consider it.

"Can I at least get an ooh la la or heeey sexy?"

"A-at least."

"Great! This'll work then." She smirked as she bounced back into the dressing room.

Glenn stood mesmerized at how much Alma had changed since he had last seen her. *She's grown into quite the woman,* he thought. He caught himself featuring her in an unflattering fantasy and had a harder time dashing the thought. "J-jake's sister. Jake's s-sister," he repeated to himself, the only mantra he could think of. He then recalled a more immediate motivating factor. "K-kody's girlfriend! Besides, I've…I have o-obligations. I can't b-become distracted so easily."

Glenn's mind slowly expanded, his focus on much of anything becoming absurd. Loose memories and fragments started barraging in and kept up the flow, though he couldn't determine why. Alma came out of the dressing room, once again in her short skirt and spaghetti straps.

"Ready?"

"N-no."

"You alright?" She leaned over, trying to see if he was okay.

"I n-need a m-moment. If you'll excuse me…"

"Where're you going?"

"B-b-bath-bathroom."

"Huh…'kay…I'm gonna go grab some stuff. Come find me if you need anything, okay?"

Glenn nodded, his hand shaking, and handed off the litter box before heading in search of a restroom. He searched around a bit before he found a male bathroom, next to Mac's restaurant. He couldn't fathom why there was a fast food establishment within a shopping facility, but this concern was secondary to the more pressing issue of the moment. He made his way into a stall and sat on the seat, holding his head and rocking back and forth.

Images flooded back, and he couldn't keep them out. He mumbled incoherently to himself, but the words were indiscernible even to him. "D-damn it!" he punched the door of the stall, trying to redirect his attention elsewhere. He saw flashes: a dark storm, an old friend's face, bloody palms. *Hey, Atticus, chill out man. You'll pass out or somethin',* echoed faintly through his head.

"A-Atticus?"

His hands shook violently. His eyes became blurry. He removed his glasses, but there was little he could do. He felt trapped, guilt-nausea rising in his stomach. Was he going to throw up? He tried to quiet his head, but there was so much noise. Far too much noise and nothing he could do. He got up and turned around to kneel in front of the toilet, hoping he'd have no offering for the porcelain throne. His hand brushed against his pocket, and he felt the small bulge of the container within. He immediately reached into his pocket and pulled out the pill bottle.

He unscrewed the cap and tried to grab two with his trembling hands. He lost several of the pills as they fell out of the shaking bottle into the toilet. He managed to grab two out of the container and forced them down. He replaced the cap and stuffed them back into his pocket, regaining his posture on the toilet. He held his head in his hands rocking back and forth. He started humming a quiet song to himself.

His breathing, rapid and shallow, began to slow down. He continued with his muted prayer as his hands began to steady and his vision cleared up. He replaced his glasses. He rested for few minutes until he could finally calm himself. He stood up, stumbling forward, falling into the door. His fist against the cold metal, he concentrated, regaining his footing. He opened the stall and stepped out, a man staring at him near the trash can by the exit.

"Hey, you okay? You didn't sound too good in there."

"I'm f-fine!" Glenn snapped.

The man could see that his assistance, while perhaps necessary, was clearly unwelcome. He backed out of the bathroom as Glenn rinsed his face off in the sink and dried it, consuming a small amount of the sink water in the process. He spit the foul rotten egg scented water out. He looked in the mirror and realigned his glasses, only briefly noticing and giving no concern to the scar that still decorated the right side of his head, just in front of his ear.

He made his way to the feminine hygiene aisle where Alma was apparently still caught up in the midst of her shopping with a full cart of clothes and goodies.

"Wow, you have good timin'—hey, you all right?" She looked at him funny.

"F-fine. C-can we go?" Glenn was clearly disheveled.

"Yeah, sure."

He took the litter box as they headed to a register and quickly checked out despite the long line. Glenn more than willingly paid for everything. They made their way back to the van and loaded everything in the back.

"You should let me drive." Alma became cautiously attentive with him.

"Y-yeah…" sweat dampened Glenn's forehead.

Alma helped him into the passenger seat. She looked around for some sign of a hospital, but other than trees there wasn't much to guide the way. It would probably be best to check in with the others first just in case. She got in her seat and started the van.

"You sure you're okay?"

"Y-yeah. Feeling b-better already." A little color returned to his face.

She pulled out of the parking lot, putting Glenn's CD back on. The breeze coming in from the open window tossed her hair about. She brushed it behind her ear as she rolled the window up. Glenn, watching this, seemed to recall something familiar.

"H-heh, you look j-just like your brother."

Alma looked over at him with an uncertain disbelief covering her face. She restored her gaze toward the road and slammed on the breaks, just narrowly avoiding rear-ending a car waiting at the upcoming stop light. She pulled the van off to the side of the road and parked it. She looked over at him. Glenn, now sitting up, seemed confused.

"Wh-what?" Glenn said.

"What did you just say?" Alma's voice wasn't a clear conveyance of any one emotion, but seemingly a desperate mix of several.

"I s-said you look like your b-brother. It's n-not like it was a c-criticism." His manner was almost lackadaisical.

"How do you know about Jake?"

"What do you mean, h-how do I know about J-jake? Oh, yes, you d-don't remember…"

"Don't fuck with me! I swear to God, I won't take it from you!" Alma took off her seatbelt, facing him and holding herself back.

"T-tell me this first: what do you r-remember about him?"

"What are you, the riddle master?"

"You mean the R-riddler?"

"Ugh, whatever! You know what I mean."

Glenn sat up, though it did little to settle his disheveled appearance.

"A-are you g-going to tell me about your brother, or m-make idle th-threats?"

"Fine, but you'd better explain everything! What do you want to know?" Fury emanated from Alma's eyes, each breath audibly filled with disdain.

"Tell me what you remember about him."

"His smile, mostly. It was always so reckless. He wasn't ever worried or scared of anything." Alma's features softened as she reminisced about her brother.

"What else?"

"I don't know! Why're you messing with me?" She clutched the armrest, maintaining her focus through gritted teeth

"I'm not. My h-head..." Glenn lowered his head into his palms. "It's an abyss. I-I-I need a g-guide."

"What? What're you talking about?"

He looked up to her. "T-tell me about the last t-time you saw him, saw J-jake."

Alma looked at Glenn suspiciously. She clearly didn't trust him, yet followed his every word without hesitation.

"The night he died," Alma sighed as she muttered, almost as if she were enacting some sort of curse.

"What h-happened?"

"We went out in his little fishing boat. There was this pier not too far from our old house that we used to love going to. Dad would never let us go without him, but it's not like that would stop Jake. He would always sneak out the first chance he got.

"It always pissed me off that he got to have all these extravagant adventures and I was always stuck behind just because I was a girl. So I waited up one night and caught him as he was leaving. I forced him to let me go with him, threatened to tell on him if he didn't. He didn't have a choice, so he let me come." As she relayed her story, Alma saw a streak of familiarity run through Glenn's eyes.

"We got down to the pier, but it was already pretty late and the weather was bad. It was so cold and I wanted to go home, but Jake would never listen. He said he was going to throw a birthday party for his friend, Atticus. He was so stubborn... once he got an idea in his head that was it. I told him he was being stupid and I wanted to go home, but he just laughed it off and said I shouldn't have forced him to bring me. His friend showed up, and we went out anyway. It started getting really bad, and even Atticus got scared, so Jake finally decided we should head back...is that enough? I really don't wanna talk about this."

She broke in between the story as she noticed Glenn start to decompensate.

"Please c-continue."

"Ugh, fine." Alma dug the nail of each finger against her thumb as she continued.

"Where was I?"

"All of you were heading back."

"Oh...right."

"We were about halfway in when the waves started picking up and rocking the boat. It started filling up with water, and Atticus accidentally dropped one of the oars. Jake went in after it, but it started thundering, and I got really scared after that. I don't remember a whole lot, but at some point the boat must've flipped over 'cause I woke up on the shore. Jake's friend tried to run back into the water, but it was too dark. There was so much thunder... It was way too loud, so I covered my head and hid. All I saw was Atticus. There was this huge wave, and he was bleeding everywh—"

Alma stared at Glenn in silence, wide-eyed, as she recognized the faded seashell scar that adorned his right temple.

"You son of a bitch! How could you drag that out and not say a word? How could you know about all of this and not tell me!"

Glenn shifted his head, reflexively trying to conceal the shameful reminder of his greatest failure. He looked at her only from the corner of his eye as he kept his head forward in what appeared as some vain attempt to remove himself from the situation.

"I can hardly t-tell what's real and wh-what's fabrication. I w-wasn't even sure that h-had happened anymore. H-hearing it from you c-confirmed it."

"Such a piss-poor excuse! So you were there then, you were Jake's friend."

"Y-yes."

Alma took a moment to reflect. "But his name was Atticus."

"It's my middle name."

Alma realized her nails were digging into her hands, and took a minute to breathe as she realized she had a golden opportunity.

"So, Atty, fill in the blanks."

"As best I can r-recall, one of the stronger waves c-caused the boat to c-capsize. I'm not much of a s-swimmer, but I was able to c-carry you back, with the help of a life j-jacket. I had hoped J-jake had already made it to shore, given he w-was a much better swimmer than I, b-but I didn't see him when I got you b-back. I performed CPR as best I c-could. You came around, eventually. B-by then I'm sure it was too late, but I t-tried to go back in for him; as you know, that d-didn't exactly pan out."

Alma watched him intensively, skeptical but hanging onto his every word.

"Huh. So, you've known about it this who—le time, huh?"

"I-in my d-defense, I don't exactly c-claim the best mental fitness."

"I guess. But it's still not a good enough excuse." Alma's curiosity began to take over. "So what happened afterward? How come you never came back?"

Glenn turned his head a little, inviting Alma into his line of sight but never looking at her directly.

"For what p-purpose? We looked for J-jake's body, but c-could never find it. I had no c-claim to your family otherwise."

"What family? After...that, there wasn't anything left. My dad completely broke down and left, and my mom...well, whatever she was before, there was nothing left after."

"I'm sorry t-to hear that; I truly am."

"Whatever, that's got nothing to do with you."

Glenn said nothing, turning his gaze back toward the brushing grass twisting in the wind. He caught sight of the sky.

"We need to get back. Whatever's wrong with you, this sure as hell isn't helping."

"That's...true. Unfortunately, it d-does seem as though cumulonimbus clouds are beginning to form, so we may want to hurry."

"What, it's going to storm?"

"P-precisely."

Alma tensed up, cracking her knuckles, debating on hitting him before she gripped her hands on the steering wheel to protect herself as much as him.

"Why'd you have to say that? Do you want me to hit you? Is that the goal here? Do you desperately seek abuse?"

"...J-just making conversation."

As furious as she was at Glenn, she could see that he was clearly out of it, and in truth, probably hadn't been right in a very long time. She took a deep breath, and got back on the road, keeping the music down low and trying not to think too much. She knew she just needed to get to the motel, and she could deal afterwards.

"Yesterday was the anniversary of Jake's death," she started. "So…that would make it your birthday, huh?"

Glenn didn't respond.

"Happy birthday, I guess."

She drove back in silence, save the brush of tree branches dancing around in the wind. They made it back to the motel, Alma walking Glenn to the room he shared with Kody. Glenn opened the door, and they saw Kody fast asleep on his bed, snoring obnoxiously with a leg dangling off the mattress. Alma walked Glenn over to his bed and helped him get his shoes off.

"W-would you l-like me to wake him?"

"No, let him sleep. He's gotta be exhausted." She looked at Kody, her heart doing its fond pitter-patter. *I wouldn't wake him for anything. At least one of us should find peace…* she thought to herself as she turned back toward the door.

"Hey, get some rest, okay? We aren't done with this, but don't worry about it for now, and don't tell anyone. This is between you and me."

"R-right."

"All right. Goodnight, Glenn."

"Goodnight, Alma."

She paused before she crossed the threshold of the door.

"And Glenn?"

"Y-yes?" he turned to her.

"At least you told me."

She walked out, closing the door behind her. Should she be furious or grateful to the man who saved her life, and kept his knowledge about her a secret? She walked over to her room and stopped, trying to decide whether she wanted to go in.

She couldn't decide what to do and just stood there. Eventually, her body began to sway, landing her back against the door as she stared at nothing. A cold draft crept by, passing between her legs. She could feel a cool summer storm coming on as the dark clouds began to roll in.

Her confusion grew as her fear left her unable to do anything about it. Her body wouldn't respond. She could feel herself starting to slide down the back of the door and did nothing to stop it. Dull, gravelly rocks dug into her butt as she hit the ground. Her face warmed as her cheeks flushed.

She tried to hold it back, forcing herself to breath while her chest tightened. She could do little to stop what was coming. She remained on the ground, short of breath, as her head dropped down into her lap and she broke down.

She burst into tears. Nothing in her head but pictures and memories. So many recollections of her brother, her father, their family. The image of her mother briefly crossed her mind and left just as quickly. She thought back to that night, remembering the cold wind howling just before the water came crashing in. She held herself a little tighter, pretending everything was just a dream. She fell back a little as the door behind her opened.

"Geez, you little fur ball! Do you have to pee on every—Alma?"

Cris looked down to see her friend covered in tears, distraught, and greatly embarrassed. She set Bixby down as she sat next to her.

"Honey, what's wrong?"

"Nothing!" Alma kept to herself.

"Did something happen with Kody?" a tinge of guilt came out in Cris's voice.

"What? No! We're fine."

"Then what is it?"

"It's nothing! I just...um...I got some ketchup on my shirt. It was my favorite shirt, you know?" Alma tried to soldier along.

"Ketchup shirt, huh? Hmm...I know what it's like to lose your favorite shirt to reprocessed fluids. Why don't we get you inside so we can get you all changed up?" Cris offered her friend a smile and hand up

"No, I'm okay. I'm gonna sit out here for a while. Enjoy the rain."

"Enjoy the rain? You hate the rain."

"It's not so bad..."

"Alrighty, honey bunny, but if you need anything you let me know, okay? I love you," Cris told her as she gave her a best friend hug.

"I will."

Alma mustered up the courage to give her a weak smile as she waited for Bixby to finish peeing on the sidewalk. Cris left Alma's key next to her as she picked the small demon up and took him back inside. Alma watched urine trickle down the sidewalk. She knew she was going to get wet if she didn't move. She tried to care, but she couldn't. The feeling wasn't there. She watched, and waited. Part of her leg became dampened.

She watched the dark, evening clouds as she heard the increasingly loud rustle of the leaves that precede any good storm. She didn't know what she was going to do if it started to thunder.

I'm gonna be strong…I have to be strong. I've made it this far. I'm not gonna hold everyone back, and I'm not gonna have them worrying about me all the time. I don't wanna end up like Glenn! She kept her focus as she dried her tears. She was shaken up as she heard the door next to her unlock and open up. She looked up at his foresty-green eyes, looking back at her once again—full of life as always.

"Hey, how's it going down there?" Kody asked.

"Crappy," she smiled at him.

She sat mopey, but trying to cheer herself up so he wouldn't see her like this. She had decided. She was going to be strong.

"Why don't you join me up here then?"

He stretched out his arm, offering his hand to her. She grabbed her key as she took his hand and pulled herself up. He smiled as he looked into her eyes, wiping the remaining tears away.

"God, I must look horrible," she sniffled, returning his glance.

"That's crazy talk; you're gorgeous." He kissed her forehead.

"Psh, it's just dark. You're too blind to see anything."

"I guess that could be, but I like the view from here." He chuckled as he lowered his head slightly to kiss her. She embraced her honey bear.

"I thought you were sleeping… How did you…?"

"Isn't it a boyfriend's job to know these things? C'mon, I have an idea."

Though still in his pajamas, but retaining the foresight to wear shoes, Kody led Alma to the van and opened the door for her, seating her in the passenger seat. He then took his rightful place at the helm as Alma handed him the keys.

"Where are we going?"

"No idea." Kody had his idiotic adventurous smile prepped and good to go. "Ready?"

"Of course." She couldn't help but return it.

It crossed her mind how much his smile reminded her of Jake's. Yet there was a certain warmth there she just couldn't find anywhere else. Kody dug his CD case out from the pile below on the floor, and pulled out an old classic. He took out Glenn's CD as he put his in, and drove off without a particular destination. Though it took a minute, when she finally did get it she recognized the CD instantly.

"'*My World Ends With You!*' You still have this?" she asked.

"Well, yeah! Like I'd get rid of such a treasure. This is the first CD you ever made me, you know."

"Yeah, but I didn't think you still had it! You usually just rip the music and toss them!"

"Normally. But this is a very special CD, you see. So I had to keep it." Kody grinned.

She smiled at him as they rode on enjoying the quiet melodies of Sufjan Steven's "To Be Alone With You." She could hear the rain start to fall and became a little anxious, her hand tight on the armrest. Having Kody nearby was the only thing keeping her calm.

Night had settled in, leaving only the headlamps of cars in the opposite lane as any source of light. Alma was curious to know where they were going when Kody turned off onto an abandoned lot, just off the main road. He turned off the lights but kept the music playing low.

"So, Mr. Lehane…what exactly are we doing out here?" She twirled loose strands of hair around her finger as she spoke.

"Huh. I have no idea. It seems like we're lost. Hopelessly stuck."

"That it does."

Kody set the CD player on repeat as he climbed into the back seat, clearing it off and making room for one more. She reached into her purse to grab a condom.

"My, my, my, do you really expect me to crawl back there with you?"

"Hmm, it does seem that way, doesn't it?"

"If I didn't know better, I'd say you were planning on seducing me, Mr. Lehane."

"Well, I was never much for plans, personally. But if I was…"

He reached his hand out to her, and she took it climbing into the back with him. They could hear the rain begin to pour down, nearly drowning out the sound of the music.

"Okay, this isn't funny anymore, Kody; I'm really scared." The butterflies in her stomach began flapping madly.

"It's okay, there's nothing to worry about, I'm right here."

"I know, but—" Kody kissed her once more, and her concerns were hushed.

She felt around his lower back until she found the bottom of his shirt and pulled it up over his head. She grinned to herself as she got a look at what she was about to enjoy. She climbed on top of him, pushing him back into the seat.

He leaned forward and began kissing his way down her neck, finding her shirt in his way. His hands slowly climbed up her backside, starting with the small of it, carrying her shirt with them. Before long, the cloth was gone.

Goosebumps rose all along her body as he hoisted her up. She welcomed his hands as he felt his way around her mid-section, sliding finger upon finger along her hips; shortly after red polka dots decorated the floor. She closed her eyes, wishing for nothing other than to remain with her precious honey bear, quiet and alone, just like this. She finally let the air leave her lungs, ready to take another breath. A flash of lightning climbed up from the ground several miles behind the tree line. The crackling thunder that came echoing out shortly after scared her half to death.

"Kody, I can't do this!" she started panicking.

Kody, now freeing himself, got her firmly situated and her nerves were immediately relieved. She grabbed her lover—kissing his forehead gently—and relaxed into a state of calm bliss as her body sank into him. She rode along with him to the quiet crooning of Sufjan Stevens playing in the background.

18. Into the Dark, or Straddling the Razor's Edge

"Funny thing about life - you never know if you're gonna succeed until you do, or you don't.
'Til then, it's just a matter of trying your hardest not to fall behind while everyone else looks like rock stars."

– Kody's Notebook

Though Glenn lay there, sleep would not avail him. Though his mind had calmed, it had not quieted. He turned on the small lamp next to the bed and searched for his pants on the floor. He found the pill bottle close by. He got up to pour himself a glass of water as he opened it. He brought the pill to his lips, forcing it through, swallowing it, and washing it down with some water. He took his place at the side of the bed, staring only at the mysterious pattern on the carpet, awaiting any secret it might divulge to him.

Nothing came. He stood infuriated at the deceitful rug and scuffed it with the bottom of his feet. This did little other than skin his foot, but in a small way, he got satisfaction. He became lost and couldn't remember why he was there.

He no longer knew where he was, nor did he care. He reached for his pocket, forgetting his pajama pants had none, before wondering where his knife had gone. A wayward glance resulting from a sneeze revealed to him that his pants had been hiding in the same place that he had found them only moments before. He came upon them with much tenacity.

He slowly removed the knife from his pocket, perhaps fearful it might discover his intention and attempt flight. He dropped it on the nightstand as the fog within his mind began to lift. The memories he had regained and forgotten drifted intertwined, neither aware of the other nor capable of interlacing. He stripped himself of his cotton confinement. Stronger, free. Naked. He scratched his wrist, gliding fingers along numerous incompetent scars upon it. He shuddered, clutching his wrist, and letting it go.

He stood up, at first unaware, but slowly realizing what he was doing. He walked in front of the mirror: the man that beheld him stared back, a callow void. Dark, empty eyes. Cow eyes. Eyes that saw into him, through him, beyond him. He was vacant. Hollow. He loathed the awkward smile grinning back at him, only to mock his internal suffering. A true self-reflection. He should be afraid, but there was nothing.

He felt himself stiffen, and watched as the stranger in front of him took hold. He enjoyed the sensation, unable to understand why he could feel what this freak before him was doing, but he gripped it and writhed with pleasure. The image of that oh-so-sweet girl he had tried so hard to forget helped him to embrace himself, and he wouldn't stop.

He was gratified. A sweet release of misery and suffering. He felt pain indistinct. He couldn't remember what was going on. He looked at the puddle before him. He felt great shame as he washed his hands and cleaned up after himself. He became aware.

He had allowed himself to relinquish control so easily. A vulgarity that couldn't be forgiven. There was no forgiveness or penance in this, his sacred space—no atoning for his disgusting, self-depreciating obscenities. He had to cover the scene of the crime before any witnesses could come. He needed to cover his culprit. He shuffled back to the bed and grabbed his pants, slowly placing one leg into them as he considered whether the other would like the same. They had little choice; they were in this together.

He sat at the side of his bed once again, trying desperately to forget what he believed to be his depravity. He reached for the knife and slowly drew the blade, observing its glean. He knew how sharp it was, but it was never sharp enough—as if one last grinding would put it over the top and allow it to achieve perfection. But perfection was not what he needed. It was the farthest thing from his mind. Something he could never behold.

He brought the blade to his forearm, breathing deeply and relishing the moment, never sure if another might yet come. He applied pressure. Nothing occurred. He pressed deeper until the blood ran crimson and drew the blade across his arm. He grimaced while the blood began to coat the dull metal. It was enough. His false restitution had been bought. He pulled a tissue from the box on the nightstand and cleaned the blade. He then brought the thin cloth to his arm, applying pressure. He waited until the bleeding stopped. For now.

He put his knife away and removed the tissue, watching only a small amount of blood seeping from the surface of the self-inflicted wound. He watched it, waited for it as it ran down his arm. He stared at the small trickle that escaped with envy, and wiped himself off. He was done.

His phone rang. He answered.

"What."

"Glenn? *Bonjour cher ami, j'ai de bonnes nouvelles.*" The voice of a sultry vixen caught him off-guard.

"Oh, it's y-you. G-give me a minute."

He set the phone down, cleaning himself off properly before putting on a long-sleeve shirt. He took a sip from his glass as he walked back to his bed and put some socks on his now chilly feet. He resumed his conversation.

"Have you c-confirmed it?" Glenn was rather inpatient.

"Almost."

He should be excited, and indeed his palpitations did increase. But he felt cold.

"Wh-where are you?"

"Laughlin."

"L-laughlin, Nevada? How'd you m-make that mistake?"

"I don't make mistakes, *mon cher ami.*"

"Th-then you're p-playing me."

"I live in a dangerous world. I trust only as much as I can afford to."

"At this p-point I believe you c-can afford quite a bit."

"Ah, so I can. And it is for that reason I am so amicable. See you soon?"

"In a matter of d-days, with any luck."

"*Jusque-là. Au revoir.*"

He hung up, and pulled out his laptop, grating his finger against the power button. He tapped his finger against the start-up screen that took several minutes to load, but after he was able to log in his work progressed quite smoothly. He updated his logs, changed the destination, and pulled up Laughlin on a map.

"The most c-convenient route from here would b-be...through T-texas."

He was set. He plotted a new route and wrote down the basics, having them ready to provide to Kody in the morning. He closed up his laptop and lay back down for a moment, staring at the ceiling. The nothing above mirrored the emptiness within. His inner abyss seemed to grow. Even the monsters in the ceiling smiling back at him provided little comfort.

"It's just a m-matter of time. Everything in this world t-takes time. It's so i-inefficient. She had b-better find him."

As he lay there, he began to realize for the first time that his companion wasn't there.

"B-bixby? Are you h-here?"

He heard no response.

"A-allister, wh-where are you?"

There was genuine fear in his voice as he realized his cat was gone. He stopped to think of the possibilities and concluded with only one likely scenario that would turn up with a happy ending. He pulled up his sleeve and dressed his arm before sliding the fabric back down. He put on some slippers, heading outside.

The cool air left behind by the storm hit him like a chilly wall, though the dew still rife on the grass outside brought his nostrils some relief. He knocked on Cris's door, waiting for a response. He heard nothing, and assumed that if she had slept through the storm then she must still be sleeping, and quite heartily at that. He pounded on the door, unable to control the trembling in his hands.

"Hold on!"

He had finally gotten a response. The sound of her voice, a calm, soothing voice he trusted began to ground him as he felt himself returning. He listened to the latch unhinge as the door opened to reveal Charisma's hair a slight mess, though he was surprised to see her face looked surprisingly no different.

"I thought you wore make-up..." he remarked.

"Uh...hey, good morning to you, too, Glenn...is there something you needed?" she said, still groggy.

"Wh-what?" He became himself again. "Oh, y-yes, right, of course! Have you seen Mr. B-bixby?"

"Yeah, he's right over there." She gestured, pointing to the purring fur ball asleep on her bed.

"Oh, he's resting! Of course he is; it's s-so very late! My apologies. I sh-should not have d-disturbed you."

"Hey…are you all right?" Cris was still waking up, but could tell something was off with Glenn.

"Y-yes, fine, of course."

"You seem a little…intense."

"I…u-uh…the storm, you see…"

"Uh huh, come on in. Have a seat." She opened the door, and he stepped aside.

She gestured toward Alma's bed, though Glenn took a seat in the chair at the little table near the door. Following his lead, she pulled out the other chair and sat down.

"Hmm, we haven't talked much since we left, huh?" Cris started.

"N-no, I suppose not."

"How are you?"

"F-fine."

"You keep saying that."

"Th-that'd be because I am."

"Really…?" Cris put on her matronly tone.

"Y-yes, really." Glenn squinted as he readjusted his glasses.

"You're not fooling me, buster. What's really on your mind?"

"As I said before…"

"C'mon, it's me. Little Crissy. Remember? You and Emmy used to call me that all the time. I'm not gonna make fun of you, and I'm not going to lie to you, so it's okay to speak your mind, all right? Won't judge. Promise."

Glenn believed in her, and wanted to trust her, but a part of him wouldn't allow himself to let anything go to someone else.

"I b-believe you. And say there was something I wanted to s-say. How would I say it?"

"You just do. You come out and say whatever's on your mind."

"I s-see."

"I know you do. You see a lot of things. But somehow I don't think that's helping you right now."

"I'm j-just…it's a hard time for me. There's a lot going on."

"Like what? Tell me about it."

"A-alma, for one."

"What's wrong with Alma?" Cris suddenly remembered seeing her friend just a few hours prior and was starting to connect the two.

"I-I…nothing."

"Glenn…"

Glenn began to fret with his glasses, the pads on the bridge of his nose starting to dig in.

"Hey, hey…calm down. What is it?"

Glenn quickly regretted saying anything at all and needed to find a way to change the subject.

"May I have my c-c-cat back, please?"

"Sure."

Cris got up and went to get Bixby. She picked him up carefully and carried him back toward Glenn, trying not to disturb the kitten's slumber. She heard a strong thud sound as something slammed against the door outside. Bixby's kitty eyes popped open, though he showed no other signs of being awake.

"What was that?" Cris turned back to Glenn, who was mildly alarmed.

"Shhh! Kodykins, keep it down! She'll hear us…!"

"Not if you stop making so much noise…"

They could hear the conversation intermixed with quiet moaning on the other side of the door.

"Okay, stop, for real! She's gonna wake up and freakin' kill me!"

"If you say so…"

"Mm…Kody, not…" Alma squealed and quickly quieted herself.

"Goodnight, Mr. Lehane."

She tried to unlock the door silently, finding it was already unlocked, and slowly inched the door open. As the door opened to reveal her face, Cris and Glenn both sat there staring at Alma. Kody stood behind her, playing innocent and looking lost as they both came into the room.

"So, uh…thanks for walking me back to my room, Kody; I very much appreciate it. I don't think I would've found my way back from the um…vending machines otherwise." Alma tried to be casual as she straightened up her hair, which was a little less organized and a little more like a rat's nest.

"Uh, yeah, of course! You know me: Good Samaritan all the way. Just tryin' to help out where I can."

"Well, um…I need to go pee, so I'm gonna do that." Alma slinked her way into the bathroom with her bags from the van.

Cris handed Bixby to Glenn as he abruptly got up and left the room. She then heard the shower turn on in the bathroom, which only confirmed her suspicions. She wasn't keen on the matter, but did her best to don the mask of humor.

"That's quite the late-night recreation, huh?" Cris smirked.

"Heh, what can I say…? I'm a gentleman." Kody, unable to hold his own grin back.

"Yeah, I can tell. Escorting a lady back from the…vending machines, and all."

"She was hungry."

"For hours?"

"Voracious."

"In the middle of a storm?"

"Determined."

"With messy hair?"

"It was so windy!" Kody shrugged. "Plus all that food…"

"Right…"

The two continued to banter back and forth with their little game. Cris eventually noticed the clock on the wall and realized the time.

"Well, gentleman that you are, don't you think you should be getting back? It's pretty late."

"You're quite right, milady. I'm on my way now." Kody started heading out the door but he turned back.

"Hey, thanks for that text."

"She's my best friend. I thought you'd want to know." Somberness started creeping back into her demeanor.

"I won't forget it."

"Yeah, I bet," Cris said, pointing out the dirty grin Kody was still wearing. He smiled and shrugged it off.

"One more thing…" Cris barely remembered.

"Yeah?"

"Keep an eye on Glenn."

"Why, what's up with him?"

"I don't know, but he seems kind of out of it. I think he might be getting worse."

"Hmm…I'll definitely check on him. Thanks."

"No problem."

Cris closed the door behind him as Kody left, finally able to drop the pretense all together. She heard the shower cut off as she looked over at her bed and saw a sleeve of the jacket hanging out. She rushed over to cover it up with her blanket.

"Sorry I got back so late!" she heard Alma call out from the bathroom.

"Don't worry about it. Feeling better?"

"Like you wouldn't *believe*." She instantly recognized the tone in Alma's voice.

"Pervert," Cris called her out.

Alma busted out of the bathroom in her new underwear as she playfully got up in Cris's face, hair still damp and dripping.

"So?"

"Careful, Alm, you're making a mess everywhere!"

Cris, sighed, wiping herself off as she helped Alma towel-dry her hair.

"You're too horny for your own good sometimes, I swear," Cris remarked, to which Alma simply scoffed.

"You're just a prude."

"Hey! I am not a prude. I just happen to have a little integrity."

"And I don't?"

They both looked at each other as Cris put the dirty towel on an empty rack near the bathroom.

"That's not the point," Alma ceded. "I want a second opinion. We could always call Kody in here and ask him."

"Oh no you don't!" Cris tackled Alma, pinning her to the bed.

A small fire lit up in Alma's eyes. "You wanna fight it out?"

"Think you can take me?"

"You know I can."

"I know you think you can."

Alma tossed Cris off and managed to get back on her feet, the two now squaring off. They stared each other down as the other planned her next move. Alma lunged first, narrowly missing Cris as she dodged out of the way. Cris countered by grabbing Alma around the waist from behind and dragging her back onto the bed. Alma flailed, trying to break free of Cris's grip. She reached down and bit Cris's hand enough to hurt, escaping her grasp.

"Hey, that's cheating!"

"I play to win!"

Alma rolled over and managed to get on top of Cris, pinning her down.

"Say it."

"No!"

Cris reached up behind her head and found one of the pillows, hitting Alma in the face with it.

"Bitch!" Alma didn't see it coming.

"Loser." Cris stuck her tongue out as she slid out from underneath Alma and flipped her over, pinning Alma with her knees while still hitting her with the pillow.

"Give up?"

"Never!"

Alma defended her face, trying to come up with another plan. She tried to squirm free, but Cris's knees had her locked in tight.

"What do you say? Do you admit defeat?" Cris stopped, giving Alma the chance to surrender.

"I will not submit!" Alma took this opportunity to reach up and get Cris's armpits, tickling her into submission.

"Stop it! Let go!"

"Say it!"

"Alm, I'm gonna pee!"

"Say it!"

"All right, All right! You win!"

"Annnd?"

"I'm a prude! Now let me pee!"

Alma considered it.

"Hmm…that'll do."

Alma released Cris as she ran to the bathroom. Alma stood the victor, gloating in her triumph.

"It's okay, sweetie; someday you'll get yourself some, too. You just gotta learn to not be so picky!" Alma reveled in her accomplishment as she began to clean up.

"Hey, it's a special thing, okay? Not all of us are willing to give it up for just anyone," Cris called out from the bathroom.

"First off, Thaddeus Williams is not just anyone. Secondly, he was a loser anyway. Now Dave on the other hand—meh, that's not the point. Believe you me: it made my first time with Kody all the better."

Alma's wide smile could not be contained. She was, however, surprised at Cris's silence.

"I'm not saying you should go screw the first guy you see, I'm just saying that it's not as big a deal as you make it out to be. You have no idea what you're missing out on."

Cris came out of the bathroom.

"I'm comfortable with where I'm at, okay? Let's just go to bed."

"M'kay."

"Um...Alm?"

"Yeah?"

"Aren't you at least gonna put on some pajamas or something?"

"It's too hot in here for that...stupid air conditioning."

"The A/C's busted?"

"Yeah, you didn't notice? The boys got the only working one."

Cris suddenly realized why she thought the room felt so comfortable. They both climbed into their separate beds and turned off the lamps.

"'Night, Cris."

"'Night, Alm."

Alma's lips curled up into a warm smile as she snuggled herself into her blanket.

Cris turned her back to Alma, facing the wall. She wrapped herself in his jacket. She held it close to her face and inhaled deeply, noticing that the jacket was losing some of its scent. She tucked it back underneath her blanket, making sure that Alma wouldn't see it. Though she was happy for her friend, she couldn't help but admit to herself that maybe she was just a little jealous. She suddenly realized she was beginning to miss the whimsical purring of chicken-flavored cat breath.

* * *

Kody locked the door behind him as he came back into the room. He saw Glenn sitting on the bed, laptop resting on his legs and the wide-eyed feline next to him.

"So, what's up, buddy?"

"Meeeerowowow."

"Not you." The cat disregarded him as Kody smirked.

"Ah, y-yes. How was your outing? D-did you finish 'patching,' as you put it?"

"You could say that."

"I s-see."

Kody kicked his shoes off as he walked over to his bed. A small note sat waiting as he went to lie down. He began to read it.

"Huh…what's this about? Nevada?"

He looked over at Glenn, now able to see the laptop screen covered with maps, documents, and a half-finished game of Solitaire.

"Glenn, what's this thing about Nevada?"

"Hmm? Oh, y-yes. I'd like to go there or at least stop through, if you don't mind."

"Sure, it's pretty much on the way. More or less. What's there though?"

"M-maybe nothing."

"Maybe something?" Kody canted his head.

"W-we'll see."

"What?" Kody arched an eyebrow.

"M-must be the lack of sleep. It's r-rather late."

"Right. This is true. Hey, make sure you get some rest! You're on deck to drive tomorrow! Or I guess later today, at this point.

"I'll be fine."

Glenn petted Bixby as he continued his card game, unable or unwilling to focus on much else. Kody lay in bed for a few minutes, debating whether to investigate Cris's claim. She had steered him right so far. Thinking about what she had told him, he thought of her face. His thoughts began to drift to things other than her judgment.

"So! Glenn! Man…" he said, trying to distract himself.

"Y-yes?"

"How are you, really?"

"I'm f-fin…" Glenn stopped as Kody sat up, staring at him.

"Don't say you're fine."

"But I…" Kody stared at him. "Wh-what would you have me say?"

"The truth."

"That b-being?"

"Well, not that I really want to get into it, 'cause every man does his own thing…but it smells funny in here, and I don't just mean the actual smell. And you're unusually defensive. Suddenly you've got a new game plan, and since when do you do much of anything other than play with your cat?"

Glenn watched Kody with a keen eye, listening to everything he had observed.

"My policy is usually to let people do their own thing. Long as they aren't hurting anyone, I say hey, whatever. But there's something up with you, and I'm pretty sure it's hurting you."

"K-kody, maybe there is 's-something up with me,' as you put it. What do you intend to do about it?"

"I dunno...help you? Can't do much if you don't talk to me."

"'T-tis true enough. Fine. W-would you like to talk then?" Glenn sat his laptop down and faced Kody.

Kody gave him his undivided attention.

"All right then." Glenn took a deep breath and threw a CD case off the bed as he got comfortable.

"What's that about?"

"*The D-devil and God are r-raging inside me.* Symbolic, if n-nothing else."

"Eh, fair enough."

"You w-want to know, Kody, about my h-head? I c-can't...I mean...it isn't always right." Glenn stopped to take slow, deep breaths and tried to articulate his troubles. "K-kody, do you believe in religion?"

Kody shook his head.

"I see. W-well, I do. I b-believe in things such as Heaven and Hell, God and the D-devil. Whether th-this is in the theological sense is irrelevant, b-because both of them exist inside of me, my h-head. Th-though they are far f-from the only things there." Glenn leaned back, staring at the ceiling before continuing.

"I...i-it's dark. I don't know w-what *it* is, but I cannot help it, I c-cannot stop it, I cannot fight it. Suffice it to say that it s-scares me."

Glenn's hands began to shake as he spoke. He set the reluctant cat in his lap and continued petting him.

"There are times when I c-can't feel anything, and times when I th-think I c-can literally feel everything. Something in my head b-breaks, snaps, shifts. It c-cracks. There's noise everywhere. It's so loud. It's c-chaotic. It hurts and wants me to die. Sometimes. B-but that's n-not me. It's just part of s-something inside me. Sometimes I wish I could c-cut it out, so I could become normal."

Kody sat in silence. Searching for anything to say wouldn't do justice; he could barely understand, much less offer him anything.

"Ever since I lost J-jake, ever since I let him d-drown...there's been s-something inside me. Something other than h-hatred and self-loathing. I am responsible f-for the loss of my best friend. And I h-hate it. I h-hate myself. It may not be my fault ex-exclusively, but it is. I let him down. I am unw-worthy of everything around me. I want to de-de-destroy everything, everyone. Every year it gets w-worse. These things are too g-great to be allowed to exist around me. Even this little one b-beside me." He cast a sorrowful eye toward Bixby.

"This little c-creature is the c-closest thing to peace I've ever known, yet still… He does not love me; he does not even c-care for me. He only c-cares for himself. But so long as I provide for him, he will not abandon me. This is true of nothing else in my life."

"Glenn, man…everyone feels alone sometimes." Kody had to say something.

"This is not th-the same! It isn't s-simply *feeling* alone. It is *being* alone. C-completely, utterly. With friends, with loved ones, with myself. I'm not in c-control even in my own head, much less out of it. I d-do not exist. I am the shell of a m-man for the thing inside of me, d-dying to get out. I've f-fought it for so long with no success! I wish I c-could just let it succeed, g-grant it victory where I fail, for then p-perhaps it would leave me be, or I c-could cease to be! But I c-cannot. For more than anything, I fear it's possible we are one and the same…I f-fear that the beast inside of me *is* me."

Kody looked at him in awe. Glenn paced his breathing as he continued to stroke the kitten's fuzzy fur. He tried to speak slowly, but clearly.

"So, K-kody, what words of wisdom do you have to impart to me? What sacred knowledge can you impart that will liberate me from this curse! Can you a-alleviate my suffering? Do you have that oft-promised solution so many people speak of but c-cannot seem to provide? Or shall you simply report to Cris as you always do, and the two of you gossip once more? Please, b-blog about it so that others may enjoy in your frivolous chatter while I continue to degrade. At least leave d-documentation of your surely amusing attempts at righteousness." Glenn snorted. "No, don't c-come to me offering worthless banter; you've nothing to help."

Kody sat back, crossing his arms across his chest. He stared at Glenn, ignoring his own reflection in his friend's dirty glasses. The two sat deadlocked, until Kody finally threw his arms up.

"Hey, man, I'm trying to help, okay? But this is all new to me! You think I've heard or dealt with this kind of crap before? I can't say I really know what you're talking about, and neither can Cris! That's why we're trying to help you! We don't know anything about this shit, but we wanna try to help. Maybe we don't really get it, and maybe it's true that we can't do anything, but if you let us in and let us try then maybe we can help, or at least figure out something."

"I've h-heard these words before, Kody. D-do you think I've not sought help? Did C-charisma ever tell you why her sister left me? Did you two ever discuss wh-what it was that brought me back from England? I've let people in, and they c-couldn't handle it. I drive p-people away, and am left to b-bear the cost. It is me that is t-torn asunder every time they r-run off. There's little left, and I c-can ill-afford to let people toy with that. My acumen is rather quite frail, in c-case it's escaped your keen notice, and I'd much prefer you d-don't toy with the remainder."

Kody cocked an eye, stroking his imaginary beard as he contemplated. Before long, he snapped his fingers leaving his index raised.

"Okay, I think I got it! So you're scared. You're afraid we're gonna bail on you like everyone else did, I guess. Welcome to the world; who isn't? You don't wanna let us help? Fine. Let's say we don't care about you and just let this go. What'cha gonna do?"

Glenn shrugged as he rolled his eyes.

"I'll d-do what I must."

"And what's that?"

Glenn offered no answer.

"So, in other words, nothing. You'll just suck it up and drive on?"

"It's w-worked thus far."

"Yeah, looks like you're doing great."

"I-I am."

"Then why are you telling me all this? Why are we here now?"

Glenn remained silent, eyes cast to the side.

"Look, I don't have all the answers. To be honest, I don't even understand the damn questions. But I know that Cris is worried about you. I'm worried about you. Maybe we can fix some things, maybe we can't, but we're here and willing, which looks a hell of a lot better than whatever else you tried so far. Let us help."

Glenn sighed. "K-kody, if you're wrong there may be nothing left."

"I don't know if that's really all that worse than what you've got going on right now…but you know what? Ball's in your court. What's it gonna be?"

Glenn hesitated. "I'll need some time to think it over."

"Sure, sleep on it. That's not a bad idea for either of us."

Glenn rubbed his kitty's fuzzy fur, just behind the ears. His arm itched. He ignored it. He closed out the projects on his laptop for the night as he prepared for rest.

"Uh…K-kody?" he looked over to the scruffy poet.

"Yeah?"

"Aren't you going to shower…?"

"What?" Kody smelled himself. "Ohh…right. Nah, fuck it. I'll be all right. I'll do it in the morning. Not going anywhere else tonight."

Glenn shook his head, lying back on the burlap sack that passed for a motel pillow. He removed his glasses, letting his eyes linger on the ceiling once more. "How am I s-supposed to have faith in kids that c-can't even take care of themselves? I c-can afford little at best," he muttered to himself. He closed his eyes as he rolled over to his side. "P-perhaps… a little faith is enough."

19. Daydream Desert

"Ain't no point in doing anything other than one day at a time. No one ever promised me there'd be a tomorrow."

– Blurbs Mr. Agramonte Jotted Down on a Dirty Napkin

Somewhere near the Mojave Desert

The rough, rugged man gazed at the ceiling, spitting out beads of sweat as they slid through his stubble into his mouth. For being so young in the ways of the world, he sure as shit felt old.

"Still better than what came before..."

The humid air made the walls sweat. There was little hope for any kind of air conditioning or a storm to help cool things off. The man sighed and cursed his eternally damned luck at being stuck in such an abysmal rat's hole.

"I can't do this shit ferever. I gotta come up with some kinda plan to get outta here," he muttered to himself as he climbed off the mattress laid out on the floor. He got up to check the hand-drawn calendar shoddily taped to the back of his door and discovered that in the cycle of days, this one claimed Wednesday.

"Clinic Day."

He looked around his room, dank and run-down, and tried to decide which of his shirts in the scattered pile on the floor could attempt to pass for respectable. He found a button-up one with only a few buttons missing and doused it in body spray, masking whatever odor curling off it. It didn't smell terrible, though it needed some smoke. He threw on some jeans—he could never tell if they were dirty or clean—and headed for the bathroom to wash his face before heading out.

He glanced toward the razor near the sink, noting the growth of his stubble in the mirror, and glanced away. He messed around with his hair with little success. He threw it in a ponytail. He made his way back into his room, ready to head out the door before he realized he was already forgetting something.

"Aw, shit…where is it?"

He searched his room, but couldn't remember where he'd left it. He checked underneath his cardboard table-dresser with little luck. There was nowhere else to check. He moved to his door, creaking it only a little, to see if anyone was still out in the living room. He was of course unafraid; there was just no reason to deal with more bullshit than necessary. With the coast clear, he proceeded to check the kitchen.

He had a hunch about what'd happened and decided to check the junk drawer. Shuffling through all the crap, he managed to get his hand into the back. He got a grip on it and pulled it out, straightening out the ugly creases that had been pressed into it.

"My I.D. badge is all fucked up…great. How that bitch ever got to living here is beyond me, but it's about time for one of us to go."

He stuffed the badge into his pocket, neatly, as he boiled some water on the rustic stove. He hated having his oatmeal without cinnamon, but it was just another aspect of his life. Something was always missing.

He poured the packet into the small pan, carrying it into what passed for the living room. He sat down to a fuzzy television that offered little other than a snowy picture. It didn't matter one way or the other—he ate only because it was necessary. He finished, heading back into the kitchen and dropped the pan in the sink.

He went back over to the living room and reached for the back of the couch, grabbing at nothing, now realizing his favorite and only jacket was no longer there. He quickly looked on both sides of the couch, taking every precaution to make sure he hadn't missed it.

"Goddamn it…she took my fuckin' jacket!"

He threw his shoes on and stormed out the door. The bright desert sun blinded him as soon as hot air hit his face. He reached for his chest pocket to pull out his sunglasses, but was reminded that he was still not wearing his jacket. He hocked a loogie.

The warm dusty sand blowing around in the air got into his eyes, making it progressively more difficult for him to continue walking to his destination. Tough shit—he had no other means to get there. He'd walked this path more times than he cared to remember, and required little assistance from his eyes in finding the way.

He made it back to the bar and entered through the side door to find his same couch-hogging whore restocking the cabinets for the coming night.

"Hey, jerk-off, didn't think you worked today. Or ever, for that matter." She didn't even raise her head.

"You pay the damn rent?" He slammed his fist against the counter.

"I ain't tryin' to get kicked out. My pretty ass is way too good for the streets."

"Not as much as you think. Where's my jacket?"

"Why, honey, you cold?"

He sighed. "Just gimme the damn thing."

"Sure thing, shug."

She went into the stock closet and dug around for a minute, shuffling through various garments of ill repute before finding a jacket that hardly came close to resembling his. She pulled it out to look it over, though it appeared more for her sake than his.

"This it?"

"Keep fuckin' around with me, Lexy. See where the day takes us."

"So gruff. Guess you woke up on the wrong side—oh, right, there's only one side to your bed."

He glared at her, his patience clearly at its end. Lexy, seeing that it might behoove her to appease him, and that further antagonizing wouldn't provide nearly as much fun as she'd hoped, reached into the closet again, somehow magically finding his jacket.

"Well, look at that: it's your stupid coat." She tossed it on the counter.

He took it and left.

He pulled out a cigarette from his jacket and lit it up as he made his way down the curb and across the street. He once again reached for his pocket; this time successfully procuring a pair of sunglasses from it. He tossed them on. Having now fallen back into his routine, and feeling the sickly sweet drag of nicotine, he finally started to calm down. He took a deep breath, inhaling the smoke, and walked along.

He headed in the direction of his apartment, passing the only convenience store he'd ever graced with his presence. He continued on, seeing that same damn yard with the huge swing set that no one ever played on. He hated the neighborhood, but it was a part of him. He still hated it.

He stopped short of his apartment, standing instead in front of a small and dilapidated clinic. He stood outside, finishing his cigarette. Shitty as the place was, it was one of the better places to be. He dropped the cigarette butt to the ground and put it out before pulling out his I.D. badge and throwing it on as he headed inside.

He was greeted by the over-the-hill, grizzled combat receptionist who had seen it all and was fazed by little. She sat comfortably in the same chair that had carried her through her glory years, complacency evident in her jaded physique and manner. Dull eyes with faded lips, and bright, lovely nails.

"Hey, Mr. Agramonte, how's it goin'?" She asked.

"Same old, Mami, how about you?" Mr. Agramonte stated as he leaned on the counter.

"Every day's a new battle in the same endless war. You know how it is around here."

"Different strokes." He had a rough, callous grin that only ever briefly exposed itself. "Is the doc in?"

"Yeah, in her office."

"All right. Anyone waitin' on anything?"

"Just a little girl that needs some stitches. You up for that?"

"That's up to the doc."

Shirley stared at him.

"So, I should go see if she's good with that then."

He pushed himself off the counter and made his way into the back, throwing his jacket off in the break room, while taking the time to carefully place his sunglasses back in the right spot. He headed back to the doc's office.

"The only person rude enough to walk into a doctor's office without knocking." She turned to face him. The refined Doctor Asher looked him over, making sure he was clean and sober before she allowed him to work in her clinic for the day.

"Mornin'. Shirls says we got a little girl in need of some stitchin'. You good with me doin' that?"

"Are you comfortable with it?" she asked.

"Yeah, sure. Nothin' new."

"So you've done them before?"

"Few times."

"Hmm, perhaps they train combat medics better than I thought." Doctor Asher handed the chart to him. "All right. Look her over and check the wound. Wait until I get there to start though."

"Will do."

He headed back to the front desk, reviewing the girl's paperwork as he walked.

"Got caught on a fence? What kind of dumbass kid…?"

The receptionist looked up. "She's a little girl. How about some sensitivity? Kids make mistakes all the time. I'm sure you did."

"Can't argue that…"

He headed out into the lobby and called her back.

"Ramirez?" he called out.

"Dani Ramirez?" the little girl's mother asked.

"Sure. Come on back."

They followed him back into the examination room. He set her up on the table to get a good look at her arm. He looked it over closely. Looking it over, he didn't see anything that he'd be concerned about.

"Doesn't look like there's any kind of infection or anything. We'll get her stitched up an' go from there."

"Excuse me, but are you a doctor? I don't think I've seen you here before."

"Nah, not exactly."

"I think my daughter should be treated by a doctor, not some—"

The man scoffed, staring the mother down. "Doc's wrapped up right now. She'll be in as soon as she can. Fer now I'm what ya got. We can sit around and wait for the doc, see if this thing can't get a little infected, or you can let me fix your little girl up nice and proper, maybe save her some trouble. What'dya say?"

The man watched as Dani looked up at her mother pleadingly, hiding behind her mother's sleeves while still holding her arm. The mother herself appeared as though she wanted to step out, but her daughter tugging at her sleeve must have caused her to realign her priorities.

"A…all right. I guess that works."

Dr. Asher walked into the room professionally, allowing no air of imperfection.

"Don't worry, Mrs. Ramirez, Dani's in good hands. Our youthful Mr. Agramonte here used to be a soldier not too long ago. Trained by the Department of Army as a combat medic. He's more than proficient enough to handle this."

A quaint smile crossed Mr. Agramonte's lips, but he dashed it off as soon as he became aware of it. He looked to the doctor, awaiting her guidance.

"So what's your assessment?" she asked.

"Looks clean. Figure we clean it out just to be safe an' stitch her up. Should be good from there."

"Good. Let me know when you're done, and I'll get her started on a tetanus series as well. Never know with the fences around here."

"Got it."

He cleaned out the little girl's wound, the mother now looking at him with renewed interest.

"So...you were a soldier?" She seemed more interested in his personal history than her daughter.

"I don't give a damn about what your last job was. Don't see what business it is of yours nosing into mine."

He pulled out a suture kit and started stitching up the girl's arm, being careful to maintain the proper interval and not hurt her too much. His hands moved deftly as he finished up.

"There, yer all done, kid."

Dr. Asher came back in with a shot kit.

"All right, Dani, this'll only hurt for a minute, okay?"

"Mommy, I don't like shots! This is gonna hurt!" Dani was starting to make a fuss.

"Hey, kid. Quit fussin'. You just got stitched up and yer worried about a little shot? What were you doing playin' around with busted-up fences anyway?"

"Huh? Oh, I was…"

Mr. Agramonte nodded to Dr. Asher, who then gave Dani the shot.

"…and then I fell. It was all Emil's fault!"

"All right, you're all done!"

Dani looked at the doctor in disbelief.

"Huh, what about my shot?"

"I already gave it to you."

Dani looked at her wide-eyed, unconvinced of such a possibility.

"Okay! You've been such a brave girl that I think you deserve an extra treat! Why don't you go up to the front desk and ask the nice lady for a sticker? I think you've earned it. Tell her I said it was okay."

"Yay!"

Dani jumped off the table and ran back to the front of the clinic. Her mother stayed behind to speak to Mr. Agramonte for a moment. She stood awkwardly, unsure of what to say.

"Um…thanks, for everything you've done for this country. And I'm sorry if I was rude before."

"Eh, whatever." He left the room.

"I apologize; he doesn't like talking about it. Dani should be fine, though. Just keep an eye on her arm for a few days and give us a call if you notice anything."

"I will. Thanks, Dr. Asher."

Mrs. Ramirez returned to the front with her daughter. Dr. Asher dropped the cheery act and lost her well-trained smile. She went into the break room to take a reprieve from her mandated professionalism. In there she found Mr. Agramonte had already started smoking.

"You know you can't do that in here."

"Eh, why not?"

"It's a medical facility. And also because I'm your boss today and I said not to."

"Fuckin'…" He put out the cigarette.

"You did good work in there, you know. Those were some fine sutures."

"Yeah, yeah…"

"They've improved since your last set. Have you been practicing?"

"I sewed some towels together an' shit. Figured it might help a little. And I was bored."

"Well, it shows. Keep up the good work. I'd very much like to see you as a colleague one day instead of an apprentice."

"I'd very much like to see shit fly, but I jes' don't think it's gonna happen."

"I'm serious! You could have a very bright future in medicine if you stick with this!"

"Like my broke ass even has a future…"

"Stubborn…you have potential." Dr. Asher became annoyed with his indifference.

"Every fuckin' kid lyin' dead in a ditch somewhere had potential. Now they're just fodder and fertilizer."

"Look, whatever you believe, you do have talent. Talent that you could use to stop some of those kids from ending up in ditches. As I recall, someone did that for you once."

He hadn't considered that angle.

"Your life may not be easy, but guess what? Neither is mine. No one's is. We all have different problems. But if you want a better life for yourself, if you really want to make something of yourself, then you can get up and do it. You're already at a good start. You just have to keep going."

"Damn…the view must be real nice from that high-ass ivory tower you're livin' in," he scoffed.

She returned to her office without acknowledging him.

He sat there for a minute, reflecting on what she had said. He had never had much encouragement in life, and few people if any ever believed in him. To hear such praise from someone of such high stature was one of the few perks of the job. That, and the money. The money wasn't terrible, though it still wasn't much.

"At least I'm good for somethin'. Could be worse," he muttered to himself as he went back into the exam room to clean up and practice on some more towels.

20. The Exit (featuring Emma Roberts)

"Sometimes, all you need is to hear the voice of someone you love."

– Cris's Journal

Nashville, Tennessee

Cris, being the only one who'd actually slept through most of the night, awoke much earlier than the others. She got up and showered, putting on one of the few pairs of clean non-various-liquid-soaked clothes she had left. She took a walk around outside, enjoying the seasonably warm morning and checking out the place as she had neglected to do the day before. She noticed a Laundromat across the street, providing an excellent opportunity to rectify the stinkiness of her traveling wardrobe. She went back into her room and nudged the sleeping Alma. She leaned down to talk to her.

"Hey, Alm. I'm going to go do some laundry. Do you have anything you want me to wash?"

"Hmm?" Alma barely stirred.

"I'm going to do some laundry. Do you have anything you want to throw in?"

"Oh, um…just my stuff from yesterday. It's in the bathroom."

"Okay."

"Thanks, Cris." Alma patted Cris's head, shuffling her hair as she went back to sleep.

Goofy girl, Cris kept to herself. *At least she's feeling better. I hope Kody can say the same for Glenn.* She shook Kody from her mind as she went into the bathroom to pick up Alma's clothes. She caught the van keys as they fell out of one of Alma's new clothing bags and took them with her, leaving Alma a change of clothes. She glanced around the motel room before heading out, catching the elusive sleeve of Kody's jacket once again trying to escape her bed. She grabbed the jacket on her way out the door.

On her way to the Laundromat, Cris stopped by the van to pick up the remains of her cat-clawed shirt and grab any dirty clothes that might be lying around. As she opened the door, trash tumbled from the van into the street. If she didn't clean it up, no one ever would. She crawled around in the middle row first, finding an odd red clump of fabric under the seat. She leaned down and crawled under the seat to grab it, and tried to figure out what it was.

"What's this…?" Cris picked it up and crawled back out as she unruffled it. "Oh, Alm! Ew, gross!"

She threw the red thong back on the floor of the van, now looking at the middle seat in a far more perturbed light.

"You've got to be kidding me…"

She worked her way around the van, avoiding the spot of the floor as much as possible. She tried to straighten up the rest of the van and clean out the trash, as well as other less-disturbing dirty clothes lying around. She finished rather quickly and was confronted only with that one last unflattering undergarment.

She had no desire to touch it, but she couldn't leave the otherwise sparkling-clean van tarnished like this. She shuddered to think of what might happen if someone else came upon it instead. They might even assume they were hers.

"Ugh, crap…"

Cris picked up the thong and threw it in with the rest of the laundry as she grabbed a change purse out of the center console. She then closed up the van and headed across the street to get started on the laundry.

She sorted out the clothing, trying to figure out what belonged to each of them before giving it up all together and just separating by color. She started a load and loitered around, trying to figure out what to do. She tried the claw-grabbing game, but found that despite her almost precise movements the claw just wouldn't grab the cute little fish animal near the bottom. Her hopes of winning a neat little cuddle prize for the harried fur-devil were quickly dashed.

She decided next to try her hand at some of the old arcade games. She saw an old favorite and jumped right in. She finally started getting a knack for Ms. Pac-man when the first washer went off, interrupting her while she was in the zone. She lost her focus and had more and more trouble trying to keep up with the ghosts. She tried a blitz and moved quickly to get the cherry and the big orb of whatever Ms. Pac-man eats before Pinky caught her, but was ambushed by the ever-so-sneaky Blinky, who had cleverly come in from the other side of the maze.

Defeated, she moved the load of clean clothes to the dryer and threw in a second load as she searched for something else to do. She watched the local news for a bit, but couldn't maintain interest in celebrity gossip and started messing with her phone. She scrolled through her short contact list containing only the names of her family or the people she was with already. *Maybe Alma's right. Maybe I am a bit of a recluse,* she thought.

Determined to prove her friend wrong, she picked a number and dialed. There was a protracted ringing period, filled mostly with Katy Perry, followed by an excitedly sleepy voice.

"Hey, little sis, what's up?" Emma was enthusiastic even when half asleep.

"Hey, Em. Not much. How're you?"

"Sleeping it off."

"Oh, I'm sorry. Did I wake you?"

"No, no. I actually had to get up to pee anyway. How's your trip going?"

"Fine, for the most part. It's pretty fun, actually."

"'The most part?' Huh? What's up?" Emma could hear the dissonance in her sister's voice.

"Nothing. Just bored. Doing some laundry in a Laundromat. Alma and everyone are still sleeping."

"Wait, what? Alma's there with you?" Emma shuffled around in the background.

"Yeah, why?"

"Her mom's freaked. She called the cops and everything. She thought Alma just disappeared or something."

"Are you serious?"

Cris hadn't really considered Alma's reasons for leaving, but Emma's insight provided her with a new perspective on an old situation.

"Yeah, it was this whole big deal. She even had Mom and Dad out looking for her a while ago. They called me to see if I'd heard anything."

"Huh… she said she was going to call her mom."

"Guess she didn't. I wouldn't blame her for bailing, though. Her mom's a nut case."

"Yeah…"

"Well, whatever with that. I'm glad Alma's okay. Tell me about the rest of your trip! Meet any cute guys?"

"Um…not really."

"What about Kody? Isn't he supposed to be a cutie or something?"

"I guess. He's not exactly available, though."

"He hooked up with some other chick already? That was fast."

"He and Alma got back together."

"Whaaaat? Alma actually wanted a guy back? As in, she wasn't done with him?"

"Looks like."

"Wow…maybe she's growing up!"

Cris watched the red thong flipping around in the dryer.

"I doubt it."

"Huh. Wow…well, hey, good for her. Listen, I'm glad you called, sis! I gotta go pee, but def call me later and let me know what's up, okay?"

"Sure, Em."

"Oh, one more thing…those are, like, the coin washers and stuff, right?"

"Yeah."

"Like the ones that sit on the ground?"

"Uh huh…"

"Just between you and me, I bet you could probably get a better view of the world from sitting on top of one of those." Emma sounded mischievous.

"What?"

"Trust me on this. You'll thank me later."

"Okay…" Cris was clearly confused.

"All right, talk to you later."

"Love you."

"Love you too, brat. Bye." Emma hung up.

"Better view of the world...?" Cris looked at the washer and then out the window, trying to figure out what Emma meant. She stood on her tippy-toes trying to get a better view, seeing if maybe she was missing something. She was at a loss and decided to give Ms. Pac-man another go. She started a new game but was quickly tagged by Pinky and decided to give it a rest. She saw the motel clerk putting out the Free Continental Breakfast sign in the window across the street. Perfect time for a free food break. Besides, she had more than a few minutes until the clothes were done.

She ran back across the street and into a small common room that was about as bland as the Laundromat. She looked around and couldn't find anything continental about it. She saw a pitcher of orange juice, which at first brought out a latent anger due to the Danny's incident. However, her childhood obsession would not be so easily dashed. She poured a small cup and quickly felt the thick, pulpy texture as she drank.

"Yes!" She began to chug her juice.

"A big fan of orange juice?" The morning manager walked in for her cup of coffee.

Cris jumped, spitting some of her juice back into the cup and trying not to spill the rest. "Oh, hi, good morning!" The manager continued looking at her cup. "You asked me about the orange juice, right. I do like it. I was just surprised there was actually pulp."

"Yeah, a lot of folks don't really care for it, but I like it, and that's all that really matters. I'm the only one drinking it day in and day out."

Cris nodded in agreement, grabbing some toast and a bagel. She wolfed her breakfast down, trying to get back to the Laundromat. She finished her cup of orange juice and said goodbye to the manager as she returned to the Laundromat to see if their clothes were still there.

Relieved that the clothes had not been stolen by a mysterious sock goblin, she took a seat in one of the chairs, patiently waiting as she began eyeing the washing machine. She generally listened to Emma, and more importantly, was completely bored.

She looked around to make sure no one was nearby and climbed on top of the washing machine trying to figure out what Emma meant. She looked out the window, but it didn't seem any different. She arched her back a bit to get a better view, but still couldn't see anything she didn't see before.

"What was Emma talking about? I don't see anything..."

She sat there, still bored but at least doing something interesting. She started humming along to one of her favorite songs before getting completely involved with it and singing aloud. Cris loosened up her posture to help with her singing, shifting around a bit. She went from sitting cross-legged to dangling her legs off the side of the machine, getting a little more comfortable. As she arched her back, Cris began to see things from Emma's perspective as she quieted down and braced herself as the machine entered the spin cycle.

* * *

Alma stretched her arms out and rolled over.

"Ow! Fuc—"

She looked around groggily as she hit the floor, finding herself with a face full of dirty carpet as she fell out of bed. She rolled around and looked up at her bed, realizing she was now on the ground.

"Seriously? C'mon…"

Alma picked herself off the ground and brushed herself off. She looked around the room for a minute, taking stock of it and thinking about what to do. She looked at the clock, seeing it was a quarter past ten and figured Kody was still snoring the morning away. After all, she'd worn him out well enough. She went into the bathroom and grabbed her bag, bringing it back to bed with her. She got all cozy as she opened it up and pulled out Kody's old notebook.

She glanced through it, laughing at her now favorite sketch of a silly duck. She had doodled little hearts in the margin and wrote her name in several times. "Kody n' Alm 4 Ever!" It hadn't occurred to her that she had incriminated herself in her petty larceny. She kept thumbing through the book, looking for more interesting passages. She found what she was looking for in a passage entitled "My Dream."

It was only me,
I was the only one ever there.
But that was all right,
For I was the only one who ever cared.

But it was not to be,
For a change in circumstance occurred.

175

She saw me,
And I thought perhaps I could be heard.

She came to me,
Like a fleeing cherub in flight.
She took hold of me,
And for the first time, I think I truly saw the light.

If at the beginning and the end,
You were the best I'd ever dreamed.
I'd know the world would be fine,
For I'd been blessed for all I'd seen.

If that light somehow dimmed,
I don't know that my heart could ever mend.
Maybe I could sleep,
But I'd never dream again.

Alma's clutched the notebook closely to her heart, kissing it and holding it tightly once more. *I never thought my life could be this good,* she thought. Small tears ran down Alma's face, reminding her how much she cried these days. Good or bad, it was more than she had felt, had allowed herself to feel, in a very long time.

She could feel how important she was to him, to this world. That she mattered so much to someone. It had been a long time since she had been loved. She was all too familiar with being wanted—there was always some guy who wanted her for one purpose or another, but she had never been needed. In becoming loved, she felt something deep inside herself burn and bring her to life.

She felt a purpose arise and began to feel a passion she had never known. Her heart beat faster every time she thought of Kody. She became nervous. She found herself thinking such unusual thoughts. Ideas about the future: what she wanted to be, what she wanted to do with her life. Did she want to get married? Did she want kids someday? Was Kody the one with whom she wanted to make all this happen? These thoughts seemed so foreign to her; she had hated the world, much less wanted to bring more people into it. But these were things that were less and less a part of her.

Even the inner turmoil revolving around her brother seemed to be settling in her heart, having found his long-lost friend and understanding the circumstances of everything that had occurred. While she'd never forget it, she felt like she didn't need to be crushed by it—she could let it go and forgive Glenn.

Glenn. She thought about him: his unusual behavior at the store, how he had been when he first met her. He, too, lost someone very important, and unlike her, he had no one to help him deal with it. Even worse, he could've done something to save Jake, but chose to save her instead. He must feel responsible. How isolated and alone he must feel in his dark and lonely world. Reconciling her pain, she began to feel what he must have felt was his pain. She knew how hard and difficult that could be. He didn't have to go through it like she did. He didn't have to deal alone. But... she needed to brush her teeth first.

Alma cleaned herself up and got dressed as she headed outside, enjoying the warm summer air. The grass looked nice after such a heavy storm. She saw some people in the common room enjoying a late breakfast and went inside to check it out. The more she looked around, the more she felt that the Continental Breakfast sign was just a bit overstated. She grabbed some cereal and chowed down. She then got up to pour a glass of orange juice. She took a sip of it but was immediately repulsed.

"Ew, it's all goopy!"

"What?" The manager looked up, being the only person in the room who seemed to acknowledge anything other than herself.

"Oh, sorry. I was just trying the orange juice. I think something's wrong with it. Maybe it's bad or something."

"Honey, that's called pulp. It's a part of the orange."

"Then it should've stayed with the orange!"

"It's actually pretty good for you."

"Maybe, but it still tastes like crap."

"To each their own."

"Yeah, yeah."

Alma left her juice there and went back outside, still trying to figure out what she was going to do. She looked for Cris, checking the van first and noticing how clean it was despite the mess she and Kody had left just a few hours ago. Seeing that there weren't any clothes lying around, she decided she'd look somewhere else and closed the door. As she turned to walk away from the van, she remembered something and whipped the door back open, looking around on the floor.

"Aw, crap! Please be kidnapped by the underwear gnomes…!"

She saw the Laundromat across the street and remembered something about Cris and stealing her clothes from the bathroom. She started across the street, but caught a glimpse of Cris washing their clothes from atop the washing machine. Alma started giggling maniacally, knowing she had just scored her get-out-of-jail free card.

She crept down the road a bit, avoiding detection by Cris as she crossed the street and snuck around to the back of the Laundromat. She slipped in through the back door without making a sound and sat there watching Cris watch the news, among other things.

"You know, I've never seen anyone enjoy the news that much before."

Cris fell off the washing machine, barely avoiding catching her face on the adjacent dryer. She popped back up to her feet and spun around, face covered in embarrassment.

"Alma!"

"Guess you aren't such a prude after all," she teased.

"Oh, God, Alm…"

"Don't worry. I won't say anything. We'll call it even. Although this might even be better than that one Christmas—"

"Nothing!" Cris shrilly silenced her.

"Hehehe. I'm just sayin'. You should do your own laundry more often."

Alma's mischievous grin crept along the side of her face, making its way up to her cheeks.

"Almy…" it was evident Cris wanted the incident forgotten. Preferably forever.

"Hmm? How's your morning been? Other than that, anyway."

"Ugh…fine? At least I've got some clean clothes now."

"Yeah, you do!" Alma smirked, unable to help herself.

"Hey, are you looking to go for round two?" Cris was getting annoyed.

"You still think you can take me?"

"I know I can. But this isn't the place."

"Yeah, that's true. Not in this sanctuary of *love*."

Cris face-palmed.

"We'll put it on hold. But challenge definitely accepted."

Alma had an evil sparkle in her eye, and Cris caught it, though she thought she saw something else there as well.

"Huh, you seem different."

Alma stopped and looked at her, cocking her head slightly.

"Do I?"

"Yeah. Whatever it is, it's working for you."

"Aw, thanks, sweetie!"

"Uh huh. Hey, are the boys up yet?"

"I don't think so. Kody probably won't get up until God knows when, but Glenn or his little kitty might wake him up sooner."

"I don't really want to leave that to chance."

"Want to go wake them up? I'll stay here with the clothes."

Alma secured her opportunity to kidnap her underwear back and escape her own embarrassment.

"Yeah, that might be a good idea."

"'Kay, you got it! Alma's on duty!" she proclaimed as she perched herself on top of the washer, taking Cris's spot.

"Alma!"

"What? You're not using it. Besides, I'm watching the news." She leaned in to whisper to Cris.

"The trick is you gotta look like you don't care. No one will suspect a thing." She winked.

"Now shoo! Looks like a *good story* is about to come on!"

Cris left the Laundromat, no longer surprised by Alma's antics in the least. She got back to the motel and knocked on Kody's door, waiting for a response. The door slowly opened to reveal Glenn, quite disheveled and half-asleep, though making far better progress than Kody, who was still face down and dressed only in his boxers.

"Um…"

She thought about coming back later when she saw Bixby squatting in a corner by the door. She rushed over and picked him up, looking for the litter box, which Glenn pointed to near Kody's bed. Cris briefly thought about whether she should place him in the box or take sweet, sweet revenge, but decided for Bixby's sake that the litter box was a better option.

"G-good morning, Charisma." He rearranged his glasses.

"Morning, Glenn. Feeling better?"

"Quite."

"Just wanted to make sure you two were up."

"Ah, yes. Well, Kody might need more p-persuasion. My efforts have been in vain."

"You couldn't wake him up?"

"More so, he refused to r-rouse."

"Hehe, I can handle this. We used to have that problem with Emmy sometimes."

"Oh? Funny, I n-never had that issue."

"What? When did you have to wake her up?"

Glenn accidentally backed himself into a corner.

"Wh-when she t -took a nap?"

"No way…"

Cris wasn't sure she was capable of believing such a thing. Not so much about her sister; she knew Emma had more in common with Alma than either of them would admit (though Emma was still a Roberts at heart). Glenn, however, Cris had a vastly different perspective on.

"W-wasn't it Kody you came for?"

"Oh, right."

She nudged Kody a few times, hoping he would stir. He barely responded, and rolled over to continue sleeping.

"Oh, no you don't, buster."

Cris went to the other side of the bed and knelt down, getting up close to his face. She had never been this close to Kody's face before and felt a little awkward, now noticing the small stubble he was beginning to develop. She hadn't thought he could even grow facial hair.

She remained focused on her mission and was determined to wake him up. She got in close and became distracted, watching him sleep. Feeling Glenn's eyes watch her more intensely as the seconds passed by, she regained her concentration and put her hand up to Kody's face. She extended her pointer finger as she leaned over to look into his nostril. Glenn looked on curiously.

"Wh-what are you…?"

"Shhh!"

She looked up Kody's nose, finding it was surprisingly clean, especially since he himself smelled ripe. She slowly rubbed her pointer finger around the bottom of his nostrils. He began to fidget, but refused to budge. She slowly circled her finger around until she gently slid it into one of his nostrils and held her position. His breathing started to pick up, and he grabbed at his nose before finding an unusual object coming out of it. He opened his eyes to find Cris all up in his face.

"Gah!" He jumped back, pulling her finger out of his nose.

"What're you doing?"

"Good morning, sunshine! Time to get up and shower! We've gotta get back on the road!" She was as jovial as ever as she backed up to give him some room. She wiped off her finger.

"Why did you stick your finger in my nose?"

"Because you wouldn't get up."

"But why did you stick your finger in my nose?"

"So you'd get up."

"But...why?" Kody shrugged, palms up.

"You're up, right? Now go shower and get your stuff together; we've got road to cover."

"I c-concur," Glenn stated, putting on some socks.

"Fine! I'm awake. I'm up. I'm getting ready. Mind giving us some man-time to get dressed and all?"

"Man-time?" Cris snickered. "Sure, whatever floats your boat, big guy, but try not to take too long, okay?"

Kody was baffled and just looked at her as she left the room.

"She certainly is...lively, i-isn't she?" Glenn stated.

"She's annoying is what she is."

"Surely you d-don't mean that."

"I hate being woken up."

"At least she didn't take notice of that."

"What?"

Glenn threw Kody's Camp Morningwood shirt at him as he pushed him toward the shower.

"She's right; we've progress t-to make."

"Okay, I'm going!"

Kody got in the shower as Glenn packed up the room. He heard the shower come on, but Kody managed to speak over it.

"So, how're you feeling this morning, buddy?"

"B-better, thanks."

"That's good. What was your whole deal yesterday? You were kinda whacked out the whole day."

"I d-don't know. I've been trying to come off my meds. I felt fine at first, perhaps due to the ex-exhilaration of our trip, but then..."

"Weirdness ensued?"

"You c-could say that."

"How about now?"

He stayed quiet.

"Hey, we talked about this. If we're gonna help you, you've gotta be open with us about this stuff."

"Unless you're incredibly p-pretentious, I don't recall an 'us' at all. That was a discussion you and I had, and th-that shall proceed when I'm ready for it." Glenn stood his ground.

Huh, he found a pair...maybe I left mine laying around? Kody chuckled to himself as he checked. *One...two...nope, all accounted for.*

"Gotcha." Kody responded.

He made his way out of the bathroom, drying off and throwing on his shirt. He grabbed some pants and they gathered their things before leaving. Glenn waited for Bixby to finish exploring his new litter box, letting Kody go on ahead. He stayed behind with his cat.

"So, Mr. B-bixby, what do you think about all this? D-do you think he can help me?"

Bixby looked up at the unusual man who always made strange sounds at him. He wasn't sure how he felt about this new box of scented sand, but since he had been thrown into it he made the best of it. He sauntered around, letting his regal paws sift through the sand. The sensation was not unwelcome. Looking back up at the man, who seemed to want something from him, he really had nothing to offer. His ear itched, and he scratched it.

"Ah, I s-suppose you're right."

Glenn picked up Bixby's litter box with the cat still inside and carried it out, setting it on the floor in the back of the van to try and minimize any odors.

"I'll give you one thing, Glenn. At least you're loyal. You stick by that stinky cat no matter what." Kody said.

"What e-else can I do? He's my friend."

Kody watched Glenn curiously. He looked in back and saw the girls' things already packed. He figured they must've already checked them out and went to turn in the keys. Heading back to the van, he heard Cris and Alma coming back from across the street laughing loudly with all their clothes in hand.

"Oh, you guys did laundry? Awesome! Thanks."

"We sure did!" Alma grinned and turned to Cris, who coyly looked away.

"Here you go, sweetums" Alma said, handing Kody his jacket.

"I was wondering where this went. You're the best, Alm."

"Maybe you could repay the favor by changing into something clean sometime soon?"

"These are clean…!" Kody pulled the collar of his shirt up to take a whiff as Alma looked at him, and then at the van. "…ish."

He pulled her closely and kissed her forehead, before seeing Cris behind her and breaking it off, instead helping to load up the rest of the stuff. Alma helped Glenn sort out the arrangement of the van. Kody leaned over to Cris, who reluctantly took a step back.

"Sorry about that," he whispered.

"What?" She looked at him, baffled.

"I meant what I said earlier: I don't want you to feel left out. I didn't really notice until now but I figure that kinda stuff—"

"Really, Kody, it's okay. Don't worry about it."

"No, it's not. I'll try harder not to do that stuff so much in public." She nodded, apparently unsure of how to respond.

"Oh, when we get some time later I need to talk to you about Glenn, too."

"Sounds good."

Kody ran back to the office to turn in the set of keys for his room while Alma rearranged the van and handed Glenn the van keys.

"Your turn. You ready?"

"O-of course." Glenn took his seat up front.

"And my co-p-pilot?"

"Well, as the current battle captain of this here shuttle, I do believe that's for you to decide." Alma cheered him on.

"Hmm, I s-see. Since Bixby can't really perform the d-duty, I'd like C-charisma to assist me."

"Me?" Cris barely heard him, still lost in her own little world while standing outside.

"Yes, unless you o-object?"

"It'd be an honor." She shook it off and smiled, taking her seat next to him.

Kody returned to the van and piled in back with Alma, sitting in the same spot they had held the night before. Cris glanced back taking note of this as Glenn started up the van.

"Ready to go, mister?"

"A-always."

Glenn straightened up his glasses as he decided on the best way to proceed.

"Oh, Glenn!" Alma called out from the back.

"Y-yes?"

"I made a little present for our kitty friend!"

"Hmm?"

Glenn looked back to watch Alma affix a small collar around Bixby's neck. The collar itself looked like it had been composed from small pieces of assorted fabric.

"It's even got your name on it so in case he gets lost someone can bring him back!"

"Oh! Th-thank you!"

Glenn brandished an awkward smile while he scratched his head. He patted his cat on the head and turned his attention back toward the parking lot, pulling the van out of it and back onto the open road.

21. S'mores and Wieners

"There's nothing I'm fonder of than my memories. They remember everything just I how I choose to, and change the things I don't, so at least something in my life is like a fairytale."

– Alma's Diary

Glenn drove for several hours along Interstate 40, surpassing the expectations of everyone except Bixby, who had no expectations of anyone or anything other than being fed frequently. Glenn surprised Kody the most with his decent selection of music, going through a few different albums that he had never heard but definitely wanted to borrow.

Alma, with little else to entertain her, couldn't stop playing with Bixby. The cat in question was unusually amicable with her, even warming up so much as to show her a rare display of affection, licking her. It crossed her mind how Glenn might respond to his cat now playing favorites, but she was having too much fun to really worry about that.

"Hey, Kodykins."

She nudged him, interrupting his writing.

"Hmm? What's up?"

"We should get a little kitty. We could name him Jynxy-cat or something!"

"Get a cat? Uh…Alm, wouldn't you need to have a house or something first?"

"Oh, you're right! We need to get a house first."

Cris looked back with a small grin at how quickly Alma misinterpreted such a simple statement into her own wild fantasy.

"Um, Alm, that's not quite what I meant."

"Well, not yet, of course! We have to get back first, and you'd have to get a better job…I might have to get a better one, too. But, I mean, I love that idea!"

"Erm…"

Kody let it go. Surely Alma's imagination would get caught up in another insane notion before long.

Cris turned Glenn, who had been nearly silent the entire time. "So, Mr. Driving Man, how're you holding up?"

"F-fine."

"Really? You seem like you're enjoying this."

"It has been a while since I've done anything so p-productive."

"Well, you're doing great so far! Keep it up!"

Cris patted his shoulder, trying to encouraging him. He flinched, and shied away. She tried not to embarrass him, but the more he interacted with people the better off he would be. Though they hadn't really discussed it, all three of them were trying to help Glenn in their own ways.

Kody, oblivious to all else, was frustrated by a case of writer's block. He kept scribbling in the margins and rereading his old notes, but nothing new would come to him. He was completely uninspired. *Heh, everything finally starts going my way and suddenly I have nothing to write about. As if drama were my only muse… maybe I should stub my toe or something.* The thoughts amused him, but did little else. He looked at Bixby and started poking him, hoping to arouse the tiny demon into some kind of frenzy. Ultimately, however, Kody's efforts only served to annoy the kitty.

"Hey, stop that! Leave Mr. Kitty-Whiskersons alone." Alma defended her charge.

"Mr. Kitty-Wh-whiskersons? I should imagine he w-wouldn't like that very much."

Bixby didn't seem to care about much of anything other than his own tail, which he stared at in awe. He watched it weave back and forth in front of his purring little kitty nose and seemed to be enamored. Kody sighed and rested his arm on the window, looking out of it hoping to find something interesting. Cris looked back, casually watching him but saying nothing. She turned back to her window and watched the grass pass her by.

As her gaze wandered, she heard a weird popping sound as she saw pieces of rubber fly off outside the window below. This caught her attention, but not near quick enough, as the tire underneath her section of the van dropped and shifted the vehicle off-course.

Kody grabbed Alma and held her closely, caging Bixby in between them as the van started swerving. Cris's head bounced off the window before she was able to brace herself into the seat and hold herself steady. Glenn tried his best to maintain control of the van, veering at first to the right toward a large sugar maple tree before he was able to guide it away from the wood line and back onto the side of the road, finally getting it to grind to a halt. They all sat in silence, checking for damage and injuries.

Glenn jumped out of the van, immediately running to the side to assess the situation. Kody's adrenaline free flowing, he let go of Alma, trying to figure out what to do first. Taking quick, frantic breaths, he looked her over to make sure she was okay. She sat trembling as she did the same for him and the little docile fur ball in her lap. She held the cat closely, trying to calm both him and herself, as even his fur stood on end. Kody looked up front to see Cris holding the side of her head.

"Cris, are you all right?"

"Yeah, I'm fine…just bumped my head." She rested her head against the seat, fatigued and shaken.

"Hold on, let me check it out."

Kody slid passed Alma, his heart racing as he got out of the van. He moved around Glenn and opened Cris's door, helping her out. He took her hand and stood her up, looking her over and checking her head to make sure she was all right. He noticed some light bleeding, but it appeared to be coming from a small cut and, as far as he could tell, she was all right. He was finally able to breathe a small sigh of relief as Alma got out of the van, still holding Bixby to see what had happened.

"There's a little bleeding, but it looks like you're okay," he reassured her.

He pulled a tissue out of the glove box and applied gentle pressure to Cris's head, holding it in place to stop the bleeding. He moved her hand up for her to hold the tissue in place as he helped her over to the side of the van, her other arm wrapped around his shoulder for support. Glenn broke down their situation.

"It a-appears as though the tire blew out. Other than some s-surprisingly minor structural damage, it looks like we j-just need to replace the tire."

"Why did the tire just blow out?" Alma asked.

"Th-they're old. I should've th-thought to ch-check them, b-but… I d-don't have an excuse."

"So, does that mean all the other tires will blow up, too?"

"It's h-hard to say. If that impact didn't affect them, then I imagine they sh-should be all right. It would be a good idea to d-double check, just in c-case, however."

"Hey, can you stand?" Kody asked Cris.

"Yeah, I'm okay."

He released her arm as he knelt down to look over the van. Cris leaned back into her seat to pull a bandana out of one of her bags, tying it around her hair to hold the tissue in place.

"I think Glenn's right. If we can replace the tire, we should be good to go."

"How're we gonna do that?" Alma wasn't keen on getting back in the van any time soon.

"Glenn, is there a spare?" Kody looked up at him as Glenn's body slowly stopped quivering.

"If there is, I h-honestly wouldn't rely on it. I d-doubt it's any more serviceable than what we're already working with."

Kody stopped to think for a minute.

"I have an idea. Someone got a phone I can borrow?"

Glenn and Cris both offered their cells; Cris's being the closer of the two.

"Who you gonna call?" she asked.

There was a dead silence as no one wanted to say what they were all thinking. Cris's mind immediately went back to Pinky the Ghost chasing her Ms. Pac-Man halfway was across the screen. Glenn was the first to laugh, marking it acceptable for everyone to proceed.

"All right, seriously. We don't know anyone out here." Alma got them back on track.

"If I'm lucky, he might be somewhere around here. That guy's everywhere, and I feel like they were supposed to be traveling themselves." Kody was a man with a plan.

"He? Aw, you don't mean…" Alma rubbed her forehead.

"Hold on."

Kody dialed the number and waited for a response. He nodded his head to the AM Taxi call tone playing in the background until a merrily gruff voice answer the call.

"Heeeeey dude or dudette I don't know, but definitely seems to be cool with calling me anyway. What's up?"

"'Sup, brother man?"

"Kody? Hey, Kody, buddy! What's up, man? …Hey, it's Kody!" he could hear G talking to people in the background.

"Nothing much. Kinda stuck in a bit of a situation. I don't suppose you're anywhere near—" Kody looked for a nearby off-ramp sign, "Looks like the Little Rock, Arkansas, area by chance?"

"Heh, not so much, man. More like Memphis."

"Seriously?"

"Hey, it's a musician's dreamland! Not to mention gorgeous. And you know how I feel about pretty things. That, and some chick Jeany knows…what, that's your mom? Oh, shit… anyway, I guess Jeany's mom is getting married…remarried? Whatever, Kody doesn't give a shit about that… Sorry, pain-in-the-ass woman. Anyway, the long and short of it is we got ourselves a paying gig, though this ain't really my thing. Who plays a wedding if they don't have to? But hell, you need some help?"

"Our van kinda chucked its tire."

"Duuuude, that blows! I totally gotcha. It'll be like auto shop all over again. Good times, right?"

"Some of the best!"

"All right, all right. We're finishing up here, but send me your addy and we'll head out as soon as we're done."

"Awesome buddy, thanks. How long you think you'll be?"

"Let's see…you're not too far, I think. Maybe a few hours? Depends when we finish up."

"Gotcha. Thanks, man."

"No problem, brother. Hey, two things real quick."

"Yeah?"

"When'd you get a phone?"

"I didn't, I'm borrowing Cris's."

"Heh, guess that answers question number two. That's my boy!"

"It's not—"

"See ya in a bit!"

G hung up. Kody handed the phone back to Cris.

"What'd Geroge say?" Alma clearly disapproved.

"He said he'd be able to come up and help us out in a few hours. Turns out they were in Memphis playing a show."

"Ugh…" While she liked the Bards, Alma's distain for her boyfriend's boyfriend was well known.

"Aw, don't worry, Alm, he's coming to help out."

"Whatever. So what do we do until then?"

"How about find somewhere to eat? I'm starved." Cris said, slipping on the side of the road.

Kody caught her and placed her arm back around his shoulder.

"You sure you're all right?"

"Yeah, just a little out of it. Sorry, I'll be fine though."

"Not taking any chances."

"You're right, you shouldn't. And you're clumsy! Let me help her, she's my bestie, anyway."

Alma stepped up, handing Bixby to Glenn and quickly maneuvering Cris's arm away from Kody, helping her walk. Kody carefully climbed back into the van, grabbing some overnight bags. The day was breaching midafternoon, and Kody became skeptical that they'd make it back before nightfall. He handed the lighter bag to Glenn so that he'd still be able to hold the cat, while he carried the heavier bag. They started making their way down the side of the road, trying to find some sort of building to mark their location and rest. Glenn took the lead, following with Kody close behind.

"She's becoming more b-bold, isn't she?"

"Who?" Kody tried to focus on the conversation more than the heavy bag.

"Alma."

"I didn't really notice a difference."

"Hmm, it c-could just be me."

"Nah, you're probably right. I've just been distracted lately."

"H-how so?"

"I dunno. Lots on my mind. Hey, guess we can relate, huh?"

"Not particularly." Glenn kept his eyes forward.

"Right." Kody realized his problems weren't exactly on the same level as Glenn's. "Sorry. We will help you, though."

"Yes, I recall. Let's focus on finding a place to st-stop for now. Cris could be concussed and will need to take it slow."

"You think it's that bad?"

"I d-don't know. But I'm hoping we d-don't have to find out."

They kept walking for a while until they came upon a campground just off the side of the road. It had a small gift shop and restaurant, but more than anything, it was surprisingly not crowded for the beginning of summer.

"This is a good p-place to rest. We can s-stay here for the night if need be."

"Yeah, can we stop? I need a break." Cris said.

"We'll break here then. Glenn, can you go see if any sites are available?" Kody took charge, setting the bag down with relief.

"O-of course."

"Alm, over here."

Alma walked Cris over to a bench in front of the gift shop and sat down next to her. Glenn handed Bixby off to Alma before going inside with Kody, who went to look for tents. Cris's phone went off, though it took her a minute before she realized it and checked it. She received a text message from G asking for the address. She sent him a picture of the welcome sign in front of the gift shop with the information on it. She slowly put her phone away and leaned back on the bench.

"How're you feeling?" Alma checked up on Cris.

"I'm good. Just a little tired. I keep telling you guys I'm fine. I just need to lay down for a bit."

"I know, I know. You're the sleepy girl. It looks like we can stay here tonight if we need to, so hopefully you'll get some rest soon."

"Yeah."

"Hey, look at the bright side: at least you aren't covered in orange juice or pee."

"This is true."

Cris hardly considered that a highlight, though at the same time she couldn't say it wasn't. The boys came out of the store, each carrying a packaged tent and two blankets.

"W-we were in luck, there's a nice spot near the back."

"That, and Mr. Moneybags here spotted the bill." Kody patted Glenn on the back, gleeful as ever.

"Anyway, the site is supposed to be near some river or something; they said it's pretty relaxing. I'm thinking it's probably full of mosquitos, though. Woods and water don't mix well. Or too well. Not sure how that works." Kody didn't need the fine print.

"Great, I'm gonna get eaten alive." Alma became a little pouty.

"Long as you keep your clothes on you'll be fine," Cris reminded her. "Eaten alive…"

Cris climbed to her feet and started heading over to their campsite.

"Hey, wait up!" Alma chased after her, holding the kitty-kitten close.

"Hey, I'm the injured girl and I'm moving faster than you guys. That should probably tell you something, huh? Now let's go get settled! I wanna lie down!"

Kody and Glenn looked at each other as they realized they'd have to pull double duty. They barely managed to carry their own bags on top of the camping gear as they caught up to the girls. They made their way to the back of the campsite as Cris and Alma got as comfortable as one can get on logs.

The girls gossiped idly while they watched the boys gladly drop all the gear and work on setting up the tents. Despite their macho bravado, the boys had some difficulty getting anything more than the base rods into the ground. Bixby, remaining indifferent about the affair, nuzzled Alma, who kindly returned the gesture.

"Those two dorks'll never get this done." She was hardly even paying attention.

"That's for sure. It'll start to get dark soon, too; they might wanna hurry."

"Eh, there's no rush. I'm just as comfortable sleeping under the stars. Not like it'd be the first time."

"Alm…I wanted to talk to you about that."

"Hmm? About what? Sleeping outside?"

"Not that. Did you ever call your mom?"

Alma looked up, startled.

"Yeah…a while ago. Why?"

"When?"

"Um… yesterday? When we were at the store?"

"Really? What did you say?"

"I told her I was hanging out with Kody for a few days, that he had a trip-thing going on."

"And she was fine with that?"

"Totally. After all, she's a wonderful mother, right? All she wants is what's best for her daughter." Alma had a hard time finishing it with a straight face.

"Alm." Cris looked at her, neither of them needed to say anything.

"She's fine, Cris."

"Emmy said she called the police looking for you."

"That would imply she noticed I was gone. And even got off her ass to do something for me, which we both know would never happen."

"Alma, you can't just run off like that. She's got to be worried sick about you."

Something snapped in Alma. She started visibly shaking and set Bixby down.

"Really, Cris? You think so? You think she's so worried about me? 'Cause I think you're getting her confused with your mom! Or maybe Tabby! My mom doesn't give a damn about me or anyone but herself! She's worried? She's pissed 'cause no one will clean up after her and she'll have to pick up her own damn mess! That's the only thing she's worried about! For once she has to wipe her own ass!"

Kody, having caught the end of this outburst, came over to help calm Alma down.

"Whoa, whoa, what's going on over here?"

"Nothing!" Alma shot a vulgar expression in Cris's direction.

"What…? Then what're you getting all riled up for?" Kody said, trying to play the peacekeeper.

"Um…" Alma was at a loss.

"She's upset because I forgot one of her shirts when I was doing laundry earlier." Cris covered her.

"Whoa, it's all right, Alm. It's just a shirt. We'll get you another one, okay? Don't eat Cris's face."

"Yeah, sure." Alma started to calm down.

"Glenn, can you finish setting up?"

"If you b-believe that I can set this up in the first p-place, then sure, why not?" Glenn shrugged, making different shapes out of the base rods.

"Thanks; Alma and I are gonna go for a walk."

Kody took her hand as they ventured off into the woods. Cris picked up Bixby and walked over to Glenn, who was struggling furiously with one of the rods that presumably went with the tent.

"How's it going? Need a hand?"

"P-please, if you don't mind."

"Sure. And really…how's it going Glenn?"

Cris took the fiberglass rod and connected it to two other ends, placing it through the tent loops before sticking it into the ground. Glenn watched in amazement.

"Much b-better now."

"My family used to go camping a lot."

"I r-remember."

"Oh, yeah, you guys used to come with us! God, how long ago was that?"

"I've no idea. A long t-time ago."

"Things have changed a lot since then, huh?"

"Not as much as I m-might've hoped."

"Still a work in progress, huh?"

"Well put."

"That's okay. Life's about growth and change. The important thing is you're out here living it."

"Not as much perhaps as th-those two."

"Yeah…" Cris trailed off, unusually grateful for the throbbing headache that distracted her.

"C-charisma…be h-honest with me, as you'd expect me to be with you."

"What? Yeah, definitely." She paid a little more attention as she started on the second tent.

"You like that b-boy, don't you?"

She blushed. She placed the first rod through the second tent as she carefully thought of how she wanted to reply.

"I-it's all right. Your face says it all. And I don't mean to embarrass you. It's just…I, I have t-trust issues. Kody wants me to open up to the both of you, but I c-can't be expected to do that if I don't feel you trust me, too."

"That's true. I don't think it'd be fair of us to ask that of you."

"C-certainly not."

"But does that mean you trust us? Are you going to open up to us?"

"I t-trust you."

Cris smiled but was hesitant.

"What about Kody?"

"He's p-probably a good man. But…"

"But what?"

"Cris Roberts! Kickin' it in the backwoods, huh? I never woulda guessed!"

Cris looked up to see Geroge and the rest of the Bards come walking up to their newly established campsite.

"Geroge, hey."

Cris noticed Glenn becoming more tense as he got up and backed up behind her, picking up his cat.

"Oh, Glenn, this is the friend Kody called earlier. Geroge, this is our friend Glenn. Glenn, those people with him are his band, um…"

"Our band," Jence corrected.

"Right. That's Jence, his girlfriend, and behind her are Daron and…Thteve?"

"Correct, as always," Daron confirmed.

"Hmm…"

Glenn shifted his glasses as he carried Bixby and went for a walk to any place but there.

"Yo…what's that guy's deal?" Geroge threw his arms behind his head.

"He's just a little uncomfortable around new people."

"Ah, too crowded, huh? Gotcha. Well, we're here to help with your van troubles, anyway. That's the one just back down the road a ways? All reddish-like?"

"Yeah, that's the one."

"Got the keys?"

Cris pulled out a set of keys and handed them to Geroge, who tossed them back to Jence. She and Thteve headed back to the front of the camp, getting in their own van before going to check out the other one.

"So, it's just us, is it?" said Daron, a fine mix of charming and slightly creepy.

"Yeah, I don't see my boy here. What gives?"

"Oh, he probably went off for a little quality alone time with Alma."

"What? And you're cool with that? Damn, you're an even cooler chick than I imagined! D, Jeany might be outta luck on this one."

"What?" Cris didn't follow.

"I'm just sayin'. I don't think even Jeany would be totally cool of me macking on another chick without her bein' there."

"Wait, you think Kody and I are involved?"

"You aren't?" G cocked an eyebrow.

"We're just friends."

"Damn, that sucks."

"Why does that suck?" she asked.

"You tell me, *chica*."

"Um...right. Can you two help me finish setting up since you're here? I want to have a bonfire tonight if it doesn't rain, but we need some more wood."

"We're on it, princess. D, you in?"

"Naturally."

Cris was unable to figure Geroge out, but felt she might be better off not trying to. She finished setting up the other tent and laid blankets down inside as Geroge and Daron went to go gather some wood. It started getting dark when she realized that she'd been alone for some time. Her fatigue began to catch up with her, and she took a moment to lie down in front of the tent, to reflect on her day so far. She got comfortable, and felt the increasing weight of her eyelids as she closed them to rest only for a minute.

* * *

She woke up unusually warm, next to a raging fire in front of her, noticing how dark the sky had become. She faintly recognized the snap-crackling of burning wood as she scrambled back to see the Bards roasting hotdogs and s'mores from lawn chairs setup in front of the campfire.

"Hey, sorry princess. Didn't mean to wake you. Thing needed some more kerosene, and Daron got a little crazy with it." Geroge smiled as he helped her up.

"No, it's fine. It's nice, actually. Is everyone back yet?" She was still a little startled.

"Uh, the weird guy's just been kinda pacing back and forth around this place. The two love birds made an appearance, but bailed to get some more snacks."

"Huh?"

"Eh, don't fret. They'll be back soon enough. Don't worry about your van either. Kod and I were gonna fix it up, but Jeany here is a beast when it comes to tearing up machines. Her and Thtevey boy looked it over and checked out the other tires. Just need to pick up a new one in the morning and it'll be golden."

"Oh, that's good...how long was I out for?"

"Since we got back? Half an hour or so. Dunno when you started your little power nap, though."

"Huh."

"Have a seat."

Geroge pulled up a chair for her next to him and handed her a stick.

"Wiener or 'mellow?"

"S'mores?"

"Yeah."

"I'll take a marshmallow."

He stuck one on the end of her stick, subtly looking her over. She glanced into the fire, waving the stick back and forth before casting it over the flame. She stared into the fire, the heat warming her skin. She felt an odd sort of peace as she thought of all the flames she'd seen before. Her marshmallow lit up, engulfed, as it erupted in a fiery blaze before it fell droopy to the ground.

"Gotta move it before it becomes a meteor, chickadee." He nudged her.

"I'll try to remember that." She smiled, grabbing another marshmallow from the bag and trying again.

"Hey, I don't normally do this, but I gotta say…I was really impressed with your singin' before. I was wondering if ya' could throw out a little tune for us. She wouldn't say it, but even Jeany's been kinda curious to hear you sing."

Jence hit his arm, trying to silence him, but he marched to the beat of his own very adamant drummer. Geroge did as he pleased in spite the knot swelling in his bicep.

"Um…it's kind of embarrassing; I mean I don't even have any music or anything."

"Sweetheart. You have an honest-to-goodness rock band sitting right in front of you. Seriously?"

"Oh, right! Um…I guess I could. What would you guys like to hear?"

"Whatever you want, man."

"Huh…well what songs do you know?"

"You mean other than the standard Bard set?" Daron inquired.

"Yeah. I'm a big fan, really. I just don't exactly know any of your songs." Cris didn't want to offend the band.

"Heh, s'all right. Hell, I don't even know all of 'em." Geroge couldn't help but laugh.

"Really?"

"Hell yeah! I forgot our closer just the other night! We don't usually close with new songs; I just couldn't remember the next one, so we just kinda winged it."

"Oh, wow. I didn't think that happened to performers."

"Yeah, all the time. Like to call it an audible."

"Or lack of preparation," Jence corrected.

"So! Name your poison, and we'll play along. If we don't know it we'll improvise."

"Hm…how about 'Honey and the Moon?'"

"Joseph Arthur? Classic! I fuckin' love it! Hold on."

Geroge ran back to their van to grab his guitar and made his way back over, taking his place between Jence and Cris.

"All right, ready when you are, princess."

Geroge started strumming the intro as Cris grabbed one of the bottles of water on the ground and took a sip. She fumbled around with the cap, trying anxiously to get it back on the bottle. Despite her shaky hands, Geroge's encouraging smile brimmed with confidence and she couldn't help but fall in line with the melody. She set her s'more stick down as she prepared herself to sing along.

She felt the song flowing through her body and became a part of the music. As she sang, she noticed a man across the campground pond holding a cat, watching her silently. She smiled to him while she sang, and continued. As she finished, she heard applause and turned around to see Kody and Alma standing there supporting her. She looked around to see even the Bards sitting in awe of her.

"Damn, girl…you're about the only lady I've ever heard actually pull that song off. Please tell me there's a way we can convince you to change your mind. I'll even let you be the front man." Geroge was doing his best to placate her.

"You'd certainly keep the audience captivated," Daron added.

"It was okay." Jence cracked a small smile. Thteve nodded in approval.

Alma ran up from behind her and gave her a strong hug.

"Cris, that was amazing! I mean, it was beautiful! I knew you could sing, but I've never heard you with actual music before and stuff! That was crazy!"

Alma hugged her again. Cris tried to calm her trembling hands. She kept her eyes on Kody, whose face was covered in admiration.

Almost on cue, her modesty kicked in. "It really wasn't much. It's just for fun."

"Maybe it shouldn't be." Kody nodded, and she blushed.

Kody took a seat on the ground next to Cris, Alma coming up behind him to wedge herself in between Kody and G.

"And a good evening to you, cutie."

"Hmph."

Geroge tried to be polite, but Alma snubbed him. G was well used to Alma's jealous habits; he made a game out of it. He offered her a roasting stick. She glared at him.

"Peace offering."

"Yeah?"

"Wiener or 'mellow?"

"Wiener."

"Always figured you for a wiener girl." He cracked a smile.

"Shut up!" she said, fighting playfully with him.

"Jency, you might wanna keep your boyfriend on a leash." Alma called over to her.

"It's in the van," Jence remarked casually without reservation.

"Err…right."

"Jeany, how about easing them into your unusual form of comedy styling? They might not get it was a joke." Geroge tried to save face.

"Who's kidding?" She started on her next s'more.

"Um…anyway…"

Alma changed the subject, shifting around while scratching her mosquito-bitten legs. She used the ground to scratch the more conspicuous areas.

Kody tried being supportive. "Doing all right there, Alm?"

"Psh, it's your fault." She had a dirty smile but couldn't stop scratching.

"What is?" Cris was now paying attention again, having had successfully formed her first s'more of the evening.

"Nothing." Kody tried to give Alma the dignity she obviously wasn't concerned about for herself.

"Classy," Daron remarked to himself, winking at Alma.

Alma ignored him, hearing Bixby meow behind her as he strutted past and started picking at one of the hotdogs.

"Hey…where's Glenn?" Alma said while inspecting the surrounding area.

"Oh, I just saw him across the pond not too long ago…where'd he go?" Cris looked around for him.

She looked off across the pond that sat in the middle of the campground, but she saw no one in sight.

"I don't like this, I'm gonna go make sure he's all right."

"I'll do it." Alma stepped up.

"What?"

"I owe him that much."

"You owe him? For what?" Cris tried to figure out what she was talking about.

"You said he was just across the pond, right? I'll go find him."

With that, Alma ran off after him. Kody looked around, seeing Thteve and Jence exchange glances, while Daron and G keenly watched Alma run off. He figured maybe he should be jealous, but if anything, it was flattering. He picked up Alma's stick, giving her lightly cooked hotdog to Bixby as he started a s'more of his own.

"Wonder what that was about?" Kody seemed unconcerned.

"I'm not sure... aren't you worried about them?" Cris tried to be supportive.

"Alma's a big girl, she'll be fine. Glenn..." he trailed off.

"That reminds me. What did you want to talk to me about before?"

"Oh, right. Let's take it somewhere else." Kody motioned away from the group.

Kody picked off his barely warmed marshmallow and ate it as they got up and headed for the tents.

"Yeah, buddy!" Geroge cheered Kody on.

"Shut up, G!" he barked as they went inside.

They got inside the tent and sat down, Cris sitting across from him. Kody relayed the conversation he'd had with Glenn the night prior, emphasizing the importance of them helping him. Cris supported him.

"I agree. I think we can help him, he just needs to learn to let us in."

"Good, so you're on board with this?"

"Of course. What do we do?"

"I dunno. Just watch him I guess. If we see something funny or out of place, we ask him about it."

"Like right now?"

"For instance." Kody slapped his head, missing the obvious cue to help his friend.

"Does Alma know about any of this?"

"I don't think so. Or at least I didn't tell her anything. She seems to know something about him, though."

"Yeah, those two definitely seem to have something going on."

"Huh." Kody stopped to think on it.

"Not like that, dork-face! I just mean that they're connected somehow." Kody looked relieved.

"Maybe something to do with Jake?"

"Probably."

"Hmm, so then I think—"

"Hey, hate to interrupt your make-out session," Geroge said, leaning into the tent and clearly disappointed he hadn't interrupted anything.

"But, uh, your cat's gone."

"What?" Cris turned back to him.

"Yeah, little guy took off for the woods. Just bolted. It was kinda weird."

"And you didn't go after him?"

"The guys did. Lettin' you know 'cause I figured you'd wanna help out."

"Yeah, of course!" Cris turned to Kody, who was already looking back at her with mutual concern. "Let's go!"

They all rushed out of the tent, Daron dragging Geroge off in one direction as Kody and Cris went to check another. They all chased after the little devil before he got off too far into the woods and ran into something bigger, more dangerous than him. That, or before Glenn found out he was gone.

22. Dead Ends

"There are moments in life that reverberate throughout our history, and forever change the course of who we are and will become. I find it sometimes regrettable that those moments shine out like a beacon, with no intention of surrender despite our best efforts and wishes otherwise."

– Glenn's Chronicles

Cris and Kody took off into the woods, running, unaware of where they should be going or how to find Bixby. They were inhibited by the darkness of the rural area, able to see only what little light the stars and full moon provided through the canopy of trees. They ran through brambles, catching minor cuts and scrapes, and getting caught in a myriad of spider webs, but they remained far more concerned about finding the teensy furry devil.

"Kody, what if we don't find him?"

"We'll find him!"

"We have to! If we don't, Glenn—"

"I know."

"That little guy is the only thing holding him together! We can't lose him!"

"We won't!"

They kept rushing through the woods, searching in vain without a method or means of actually finding the cat. Kody tripped over a branch, falling face-first into a mud puddle, forcing them to stop and reevaluate their progress.

"Are you all right?"

Cris knelt down to help him up. She pulled him to his feet as he tried to wipe the mud off his face.

"Yeah, fine. Just this crappy mud."

"Hey, come here."

Cris moved close to him, examining his face and brushing off the mud.

"You've got it all over your face…you've got to be more careful."

"What can I say? Planning was never really my strong suit."

"Yeah? It shows. Hang on."

Cris untied her bandana, licking the back of it and using it to wipe his face. She leaned up and stood on her toes to make sure she could reach all of his face.

"Hey, turns out you're under all that dirt after all!"

She laughed at her own dumb joke, creating an awkward air between them as she continued to clean off his face. She finished and tied her bandana back on, the tissue that had been held underneath it soiled and now falling to the ground. She shied away from Kody, unsure of what to do next.

"Thanks."

"Don't mention it."

He held his ground for a moment, looking her over as she stared back

"Hey, should we be moving this fast? You should probably be taking it easy, what with the head wound and all."

"No, it's fine. I'm okay, and we should really find Bixby."

"Ok, ok. How about this? We're only gonna scare him off if we keep running. Maybe we should just move slowly and listen for him?"

"I guess that might be a better idea. We aren't having much luck anyway."

They slowed their pace, navigating slowly through the dense woods, trying to find their way through. Kody moved first, making his way up hill in an effort to get a better view. Cris stayed back watching him when she heard other voices echoing nearby. She tried to move around to get a better look, and barely caught sight of Jence's short, wild hair against a tree. She moved down trying to reach her when she saw Thteve holding Jence up against the tree, comfortably.

"Cris, what're you doing down there?" Kody called back to her.

"Sorry, coming!"

She and Jence briefly caught eye lines, Jence's lips curling into a wicked smile as Cris made her way back up the hill and out of sight. They continued in hopes of finding their dear kitty before the night got any worse.

* * *

Alma searched the other side of the camp, but could find no trace of Glenn. She started asking around with the hopes that maybe one of the few other campers in the area might have seen him. She caught a lead about a disheveled man with glasses that had headed toward a river in the middle of the woods not too long ago, and was directed to the path by a little boy who had been playing soldier with some of his friends.

"The river? Oh yeah! It's right past our outpost! It's got a big flag and lots and lots of guards, so be careful!"

Alma was skeptical about the guards, but paid close attention as the little boy leaned in close to whisper.

"The password is 'taco.' Don't tell anyone, okay? It's a secret!"

"Deal."

Alma nodded and patted the kid on the head, making a pinky promise with him before heading off down the trail toward the river. She couldn't see very well, but found a worn-down path that helped to guide her way. She continued down, walking briskly but at the same time trying to be quiet, hoping not to rouse any of the monsters that might be lying dormant in the woods.

"It's okay; this place isn't creepy at all," she said to herself in an effort to keep calm.

"After all, there are plenty of tasty kids here to eat; why would anything want to bother with me?"

She heard a strong rustling in the leaves as a warm draft blew passed her. A small branch fell off a tree, crashing down several feet deeper into the woods.

"Not gonna die, not gonna die, not gonna die!"

Alma crept faster through the woods now, debating whether she should turn back and leave Glenn to find his way home.

"He'll be fine. He's a tough guy, right?"

She contemplated it.

"Smart, anyway! I'm sure he'll be okay."

She turned around and headed back. The woods were pitch black, and there would be no way for her to find him. Worse yet, she might get herself lost and only add to everyone's problems, most of all her own. Though it took some time, she found her way out of the woods, only briefly looking back once more when she lightly stepped on a pair of glasses on the ground near the entrance. Curious, she picked them up and inspected them, realizing they were Glenn's.

"Damn it!"

She thought about how Glenn must have felt carrying her back to shore, fighting against those strong waves in the dead of night. She thought about how difficult it must be for him to find his way in the dead of night now without his glasses.

"Not gonna die, not gonna die, not gonna die!"

Alma rushed back into the woods, ignoring her fears and following the trail all the way down. She didn't stop until she began splashing through small rivulets. She then started looking around to find the main river.

"Now, if I was a river…"

She looked around but couldn't see anything in the deep brush surrounding her.

"I'd be all dark, wet, and alone in the middle of the woods. Good job, Alma. Really. Right in the monster's den so they don't even have to come and find you! They can just mosey right along and eat y—"

The sound of someone else broke her attention. She listened closely.

"I…it…I…"

"What the fuck is that?" she panicked, keeping quiet and low to the ground.

"I…ugh…damn it! Damn it!"

The adrenaline screaming through her veins supercharged her senses. She lay still, trying to make sense of the sounds coming from nearby.

"I w-won't always live with my regret…it might not be true."

She got up and started moving in closer.

"Shh… shh…all q-quiet…stay q-quiet…I just, I j-just…I don't. Everything is all right if it's j-just quiet. Just stay quiet. S-stay quiet. Stay quiet."

She identified the voice. She rose and moved in closer.

"Glenn?"

"W-what?"

The tumultuous crack of twigs snapping echoed out as she moved near, accompanied by rapid and violent shuffling.

"Glenn, sweetie? It's me, Almy."

"A-Alma? Wh-what're you d-doing here? What d-do you want?"

She continued closer, barely able to recognize his visage under the dull starlight.

"Just wanted to check on you. See how you're doing. You okay there?"

"I'm f-fine. Just out for a w-walk. Please leave."

"Mind if I walk with you?"

There was no response. She could see him now and stepped in front of him.

"Hey, why don't we sit down for a minute?"

"I c-can't. I c-c-c-can't."

"Shh…it's okay."

She took his hand and guided him over to a nearby rock, sitting down upon it and sitting him next to her. He looked away, keeping his line of sight low to the ground.

"It's okay. Talk to me. What's going on?"

"N-nothing! N-nothing is going on! I n-need to leave."

She placed her hand on his shoulder. He lifted his head slightly. She gently but firmly placed a finger under his chin, guiding his face toward hers.

"Sweetie, listen to me. Something's wrong. And you know it. You know it like I know it. It's okay not to know what it is. When it was me dealing with issues, I didn't have a clue. But you can't pretend it doesn't exist because it does."

His eyes widened as a faint spark of recognition crossed his face.

"I know what it's like to lose yourself. To have no control over who or what you are, or even worse, to not want to. To not care about anything and know that you don't matter. I lost him, too."

His breathing became softer, almost still, like that of a specter.

"It's so scary…you never know what's you and what's not, what you'll do, or who you are."

"I-it's…it's not j-just that."

"What is it?"

"There's…a voice, a n-noise. No, I d-don't know…"

"It's—"

"I don't know! It's loud, it's q-quiet, it's not a sound! It d-doesn't have w-words—not a face, not a person. It *is*. It wants to c-consume me. I want to let it. I want to be g-gone."

"Shh, sweetie…it's okay."

Glenn burst into tears, barely able to hold his head up as he fell off the rock to his knees.

"It's not okay! It w-wants to kill me and I w-want to let it! I'm so s-s-sick of this… How is that okay?"

"Because we won't let it."

He looked up sniffling, tears still running down his face. She took his head and placed it in her lap, stroking his hair softly as the tears flowed between sniveling sobs.

"I see you, you know. There's something deeper than what you let on, and it's tearing you up inside. But that's why I'm here. Just listen."

She breathed quietly in unison with him, the rippling of the river singing in harmony with his sniffling—nature's accompaniment to their effusive exposition. She held him, continuing to brush her fingers smoothly through his dirty and ruffled hair, wondering what Kody was doing. She wondered what her brother would think of this. She was trying her best to honor his memory, to live up to his expectations. She would take care of the things that were once closest to his heart.

"A-alma…"

"Hmm?"

He said nothing. His tears gradually stopped flowing, but he did little else. He turned his head to look up at her, she casting her gaze upon him with kindness in her eyes. He raised his head, now eye to eye with her. He leaned in, his lips grazing lightly across hers.

"Hey," she said, backing away.

She continued: "I'm sorry, sweetie, but that's not okay."

He pulled back, head bowed and low to the ground.

"I didn't mean to give you the wrong idea. I'm here for you, I want to be here for you. But not like that. I'm with Kody."

He said nothing.

"What would be a better way to put it? I can be the spark that brightens up your day, but I can't be the fire the lights your life. Do you get what I mean?"

He nodded.

"Good. Are you ready to head back?"

He stood up without saying anything.

"It's gonna be hard to find our way through this."

Glenn pulled out his phone, opening it up to use it as a flashlight.

"Oh, great idea!"

They found the trail and started heading back. They trudged along, listening to the rhythmic tones of the cicadas along the wood line. Alma couldn't contain her curiosity of what might be passing through Glenn's mind and tried to manage her own surprise in his attempt to kiss her. It should have been awkward, uncomfortable, but his contretemps only strengthened her resolve to help him.

Neither spoke a word as their sluggish pace finally brought them near the campsite. As they approached, they could hear the sound of people running up to them, though it was a few seconds before they could make out the image of anyone.

"Alms, Glenn—glad we found you guys." They recognized Geroge and Daron as they approached.

Glenn glared at G as his only response.

"Right, stiff upper lip. Got it. Here's the thing…" they could see Geroge was clearly out of breath.

"What's up, G?" Alma inquired.

"Dude, your cat's MIA."

Glenn's face immediately slated.

"We've been searching the woods high and low, but zero joy, man."

Alma tried to establish who was doing what. "What about Kody and Cris?"

"Same thing. Ain't seen them in a while either. These woods are pretty damn thick, though, and doing this by moonlight sure as shit ain't helpin'."

"Glenn, what'll we—"

Glenn turned around and headed back into the woods, pocketing his phone and waiting for no one as it started to drizzle. Alma's attention became divided between Glenn and the storm.

"You gotta be fuckin' kiddin' me. This just ain't the night, is it?"

Geroge looked over to Daron, who instead kept a keen eye on Alma.

"No, no, no, no, no. Not now! Not again!" Alma started shaking.

"We should get you back." Daron pulled off G's jacket, wrapping it around Alma.

"I'm not cold: I just hate storms."

"Either way, you'll catch cold. C'mon. Let's get you inside."

She turned back toward the woods, Glenn's silhouette fading from view.

"Hmm…damn it… No, I'm not leaving him out here. If you guys aren't up for it, then go ahead and head back, but we're gonna keep looking."

Alma ran off after Glenn, leaving Geroge and Daron standing there.

"Well, you heard the girl."

"On we go."

They ran off onto a side path, trying to find Mr. Bixby as quickly as possible.

23. Falling from the Stars

"Right or wrong, good or bad. Always such one-sided arguments. Isn't it possible that both choices could be right or wrong, depending on how I handle them?"

– Kody's Notebook

The damp bark of the tree grated against Jence's back as the storm rolled in. She bit Thteve's lip and pushed him off.

"Hmm?"

"That's enough."

"Not feeling conscientious now, are we?"

"Don't be ridiculous. I'm bored."

Jence's wicked snarl faded as she brushed herself off and made her way past him. She began meandering through the increasingly dense woods, trying to get her bearings. However, the dark had now established its dominion, and the winds were only getting worse, preventing her from making any real progress. She was starting to feel tired. This is what her scruffy man-pillow was for. She followed what she believed to be the path back as best as she could, but could make out very little with hazy rain now obscuring her way.

"So, back to the boss? Or do you have something else in mind?" Thteve overtook her and asserted himself.

"Hmph." She brushed passed him and continued on.

Thteve continued to follow her, Jence confident in her self-confidence. He followed her for a short while longer before breaking off and heading in a different direction.

"Hey, where are you going? I didn't say you could leave me."

He continued.

"Thteve, where are you going?"

"If you wanna head back to camp then go for it. This is a beautiful night and I intend to make the most of it."

"And how're you gonna do that?"

Thteve stopped and turned around, making his way back just close enough to grab Jence's arm before dragging her along with him.

"You wanna know? Then come see."

He embraced the airy scent of the grassy rain as he carelessly lost himself in the woods. She attributed Thteve's fearless approach to the wilds of nature to his JROTC land navigation training rather than his Native American heritage. Jence watched him, seeing him stare at the ground and following some sort of pattern she was unable to discern. She didn't like being kept out of the loop, but found herself reluctantly aroused by his aggressive determination. Her thighs warmed as they continued along, trudging up through brambles.

"Thteve, where are we—"

He turned and glared at her, providing more than enough intensity to keep even her quiet, though by no means sated. He let go of her arm and continued upward, now climbing a somewhat steep hill. She watched him climb until he finally reached the top and lay on the soggy ground above. She deliberated whether he was even worth the trouble. She'd much rather be with her man-toy at that moment. She had no way to get back to him, though, and had no choice but to make the most of it.

She managed her way up the hill, finally getting to the top despite Thteve's lack of consideration. She kicked him in the ribs, and found herself a spot to lie back on the grass, trying to appreciate the rain.

"That was uncalled for." Thteve didn't seem to care for her attitude, or anything else.

"You're uncalled for. Yet here you are."

"Aw, don't like me anymore? And here I was thinking we was such good friends."

"What can I say? The whole five minutes a day you're appealing ended a long while ago."

"You know, I think one of these days you'll develop a better appreciation than the simple use-me, lose-me approach."

"Long as it isn't today. Besides, you know it just like I do that you strictly aren't long-term anything."

Thteve let out a deep sigh. He audibly contemplated the shape of the stars as the haze fell coolly upon them, dampening their skin. He thought aloud.

"Guess I could do worse. At least I get breaks. Poor Geroge, I dunno how he does it full-time."

He took remorseless pity on his friend.

"Funny. That's real cute."

"Hey, it's your new favorite person."

Thteve motioned toward some crackling sounds in the woods. Jence squinted, trying to see what was over in the distance but couldn't make anything out.

"Who?"

"Cris."

Jence moved a little closer, quietly, and realized she could make out the faint visage of what she believed was Kody moving through the woods. She laughed to herself as she watched him.

"Huh, guess we aren't the only ones with extracurricular activities."

She looked back over to Thteve, who simply ignored her and kept his eyes on the dew-stained leaves above. She continued to watch the two, hoping for something more exciting than the prospect of the rest of her otherwise boring night. Her interest quickly waned as they did nothing scandalous enough to keep her attention, and she rested her head on the tough bulk of Thteve's chest. Together but alone, they watched the night continue to unfold.

* * *

Alma caught up to him as he mindlessly charged through the forest.

"I'm gonna help you find him, but do you have a plan?"

"I'm g-going to look. Eventually, I'm g-going to find him. And then I'll bring him b-back."

"Might help if you had these, huh?"

Alma pulled the glasses she had found earlier out of her pocket and handed them to him.

"Where d-did you find these?"

"On the ground out front. Did you even notice?"

"No."

He was cold and distant. Mechanical and calculating. He was on a mission. He looked around with what little he could see and followed the beaten path. He started to veer toward the river, but shifted to the other direction and kept heading downhill.

"Glenn, where are you going? Do you know where Bixby's at?"

Glenn kept trudging, slipping in a puddle of mud and sliding down a hill. He maintained his balance, never relenting. Alma carefully worked her away around the puddle and down the hill, barely able to keep up.

"Glenn!"

"Allister!" Glenn's voice rang out in the quiet forest. "Allister! Allister Th-theodore Bixby! I k-know you're out here, and I know you c-can hear me."

Glenn stopped and waited, looking around questionably yet shrouded in a veil of certainty that left even Alma with faith he knew what he was doing. She almost expected the cat to—

"Mereow?"

Glenn stopped, standing before a small clearing in the brush and pushing his way through. Standing behind him, Alma could barely make out the form of their kitty, who was apparently a very frisky kitty. They could see Bixby had found another cat.

"Whoa…how did you do that? And…is Bixby getting it on?" Alma was in disbelief, particularly as she had never seen a coital cat firsthand. She couldn't help but giggle, more to relieve the tension of the situation than at any mere amusement, but it helped. Glenn stared at Bixby, who proceeded to ignore him. Alma got down on her knees and thought she might try something better.

"Hey kitty, kitty, kitty. Here kitty, kitty, kitty."

She caught Bixby's attention, the cat now finished with whatever business he may have had. He meandered over toward her.

"Moereeow."

He yawned a cat yawn, now exhausted for the evening and wishing nothing more than to be pampered. Alma picked him up and offered him to Glenn. Glenn turned about and headed back to the campsite. Alma did her best to follow closely. They trudged their way back uphill, brushing through the leaves and plants. Alma pressed, trying to get out of the rain, and they finally both arrived back at the campsite. Alma offered up Bixby once more, and this time Glenn took him as he disappeared behind the tent zipper-door.

"Whew…exhausting."

Alma looked around, not seeing anyone else back yet, and from her tent witnessed the campfire die down in the somewhat heavy drizzle. She waited impatiently as the rain beat down against the fabric, watching out the window for the others to get back. After a short while, she saw two people heading back over and called out to them through the window.

"Hey, Kodykins!" she ran out and cheered, jumping up and down, until she realized it was two others.

Daron was quick on the uptake. "If only I could always receive such a reception."

"Sorry; thought you were someone else."

"I am. Let's get you out of the rain. Come hang out in our tent for a bit, at least until your boy gets back."

"Sure, I guess."

They all headed into the Bard's much larger tent, waiting out the rain and hoping their friends would come back soon.

Daron tried to strike up conversation. "Hey, Alms."

"Hmm?" she said, distracted with thoughts of Glenn and Kody.

"Sorry you had to miss our show. It was quite a good one."

"What're you talkin' about? She didn't miss it." Geroge was boisterous as ever.

"Um…yeah, I kinda did, actually."

"What? Kody didn't show you the tape?"

Alma's curiosity was piqued. "What tape?"

"There was a tape. A, uh…whatchamacallit…a video. On my camera. Weird as that sounds. He should still have it somewhere."

"Huh? Hey…hold on."

Alma got up and went into Glenn's tent to find Kody's bag. She caught sight of Glenn curled up in a corner, seemingly already asleep. He must've been more tired than he let on. *All this must really take a lot out of him,* she thought. She quietly crept over to Kody's bag, trying not to disturb Glenn, and dug through it until she found a camera stuffed in an old coat pocket. She glanced back at Glenn, who looked like he was now sleeping somewhere close to serene. *I wonder if he ever finds peace.*

She looked around for the tenacious cat, spying Bixby cuddled up next to Glenn for warmth. She was glad they were at least able to find the kitty cat. She ran back over to the Bard's tent and handed the camera to Geroge, who showed her how to work it.

"Let's see…it goes something like this…"

Geroge messed around with the camera until they got it to play. The three of them huddled closely around to keep warm as they watched the show. They watched the opening of the show, noting they could barely hear Kody's commentary in the background.

"Aw, look at that. He knows me so well!" Geroge remarked to himself.

"What?" Daron was trying to figure out what he meant.

"You mean the deal with 'I'll Be Seein' You?'"

"Yeah, I mean that, what else?"

"I thought you only opened with it because you liked irony."

"Nah, that's just a bonus."

"Guess we all learn something new."

"See, D? Just gotta pay attention."

"Yeah? And do you think I'm from Romania, too?"

"Close enough."

Daron scoffed, putting up resistance only for show. Alma ignored their banter, paying equal attention to Kody's commentary as well as the show.

"Wow, you guys really turned it up for this one."

She mostly talked to herself as she watched on. She recognized parts of some of the songs from notes she had read in Kody's notebook and was surprised to find how close he and G really were. She was even more surprised by, and less keen on, G referring to Cris as Kody's girl.

"What the hell, G?"

"Ah, quit your bellyachin' and just watch the next part."

Alma pinched him, but didn't fuss much for fear of missing anything else. She watched on, listening to "I Heard," unable to decipher how she felt about it. She hummed along to the catchy melody as the song finished.

"Was that really written about me?"

"Maybe." G kept quiet.

"Which parts?"

"Whichever parts you liked the best."

"G!"

"Didja like it?"

"It was a great show, I'll give you that."

"Damn straight it was. That's how we do."

"Hmm…"

"What's up?"

"Nothing."

Alma got up and left, keeping her thoughts on the matter to herself. She went into the empty tent and waited patiently for Kody and Cris to get back. She tried not to let her emotions get the best of her, but it had already been a weird night and she didn't like the notion of anyone being called "Kody's girl" except her, even if it was Cris, and even if it was just a joke, which she had assumed. She couldn't help but wonder where they were right now and how Cris must've felt about hearing that.

Alma had to do something. All this sitting around was getting to her head and she didn't like it. She got up and stepped outside. The wind started to pick up, rustling the trees around and slamming branches violently against one another. The warm air met the cool summer rain as they smacked against her skin, pushing her backward. Her fear came creeping back—she couldn't brave the storm. She thought about Kody, about Jake, about Glenn.

She hated the rain, abhorred it. But she wasn't going to let it stop her. There was something more important than her personal qualms at stake. She tightened her grip on G's jacket and headed off back into the woods to find Cris and Kody as the wind started to pick up. Clouds blocked the stars from sight, leaving her on her own in the dark.

24. Rebuilding Haven

"Show me your fire and I'll show you the stars."

– Scribbled in the Margin of Alma's Diary

"Kody, we've got to get back!"

Cris was forced to yell over the winds just to be heard. She tried to hold her bandana in place as the winds threatened to blow it away. It lifted off her head and started drifting on the gust, but Kody managed to catch it and stuff it in his pocket.

"C'mon, this way!" Kody led her up the hill.

"Isn't the camp the other way?"

It was too dark to tell for sure which way the camp was, but Cris was certain they were headed in a very different from the way they had come.

"Kody, where are you—"

"Even if we make it back, the tents might not hold!"

"So what do we do?"

"Keep moving!"

The rain pelted their faces and further reduced their almost nonexistent visibility. Cris kept a firm grasp on Kody's hand as they made their way up the hill. He slipped down the muddy slope. Cris barely managed to catch him and help him back up. They kept pushing on and found a small alcove barely large enough to block some rain. They tried to squeeze in, finding a small, dry spot covered from the rain, and crouched under it, taking shelter.

"Do you think this'll work?" she asked.

"I dunno, but it's the best we've got. The wind is blowing the other way, so it's keeping some of the rain out at least."

"Good. I need a break."

They settled down and huddled together to keep warm.

"Are you..."

"Quit asking me if I'm okay! I told you!"

"Gotcha."

"I am a little worn out, though." She offered him a reluctant smile, to which he responded in kind.

They sat there for a few minutes in silence, taking the time to catch their breath.

"Do you think he's all right?"

"Who? Bixby?"

"Yeah. This is a pretty bad storm. A little cat like that..."

"He's fine. Guy's a fighter, remember?" Kody poked the faded scratch marks on Cris's face as proof, to reassure her.

"Hey, I so could've taken him."

"Not without losing an eye."

"Not the point." She smirked.

"Yeah, yeah."

She tried to ignore the weather, keeping her mind focused on other things, like what they'd do when they got to California. Beautiful white sand beaches. All sorts of—

"I liked your singing."

She blushed

"Thanks."

"Seriously...you're amazing. I'd really like to listen to you sing again sometime."

"Yeah, maybe..."

Cris started shivering, keeping her arms close to her body to try and get it under control. Kody pulled her close and wrapped his arms around her.

"Kody...what're you...?"

"You're cold."

"Well, yeah, but..."

"I said I'd look out for you, remember? And that's what I'm gonna do: I'm gonna keep you safe."

She bit her lip. Feelings began to surface she had previously entertained only in passing, and this time they weren't fleeting. She felt the warmth of his body, his strength, and tried to keep to herself as much as possible.

She hummed a little melody, trying to keep her mind quiet. She remembered what Alma had said only a few days ago on the hillside. Then she remembered Alma. She wasn't going to betray her; she refused to be the source of her best friend's heartache. She began to feel light-headed as her grip weakened.

"Cris?"

She flinched at the sound of her name. The sudden spasm of her body scared them both, and they reflexively held each other tighter. She looked at him—his deep dark eyes—and gazed with wonder. They seemed very dark. Too dark. They weren't supposed to be dark. She could barely make out their shapes as everything became black around her. She collapsed.

"Cris!"

Kody checked her pulse, making sure she still had one. She was breathing. He noticed the small welt on her head and checked it over. It was small and healing—it had stopped bleeding. But she had still lost some blood. "All this excitement and she still hasn't had a chance to rest," he thought.

He took off his soaked button-up and under shirts and wrapped them loosely around her. The cold dirt of the alcove grated with the rain assaulting his bare skin. But he couldn't let this detour him—she was far more important. He shifted her body, resting her head on his shoulder. He wrapped his arm around her.

He shuddered, soaking wet and afraid for both of them. He couldn't keep from shaking, being lost so deep in the woods late at night in the middle of a harsh storm. He didn't know how long they could hold out, or if some wild animal might decide their spot should serve as its own shelter. He tried to stop his teeth from chattering as cold shivers overtook his body. He hoped for the very best as he looked down at Cris, but knew regardless that he'd protect her. He wouldn't let any harm come to her. He held her hand as she rested, keeping her warm and safe.

* * *

Alma had no luck in finding either Kody or Cris, which only served to piss her off and strengthen her resolve. She shoved her shoe through a decayed log as she stomped through the woods.

"I'm not gonna let some damn rainy windy forest beat me!"

She trudged on, finding it was hopeless and too dark to accomplish anything further. She knew, though she wouldn't admit it, that she'd have to wait until morning if she wanted to go any deeper into the woods. The trees in the area blocked most of the wind and rain, but she could see that going any further out would've gotten her stuck with all of the slippery mud. She wandered around a bit more, but found no success and started heading back. She crossed the spot where hours ago Glenn had tried to kiss her, and took a seat on the rock once more.

"I wonder how he's doing."

Her thoughts kept wandering back to Glenn, no matter how much she wanted to focus on anything else. "He was so torn up...that poor boy. How long has he been like that? It must be unbearable."

An overwhelming warmth rushed to her face. She found herself fighting back the tears she hadn't known were there. Though she couldn't know his darkness, she had felt his pain. It was not so unlike her own. She understood some of what he was going through. She took a deep breath. Even now, she was overcoming her fears. She was determined to become strong. She looked over toward the river rushing slowly by.

"Water...it's not so big and bad. Just like this rain. Just drips and drops. Splishes and splashes."

She walked over to the riverbed, taking her shoes off and dipping her feet in. She was surprised to find that the river was warm, even in the middle of a midsummer's night shower. She wiggled her toes, pretending they were little fishies, before realizing there may be actual little fishies in the water that wanted to bite them off. She quickly pulled her feet out, but looked around and thought about all of the monsters that were assuredly hiding in the woods.

"Hmm...monsters...well, I guess if there really were monsters here, they would've attacked me by now. Unless the guards are here, too. Guards of a noble outpost, ready to stand and defend such a fair maiden.

"Guards, in case you're listening, the password is taco!"

She giggled to herself, her confidence reaffirmed. She checked to make sure there weren't actually any guardsmen in place. She pulled off G's jacket and dropped her shirt along with her skirt, stripping naked. She climbed into the riverbed. The flow of the stream left her cool and free, liberated. She dipped her head back, soaking her hair. She felt the rush of the weak current push past her, gently carrying her body away as she lifted her feet up. She firmly planted them and walked against it, only to let them go and carry her down once more.

It was an odd mixture of rain against the river, and she somehow knew—regardless of any truths—she was the first person to become a part of nature. She could no longer understand her fear of the wild, for she was now an aspect of it, and sat in the shallow edge of the riverbed, avoiding rocks, as she began to reflect on those many nights she cried herself to sleep alone at the old pier.

"I was so obsessed…I couldn't get away from it. It was always about Jake." She talked aloud, organizing her thoughts.

"I lost him. Then Dad. He tried, but it was too much. He stopped being himself. He became a shell… Mom was so horrible to him. I know she tried her best. I lost my brother, and they lost their son. I think then, my real mother died, too. And the monster drove my dad away, and I was all alone.

"Guy after guy, bed after bed, it didn't matter. I just wanted to be wanted. And then there's Cris. The only person who didn't judge me. Even she must think I'm pretty disgusting. But she keeps it to herself. She puts up with me. She doesn't talk trash about me when I sleep with a guy, and she's still there for me after he breaks my heart. It's always breaking. I wonder, with all this breaking, when did it ever mend? How can it have been broken so many times when it was never whole to begin with? Are there even enough pieces left?"

She dangled her toes in the stream, feeling the warm water pass between them. She dug them into the dirt, feeling the warmth and heat of the earth. It felt right, natural. It felt like home.

"Cris…am I a slut because I fucked men just to make myself feel better? Am I a whore because I can't understand how you've never slept with a guy? Or maybe you've just been lying to me the whole time, too afraid to admit it, too ashamed of yourself, like me." She looked up through the canopy of the trees, to the stars.

"But I'm nothing to be ashamed of. I'm me. Alma. Almy. Alma Grey. Maybe I'm not the prettiest girl in the world. Maybe I wouldn't make a very good mother, or wife, or girlfriend. Sometimes I can't even take care of myself. God knows I'm not perfect. But I'm a good person at heart and I care about the people I love. I don't betray my friends and I stick by them no matter what. Even if my heart gets a little confused sometimes. I think I'm a good person. I can be strong."

She felt something wriggle around her lower back. She jumped up, moving to the other side of the riverbed. It felt like it was just a minnow, but she didn't want to take any chances.

"My Kody, Kody, Kodykins. You'd never betray me, would you? I've given you every good reason to. I've broken your heart; I've caused you so much trouble, so much pain. But I've also loved you. I wonder if that's enough..."

She looked down at herself, evaluating her own body. She spent too much time judging herself so harshly because of how everyone else looked at her. How everyone else looked period. Most of all Cris. She could never compare to what her best friend had. But maybe she didn't need to. It wasn't about Cris; it was about her. It had been too long since she had taken a good honest look at herself. Who she was, body and soul. She had forgotten where she stood.

"I am me. The daughter of Maria, lover of Kody, the best friend of Charisma. And now, the caretaker of Glenn. Even if my mother's no longer who she was, I am who I am. Because of her. I should apologize. Sorry mom."

She knew her mother couldn't hear her, and that her real mother never would. But the Maria Grey that lived on within her knew. The rain began to ease up as the wind died down. Alma regretted that the storm began to wind down. The stress of the long night started catching up to her as her adrenaline began to fade. She was deep in the woods now, and certain no one would ever find her. The walk back seemed like such a long trip, and she was so very, very tired. She crawled out of the river, and lay next to her clothes. Naked with waning euphoric, she decided to rest her eyes, just for a moment.

* * *

"Merrow!"

"Hssss!"

Glenn opened his eyes to discover that he had been resting on Bixby's tail. His hypothesis was confirmed when he felt Bixby's gnawing teeth gnashing violently at his hips, trying to get him off.

222

"Oh, I-I apologize, Mr. Bixby."

Glenn quickly shifted his waist, releasing the cat's tail, though not his wrath. Bixby glared maliciously at Glenn, his eyes now demanding to be fed immediately as restitution. Glenn reached for Kody's bag and searched through it hoping to find some more cat food. He found nothing in the front pocket and made his way through the back, which had apparently already been sifted through.

He took the liberty of searching for edibles, finding his actions easily defensible in the name of nourishing his regally eager pet. With a stroke of luck, he stumbled upon a second can of the turkey/chicken hybrid that Bixby seemed to like so much, and opened the container. He couldn't explain why Kody had a can of cat food on him, but was gracious in accepting the small favor that appeared to have been granted from on high. The soft rumbles of Bixby's furry kitten tummy implied absolution as the cat chowed down.

* * *

Cris snuggled closer as she realized she was snuggling and pressing up against dirty, warm flesh. She opened her eyes slowly, unsure of what to expect when she caught her first sight of the day. She was covered in shirts, and recognized the somewhat wafty yet relaxing scent that was mixing with the dirt of the forest around her. She looked up to see Kody resting on her as the sun started to rise. She noticed for the first time a simple tribal necklace tied around his neck. There was no clasp, so she wondered how it got there in the first place, or how he got it off.

She began to recall the night before: the dark night, the long harsh storm, and the lost kitten. She remembered freezing and fading, but not being nestled or wrapped up in Kody's warmth as she was now. The feelings of the night before came creeping back, but she knew this time they couldn't stay. Still, she could not forget his efforts and leave them unrewarded. She reached up, her lips softly grazing his neck as she gave him a light kiss. She tasted the suppleness of his skin. Dirty but nice—better than she had imagined. This one minor indiscretion was worth it. If she was going to sacrifice what she was now beginning to hold dear for the sake of her best friend, she had earned this. He began to stir, and she immediately pulled back, wide-eyed and breaking free of his grasp, leaving his shirts in his lap.

"Uh…?"

He stretched, scratching his head and wondering why he was cold, before seeing Cris sitting in front of him. He looked down and saw his shirts in his lap. He quickly covered up and clumsily fumbled back into them before trying to reassess the situation.

As her dream-like haze began to lift and reality set in, she started feeling sick. The butterflies in her stomach were at war. She had just kissed her best friend's boyfriend, even if he himself had been unaware of it.

"Hey, morning! How's it going?" Cris tried to play off her behavior as casual.

"Heh, exhausted. You?"

"Uh…great! Sleep well?"

"Yeah, not too bad, I guess."

"Yeah?"

"Yeah."

The memories of the night before quickly caught up with Kody as the two shared their awkward sunrise. He wanted to be there for Cris, like she had been for him. He didn't want anyone to be alone. But he was beginning to worry that being around her was clouding his judgment and affecting his behavior toward Alma. He needed to figure out how he was going to manage this. They both got up and looked around. They could see the sun rising up behind the trees, and the path back to camp came into view.

"So, I guess we were out all night?" Kody started.

"I guess we were."

"What do we tell them?"

"Them?"

"You know, everybody?"

"You mean Alma?" Cris had only one concern.

"Well, she is part of everybody."

"We'll tell them the truth. That we were looking for Bixby. We just couldn't find him."

"Heh, makes sense. That sounds like a good reasonable plan."

"Good! Shall we head back then?"

"We shall."

Kody reached for Cris's hand before quickly retracting it and heading down the hill by himself, leading the way. Cris followed a few paces behind him, unsure of what had just happened. She didn't know what would be a proper following distance or whether she should be close to him at all. She didn't like the sudden change in his behavior toward her or that she couldn't rid herself of lingering affections. She didn't know where she stood in any of this and she wasn't a fan of such.

Kody came bustling through the woods to find Daron and Glenn cooking hotdogs by the reestablished morning campfire.

"Welcome back, friend," Daron nodded.

Glenn watched Kody, waiting for his counterpart who came stumbling sheepishly up behind him in dirty shorts. She lost her footing and caught herself on Kody's back before regaining her balance and stepping back, putting a little distance between the two of them. Glenn smiled in unison with Daron, who was now checking her out while eyeing Kody. Cris caught this and immediately rushed into her tent to change.

"Much respect." Daron shook Kody's hand and pulled up a seat.

"I-it's not like that," Glenn said, mocking Kody, earning a chuckle out of him.

"You do impersonations now? Since when do you do impersonations?" Kody tried to figure out what was going on.

"S-since my friends spent the entire night t-trying to find my lost kitten for me. Th-thank you."

"So you heard about that? Sorry man."

"For what?"

Bixby sauntered out of the tent, chicken and turkey heavy on his breath, literally. The cat carried and then dropped the can outside. Kody's heart sank just a little inside as he saw his secret stash had been violated and desecrated, though he was glad to see the prankster returned and well nourished.

"Oh, never mind then."

"Hopefully your efforts w-weren't entirely in vain?" Glenn looked Kody in the eye.

Kody said nothing, which left the normally pensive Glenn expressionless. Instead, Kody got up to go change as well. Cris climbed out of her tent, having dressed herself out of Alma's bag. She had a brown mid-length skirt and a dark green shirt, both of which were a little too big, but Cris managed to work them to her benefit.

Kody came out shortly thereafter, wearing dark brown cargo pants and a fitted green Strong Bad t-shirt. They looked at each other only through passing glances. After a moment, each of them caught on that they were matching, and looked in any other available direction. Kody retook his seat next to Glenn, while Cris sat on the other side of Glenn next to Daron.

Geroge came out in boxers and a robe, followed closely by Jence, who wore only a long t-shirt and underwear. Thteve followed the two shortly after, sporting lounge pants and a wife-beater, with what appeared to be rope burns around his neck. No one asked any questions as they all sat down to cook their breakfast.

* * *

Alma felt a cold, clammy sensation running in short, jolty bursts along her back. It stopped and jumped on her butt as she started to wake up. She rolled over, watching a squirrel fall off and run up a tree. She sighed as she got up and brushed herself off.

"Note to self: next time you have a spiritual journey of self-discovery; don't fall asleep naked in the middle of the woods. Or, at least put your clothes back on."

Despite her own advice, and innumerable mosquito bites, she jumped back into the river to wash the mud off. She took special care to keep her hair as dry as possible while still cleaning it, not knowing the next time she'd be able to get a real shower. She thought the river felt oddly colder now than it had the night before.

"This is a good way to start the day."

She waded around a little, enjoying the chirping of the assorted birds among the trees, before climbing out and drying herself off as best she could. She slowly put her clothes back on and made her way out of the woods. She broke through the clearing of the covering brush to see everyone across the pond up and having breakfast. She rushed back to join them. She found a spot open near Kody and plopped down next to him, grabbing his arm and leaning up against his shoulder.

"Morning, snuggy bear!" She kissed his cheek, as gleeful as ever.

"Morning, piggy toes."

"Seriously? Piggy toes? Wait, do pigs even have toes…? Silly boy!" she put on in her most playful voice. She kissed his cheek.

"You're peppy this morning."

"Uh huuuuuh. Can you guess why?"

"You found some tasty mushrooms and had yourself a nice little picnic?"

"Ugh, no! Not even!"

She slapped his arm playfully as she latched onto it once more, leaning in for a bite of his hotdog as he tried to get a piece himself.

"A picnic would be lots of fun, though… Anyway, I had a wonderful night! I spent it in a river!"

They all just looked at her. Alma, seeing the underdressed Bard trio, Daron, and her best friend in clothes that didn't even fit her, decided that they were in no place to judge her. She slipped off Geroge's jacket and threw it back at him. Looking Cris over again, she concluded that Cris was in fact wearing her clothes and decided to investigate.

"Ms. Roberts!" Cris jumped as Alma stood up erectly and called her to attention. "Are those my clothes you're wearing?"

"Um…yes?"

"Ms. Roberts!" Alma demanded attention. "Why are you wearing my clothes?"

"Because all of mine are back at the van?"

"Ms. Roberts!" Alma would accept no less. "Is…is that my bra strap? Are you wearing my bra?"

"Could we not talk about this here…?" Cris tried to keep her voice down.

"Ms. Roberts!" Alma was on fire. "I find that to be not only an acceptable, but reasonable request! I accept!"

Alma took her seat next to Kody once more. At this point, Kody was now certain she had been far too close to some colorful mushrooms and had a little midnight snack. Glenn watched her in awe, unable to look away. Geroge and Daron both enjoyed the show, though Thteve remained uninterested. He scratched his neck and grabbed a bottle of water as he went back to his tent. Jence followed him in soon thereafter.

"You guys look so worn out! We need to get everyone a shower and a real meal! So, when do we fix the van so we can get this show on the road?" Alma couldn't calm herself down.

"Uh, we took care of that while you were still beauty snoozin', *chica*." Geroge nodded to her, trying to figure out what (or who) exactly had gotten into her.

"So we're ready to go then?"

"Yup." Kody looked over at her, finding a very noticeable glow about her.

"Awesome! Let's go, baby!"

She reached up and smooched him—noticeably loud and garnering much attention. The entire group had no choice but to acknowledge it. Even Kody was a little embarrassed at having been a part of it. Cris kept her face down as she tugged on Glenn's sleeve, catching his eye line. They both got up and started packing. Kody got up and said his thanks to G.

"Thanks, man. I can't tell you how awesome it is you came all the way out here for us."

"No problem, brother. You know I'd do anything for you."

"Likewise." Geroge started heading back into the tent.

"Uh, G…about Jeany and Thteve…"

"Hey, man, we gotta get our inspiration from somewhere, right? She's a creative girl, and I'm a hella of a guy. Long as it's my bed she's crawlin' into at the end of the day, I don't really ask too many questions. Besides, believe me when I tell you it works out just as well for me."

"Heh, gotcha."

G leaned in close. "Best of luck, buddy." Geroge whispered into Kody's ear, "but from what Daron says, you don't need it!" He held a dirty throaty laugh to himself.

"Either kiss him or get the hell away from him!" Alma charged in, pushing Geroge back and breaking the two up.

"Damn, all right, all right. You win this one Alm'ster. But you keep that up and I might just come back for you myself."

Geroge slapped her ass as he headed back into the tent. She scoffed, staring wide-eyed at Kody, who just stared back.

"What? He thinks you're hot. I'm supposed to be mad at him for it?"

"At least do something about it!" Alma wouldn't settle for inaction.

"Meh, all right."

Kody slapped her ass as he went to go get the tents packed up. As he turned around, Alma's face flared up. She ran up behind Kody and jumped on his back, throwing him off-balance.

"Oh, hell no you don't. To the van, mush!"

He looked at Cris, pleading for help, but she found no sympathy for his plight. She left him to his fate.

"All right, guess I'm going to bring the van around. Have the stuff ready?"

"Will do, Captain." Cris nodded as she headed back inside the tent.

Kody shuffled on out of the campsite, with the few campers and Alma's soldier troop watching him go. She ruffled his hair and played with his head as he marched back to the van. They finally got back, finding the van in good repair and slightly shinier, as G had told him that Jence had worked her special on it, whatever that meant. He let Alma down as she turned him around and looked up to him.

"You're so goofy, my silly boy."

"I'm goofy? You were the one riding me like a sleigh dog."

"Oh, not yet, but I plan to." He could hear the sinister tone in her voice once again.

"That right? Crazy girl."

"Mhmm." She smiled like an innocent devil ready to collect her debt.

"But that's okay. That's why you love me. I love you, too, snuffle bug."

Kody stopped, to which she cocked an eyebrow. "What? I know the whole dog thing was kinda kinky, but, I mean hey, there are all sorts of ways…"

"You love me?"

"I do, Kody Lehane. I'm in love with you. Utterly and completely. And I'm gonna prove it to you."

She pinned him up against the van and kissed him, wrapping her hands around his head to stop him from getting away, not that he was trying to escape. She let him go only for a moment as she opened the door of the van to toss him in, and then climbed in after him, slamming the door shut behind her.

25. Tumbleweed Brushfires

"Reflectin' don't get'cha nothin' but stuck lookin' in the mirror. And I ain't pretty enough to be starin' at myself all day."

– Agramonte's Dirty Napkin

Somewhere near the Mojave Desert

Smoke filled the air, and his only regret was that it wasn't his. He cleaned up the glasses lying around the bar as he got up to lock the door for the night. He went in back to get the broom and started sweeping, knowing it wouldn't make shit for difference. The floors were covered with sand, and they always would be. But he got paid to sweep, so he swept.

"Hey, sugar."

She came in from the front of the bar, locking the door behind her. Just hearing her voice was enough to ruin whatever was left of the rest of his night.

"What do you want, Lexy?"

"I'm lonely. Spend some time with me."

"I'm busy, workin'. Go away."

"Yeah, you're workin' real hard. All that sexy sweeping, makes a girl all soft and sweaty. Weak in the knees."

"It's hard to believe you have an issue with whorin'."

"Only with the wrong marks."

He scoffed. He kept sweeping, following the routine no matter how pointless it seemed. Lexy watched him closely as she made her way behind the bar and poured herself a drink.

"I already closed the fuckin' drawer, what're you doin'?"

"If you won't keep me company, someone has to. Looks like it'll be my friend Jack tonight."

"Stupid bitch…gimme a few minutes."

The soft glow of the dim lights harshed his eyes. Dim lights reminded him of being confined, restricted. Lexy turned the bar music down low, changing it from the usual crowd's country to a more mellow folk rock. He put the broom away, moving up toward the bar and taking a seat on the stool.

"What can I get for you, padre?" She tried to be cavalier.

"Whiskey sour, straight up. And you're payin' for it."

"And you call *me* a whore."

"It's closin' time. That means I should be on my comfy ass snoozin' the night away. But here I am. Quit wastin' my goddamn time."

"Quite the gentleman."

She poured him a drink and continued to throw back her own, though she was already well on her way. He took the whiskey straight and felt the slow burn all the way down, tingling his insides and making him warm.

"So tell me about yourself, stranger."

"What's with the sudden need to know?"

"I figure if we're gonna be lovers I should know a little something about you first."

"Shit ain't made a difference so far."

"Makes a difference now."

He looked her over, trying to decide if she was even worth his time. He reached into his breast pocket to pull out another smoke. She leaned over the counter with a lighter, exposing the minimal amount of cleavage she had to offer as she lit his cigarette. He took another drink and looked her over again, getting more comfortable and starting to feel the music he didn't give a shit for.

"What'dya wanna know?" he asked.

"Tell me everything."

"Lived in a lot of different places, lots of stories to tell."

"Why?"

"Dunno. Never got along with people, I guess. My first family didn't work out. Didn't have much of a whim ta' head back and give 'em a second go. Got a better offer, so I took it. After a while I just got bounced around."

"Sounds like a rough childhood."

She slid around the bar, taking a seat next to him.

"That's life."

"So what after that? The boy had to grow up sometime, right?"

"I wasn't never a boy. Was born a man. Got kicked 'round and 'round 'til I found some blood kin down south. I stayed with them for a while, but shit started gettin' hairy. Got a lot of good people into bad trouble, ya' know? So I left."

"You, getting people into trouble? Now that I can't imagine."

"Yet you keep runnin' yer mouth like you're lookin' to find out..."

They both raised their glasses, having another drink as the night dragged on.

"You were saying you caused a lot of trouble at home."

"Yeah...so I left. Joined the army, of all things."

"Really...someone like you, a soldier?"

"Heh, they said the same goddamn thing. Hell, so did I. Did it anyway."

"How come?"

"Why does anyone do it? I needed the money. I fuckin' hated that lifestyle. Go here, do this shit, go fuckin' shave, wear a shiny belt and stand at attention. Got out the first chance I got. Ended up here."

"Friends, family?"

"Nah, nothin' like that. Just drifted until I stopped."

"What about your family down south? Why not visit them?"

"And give up this sweet gig?" He was sardonic, as usual.

He leaned back, taking another drag of his cigarette and staring at the floor. He spent so much of his life looking down on things it became a natural habit for him. It might not be earth, but at least it was wood, and covered with dirt. She placed her hand on his knee and held no reservations about sliding it up further. He took another drink.

"I fuck up lives; I don't fix 'em. At least I don't know anyone worth fuckin' up 'round here."

"Acting like you've forgotten about me while I'm still here?"

"You must be the most self-depreciating bitch around if you think I'm what ya' want."

"That really sounds like something for me to worry about."

"Yeah? Ya' might wanna start."

He felt a sleight of hand coming on and grabbed hers, violently throwing it aside as he got up to take a piss. He got into the bathroom and made his way to the urinal, trying to find some kind of peace. He took a leak, leaning forward, resting his head against the wall trying to keep his balance. The wall wouldn't stop moving.

"I can't be drunk already...I ain't even drink that much. Few shots here and there plus that whiskey..."

He thought about the drink she had poured for him and didn't put it past her to pull something sly.

"Well shit...don't that just beat all...?"

He finished up and tried to put it away when he felt a soft, refined hand reach around from behind.

"Hey, baby, we aren't done yet."

"I ain't your baby, and what the fuck're ya' doin' in here?"

"Like I said. We aren't done yet. I haven't got what I came for."

"And what's that?"

"A good night kiss."

She ran her hand up and down, releasing him to turn around. He looked at her, his eyes glazing over as she knelt down before him. She leaned forward and he caught her throat with his hand as he picked her up and pushed her against the wall.

"What're you playing at?"

"What makes you think I'm playing?"

He tightened his grip, making it harder for her to breathe. She could only barely get out the words he was so eager to hear.

"What's the game, Lexy?"

"You know...I like it...rough."

He started feeling dizzy and fell back, letting her go and grabbing the sink for support. She fell to the ground, gasping for air. He lifted his head and straightened himself up. He cleaned himself up and washed his hands.

"Let me make this clear: you don't got nothing I want."

Taking a minute to recompose herself and catch her breath, she arose again to her feet.

"Honey, you don't seem too clear on what you want. You should let me remind you."

She moved closer again.

"Remind me? My long-forgottens are best left buried, sweet cheeks."

He walked out of the bathroom, grabbing his jacket off the back of the chair as he left the bar. He stumbled down the street, trying to maintain his balance as he followed the glowing light of the convenience store sign.

He felt around for his cigarette but couldn't find it. He fell onto the sidewalk, trying to find his pack of smokes and a lighter in his jacket. Lexy pulled him to his feet and hoisted him onto her shoulder, walking him home.

"The fuck're you...?"

"You're in no shape to walk. I tried to make this easy for you but you just insist on being a pain in the ass."

"What? What are you?"

"Keep it down, I'm taking you home."

She walked him around the block, passing the rickety swing set left abandoned in front of the semi fenced-in house, and half-carried, half-dragged him up the stairs. She pulled out her keys, unlocking the door, and carried him inside before locking it behind them. She walked him to his room, dropping him on the bed and stripping him down. She pulled out a syringe and a small vial as she climbed on top of him.

"Lexy, what the fuck is going on?"

"*Pas de soucis, mon chéri*; you won't remember a thing. Sit back and relax, *Mr. Agramonte*, I just need to borrow something from you. Don't worry, you're about to have yourself a real good time."

26. Ode to Melody

"I'm a little ashamed to admit that most of what I know about philosophy I've derived from books. I spent more time reading than I ever did getting out. But it has served me well."

– Glenn's Chronicles

Little Rock, Arkansas

Cris and Glenn waited patiently, having finished packing up the campsite, and continued waiting for Kody and Alma to arrive. They sat curious as to what was taking the couple so long, though they didn't need many guesses to figure it out. Cris set one of their bags down in front of the pond, taking a seat on it as she stared into her reflection in the water.

"D-deep thoughts?"

She looked up. Glenn stood before the pond, looking beyond it at nothing in particular.

"It's not what everyone thinks." There was a bitter defensiveness in her voice.

"So you mean something d-did happen between you and K-kody back there?"

"What?" She looked up at him.

"Charisma."

She glared.

"C-cris. Neither I nor Alma believe anything happened between the two of you."

She was attentive now.

"Kody, for whatever p-poetic aptitude he might possess, lacks social grace nearly as much as I d-do, if only in more subtle ways. He's trying t-too hard to avoid you. Far too much effort expended for someone he'd be p-purported to have had sexual c-contact with."

She cast her gaze back toward the pond, back to her own reflection that looked upon her wrapped in indecision.

"So your theory with Kody is that he's trying to avoid me for my own good?"

"You c-could say that. However, it's *your* 'own good' that I'm concerned with."

He placed his hand on her shoulder. She turned away.

"You two share a b-bond that affects you more than you've been l-letting on. You've always been a light-hearted girl, Ch-charisma, so it worries me to see you with s-such heavy thoughts."

"My heart's fine." She scoffed.

"It's funny…it's b-been my experience that the p-people who tell you they're fine are usually the ones that a-aren't. Wasn't that the sum of the p-point you made to me?"

She cast her eyes to the side, nodding.

"Let's assume that I was in s-such a situation. P-perhaps, that I was in love with a woman whose h-heart was not free. Let's say I was f-forced to witness her k-kindness and charity without being able t-to make a move, or even express a word of my f-feelings for her without hurting a friend. In either c-case, whether I fought against my f-feelings or indulged them, I would only c-cause more pain. If this were the c-case…" hesitating a moment, "it isn't a s-situation I would undertake lightly, or attempt to handle on my own, even g-given its nature as a personal matter."

"I am on my own."

"Only if you ch-choose to be. You have friends, Cris. Trust them."

"Trust my friends? Little hypocritical, don't you think?"

Glenn chuckled. "I'm t-trying. A solid example c-certainly wouldn't hurt."

"Hmm…okay." Cris sat up to face him. "I do trust you, so tell me this: do you think I'm in love with Kody?"

Cris awaited his response, contemplating everything he had told her. Glenn held his tongue, gazing out over the water.

"Glenn, am I in love with Kody?" There was a pleading desperation in her voice

"You're in an arduous p-position. I don't envy you. I c-can't speak for you; I can only listen. But maybe I c-can help put things in p-perspective. Alma's your b-best friend. You've been everything to her for q-quite some time, and I imagine she holds a similar post in your life. Kody is s-someone new, someone special. You feel for him in ways you n-never have before. It's exciting, f-fresh. But it's also volatile and d-dangerous. The thrill of the u-unknown may supersede your own sense of rationality."

She lowered her head, watching his reflection. She blew tresses out of her face, looking to him from her periphery.

"Have you fallen in love before?"

"I d-did have a life before this, even if it wasn't m-much to speak of."

"That doesn't exactly answer the question."

"No, it d-doesn't. I…c-cared for someone, once." Glenn took his glasses off, wiping them on off on his shirt.

"What'd you do about it?"

"Nothing."

"So you just let her go? And everything was fine?"

She raised her eyes, searching, hoping for the prospect of hope.

"Nothing is fine, u-unfine, or anything in b-between. Th-things simply are as they are. It's your c-choice if you accept or d-deny that. Things only hold meaning if you b-bestow such upon them."

She leaned back, sighing violently into the sky. A wild breeze lifted her hair up onto the wind, and she mussed it about, shaking her head around to let her hair fly free. With the draft dying down, she let out a deep breath, leaning forward to stare at the rocks on the ground. She ran her fingers through her hair, slowly combing it back out.

"Too much of this craziness. At least you seem like you're doing better."

"It w-would appear so."

"What happened?"

"I've stopped t-taking my medication."

She looked up at him, he still gazing at nothing, trapping himself in his own pensive repose.

"I'm glad to hear that…I think. But is that okay? Can you do that?"

"I've n-no idea. But I s-suppose we'll see."

"That sounds kind of dangerous."

"Any more d-dangerous than abusing it as I have b-been?"

Cris shrugged, kicking a nearby rock about.

"Who knows? Why now though? Why the big change?"

"Life is about c-change. Do we n-need a reason to progress along our own p-paths?"

"I guess not…"

"Meroew."

Bixby started climbing up Cris's back, perching himself on her shoulder. The feline made himself comfortable. She turned to look at him, seeing him only out of focus, as he stared back at her and licked her face.

"I missed you, too, little guy, I'm glad you're all right."

He stopped to yawn, canting his head and rubbing it softly against her skin. His furry face leaned in, painting her cheek with his wet sandpaper tongue.

"Are you trying to say you're on my side, little guy?" She brightened up a bit.

"He recognizes the p-plights of individuals. He's a rather c-clever cat, even if he doesn't look it."

Bixby continued licking Cris's nose, causing it to become itchy. She felt a sneeze coming on and did her best to hold it back. Bixby bit her nose before jumping back to the ground and pawing his reflection in the water.

"I think you give him too much." She couldn't hold it back anymore and let the sneeze fly free. "You give him too much credit."

"P-perhaps."

They finally saw the van rolling around and gathered up their things as they prepared to load it up.

"J-just as you've been here for me, I'm here f-for you."

She nodded as the van came rolling to a stop in front of them.

"Heeeey! Are you guys ready?"

Alma jumped out of the passenger side, invigorated as ever.

"We've had more than enough time to p-prepare. If you don't m-mind…"

Glenn addressed her lack of punctuality as he gestured toward the bags. She helped him carry them as Cris got up to load the bag she had been sitting on. Cris tossed her bag in the back and went back to grab Bixby as

Glenn took a seat up front. Alma came up slowly behind Cris and gave her a big hug.

"Heeey, bestie! Missed you!"

Cris tensed up and tried to conceal her irritation, but Alma could feel the tension in Cris's body.

"Hey, what's up?"

Alma let Cris go and moved around in front of her, trying to read her body language.

"Sweetie, what's wrong?"

"Nothing, Alm. Did you and Kody have a good time?"

There was venom in Cris's voice, the likes of which even she did not intend. She immediately regretted it and tried to pull herself together.

"Is that what's bothering you?"

Cris looked up at her, unsure what Alma meant.

"I'm sorry we took so long; I really didn't mean to lose track of time like that. There was just some really important stuff I needed to talk to Kody about. I kinda couldn't...Er, it couldn't wait." She corrected herself.

"Talk to him about? Like what?"

"It doesn't matter; it's all settled. Now, are you ready? There's a motel not too far from here, and I don't know about you, but I need to get showered up!"

"Yeah, let's get going."

Cris climbed into the back of the van as Alma walked up to the passenger seat, standing outside, staring at Glenn.

"Hey, you're in my se—at," Alma sneered at him.

"So I am. As it t-turns out, I've claimed this seat for myself t-today. You're more than welcome t-to find an accommodating seat b-behind me, though. I hear there are lovely selections available t-toward the rear of the van." Glenn became callous with her.

"Are you serious?" She looked around him to Kody.

"Sweetie cakes?"

"Sorry, he called it."

"This is crap!" Alma protested.

"I'm sure Cris'll hook you up with something nice back there, maybe first class?" Kody tried not to laugh.

"Go on, smart ass. You'll pay for this."

Alma grinned evilly at him as she proceeded to take her newly furnished seat in what was apparently considered First Class. She shuddered to think at what Economy might look like. She closed the door and they took off.

She started petting Bixby, who now slept in Cris's lap. Cris tried her best to ignore Alma being so close, but had little to distract her. As they continued down the road, the ride was quiet. No one wanted to be the first to break the silence. Kody's short attention span quickly got the best of him however and he threw in a mix CD. Indie pop slowly reverberated through the speakers as he started singing along to the Rocket Summer's "Hills and ValleysBonfire."

Glenn looked over at him; Kody simply cracked a smile and waited for the chorus. He hummed along, waiting for Glenn to speak up, but he never did, so Kody took the initiative.

"The Rocket Summer."

"Wh-what?"

"It's the Rocket Summer. The band. Or man, I guess."

"Ah." Glenn reserved his opinion regarding the music.

"You like them?"

"I'm not o-opposed, if that's what you mean."

Kody laughed to himself as he realized what he needed to do next.

"Nah, man, it's not that simple! It's time to take you to school, buddy."

"As if I h-haven't already been."

Kody tapped the side of his head with his finger.

"Heh, it's not that simple. It's not about the book smarts. Like there's anything I could teach you about that."

Glenn released a small smile, vindicated.

"No, no, buddy. This is about music. This is the School of Soul. You gotta feel it."

"You think I d-don't?"

"Huh, fair enough. Let's find out. Pick a song."

"E-excuse me?"

"Pick a song. Anything. Find a CD around here you like and pick a song."

Glenn shuffled through the albums, trying to find a CD he recognized. Most of the CDs were unfamiliar mixes. Just as he set the albums down, a binder appeared next to him. He looked back to see Alma passing it up to him cheerfully. He searched through his own CD case and found one he thought to be suitable. He ejected Kody's CD and put it in.

"What's this?"

"'T-tales of Brave Ulysses.'"

They all stopped to listen, Kody finding Glenn's taste in music once again surprisingly decent. Kody let the song play through, stopping the CD after.

"Tell me about the song. Why'd you choose it?"

"B-because I like it."

Kody could hear Alma snicker in the background, but chose to ignore her in favor of continuing the lesson.

"Good, good reason. But tell me more about it. What does the song say to you?"

"It's about the t-tale of Odysseus. P-particularly his encounter with the sirens—"

"No, man, no. I don't mean literally. When you hear the song, what does your body tell you?"

"My body? N-not much, other than I like it or d-don't."

"Huh…how should I put this?"

Cris sighed, seeing Glenn struggling with what Kody was failing to explain. She searched through her bag until she found her mp3 player and passed it up front with a car adaptor.

"Hey, plug this in."

Kody hooked it up and pressed play. Cris began her block of instruction.

"Okay, Glenn, listen to me and pay attention."

They all sat quietly, listening to the introduction of "Lucky Denver Mint."

"Ooh, I love this one!" Alma got excited and joined in as the chorus kicked off. They listened through the first chorus before Cris continued her lesson.

"All right, Kody, pause it."

He stopped the song as Cris leaned forward.

"What did you feel when you heard that?"

"A little b-bad about myself, I guess. Apparently I'm not b-better than whatever's going on."

"Okay. Next time the chorus kicks in you're going to sing along with us."

"I'd rather n-not."

"Just do it. It'll be fine."

Glenn accepted the command with hope Cris was making an actual point. She reached forward, resuming the song. She and Alma sung along as the second verse played through. As it finished, Cris nodded to Glenn at the beginning of the next chorus. Kody joined in as well. She reached forward and paused it once the chorus moved along into the bridge.

"Now, Glenn, what did you feel?"

"I felt as if I was i-insignificant. I'm n-not sure what else beyond that, but that's all that makes sense."

"Now you're getting it! Going a little further, I think it's more than just that. You don't take music for just the album, or even just the song—though these are both important, too. You listen to each line. You hear it and feel it. It doesn't always have to make sense to you, and you might not even agree with the lyrics, but singing brings a little piece of your soul out with each melody, and lets you connect to the music as if it's going to become one with you.

That's why it means so much, why it's so important. To simply analyze the message and come up with an explanation might help if you've never heard a song before and don't understand it; but with music like this, you have to feel it, even if the words don't suit you."

All eyes were on Cris. Only one set of which she noticed, but she didn't allow herself to pay attention.

"Let me put it like this: think about how the 'Lucky Denver Mint' chorus goes. Now, do you really think that I believe I'm not as good or better than anything, or that I simply can't accept something? Of course not. But I don't believe that's what the song is really about.

For me, it's about believing that life is something greater than all of us. For me, they're saying, 'You're not bigger or better than life or the things that happen. You're just human, like the rest of us. Why can't you figure that out?' and once I did get that, it was 'You're a part of this, just like the rest of us. You're a part of life in our world. You aren't alone because we're all going through something: we all suffer, we all struggle, and we all make mistakes. It'll be okay. Just remember to keep your perspective and don't forget this lesson because we all lose sight of the big picture sometimes.'

"In truth, it doesn't really matter so much what they say, it's more about what I feel through it. Through that, I can express what's in my heart, even if I can't figure it out or say it…"

She stole only the slightest glance of Kody. "Now listen with your heart instead of your head." She reached up to turn the mp3 player back on.

They all listened as the song played through the last chorus to its conclusion.

"I—"

Glenn started, but Cris cut him off.

"Whatever you felt, whatever you feel…that's just for you. Share it only when you're ready and only with the people you feel you should."

She reached up front and took her mp3 player back. She exhaled, sitting back with a wide grin, petting Bixby.

"That was pretty impressive, Cris. You may be worthy of my music library yet," Kody said in an encouraging voice.

"Hey, and I'm not?" Alma wasn't content with being excluded.

"Alm, you built half of it."

"Oh, yeah." She giggled, the incident quickly forgotten.

"C-cris…" Glenn spoke up.

"Yeah?"

"If you don't mind, c-could you p-put on another song? I'd like to try and get a feel for th-this."

She was delighted to see she had gotten through to Glenn. She selected The Spill Canvas's "Secret Oath" before passing the mp3 player back up to Glenn. They all listened through her playlist, singing along to the songs they knew, and humming the rest. Only Bixby excluded himself from the activities, feeling such behaviors were both adolescent and beneath him.

The mood much lighter, they continued down the road in search of a place to get cleaned up and eat. They stopped for a meal at a small mom and pop shop, messing around in a nearby gift ship before getting back on the road. They passed a few motels throughout the late afternoon, and Cris, her former zeal now restored, was the first to point out that Kody didn't seem to be heading in a discernable direction as they continued on through Arkansas.

"Um…Kody? Where're we going?"

"It's a surprise."

"What? What kind of surprise?" Alma had to know.

"The surprising kind."

"Listen here, bucko! If you don't tell me exactly what it is you have planned, I'm going to…"

Alma leaned forward and whispered the rest into his ear.

"Whoa! Hey now! That doesn't even sound legal, let alone like something I'd take any part in."

"I didn't say I was going to give you a choice." Alma smiled deviously.

Glenn and Cris looked at each other, concerned and confused.

"Due to a sudden change of circumstances provided by this lovely young lady behind me, the surprise I had planned is now cancelled, to ensure the safety of everyone here, among other things." Kody smirked as he announced.

"Whhhhaat? That's so not what I wanted! Take it back!" Alma was devastated.

"P-perhaps you'd like to let me handle th-this?" Glenn suggested.

"Sure, go for it."

"For th-those of you still interested in th-this little endeavor our self-d-designated c-captain has decided to undertake, I'd recommend that you k-keep your behavior and attitude under c-control. If that sounds like t-too much for you to handle, we can c-cancel the event all together and you can remain with only the c-curiosity of what might've been."

"Wow, Glenn, never knew you were such an authoritarian. Glad you aren't my dad," Cris commented.

"I know, right? We'd never have any fun that way," Alma threw in.

"Guess we have to be good girls or papa bear over there is gonna take all the fun away."

"For sure, but we'll totally get our porridge before the day is done! Right?"

Cris couldn't help but to burst out laughing at Alma's oddly stated remark, unable to even understand what she was talking about.

"Are you serious? Did you really just make what I'm pretty sure was a Goldilocks reference?"

"Hey, you said 'papa bear.' I'm hungry and porridge totally made sense!"

"Oh my God, Alm, I'm really starting to wonder about you."

"If you just now started you already missed the train, sweetie!"

Alma and Cris couldn't stop giggling back and forth. Even Kody couldn't help but chuckle at those two and their bizarre bantering.

"This d-doesn't seem strange t-to you?" Glenn looked at Kody inquisitively.

"You get used to it. Hell, after a while you come to appreciate it."

"I s-suspect it'll still be a while yet for me then."

"You'll come around. Oh, hey, sweet! There it is!"

Kody got off the expressway and pulled into the parking lot.

"No way...we're staying here?"

Alma pressed her face up against the glass, trying to get a better look at the place. She marveled as she read the luxury hotel sign, and couldn't contain her excitement.

"Yeah. Figured we earned ourselves a nice little treat for the night. The best part comes tomorrow."

"What's tomorrow?" Cris asked.

"Not a day like all the rest. That's for sure." Kody grinned as he parked the van.

They all grabbed their evening bags as they got out of the van. Though it pained him to do so, Glenn carefully placed Bixby in his cargo pocket, trying to keep him out of sight until they got into their rooms. They entered the lobby, with a crystalline fountain showcased in the center, and noticed the glass elevators on both sides of the seating area. The lobby paled in comparison, however, to the glorious indoor swimming pool and spacious hot tub surrounded by actual live plants placed just on the other side.

"This is the most beautiful place I've ever been in my life!" Alma was nearly breathless." This is gonna be soooo sweet!"

She hugged Cris, and then Kody, and then Glenn. Though Glenn was still getting used to physical affection, he wasn't prepared to receive it from Alma, and was grateful that she released herself when she did. The soft warm feel of her voluptuously inviting body was a bit much for him, and it showed.

"This place is very nice, Kody, you've really outdone yourself," Cris said.

"I c-concur. Well done," Glenn pitched in.

Kody went up to the front desk, with Glenn following closely behind. Kody got out his wallet, getting ready to inquire about availability when Glenn stepped in front of him, reserving two suites instead. The clerk, far too busy behind the counter, took little notice and handed Glenn the card keys after running his credit card. They both stepped back from the counter when Glenn pulled Kody aside.

"I'll c-cover this one. C-consider it an expression of my g-gratitude."

Glenn went first, heading over to the elevator as the others followed suit. They all got on, and watched the lobby as it began to get smaller with the rising of the elevator. Bixby peeked his head out of Glenn's pocket, amused and pleased with the surroundings he felt were finally adequate for a cat of his stature. They split off into their separate groups as they made their way to their rooms to prepare for the night ahead.

27. Historically Inaccurate Drunken Fairytales

"Alcohol is a fascinating substance. Despite all the horrors attributed to it, only when someone is drunk do I ever trust that they're telling me the truth."

– Glenn's Chronicles

Kody and Glenn got down to the end of the hallway, opposite of the girls' room down on the other end. The halls stood lined with railings that oversaw the lobby, and through the glass separating it, the pool. The rich, warm colors used to decorate the walls and floors accented the place well. Kody felt it was a place better suited for royalty than everyday guests. He pulled out his key card and opened the door, letting Glenn go in front of him before following suit and closing the door behind him.

They both looked around the room, finding two full-sized queen beds facing an impressive flat-panel television display. The room itself had automatic lighting and a mini kitchen with a fully stocked bar as well as a full-size couch to supplement the beds. The bathroom contained a luxuriously large tub, which Kody suspected was intended for more than one person, and a mirror spanning the entire opposing wall.

"Kody, this p-place is phenomenal. Excellent c-choice."

"Thanks. And thanks for covering the bill, but you know I could've handled it, right?"

"I'm sure, but out of c-curiosity…how on Earth did you plan on p-paying for this? I'd be s-surprised if they'd even let you rent a room, p-particularly one with a bar."

"I have my Christmas money and the money I had been saving up for Alma's birthday present before she dumped me. And let's just say Geroge is well connected."

"Geroge has c-connections as far as Arkansas?" Glenn readjusted his glasses.

"No. Fake IDs." Kody laughed at the thought. "How about you? How're you forking out cash left and right? I somehow doubt you made that much back when you were still working at the ice cream shop."

"Ah, no. That job was j-just to get out and do something. My father set up a rather excessive t-trust fund when seeing a p-psychiatrist didn't solve my problems—his solution to p-parenting."

Kody gave Glenn a funny look, the latter immediately remembering the tiny fur ball now scratching at his leg. He opened up his cargo pocket, freeing the mini devil from his cotton cage as he shot out and immediately claimed the couch.

"Hey, fur face. You better not mess up anything in here, got it? This place is expensive! Capital on the ex."

"He'll b-behave, I'm sure." Glenn defended the integrity of his regal friend.

"He better."

The men got settled in, choosing their beds and unpacking their bags as they turned on the television. Kody flipped through the channels until he found an episode of *Futurama* and left it playing in the background. They both pulled out their shower stuff and looked at each other, trying to figure out who would go first.

"So, uh…how do we do this?" Kody looked down at himself, still reeking of muddy residue and the stench of stagnant rainwater.

"I don't have a particular p-preference."

"Eh, what the hell. You go first. I got something I need to work on anyway."

"Oh? Is it more of your p-poetry? I actually r-rather liked it."

"When did you hear my poetry?"

"I r-read some in the van while you were s-sleeping."

"You stole my notebook?"

"Says the p-petty larcenist." Glenn smirked.

247

"Huh?"

"D-did you forget? I did notice the absence of a c-certain photograph from my belongings."

Kody took a minute before he remembered what Glenn was talking about.

"So! My poetry! Big fan, huh?"

"Mediocre."

"Fair's fair. You'll have to give me a decent rundown on what I can do to fix it up then."

"Maybe after."

Glenn dropped his pants and tossed them onto his bed, causing Kody to avert his eyes.

"Aw, c'mon man! I don't need to see that! Man-junk, really? How about a little warning next time?"

"Oh, right, s-sorry. Still not used to others b-being around."

Glenn finished stripping naked and wrapped himself up in a towel as he headed for the bathroom. Kody searched around his bag, trying to find something as he listened to one of Fry's self-depreciating jokes. He dug around and couldn't find it anywhere.

"Maybe I forgot it? I wouldn't be that surprised..."

He dumped the bag out and didn't see it anywhere, deciding instead to let it go. He kicked his shoes off, getting comfortable on the bed, when he noticed a small microfiber pouch now sitting on the floor.

"Aha! Sneaky little bastard!"

Kody picked up the pouch and cleared off the rest of the bed. He opened it up carefully, pulling out a small set of sheers, some hemp string, and a bunch of small wooden beads. He measured out the string, loosely wrapping it around his neck to get a good idea of the length. He then started interlacing wooden beds with metal separators. He continued this process as *Futurama* ended and *Family Guy* began. He heard Glenn singing in the shower and found himself mightily pleased.

He heard Glenn's phone go off, vibrating out of his pants pocket and falling onto the floor. He got up carefully to pick it up, taking special care not to disturb his beads when saw that it was a text message from Cris. Being the petty larcenist that he was, he had few qualms with reading it.

"Girl's night out! No boys allowed! >;P Mwuah to Kody for me ~<3 Alm"

"Huh."

Kody had a devious idea, and texted his response. He set Glenn's phone back down and climbed back onto his bed, beads still in place. He heard the shower turn off and saw Glenn emerge from the steamy bathroom a few minutes later. Kody averted his eyes as a safety precaution.

"That might have b-been the most refreshing shower I've ever h-had."

Glenn was cheery and chipper, even smiling.

"Huh, glad you enjoyed it. Alm said they're having a girl's night or something, so it looks like it's just us tonight."

Glenn dropped his towel, getting dressed into flannel pajamas as he took a seat on his bed. He propped himself up trying to get more comfortable.

"I d-didn't hear anyone come by."

Kody lifted his head up, continuing his beadwork.

"Not that you would've with what sounded like The Who coming from your shower."

"Good c-call. What're you doing?"

Glenn looked over Kody's beadwork, trying to discern what he was working on.

"Oh, this?" Kody held it up, losing a few beads in the process. "Aw crap. It's a necklace for Cris."

"Why're you m-making a necklace for C-charisma?"

"She's been kinda lonely lately, and I figured this might cheer her up."

"Hmm, is th-that right?"

"Yeah. Me and Alma have been so couple-y and all lately, you've got that flying fuzz ball of death," Kody nodded toward the sleeping fur ball on the couch, "but Cris doesn't really have anyone. I just feel kinda bad for her, ya know?"

"I d-do. It's g-good to see you looking out for her. The shower's free, if you w-want it."

"Soon as I'm done."

Kody got up to find the beads that had fallen off and then sat back down to continue piecing the necklace together.

"D-do you mind if I ch-change this?"

"Not a big *Family Guy* fan?"

"J-just want to see what else is on."

"Yeah, go ahead."

Kody tossed him the remote. Glenn flipped through the channels. He passed a few interesting infomercials, but eventually stopped on a program about ocean life. Kody didn't like it at first, but he quickly got into the immersive world of sharks. He was so absorbed he didn't even realize he had finished his necklace until he tried to thread a bead onto his finger. He stopped and cut the thread, tying off each end of the necklace, before setting it down on the nightstand next to the bed. He got his shower stuff out as his notebook fell to the floor.

"Oh, hey, if you get bored would you mind looking something over for me?"

"Wh-what is it?"

"A little thing I've been working on."

Kody picked up the notebook, flipping through it until he found the right page and handed it to Glenn. He read the heading aloud.

"'C-cantankerous Cat: The Junior Feline C-catastrophe.' Intriguing."

"Thanks."

Kody headed off into the shower. Glenn fumbled around his bag for his glasses until he found them and read over the draft, amused more than anything else. He took some notes in the margin and left the notebook on Kody's bed. He pulled out his laptop and started it up when his stomach started growling. It occurred to him that Bixby had eaten more recently than he had. He looked over to his cat, still resting comfortably on the couch.

"He's g-going to need his litter b-box. I'll wait until later t-tonight when there's less s-staff around."

He continued looking around the room until he found a room service menu in the kitchenette. He scanned the options, unsure of what Kody would like, and decided on a set of cheeseburgers for the both of them. He ordered two and took his spot back on the bed.

He shuffled through various folders on his laptop without any specific aim until he came across his pictures folder and started going through it. He had numerous labels and dates scattered throughout for proper filing and reference, though he couldn't identify a particular need for having done so. He was going through a set of school pictures from his time in England when Kody came out of the shower.

"S-so?"

"Best shower ever. Hands down. What'd you think?"

"It's a good d-draft."

"Draft?"

"Oh, w-was that the final?"

Glenn looked over Kody's posture, assessing whether it was indicative of some type of offense he was not yet familiar with.

"No, no. I guess I didn't think about it like that."

"What d-do you mean?"

"I just kinda write."

"As in you don't revise or re-rewrite?"

"Not really. Just kinda write stuff down as it comes. I like it to be pure, raw, unedited. Gives a truly cut and clean feel, ya' know?"

"No, n-not at all. That was essentially a c-contradiction."

"Or that."

Kody threw on some lounge pants and kicked back on his bed, looking over to the couch to make sure the not-so-Cheshire cat was behaving himself. Bixby claimed no maladaptation, and instead passed his downtime in the most leisurely way possible: a catnap. Kody leaned over, trying to get a glimpse of what Glenn was doing when he saw a picture of a marginally attractive redhead.

"Hey, who's that?"

"Hmm?" Glenn looked up from his screen. "Oh, A-alexandria, one of my c-classmates from England."

"Alex, huh? I always thought that was kind of a hot name for a chick."

"Hmm, maybe. I s-suppose it suits her, though I think c-criminally insane is a better d-description than 'hot.'"

"Uh huh…you two still keep in touch?"

"On occasion."

"I see, I see…and I assume you boned her, yes? Boned her hard?"

"E-excuse me?"

Glenn looked over his glasses at Kody, trying to figure out exactly what he meant and what his angle might be. Kody threw him a friendly grin.

"C'mon, man, I know you're not just a boring stiff! No pun intended, of course. You're a guy, you got guy parts, and we both know how those work. It's no secret so there's no point in being shy about it, right? Not like I'm gonna tell anyone anyway."

"Why w-would you even be interested in something like that?"

"I dunno…I guess because it's just that everything about you is like a secret or something. It's a little weird. Knowing you at least get horny and lust after chicks makes you human, ya know?"

"I s-suppose." Glenn was somewhat reticent.

"So—Alex. Didja bang her?"

"I'm not n-nearly that reckless. Besides, in her c-case, I'm sure it'd be her that did the b-banging, as you put it."

"Huh, she does sound hot."

Glenn didn't respond.

"Okay, so it didn't play out with her. Didn't you date Cris's sister for a while? What about her? Insane or not, there's no way you'd say no to her."

"W-would you like to d-detail your sexual c-conquests with Alma?"

"Not really, but not because I'm shy or whatever; there just isn't much to tell. She likes to have sex. A lot. I don't think that's a secret."

Glenn cleared his throat, focusing back on his laptop screen. After a minute of watching Kody stare at him like an eager child from his periphery, Glenn set his laptop down.

"If I t-tell you, will you let this go and keep it a secret from C-cris?"

"Yep!"

"M-more importantly, are you actually capable of k-keeping a secret from Cris?"

Kody sat up.

"Hey. If I tell you I'm good for it, I'm good for it."

Glenn wiped off his glasses as he addressed Kody.

"Then yes, E-emma and I did sleep t-together."

"Holy shit, man! Are you serious?"

"It was a long t-time ago. We were foolish k-kids, not unlike you and Alma."

"We aren't foolish."

"You may not th-think so now, but you'd be s-surprised how easily a few years can c-change your opinion of yourself."

They both heard a knock on the door. Kody, having just spoken of her, thought for a moment that maybe Emma had come to make her own claim, as though she had come to prove Glenn's assertion or disavow it, but he soon realized how foolish such a notion was. He returned to reality and assumed Alma had changed her mind about her girl's night, deciding to come over for some extracurricular activities instead. He was considerably disappointed, however, when he opened the door to find a cart with food on it.

"Oh, I ordered d-dinner for us," Glenn announced.

"I see that."

Kody thanked the man with a considerate tip as he took the cart inside and rolled it up between their beds. Each of them started devouring well-cooked cooked burgers. Kody maintained his fascination with the subject of the hour.

"So what was it like?"

"Mostly ch-cheese and ketchup. Some p-pickles as well. And I th-think some spicy mustard."

"What?" Kody realized Glenn was talking about his burger. "Oh, heh, not that. I meant with Emma."

"What d-do you think? It was sex, like all s-sex. The fundamentals are the same and, as you seem well-ac-acquainted with the matter, I don't imagine there's much th-that would require explanation."

"C'mon, don't go all robot on me. Emma Roberts, buddy. She's a legend! They still talked about her when I got to high school."

"She's a fine woman, th-though—and don't tell Emma I said this—C-charisma is probably more attractive than her older sister."

"Seriously?"

"You've n-never met Emma?" Glenn cocked an eyebrow.

"Nah, just heard about her."

"I see. Well, if you're so enthusiastic about f-finding out what sex was like with E-emma, why don't you just approach C-charisma? They are sisters, after all."

Kody stopped eating his burger, eyeing Glenn suspiciously.

"That's not even funny. Don't joke like that."

"Why w-would you assume that I was joking?"

Glenn's manner was straightforward and humor free, as always.

"I'm with Alma, I love Alma. You know that."

"I know you c-claim that. Yet you c-came back from an evening in the woods with C-charisma. I find that interesting."

"Because we were looking for your cat! We got stuck out there because of the storm, that's all!"

Kody was getting frustrated and pissed off with Glenn, intolerant of being accused of defecting loyalties to his precious piggy toes.

"You're the one that's s-so interested in sex with other women. I merely made a c-comment regarding your interests. If that's a c-course of discussion you find offensive, p-perhaps you should leave it be."

"Yeah, that's enough for now."

Glenn set his plate down, observing Kody destroy the remnants of his fries. "Kody, I am c-curious about something."

"What's that?" Kody said, muffled, as a fry fell out of his mouth.

"C-could you tell me about your relationship with Alma?"

"Why?"

"You two seem to have a c-complicated and intricate history. And t-to be honest, I love stories. You're a writer, aren't you? C-consider this a practicum."

Kody stopped to consider Glenn's rationale as he licked ketchup from his lips.

"Hmm, I guess."

They continued talking throughout the night: Kody talking about his history with Alma, Glenn sharing stories about his time in England. The two passed a quiet, boring night with only marginal interruptions and a brief phone call, eventually dozing off with the television still blaring.

* * *

The girls watched the boys head off to their room as they made their way to their own. They opened the door, marveling at the pristine presence of the room itself.

"Cris, this place is amazing! I never wanna leave. Can we just live here? Can we do that?"

"Sure, if you start working in the kitchen, and also date one of the managers."

"Just one? I can handle that."

Cris kept quiet as she placed her bag on her bed, stretching out before lying down.

"Kidding! I was so kidding."

"It's fine, Alm."

Alma dropped her bag on the floor near her bed as she flung off her stinky clothes and plopped face-first onto the bed in her underwear. She turned her head to the side, watching Cris lie there staring at the ceiling.

"So hey, what's been up with you lately? You've been all weird and you still haven't told me why you're wearing my clothes."

"Huh? Oh, yeah…remember when we went looking for Bixby? We got stuck in the woods that night. My clothes got drenched so I borrowed some of yours."

"You and Kody?"

"Yeah…"

"Okay, about that…" Alma rolled over and sat up. "So, I don't want to ask 'cause it'll make me sound like the worst person ever, but it's been on my mind ever since G brought it up, so I have to: is there something going on between you two?"

"Me and G?" Cris cocked an eyebrow.

"No, you and Kody."

Cris continued staring at the ceiling not seeing anything. She sighed before continuing.

"No, there's nothing."

"Good. That's good enough for me. I know you would never do something like that, especially not to me, but when G called you Kody's girl it kinda got to me."

"What? When did G do that?"

"At the concert."

"The Bards concert?"

"Yeah."

"You were there?"

"No, G showed me the tape."

"Oh, huh…"

Alma got up and noticed the minibar for the first time.

"Oh, freakin' sweet!"

She ran over to it and inspected it thoroughly. It passed her inspection with flying colors.

"Alm, why are you messing with the alcohol? You aren't even old enough to drink."

"So? Why would a girl say no to free alcohol? That's just dumb."

"Um…right. I'm gonna grab a shower."

Cris got up and took her shower bag into the bathroom, closing the door behind her. She heard Alma making a commotion in the room.

"Hmm…don't want the fun-police showing up and ruining this…better handle that first. Cris, where's your phone?" Alma called through the door.

"In my skirt. Why?"

"You mean *my* skirt? I wanna use it!"

"Ugh, hold on."

Cris opened the door, handing the skirt to Alma. She closed the door and looked at her head in the mirror, lightly brushing her hair aside to look at the small welt that had been throbbing all day. She could see it had been bleeding a little, but not badly, and it was barely even noticeable unless she moved her hair out of the way. It was healing nicely, but she didn't want to take any chances.

She opened her shower bag and pulled out a small bottle of peroxide, cringing at the sight of it. She pulled out some Q-tips and dabbed one in the bottle as she brought it to her head, clearing her hair out of the way. She took a deep breath and hesitated, knowing how badly it was going to hurt. She gritted her teeth and gently dabbed it on the wound. She waited a few seconds until it started tingling and felt her head start to burn terribly.

"Damn it!" she screamed, though she hadn't meant to.

"Cris, sweetie, are you okay?" Alma was right outside the door, ready to bust in.

"Yeah, sorry. I'm fine. Just bad cramps."

"Wow, uh…'kay. I'm right outside if you need me."

"Thanks." She started the shower and stepped in.

Alma, done texting with Cris's phone, decided to order a pizza as she poured herself a drink. She mixed some vodka and orange juice, knocking back her concoction as she waited for Cris.

She sat around the room looking for something to do. She went over to the window and looked outside, watching the sunset. She couldn't figure out why, but it made her more excited. She loved sundown and felt as though she was more alive at night. She got a brilliant idea and rummaged through her bag until she found her third-choice bikini.

"Glenn so owes me…"

She changed into it and continued working on her bartending skills as she waited for her BFF. She looked over the minibar, trying to find something a little more suitable for Cris, and found some wine coolers she thought might work. She poured one into a glass, mixing in some vodka—not like Cris could tell the difference. She went back to Cris's bag and found her swimsuit, laying it out on her bed.

There was a knock at the door as a rather impish man with a cart arrived with a pizza. She shot him a flirtatious wink as she took to the pizza and closed the door, not waiting for any kind of response from him. The smell of freshly cooked pepperoni and cheese filled the air as Cris came out of the bathroom.

"Okay…the pizza I understand. Why is the alcohol now open and why are you in a swimsuit?"

"You saw that amazing hot tub downstairs. There's no way we don't get in there. And I wanted a drink. Don't worry; I made a lady drink for you."

"Alma, you know I don't drink. How do you even know how to make drinks?"

"How quickly you forget my mother," Alma said, playfully dangerous.

"Right…"

"Sweetie, we're on vacation. We're on the road, with no rules or limits! And you've been way too stressed out lately. You need to relax. Unwind!"

"Almy, I'm just not comfortable with it."

"Of course not, prude."

"I'm not a prude. I just…I don't know about this."

"It's all right; I'll be here with you the whole time. I'll make sure you make it back here in one piece. Now hurry and get changed! The Jacuzzi's a-callin'."

Finally clean, Cris didn't have it in her to argue with Alma. The burden of being the responsible, mature one had gotten old, and taking a load off for a while actually sounded like a decent idea. She took the drink Alma offered her as she saw her swimsuit laid out and waiting on her bed.

"My suit's already out? What if I had said no?"

"I would've made you do it anyway."

Cris took a sip of her drink, recoiling and setting it down before getting changed into her one-piece. As she watched Alma, she recognized a small hemp necklace similar to Kody's tied around her neck. She wanted to ask, but decided it better to forget about Kody for a while.

"How do you drink this stuff, Alm? It's so nasty! It just burns your throat!"

"It's only bad at first. Trust me; it gets much better the more you do it. Kinda like your first guy."

Cris scratched her head, shaking out any lingering doubts. She finished changing and forced herself to down her glass in one shot.

"Whoo, Cris! All right! There's my girl! Just make sure to take it easy!"

"Oh, God, that's horrible!"

Cris sat down for a minute, letting the alcohol work its way down her throat as she lay back on her bed. The room began to spin a little, but she otherwise felt fine. Alma made her another drink and they sat down together, gossiping and knocking them back until she felt Cris had loosened up a bit.

"Okay, pretty good, but remember to take it slow. We can't go anywhere if you get too trashed."

Alma looked at the size of Cris's glass and considered that maybe she had given Cris a little too much. She decided Cris had enough for now and brought the pizza box over to her bed. She offered Cris a slice. Cris refused.

"Are you sure? Have you even eaten at all today?"

"I'm just not really up for food right now."

"All right, we'll just skip to the fun part then!"

Cris felt a little funny, but chalked it up to the last few days and let it go. Alma grabbed her hand and helped her up, leading her to the door. Alma picked up her drink and finished it before opening the door and heading into the hallway.

"You meant now? I thought you meant later." Cris said.

"C'mon, look at it! The Jacuzzi's completely empty! It's totally a golden opportunity."

They both leaned over the railing, looking through the glass and seeing the steamy hot tub, water bubbling around, waiting for someone to come relax in it. Alma dragged Cris along and they both took the elevator down. They reached the lobby and strutted through on their way to the pool. Cris tried to ignore most of the men, and some women, staring at them as they went, though Alma enjoyed the extra attention from flaunting Cris around as a showpiece. Their time in the spotlight was cut short as they entered the pool section and climbed into the hot tub.

"There is nothing in this life more wonderful than this!"

Alma dipped her toes in first, slowly sliding her legs in and letting her body sink into the tub. Cris climbed over the side and dangled her legs, first getting used to the water before Alma pulled her in.

"This isn't a pool, Crissy; you just gotta jump in and live a little! This is life, right here!"

"In case you haven't noticed, my life has pretty much been in a place where jumping in and living a little are generally bad ideas." Her words were becoming entirely too long.

"You'll be fine, hun; we all get overwhelmed sometimes."

Cris lay back in the tub, sitting next to one of the jets and listening to the bubbles fizz as they glided along her back. They crawled along her skin, popping at the surface of the water. She lifted her hand, noting she couldn't feel it all that well. She found herself surprised at how slowly it moved. Alma kicked back, relaxing and enjoying the bubbles a little more than her friend as she shifted around trying to find the best spot in the tub.

"Wow, good bar. A few Screwdrivers and I'm already tipsy."

"Uh huh," Cris said, tranquil, trying to maintain control of her limbs. "How'd you like my little drinky?"

"What about your pinky?" Cris slurred a little.

"What? I said, how'd you like my *drinky*?"

Cris giggled at how Alma said "drinky," not caring or paying attention to the question itself.

"Looks like I'm not the only one who's buzzed."

"Buzzed? What're you talking about? Buzzed. Buzzzzz."

"Silly girl."

They lounged about in the Jacuzzi, waving their feet in the water and playing with the bubbles. Alma scratched her neck, bringing Cris's attention back to her necklace.

"Alm…"

"Hmm?"

"Almmmm, Almmmy, Almmmmy, Almmmm."

"Okay, clearly no more drinky-dinks for you," Alma giggled.

"You have a pretty neck."

"Why thank you!" Alma laughed at Cris, bringing her hand to her chest in an exaggerated gesture.

"You have a pretty necklace."

"Huh?" she looked down. "Oh, I do!"

Cris looked at her, clearly wanting an explanation.

"What, you want to know where I got it?"

Cris nodded.

"Kody made it for me a while ago, back when we first started dating. He's got one, too. He said it represents his inner strength. Something like self-reliance or I don't know. Back then I didn't really buy into all of his poetry crap."

"His poetry isn't crap!"

"I know that now. But at the time I really didn't care. I just thought he was hot. I didn't even know why he made me this thing. For a long time the only reason I wore it was because I couldn't get it off without breaking it. And I wasn't gonna risk hurting his feelings before I got a chance to ride him like a stallion."

Alma's devilish smile returned, her thoughts clearly starting to drift elsewhere as she looked up toward his room.

"You can't just use him like that!" Cris started getting loud and visibly upset. "He's a sweetheart! He's got a heart of gold, Alm! You'll hurt him with that attituuuude!"

"Which is why I don't do that anymore! Why're you yelling at me, Cris?"

"I dunnoooo!"

"Well stop, I don't like it. It's not like you, anyway."

"I'm sorry, Almy; I didn't mean it! I didn't mean to do that to you!" Cris started getting teary-eyed.

"Oh, hey, sweetie; it's okay! I'm fine, really! No big. All better, see?" Alma smiled, pointing to her rosy lips.

"I was just tired and it was so confusing...smelled so good."

"Um...Cris, that's just chlorine. And you probably shouldn't be huffing it."

"I didn't mean to, Alm, I didn't! You're my best friend!"

"Okay, you know what? We're gonna go back upstairs to lie down and watch a movie or something, okay?"

Cris looked into Alma's eyes, nodding along with her. Alma helped her out of the hot tub, stumbling a bit herself. She managed to get both of them out without incident, and they slowly made their way back to the elevator, leaning on each other for support. Now sopping wet and dripping in the lobby, they had the attention of the entire lobby. Cris, jovial and uninhibited, tried to talk to anyone near her. Several men tried to get close to her as Alma ran interference and tried to cover up her friend; however, one of them approached Cris as the elevator opened.

"Hey there, gorgeous. There's a pretty cool party going on with a bunch of fun guys upstairs. Wanna come?"

"Hell yeah I wanna come! Hey, do you think we could invite K—"

Alma grabbed her and pulled her back onto the elevator as they rode up to their floor.

"Cris, honey? Rule number one is not to take offers from strange men you don't know, no matter how good looking or nice they may seem, 'kay?"

"But he was having a partyyyy! I wanna go to the partyyyy and have some fuuuun!"

"If you wanna party then we can have a party in our room, where it's nice and comfy and safe."

"Oooh, our room is comfy! We can have a party in there?"

"We sure can, now come on."

Alma rubbed her forehead, her fun night out becoming oddly reminiscent of an evening dealing with her mother. At the very least, she was grateful for her deftness in dealing with drunks, though it was not how she'd planned to spend her night. She couldn't help but feel guilty, being the one responsible for the mess, but she had to focus on dealing with the matter at hand.

She walked Cris back to their room. As Alma closed the door behind them, Cris stumbled over to her bed, taking a cold slice of pizza from the box and scarfing it down. Alma grabbed a towel and tried to dry herself off, falling over and leaning on the wall for support. She managed to regain her balance and brought the towel over to Cris, trying to dry her off. She may have been more sober than Cris, but she wasn't sober.

"Look at that, you're making a mess everywhere!"

Alma tried to clean up as best she could.

"It's okay, housekeeping will come fix it! I'll call them!"

Cris tried to reach the phone on the nightstand, but missed and fell to the floor. She dropped her pizza and tried to pull herself up the nightstand, reaching for the phone. Alma got to the phone first, keeping Cris away from it and helping her back onto her bed.

"Cris, stay here, okay? I need you to just lie down for a while. I'm gonna go take a quick shower, okay? Can you stay here for me?"

"I can do that."

"Are you sure?"

"Yes, I'm sure…mother."

Alma balled her fist, catching herself before she started reeling it back. She took a deep breath, and she leaned her back against the wall for support.

"Okay, I'll be quick."

Alma shook her head and tossed her bathing suit aside as she went into the shower. Cris lay on her bed, trying to keep her balance as the room started spinning. She saw her phone on the nightstand and thought of lots of people she wanted to talk to. She opened it up and saw a text message from Glenn.

"Glennnnn? I love Glenn! Hiiii, Gleennnn!"

Cris started talking to her phone as she figured out how to open her text messages. She read the one from Glenn's phone.

"Hey, Alm. Guess you'll be missing out. 8:::::::> Kody."

"What the hell? I'm not Alm, stupid Kody! She wants to go fuck all the fun party guys in the lobby anyway! You should come hang out with me instead."

Cris realized she could send messages out as well as receive them and started sending them to different contacts. She soon found the keys cumbersome and difficult, deciding instead that she wanted to talk to one person in particular. She hit speed-dial.

"Hellllooo? Helllllllooooooo."

She couldn't figure out why the person on the other end wouldn't answer her and only kept making the same strange ringing sound. She wondered how they did that and tried to reciprocate, though with little success. She realized as the person answered, however, that it was the phone itself and not the person she had been hoping to talk to that had been ringing. She answered to a bad, static-y connection.

"Hey, Cris."

"Hellllllllllooooo? Oh, heeeeey, hi! Koooooooooodddddddy!"

"Um...Cris?"

"Hi, baby! I misssssed you! Did you misssss me toooo?"

"Cris, are you drunk?"

"I've got a seeeeecret! Do you know what it is? I beeet you doooo! 'Cause you're so smaaaaaaart and hannnndsooommmme! Wanna guess what it is?"

"Not particularly."

"No? What do you mean no? Toooo baaaaaad! I'm gonna tell you anyway!"

"Cris, you should just get some rest. We'll discuss this tomorrow."

"It's that I looooooooove yooooou! I said it! I loooooove yoooou!"

"Charisma. Go to bed. We'll speak tomorrow, all right?"

"Oh, God, I wasn't supposed to say that! Never miiind. Forget it! Byyyyyyye! You have such a cute butt!"

She snickered as she hung up the phone and turned it off. She couldn't lie down anymore; she had to sit up to stop the room from spinning. After spending a few minutes trying to regain her balance and settle her stomach, Cris caught sight of Alma coming out of the bathroom.

"Who were you talking to?"

"Whaaaaaaat?"

"Who were you talking to just now, Cris?"

"Wait, is someone heeereee? Oh, hey! Are the party guys...urk."

"You said 'I love you' to someone—"

Cris ran to the bathroom, pushing past Alma, and plastered the floor as well as many parts of the toilet in cheesy tomato sauce.

"Oh, Cris, honey!"

Alma poured her a cup of water and got a wet rag. She went into the bathroom, avoiding the more sticky spots on the floor and held Cris's hair back as she directed her to the toilet.

"Alm, I…urk!"

Cris heaved into the toilet.

"Don't try to talk, just let it pass."

Cris continued to heave, expelling anything and everything she might have consumed. Alma sat with her, trying to wipe off the smaller spots on the floor with one of the hotel towels. Cris finally finished, and Alma helped her up, handing her a cup of water.

"Feel better?"

"That's *not* how I would put it."

Alma walked her back to her bed and laid her down, setting a warm towel on her forehead. She set a bucket next to the bed and stayed up watching Cris.

"So, this is what I've been missing out on, huh?" Cris looked miserable.

"It doesn't usually go like this. Well, not always, anyway."

"If this is what I have to look forward to, remind me to never hook up with a guy, ever."

"It's not exactly the same."

Alma thought about Cris's remark, and began to see a few more parallels than she previously would've thought. She lay there keeping an eye on her best friend and trying to keep the contents of her own stomach down. She had just wanted to have a carefree night of kicking back and relaxing; she hadn't intended to get Cris wasted, or to get as drunk as she did. She needed to find a way to deflect her guilt.

She stumbled over to her bag, pulled out Kody's old notebook, and tried to read it while watching Cris lay on the bed next to her. She read some poetry aloud until Cris fell asleep, and held the book tightly as she passed out shortly thereafter.

28. The Morning After

"When in doubt, stick to what you know. Maintain your bearings until you can find the way through."

– Kody's Notebook

Hope, Arkansas

Cris woke up to a splitting headache. The world was bright, loud, and generally unforgiving. Her bed was wet, and she tried to figure out what she was doing in her damp swimsuit as she tried to get up. She quickly found this task to be overbearing, and lay back down, looking over at Alma, who was still passed out. She remembered drinking with Alma, but little else. She quickly realized she needed to pee.

She struggled to get to her feet once more, this time taking it slow and bracing herself against the nightstand for support. She took a few practice steps and found that as long as she didn't move too quickly she could walk all right. She made her way to the bathroom, stepping in putrid-smelling cheesy reminders of the night before. As she shook her foot off, she began to remember what she wished she could forget.

"How does Alma do this?"

She turned the lights down low as she grabbed one of the hotel towels to clean up the rest of the floor. She sprayed some air freshener, waiting to see if it would be enough as she tucked the towel under the sink. She started to take off her bathing suit when she noticed her phone was sticking out her top.

"What? How did this…?"

One of the many mysterious aspects of the night before, she left it unsolved. She took off her bathing suit and handled her business, setting her phone down on the back of the toilet to keep it out of the way. She then drew a warm bath with lots of bubbles, getting in and soaking the remnants of the night away. She leaned back, resting her head on the far wall, waiting for her headache to lighten up in the dim bathroom. She drew her fingers through her hair, checking her head, and found that the cut was healing much better. At least her head wasn't as bad as it had felt.

She looked to her phone, surprised there were no messages since sometimes Kody texted her a joke at night if he couldn't get to sleep. She reached over, opening it up to double check. It was turned off. She turned it back on, curious to see what awaited her. She set the phone down, waiting for it to start up, as she stretched her leg out. She let it rest over the side of the tub as she continued to soak. Her phone finally started, and she checked it to find she had some new text messages. She read them in order.

"LMAO! First night out huh? You so have to tell me about it tomorrow. Love you sissy!"

"Emmy? What did I…?"

She read the next one.

"We need to talk." It came from Glenn's phone.

"Need to talk about wha—Oh, God, I told Kody I loved him!"

She felt as though her heart stopped. She struggled not to hyperventilate. She had no solution for her situation. She began thinking about damage control and how she could explain this to him. Then she realized she'd have to explain it to Alma. She had no idea what she was going to say. Even if she said she was drunk, it still wouldn't help. Especially not with Alma. Cris took a deep breath and calmed herself.

"Don't panic, Cris. You're a strong girl. You can handle this. You're a mature, responsible young woman who is completely screwed! Crap. I need to call Emmy."

Cris called her sister, but was redirected to voicemail.

"C'mon, Emmy…even I'm up now, and there's no way your hangover is worse than mine!"

Cris began to realize that this was commonplace for Emma, that this type of morning was the kind she dealt with all the time. She wondered how her sister managed it time and again, and why. Cris received a little insight as to how she became the favorite daughter. She continued to relax in the tub, deciding that the Kody issue could wait until she had time to deal with it. Stressing now would only ruin her bath.

She soaked a little while longer before deciding to get out. She brushed her teeth and straightened herself up, wanting to be extra fresh to compensate for how crappy she felt. She went back into the room, going through her clothing bag and looking for something special. She had decided that today she wanted to make it memorable.

"I feel pretty today. I want something pretty."

She cheered herself up and found a somewhat wrinkly sundress in her bag. She took it back to the bathroom, doing her best to straighten it out before putting it on. She managed to get it straight as she drank copious amounts of water and took some aspirin while doing her hair. She started to feel a little better. She decided, as Kody had told them the day before, that since today was special, she'd do something special. She decided to wear her hair up, taking some time to put it into a nice chignon. A few stray strands got away from her, but she was mostly pleased with how it set.

She went back into the room, looking out the window to see a gorgeous day outside. It'd be a shame to waste it sitting around waiting for Alma to wake up, so she grabbed her key card and she snuck out. She made her way toward the elevator when she noticed someone she thought she'd seen before looking up at her from the lobby.

She couldn't place his name, but his lewd looks did not make her comfortable. She turned around and leaned against the railing, waiting for him to leave. She tried her best to be nonchalant and oblivious to everything around her. A lazily dressed but pleasant smelling man brushed passed her and drew her in with his musk. He moved to apologize for bumping into her.

"Oh, sorry. Excuse m—Cris?"

Kody stopped and looked her over, completely enamored. Her light perfume, her elegant form-fitting dress, the way the few strands of hair fell gently upon her neck, accentuating it gracefully. They locked eyes as their breathing slowed.

"Uh...hey..."

"Oh, hi, Kody." She blushed and shied away.

They stood there like children, chaperoned and paired off at a dance neither had chosen to attend. Neither spoke a word, nor did they seem to know what to do. They knew the moves, but they hadn't the courage to step up and dance. Something deep, primal sparked between them, and they did little to resist it. Cris began to quake as Kody warmed her with his presence.

"K-kody!"

Glenn caught them both as he made his way back to the room.

"Glenn! My buddy and friend! Hey, it's you! How are you?"

"Q-quite well, which hasn't actually c-changed in the two minutes we've been apart. Would you excuse us for a m-moment?"

"Uh, absolutely! Got more stuff to do!"

Kody rushed back to his room.

"C-charisma, you look lovely."

"Thanks. Thank you so much. That was a little intense."

"D-did you have a good time last night?"

"Oh, God, I didn't even think about that! Glenn, I'm so screwed!"

"First time getting d-drunk?"

"Ugh, and probably last, I hope. I just…wait: Kody told you about that?"

"I d-don't imagine how he c-could've. He d-doesn't know."

"What? But I…"

"C-confessed your love for me and my adorable b-buttocks?"

Everything in her relaxed at once, the tension in her body defused. She rode a wave of tranquility as her breaths flowed loose and free. She fell into Glenn, hugging him close with the gratitude of a princess whose lands had just been liberated.

"Oh, thank God! Glenn, I love you so much right now I could kiss you! You don't even know!"

Cris pulled him close, hugging him even tighter. He reciprocated while eagerly releasing himself. She straightened up and regained her composure.

"Glenn, seriously…thank you."

"Yes, well…for wh-what little part I p-played, you're welcome. B-but you do realize your feelings are c-coming through whether you'd like them to or not. And it d-doesn't seem as though the young man is t-turning away."

"This can't happen. I can't do this to Alma. What do I do?"

"At this p-point it seems like there is little choice but to c-confront him."

"What? But I can't do that! He doesn't know I like him…I think. If I confront him, that'll mean fessing up, which will create issues with Alma no matter how it goes."

"Maybe. B-but if you can't get this situation under c-control otherwise, that's bound to happen anyway, and much worse."

"You're right…I just need to get this under control." She stopped and contemplated for a moment. "Hold up. You said he doesn't seem as though he's turning away. What do you mean? And if he never got my message, then why was he…? Does he…does he like me?"

"Charisma."

She shot him a look.

"C-cris. Let this go. K-kody promised us all a surprise today, yes? I suggest you help Alma g-get rid of her hangover, w-which she's sure to have if she drank anywhere near as m-much as you, and help her get ready for today. And though you d-do look ravishing, I suggest c-caution in not luring him any f-further."

"Lure him? I just wanted to wear my pretty dress!"

"It is a lovely dress, on an even more e-elegant young woman. And in c-case you've failed to notice, most of the men here seem to th-think so, too."

Glenn nodded toward the man in the lobby, who was still standing there, watching.

"Ugh, what a creep. Okay, I see your point. I'll go get changed."

Glenn watched Cris walk away as he made his way back to his own room. He entered the room, seeing Kody sitting on his bed staring at a blank pad of paper.

"So much for early morning hot tubbing after picking up the supplies, huh?"

"I d-don't see why we c-can't still go. The girls won't be ready for a w-while yet."

"Yeah, I dunno…I just don't feel like going. Why don't we just focus on our little surprise for later today? Good idea, right?"

"I suppose."

Glenn and Kody got changed, both dressing up for the occasion. Kody wore a nice dark blue button-down dress shirt with dark cargo pants while Glenn went with the more traditional Henley with lighter khakis. They finished packing up their bags and carried them downstairs out to the van. They loaded it, hiding the groceries and their surprise supplies behind the far back seat.

Glenn checked around for his masterful pet of disguise, unable to find him anywhere. He remained concerned, but learned to trust his cat's intentions and knew the fur ball would reveal himself before long. If nothing else, he'd become hungry.

They waited around outside, Kody leaning against the van while Glenn stood in the parking lot, practicing the long-forgotten art of hacky sacking. Kody watched him; both surprised and entertained, while contemplating his situation.

"Hey, Glenn."

Glenn continued to hacky sack as he passively looked up at Kody.

"Hmm?"

"Nothing."

"Wh-what is it, Kody?"

"I dunno…what's up with you, man? How've you been?"

"All things c-considered, fairly well, I suppose."

"Yeah, it does seem that way. Good to see you turning around. Definitely a nice change of pace."

"I should like to th-think I have all of you to thank for th-that."

"I guess, but you did all the heavy lifting. We just helped."

"You've all c-contributed in your own way. Especially Alma."

"Alma? What'd she do?"

Glenn missed the hackey-sack, watching it drop to the ground. He knelt down to retrieve it, looking up to Kody as he did.

"Nothing m-much. She looked after me b-back in the woods."

"What? What do you mean?"

"She found me, h-helped me out. I wasn't d-doing well. She b-brought me around and helped me find B-bixby."

The expression Kody wore must've made his feelings plain. Though he loved Alma, he wasn't ignorant of her history. He remembered the stings she had cast upon him in the past. Still, he was a man of faith, even if he didn't believe in higher powers.

"We're f-friends now, yes?"

Kody nodded.

"And I'd e-expect you'd be honest with me."

"Definitely."

"Very well. She asked that I n-not tell you this, b-but it should be all right. You've a right t-to know, after all. Just k-keep it to yourself.

"You r-remember what you asked me b-before, about Jake?" Kody nodded. "Alma and I were b-both with her brother when he d-drowned. There was an accident on th-the lake, and I b-brought her to shore. D-did what I was able to k-keep her alive. I b-believe for this reason she feels indebted to me. That's why she t-tries so hard to help me. R-repay the favor, I imagine."

Kody took it in, but for once had nothing to say. He tried to understand where she was coming from, thinking that maybe it was such a close and personal event that she just couldn't share it with anyone who wasn't there. But from what he could tell, she'd closed herself off from him, and he couldn't do anything except watch as Glenn continued hacky sacking.

* * *

Alma rolled over, finding a clean and surprisingly fresh-smelling room. She stretched, instinctively reaching over for the side of the bed to catch herself, but found that the bed was so large that she was nowhere near the edge. She smiled to herself, having evaded her usual fate and achieving victory as she rolled over to the other side and fell off.

"Ow, fu—! Again? C'mon!"

"Morning, sleepy head."

Cris helped her up and handed her a glass of water with some aspirin. She took them and made her way to the bathroom. She came back to find a set of clothes already laid out for her. Her outfit was similar to Cris's, both of them being blue jeans and t-shirts, though Alma's was quite a bit frillier. Alma stopped to look Cris over, dressed down and inconspicuous, wearing her hair in a ponytail.

"What's up with you, girly? You seem so...casual."

Alma recovered much faster from her hangover than Cris.

"Nothing. Just felt like kicking back today, you know? Nothing special."

"It is something special! Kody promised us that thing today, right? We've got to get dressed up!"

"You go ahead, I'm gonna stick with this."

"You sure?"

"Yeah, it's comfy."

"M'kay, your call."

Alma stuck with the frilly shirt, but searched for a frillier skirt to go with it. She found one, though it was shorter than she would have liked. This was a little problem at most, and perhaps even a better solution. She got dressed and went into the bathroom to freshen up as Cris packed their things up.

"How're you feeling this morning?" Alma called out from the bathroom.

"A little bit of a headache, but other than that, fine. Got a nice bath this morning."

"Ooh, sounds nice. Hmm…do I have time to grab one?"

"I don't think so. I think the boys are already waiting outside."

"Oh, crap! Okay, lemme grab my stuff, and we'll head out."

Alma gathered her things and they both made their way downstairs, Cris being relieved that the creepy man in the lobby was finally gone. They saw a small gift shop on the way out, and Alma insisted that they check it out first.

"Almy, they've probably been waiting a while."

"I know, I know. I'll be quick. I just want to grab something."

"Fine. Hurry up."

Cris stayed outside, watching their bags. Alma went inside and searched around, looking at all the neat stuff they had. She caught a stern glance from Cris and hurried up, moving over to the junk food aisle and looking through the cookie selection.

"Hmm…"

"Can I help you find something, miss?" the gift shop employee asked.

"Hmm…maybe. I'm looking for some amazingly delicious chocolate chip cookies. Do you have any of those?"

"Uh…we have the regular cookies with the little chips in them."

"That's not really gonna cut it. You see, these are for my sweet honey bear. He does love his cookies so, and they really must be the best. Is this all you have?" she asked, holding up what looked like a day-old cookie.

"I think so."

"Then they'll have to do, I guess. Thanks."

She grabbed a number of cookies, placing them into a small bag with a Mad Bull as she paid for her things and left. She rejoined Cris in the lobby.

"Cookies? Hungry much? We're probably going to eat soon, you know."

"They aren't for me."

"Oh, right. They're for the cookie monster outside, right?"

"Yeah…" Alma trailed off.

She walked a few paces behind Cris on their way outside, keeping a keen eye on her bestie. No one was supposed to know about her cookie bear's obsession except her. Alma's insides lurched as she was overwhelmed with a weird irritation she couldn't describe. She chugged her Mad Bull and shook it off, continuing.

As they passed the checkout desk, Alma stopped, digging in her purse to turn in her key card. She looked over at Cris, who checked her pockets and shrugged before they continued outside. Alma stuffed the cookies in her bag, hiding them from sight.

"Lost it?"

"I guess…I swear I just had it, too!"

They got out to the van, where Kody was failing miserably in his first attempt at hacky sacking. They both noticed how fine the gentlemen looked, With Cris out of place and underdressed.

"Morning, ladies," Kody nodded to them.

"Morning, snuggle-cuddles!"

Alma ran up to him and hugged him especially hard, extending the embrace to hold him close. She pressed up against him and kissed his neck, leaving a faint imprint of lipstick. She watched Cris out of the corner of her eye, looking for any kind of reaction. She was more surprised at the painful expression she saw on Glenn.

"Missed you, too?" Kody replied, looking down to her. "Where do you come up with these names, anyway?"

"Just the first things I think of when I see you!" She nuzzled him like a puppy.

"R..-right. We're running b-behind, yes?" Glenn took a deep breath

"Yeah, he's right. We gotta get going. Big day ahead."

Kody took Alma's hand as he led her over to the van, the two of them piling in the back. Glenn resumed his position up front with Cris as his copilot.

"Mew, mew, mew" Glenn called out.

Cris looked at him. "What're you doing?"

A little claw dug into the back of Glenn's heel as a small gray fur ball found its way out from underneath his seat.

"So *that's* where you've b-been hiding. C-clever trick," Glenn chuckled.

Bixby climbed up the seat and crawled into Glenn's lap. The cat's purr reverberated as he got comfortable. Glenn petted him and started the engine.

"Uh…what was that?"

"B-bixby and I have worked out a system, in c-case he d-disappears again. Hopefully it'll save us some t-trouble."

"Hey, yeah, I had a question about that!" Alma called up front.

"Hmm?"

"When we were looking for him before…how did you find him?"

"What's up, Alm?" Kody became interested.

"When we were looking for Bixby, Glenn pretty much walked straight to him, like he knew where he was!"

"Oh, th-that?" Glenn's lack of interest became apparent. "I th-thought like him. If I was lazy, t-tired, and generally uninterested in anything other th-than myself, why would I wonder off in the m-middle of the night?"

Glenn nodded to Kody, who grinned at the implication.

"After th-that, I just took the p-path of least resistance. All downhill."

"Huh." Alma accepted his answer and snuggled up to her honey bunny.

Glenn looked back, and glanced over in Cris's direction. Cris turned away. He resumed his tasks, looking in the rearview mirror once more. Cris watched Glenn, and in particular, watched him watching her, Alma. She began to suspect he had ulterior motives for being so involved in her plight, but couldn't argue that he was all she had right now.

She began to wonder about the male fascination with Alma. She couldn't help but wonder if maybe she was always second-rate to Alma because she didn't expose herself at every opportunity. Or that she didn't hang off of every guy she found. She began to wonder if she should use her womanly wiles to win men's affections. If Alma was so determined to challenge her, then perhaps it was time she fought back. After all, even if she didn't have the experience Alma did, watching Emma taught her that she too had a natural grace and charm that few women could rival.

She shook her head and cleared it of such notions. She hated these thoughts. This wasn't her, and she wouldn't let it be. She focused ahead, humming a melody and trying her best to keep such ideas from her mind. She was better than this. She wasn't a saint, or a martyr, but she wasn't a home wrecker either and would not interpose in her best friend's happiness. She couldn't think so badly of Alma, or Glenn. Especially not him, as he was the only one she was sure had her back. Even if she doubted him, he was much like a brother to her, and Robertses always stick by their family.

29. Camisado Reverie

"The things we do for our friends, and ourselves, are what make us who we are. Even if we never understand why."

– Alma's Diary

Kody doodle, doodle, doodled in his notebook, writing whimsically for amusement more than any real purpose. A powerful buxom creature rested on his arm, snoring peacefully to herself, with only slight hints of waning alcohol curling from her breath. His drunken little angel. She murmured in her dreams, and he listened. He wondered what fanciful images danced in her head when no one else was watching. Was it a place she liked to be, or did she secretly abhor it? Camisado reverie. He recalled his charge to her, his oath. The girl who loved him. Who was in love with him.

He continued writing. The duck in the margin watched the pencil move with anticipation, unsure of whether to expect a new friend or an old foe. Loops and curls to form words instead of images: these were things the duck did not understand so well. A gulp with tension slid down its throat, and the feathery bird ball became rife with fear. He was not called the "combustible duck" for nothing.

Kody cast his eyes ahead to see where the day was taking them. He saw the sights, fewer woods, and more open fields. They were close. He was glad he could share this with his friends. His friends. Eyes right. Sitting there in her world, ever cold and still more lonely. He could feel her chill. No wonder she was always cold. Bright and cheery only because it was the heat that sustained her. Any less and she might freeze to death. He saw her spirit; he swelled with pride. Strength was her asset, though not her greatest.

Continue writing, eyes wander. Not words, meanings. Not expressions, impulses. Phrases, not actually phrases, but reminders of things common to the human experience one could recognize by the symbols on the page. Ideas more talky-talk talking, reality comes crushing in to teach the final lesson. If he could understand he would, but he was only a man, and a young one at that. Eyes down. Back to the paper.

He had five fingers on his hand, and two hands to count by. Mark those feet as well. Torso and a head, and other man parts, too. By anatomy, they could say he was complete. He would not agree.

"Kody, it's j-just up here, isn't it? Not t-too far before Texarkana?"

His head rose as Glenn called to him.

"Huh?"

"The p-place. It's the ramp before T-texarkana correct?"

"Oh, yeah. The 549 just off I-30." In his head no longer, he was needed elsewhere. "So, you ready, buddy?"

"Entirely. This should s-serve as quite a pleasant outing."

"Okay, if you guys aren't going to tell us about it that's your choice," Cris began, "but could you at least not talk about it? You're just teasing us." She wasn't feeling the pleasant ambiance of mystery as she looked out the window. Majestic green giants lined both sides of the road, their sagacious leaves and branches creating an air of enchantment.

Glenn looked back, watching Kody stroke the hair of the sleeping, dutifully anti-maiden.. Glenn continued to drive on as they closed in on their destination—the surprise. He pet the sleeping demon resting in his lap, who now seemed to define this one man as a friend.

Cris put her headphones on, finding herself uncomfortably out of place with the lack of melodious inspiration surrounding her. Johnny Rzeznik invigorated her with the tunes of "American Girl." Kody could easily overhear, as Cris did not rock out quietly. The two enjoyed the song as a disjointed pair.

Violently shuffling about as she produced an unusually loud snore, Alma scared herself awake. She looked up to see her shaggy snuffle-bug smiling down at her and couldn't be happier.

"Mo—rning!" She reached up and pecked his cheek.

"It's actually afternoon now, sweet cakes," he said, trying to break the news gently.

"What? Oh no, did I miss lunch?" she looked up to him wide-eyed.

"Nope, actually it looks like you're just in time."

Kody looked out the window as Glenn pulled off the western Arkansas interstate. They traveled down concealed back roads into an open, grassy field when they came upon a small state park. It was complete with idyllic wildlife, rivers, and the requisite worn-down and under-maintained wooden bench at the edge of the river.

"What? A park? It's so pretty!"

Alma was up, alert, and as boisterous as ever. Her piety overwhelmed the remnants of her hangover as she struggled to contain her excitement. Glenn pulled up and parked in the desolate parking lot.

"I wonder why it's so empty?" Cris remarked to herself as she put her headphones away.

"Too far off the beaten path, I guess," Kody shrugged. "Dunno why they even put a park this far back. It's in the middle of nowhere. Figure most people wouldn't ever find it. But…it's nice," he grinned as the engine stopped.

They all got out, stretching their legs and walking around the parking lot for a minute. Cris felt it unfair that she didn't get to wear her pretty sundress on such a beautiful day, but looking at Kody reminded her why such precautions were necessary.

The man walked his lady around as she wandered, enthralled with the beauty of the land. She was used to piers and woods; open fields with sparse trees and rich overgrown flowers were something new to her. She took her shoes off and ran through the grass, enraptured with the feel of fresh greenery beneath her feet. She dropped herself onto the ground and rolled in it, enamored with the feel of the earth and the hearty aroma that sprang from it.

Escaping from his man-friend's grasp, the agile fur ball joined the nature-rolling girl in her outdoor delights. It had been a long time since he had roamed free to stalk the bugs and plants of the wild land, his last instance being right before this season of his life began. Though he did not long for past days, the feel of dirt against his rough, padded paws was one of welcome comfort. He pounced on the girl, marking her as his prey, and she nuzzled him with enjoyment.

The three relatively sane remainders of the coterie stood standing in the parking lot. They took some time to plan their afternoon, filling Cris in on what they had in store. They unpacked the blankets and groceries as Alma regained enough of herself to join the hairy prince in his curiosity of what was taking place with the strange people friends.

"Hey, what'cha guys doin'?" she asked.

"I seem to recall something about a picnic?" Kody pulled out a cliché wooden basket that he had picked up for decoration.

"Are you serious? I freakin' love you!"

She ran up and jumped on him, nearly knocking him into the trunk of the van. He caught her, barely able to hold his own balance as she kissed him. She dropped down, running back into the field to find a place for them to eat.

"Looks like you might just win boyfriend of the year yet," Cris remarked sardonically.

"I thought this might be a nice change of pace for everyone. Figured maybe we'd get out without actually getting caught in a storm or some kind of chaos for once."

"Let's see if everyone can stick to the plan." Cris winked at him, forcing herself to stay upbeat.

"Hey, hey! Over here! Over he—re!"

Alma plopped herself down in a small, flat patch near the lake. Glenn grabbed up the blankets and food as he started over there. Cris dug around in the trunk, grabbing up some food to take over to the picnic spot.

"Hey, how's it going?"

Kody sidled up next to her, startling her.

"Hey! Try not sneaking up next time? Anyway, I'm fine. You?"

"Really?"

He looked at her. She noticed.

"Hmm…are you watching me?" she asked.

"Why, should I be?"

"No, not so much. And yes, I'm fine. Really. Don't you have more important things to be worrying about right now? There's a happy young woman sitting on a blanket all by her lonesome over there waiting for you, you know."

"I know. She'll be fine." Kody took on more chivalrous air. "I told you that I'd—"

"I'm not a charity case, okay?" Cris refuted him. "I don't need you looking out for me all the time, Kody. Quit running around pretending like you're my boyfriend or some valiant knight when you're not, okay? It's just not fair."

Cris couldn't hold it back anymore. Kody took a step back, taking a moment to think.

"Is that what you think this is? That I'm just looking out for you because I feel bad for you?"

"It doesn't really matter now, does it, Kody? Alma loves you. She's in love with you. And you love her, too. So that's where you're at, and that's what matters. Just go. Be with her, please."

"Cris, what're you...?"

She handed him the basket and pushed him gently over to the picnic blanket. She turned her back to him, leaving him no choice but to go. She sat down on the bed of the open trunk and took a deep breath.

She sighed, looking out at the abandoned parking lot and wondered what she was doing there. She pulled out her phone, giving her sister another try. It rang, but only briefly as she received a quick response.

"Emmy?"

"Hey, Crissy! How are you, baby sister?"

Hearing her sister's voice triggered an old, comforting familiarity inside, causing her spirits to drop suddenly. She missed her sister terribly, and it was evident in her voice.

"I don't know what to do anymore, Emmy."

"Cris, what's wrong? What happened honey?"

"I..." she said, trying to recompose herself. "I don't know what to do anymore."

"Okay, calm down, sweetie, and tell me what's going on. Did someone do something to you?"

"No."

"Then what is it?"

"I just...it's so hard, you know?"

"I'm trying to, but you have to give me a little more to go on than that."

"I'm sorry." She managed to calm down a bit and figure out what she wanted to say.

"You remember that boy I told you about?"

"Kody?"

"Yeah."

"What about him? Oh my God, did he touch you? I swear to God I'll kill him!"

"No, no, it's not like that. I...I think I'm in love with him."

"Oh! Wow...um, wow...ok, that's Alma boyfriend, right?"

"Yeah, and I don't know what to do. I don't want to hurt Almy, but I can't keep being around him like this all the time. It's driving me crazy!"

"I'm so sorry, honey. Do you want me to come get you?"

"Em, I'm halfway across the country."

"I don't care! You're my baby sister. I'd drive halfway across the world, even if that means hopping ferries and a long-ass boat ride."

Cris chuckled.

"No, don't. I'll be okay. I've just got to figure all of this out."

"Okay, listen up, Cris! Roberts women are tough. We can survive anything, no matter what comes at us. I have complete faith in you. I believe that you'll make the right decision and do what's best, even if it's not exactly what you'd expect. Do you believe me?"

"Ye—" She stopped to take a deep breath. "Yes."

"Good. You'll come out of this on top."

Glenn came around the corner of the van, standing a respectful distance, waiting for Cris to finish her phone call.

"One second, Glenn," she said to him, then returning her focus to the phone.

"Hey, Em? I gotta go, okay?"

"Why? What's up?"

"Nothing. I think they're waiting for me."

"Is Glenn there?"

"Yeah."

"Put him on the phone for a minute."

"What? Okay."

She got up and walked toward Glenn, handing him the phone.

"Hmm?"

"Emma wants to speak with you."

"O-oh."

He stepped around the corner of the van for privacy.

"Emma, h-how are you?"

"How's my little sister?"

"C-charisma? She's—"

"Be honest with me Glenn."

"She's been b-better."

"What's the deal with this kid, Kody?"

"She b-believes she's in love with him."

"And what about him? Does he love my sister?"

"It's im-impossible to say.""

"Listen. I'm trusting you here, so don't fuck this up. You *will* look after her and make sure she's taken care of, got it? I don't care what you have to do, but you will get it done. You owe me that much."

"And I assume this is all about your s-sister and has nothing to do with the p-past?"

"Put her back on the phone."

Emma was curt and cold-blooded when it came to dealing with Glenn. Unwilling to cross her, he gave the phone back to Cris.

"Em?"

"I'm not going to keep you, okay? But you let me know if you need anything, got it, little sister? I'm serious."

"Will do."

"Good, keep me in the loop. Love you bunches and bunches brat!"

"Love you, too, sis."

Cris hung up. Glenn took a seat next to her, offering her a shoulder to rest on. She took the opportunity for a short reprieve, calming and collecting herself. Despite the beads of sweat rolling down her back, the hot summer sun did little to warm her chilled spirit. She looked up to Glenn.

"Why'd you come over here?"

"S-something seemed off with Kody. Seemed only n-natural you'd be the cause."

"Heh...thanks."

"I meant that in a g-good way, of course."

"Uh huh...what'd Emma want to talk to you about?"

"She just wanted t-to know how the trip was going."

Cris stared at the pavement, watching a small squad of ants carry what looked like crumbs or small ant boulders into the grass.

"I h-have an idea. Do you have your dress?"

"What?"

She stared at him, clearly lost.

"D-do you have it?"

"Yeah, it's in my bag."

"P-put it on."

"Glenn, what're you—"

"You w-want to wear it, right? That's why you c-chose it this morning. Because today is a special d-day. For you, and for all of us. And it's far too lovely t-to spend it upset when you can t-truly enjoy yourself. I've spent t-too many solitary nights in the d-dark to do anything other than pass on this lesson. Now get c-changed. I'll go finish setting up."

Glenn lifted her head up, offering a callow smile. He dried her face of a tear or two that may have escaped, and helped clean her up. He nodded to her, and she let her hair down as she climbed back into the van. Glenn made his way back over to the picnic site.

"Heeeeey! Where's my bestie?" Alma was covered in grass stains, though it was evident she couldn't care less.

"She'll be a m-moment."

Glenn got back to see Kody making sloppy peanut butter and jelly sandwiches. Bixby wandered near the water's edge, searching for something. Alma lay on her stomach on the blanket, eating one of Kody's sandwiches while dangling her feet back and forth through the air.

"Hey, Kodykins, I like the things you doooo. Hey Kody, if I could I would be yooooou…" She sang to her sandwich

"Alm, what're you talking about?" He looked down at her.

"Nothin'." She continued to wave her feet in the air.

Glenn sat down as Alma caught sight of her bestie finally making her way over. Following Alma's line of sight, Kody now saw Charisma, redefined by the lovely summer dress he had caught her in earlier in the morning. Cris took her seat next to him, cheery and pleasant as ever.

"My, my, my! Who's this foxy lady?" Alma playfully nudged Cris as she tried to catch the crumbs that were falling out of her mouth.

"It's such a pretty day…I figured 'why not?'"

"Good choice!" Alma gave up hope of salvaging the pieces of her lost sandwich and grabbed another one.

Cris and Kody looked at each other: Kody with wonder, Cris with reserved pride. He offered her a sandwich, which she accepted. Glenn took one as well, and the four of them sat there through the breezy summer afternoon enjoying a quiet little picnic. They played Frisbee, teased the cat with cattails, and lay on the grass picking images out of clouds. They stared off into the sky, catching drafts of wind and feeling the subtle rotation of the Earth. They carelessly let the afternoon to pass them by.

"Qwaack!"

Alma sat up, seeing a small flock of ducks drifting along the bank of the river. She watched on as the courageous feline defender guarded his flank before preparing for an assault. She tugged at Kody's sleeve, causing him to sit up. He glanced over at her before following what she was looking at. He nudged Cris, who then helped Glenn up, and they watched on to see just how devious their latently Spartan ally was.

Bixby chased after one of the younger ducklings, unable to catch it. He couldn't understand its waddling ways, but wasn't going to be defeated by some small yellow-feathered rat. He disappeared behind the river brush, crawling along the banks as his claws stuck in the reddish-brown mud. Brushing against the weeds, his whiskers tingled as dust escaped through his tiny kitten nose. The sound of the sneeze alerted his quarry, but he was faster than the little squeaker and they both knew it. He pounced, and his victory was assured.

"Qwaack, quack, quackkk!"

He was roughly tossed aside by one of the larger, funny furried birds as it nurtured its young and returned it to the flock. This insult to his feline pride was too great, and he could not overlook this slight.

The over spirited meow-meow was primed as several much larger quack-quacks surrounded him. He bared his fangs and sunk his claws in deeply.

He felt an enormous force lift him from the Earth, and he lashed out with all his fury. Glenn winced as the cat cut through his sleeve and right into his arm. Glenn brought the calming fury ball back over to the blanket. Bixby refused to retreat, but was more comfortable with the concept of regrouping for the time being.

As the afternoon carried on, Alma remembered a little surprise she had planned for her sweetheart. She ran back to the van barefoot, pulling out her semi-fresh cookies from the hotel gift shop. She placed them in a ruffled white bag with a cutesy tag bearing Kody's name. She brought the bag back to the group, keeping it a secret surprise from her snuggy-wuggy.

"So, sweetiekins…I got a little something for you." She showed him the bag, but kept the contents hidden.

"Hmm? And what might that be?"

"You'll have to guess…but I'll give you a hint."

"'Kay. What's that?"

"It involves choc—"

He tackled her and wrestled the bag from her, running a safe distance before opening it. He pulled out the contents and ripped open the bag, devouring cookies individually without taking bites.

Glenn was astonished. "W-wow."

"Boy really likes his cookies." Cris was aware of how much Kody liked cookies, but she had never actually witnessed him firsthand. Alma rushed him, knocking him to the ground and wrestling the bag back from him.

"No! Down, boy! We eat our cookies slowly around here!"

"But…so good…!" Kody tried to get them back, but she kept them firmly out of his reach.

Kody, having over gorged himself on cookies, was debilitated. He was unable to fight back and was left at Alma's mercy. She helped him back to the picnic blanket, laying him down. He could barely move, though a blissful expression was strewn across his face. Alma smirked, having outsmarted her clever boyfriend once again. Cris looked him over with reservation, but Alma's lack of concern for his condition implied he'd probably be okay.

Glenn cast his gaze to the ground. He dug his nails into his palms, breaking the skin as his concept of self-image faded from the scene. Apprehension gripped him, and the existential facets of living his life ripped at his core. The faint blood seeping from his cat-friend's inflicted wound awoke within him a primal lust for his own demise. Mockery, self-depreciating loathing. Abhorrent self-hatred. An insult to his mental frame. He got up and left.

Back to the van he went, camped out in the front seat, debating, debating, debating what to do next. Fluorescent sun beaming too bright: someone ought to turn the light down. Air thin, weak, not made of water or gas, just a paper concept like the grinding of gears.

"Glenn!"

Eyes up. Who's there? Oh. The girl. The not-Roberts girl, he thought. He held no obligation to her other than his own carnal desires.

"Glenn! Hey, can you hear me?"

He could use this. For him, and for her. The assignment of one who charged him. Restitution for another forgotten crime he was guilty of. Toward the elder Roberts. A crime they committed together. Why did only he pay the price? But he always paid the price. Shaking, shaking, shaking; why is he shaking? Oh, the girl is shaking him. Why doesn't the girl stop shaking him?

"Glenn, snap out of it!"

Oh, she wants his attention. Not him. His attention. Its attention. She just wants the attention of it. It's waking up.

"Hmm?"

He looked up. He saw Alma with an unusual look of fear upon her face, as though she was concerned about something. He couldn't fathom what. He realized now his head was in his hands.

"Glenn, are you okay?"

"Of c-course. I'm fine. Why d-do you ask?" He couldn't remember.

"You just left. You came back here and started rocking back and forth. You don't remember?"

"Silly girl...of c-course I am. I'm right as r-rain, see?" He smiled a decrepit smile. "If you'll e-excuse me, I'd like to go for a d-drive. It's secluded b-back here, I imagine it'd be a nice place to g-gather my thoughts. Fresh breeze, low t-traffic and all."

"Whoa, hey there on that train of ideas, bucko. If you think I'm letting you drive after something like that then maybe you really have lost your mind. Are you even fit to drive?"

"I've d-driven this far."

Alma could see she wasn't going to win any debates with him right now.

"Okay, fine. Well, guess what? I wanna drive now. And since I haven't gotten to drive in a while and I'm a lady, I'm thinking it's my turn. You can ride along if you want."

She'd out maneuvered him.

"A-acceptable."

Or had she?

She started up the van as she yelled out the window, "hey, we're gonna go for a little drive." Cris recognized the urgent look in Alma's eyes and trusted she knew what she was doing. Cris nodded and waved, looking after Kody in his cookie coma. Alma put in a CD as she and Glenn pulled out of the parking lot and left.

30. The Breath in Your Lungs

"I'll never forget that amazing moment when I finally knew I was falling in love."

– Cris's Journal

Through the trees and around the bend, the van rickety-raddled its way through the woods. Thump, thump, bump, thump, over the rocks and branches that covered the back paths and trails. Though it had once been well paved, it didn't seem as though anyone had cared for this area in a long time. Alma looked over, Glenn sitting in the seat in which he sat. He was quiet, even for him.

"Hey, you all right?" It was a simple enough question.

"I'm f-fine." A simple enough answer.

"You don't seem fine."

"Hmm…"

He stared out the window. His eyes fixated upon something, though he saw nothing. He felt out of place in his skin, a shell unmeant for habitation. He was the invader, the intruder, and soon the warning bells would ring. He had nowhere to hide, for he himself was his hiding place. A horrible disguise, he knew, but he was a master of little else. A jerk and a stop. His corpse shifted forward, restrained by the fabric harness in this the conveyor of motion. What had happened?

"Glenn, get out of your head and talk to me! What's going on?"

Words. He understood words. He had been taught as a child. He was a child once. He used to make sounds with his mouth—gurgles, urgles, squeams, and squeals—until he got what he wanted. It had been so long since those glory days; he had forgotten it served other purposes as well. He could make his ideas into sounds, and for little worth, sometimes people could guess what he meant. This, he believed, is what the girl wanted now.

"What's g-going on? You wish me t-to speak?"

"Something, at least! I'm really worried about you! I thought things were okay now, but you look worse than ever!"

Eyes wandered all over, they were so horrible at following directions. But with the ears they worked together and used the brain to get "words." A rumor about appearance less than appeasing. They accepted his request to verify this, and made their intent toward the mirror. They reported trembling and an uncertain disposition. His arm still reeked of blood.

"Oh, right...s-sorry. No r-really, I'm fine."

He turned and smiled. But the face he beheld did not return such a kind gesture. A face that always smiled. He was rejected even now. Had he truly failed at such a simple task? It was impossible to tell. He might've frowned. He scratched his arm.

"Oh my God!"

Religion invoked in his name. Now this truly was a first. He looked up, but there was no god in sight. He remained disappointed.

"Glenn...why...did you do that to yourself?"

It was talking to him again. No, not it. Her. The object of his infatuation. The ever-loving tease. The existence brought forth to test his willpower. Odd, he would've thought to fail by now. He felt pressure on his sleeve as it came back. She was pulling it. Why? Oh, there were marks. Scars. She was seeing the scars. Was this her first time? It must've been. That's why she seemed to care. People always care the first time. It was less than comfortable. He pulled the sleeve back down.

"Art, of c-course. I'm an a-artist. A bit of a self-d-decorator, really." He laughed to himself.

"That's hardly how I'd put it. Glenn...that's not okay. How long have you been doing this?"

"M-my works?"

"I guess."

"Isn't an artist always an a-artist? One is b-born such, and yet d-doesn't realize it until the first time he finds his instruments: be it a p-pencil, brush, chisel, or knife."

Alma shook her head.

"Glenn!"

He scratched his arm again, the itch now more apparent with other eyes on it. It wouldn't go away. He kept scratching. Itch, itch, itch; scratch, scratch, scratch; blood, blood, blood. He broke the skin.

"Glenn, stop it!"

Alma grabbed his hand, pulling it away from his arm. Soft, firm, delicate unloving hand. She only wanted him when he didn't want himself. He could think of torment no better.

"Don't t-touch me! Like you c-care! Why should I st-stop anything? Not as though it m-matters…"

She was taken aback.

"This is no p-pain of yours! I b-bleed by my own right! I c-chose this! It is the only thing I chose, so let me b-bear it in peace!"

She was scared and afraid, unsure if it was more for herself or for him. But this couldn't continue. She stood her shaky ground.

"What peace?"

They stopped, the both of him. They considered her quandary. Were they ever at peace? *They*? He meant him. There was no one else here. Was *he* ever at peace?

"So what? What do you p-propose? Do you have some sort of m-magical solution that so many others c-could not find? Kody, C-cris, Alex, Emma: they offered little if anything."

"I don't know, Glenn. I'll be honest. I don't have an answer or solution. I can't promise you anything. Have you tried seeing a doctor about this?"

"Of c-course. For all the good it did. My d-doctor so well trained. D-despite her own proficiency, I think her time was b-better spent planning p-plastic surgeries for her retirement than playing around in my head. M-medications, pills…sometimes they p-put me to sleep, sometimes they wake it up. Never helpful, n-not for long."

"Okay, so what do you think would help?"

"I think—wh-what *do* I think? What do *I* think? Is there solace to b-be had? Will there ever be p-peace? C-can I be salvaged? Or am I waiting to p-plunge into the ocean? Take a deep breath. What d-does it find? It finds air.

That's new. The world has started b-becoming the world again. When d-did this happen? When she started speaking. She—"

"Hey!"

She guided his face with her hand, he unable to look away now. He looked into her eyes. He looked at her. He saw her.

"I n-need you."

Her heart raced as she recalled the night in the woods. The cool winds and the quiet of the rippling creek. She remembered the desperation on his face then, just as she saw it now. She remembered her strength that night and felt it surging through her once again.

"Glenn, we've talked about this."

"D-don't touch me like that."

"What?"

"You ask, you asked m-me. You said t-to him 'What d-does he think would help?' He tells you, and you r-refuse him. Again. C-cruel. If you wish to c-cut him, go ahead. He d-doesn't mind. He finds mercy in it. Better than f-forgetting him." He pulled back his sleeve, offering up his desecrated arm.

"Glenn, knock it off!" She smacked him upside the head. He stopped. Silence struck him quite suddenly.

"Now quit being such a damn baby! If you have problems, fine. Talk to me about it. I want to help; I do. But don't go losing your mind and throwing a fit every time I tell you I won't make out with you. It's *not gonna happen!*"

He sunk into his seat. Shame covered him. He began to weep.

"Oh, for Christ's sake!"

She started up the van and continued on the trail. She only now realized how curvy the path had been. She wasn't sure which way led back to the others.

"Great."

"I-I...I'm sorry."

"Huh?" She looked over at him.

"Alma...you're trying to h-help me...," he said, sniffles and tears receding.

She waited to hear if he had anything more to say. Whether he had simply forgotten he spoke up, or had nothing left, she couldn't tell.

"Yes, Glenn, I am trying to help you. And I will if you let me. But I'm not going to spend the rest of my life picking up the pieces and cleaning up other people's messes. I've spent way too much time doing that already."

Her mother came to mind.

"I d-didn't—things get clear and things b-blurry, fade away. When I c-can't see myself anymore…the things that matter are all that's left. I c-can still see you, and I c-can't look away. B-but if you disappear—p-please don't give up on me."

She listened to Glenn's earnest appeal. She thought back to that cold night on the shoreline and wished she could forget it. Her conscience refused to shut him out, even if she was beginning to believe she should.

"I'm not gonna give up on you, all right?"

"Th-thank you."

"Yeah, yeah…"

"Alma."

"What?"

"There's one m-more thing…"

"What is it?"

"I…I can't."

"You can't what?"

"N-never mind."

She looked him over, quickly shifting her line of sight back to the paths and narrowly avoiding a squirrel.

"Don't play with me, Glenn. I don't have a whole lot of patience left right now. If you have something to say, say it."

"It's important, but I c-can't offer it up without a pr-price. Too much work to let it g-go for free."

"What…? What are you talking about now?"

His lips curled back.

"What if there was a w-way to bring your b-brother back?"

Alma stopped the van once again, her throat tight at the simple suggestion that she might see her brother again. She was all too aware of how impossible it was; she had wished it every waking moment for years. Even so, the desire had not waned.

"Glenn, you've clearly lost it. Stop with this madness and let it go, all right? Jake's dead. He can't come back from that."

"Are you s-sure?" he cocked an eyebrow. "K-kiss me, and I'll tell you w-what I know."

"Damn it, Glenn, for the last time…!"

"I can provide p-proof that it's possible."

This caught her attention, and the longing rose up once again.

"You gotta be kidding me. You realize that if you are in any way fucking with me, I might actually kill you."

"Y-yes."

"Keeping that in mind, and for the last time, what the hell are you talking about?"

"The p-price."

Alma looked him over. She debated whether she could trust him. He didn't seem altogether stable but, at the same time, he knew more than any other about her brother and most everything else. Whether he was messing with her or not, this was the best opportunity to get information out of him—whether it was to help him, or find out about her brother. Once again, she looked him over.

* * *

Kody lay there, staring up at the sky. His stomach was terribly upset, and despite his best efforts, he was unable to accomplish much of anything. This must've been apparent as he had been marked as prey and thusly sat upon by a virile kitten with an overambitious attitude. The cat landed nimbly on his chest, and started pawing at Kody's chin. Though clearly annoyed, Kody was unable to accomplish much.

"You're gonna take that from him?" Cris watched on, cheery as ever.

"I…ohh…cookies…"

She got up and plucked the bitty kitty from the lazy boy's face. She dropped the cat off to the side, where he continued to play as he amassed a collection of bugs. Kody would've extended his gratitude, were he able.

"My, my, my…what're we going to do with you, Konrad?"

"You still…uhh…"

"Aw, you want me to hold you?" She patronized him.

"Nah, I'm…ugh…I'm good."

He tried to sit up, and with much effort, and slight intestinal catharsis, he managed to do so. Cris left him his dignity by kindly not taking note of his less flattering bodily functions as she took a seat next to him.

"So, here we are," she started.

"Yup. We are here."

"It really is a lovely day."

"Heh, yeah…"

He took a moment to admire her dress.

"So, hey, I'm really sorry about earlier. You were right. It was wrong of me to assume you just needed someone to look out for you or whatever. You're a strong girl and you can handle your own."

"Yeah, you're right. I am."

"Heh, anyway, I didn't mean anything by it. I was just worried about you."

"I know. And I appreciate it. Sorry for giving you such a hard time about it. I guess I'm just not used to people trying to look out for me. It's always been the other way around."

"Sounds tough."

"Not as much as you'd think. I've got some good friends."

She grinned, brimming with a calm warmth. Her own confidence served as a wave of comfort to those around her.

"Sorry I've been so crazy lately. I've had a lot on my mind, and I guess I just wasn't thinking straight." Cris began to reflect.

"Lot of that going around. Take our buddy, for example."

"Yeah…I hope he's okay."

"As okay as he can be, anyway. He's in good hands. Alm'll take care of him just fine."

"Yup."

She could do this. They had been friends long before anything else; she could continue on this way. She didn't have to hurt anyone. She was refreshed and relieved.

"Oh, before I forget…"

Kody leaned back, digging his hand into his pocket. He lost his balance and fell backward as he found what he was looking for, pulling a beaded string out of his pocket. Cris helped him up, and he took a deep breath to help his stomach settle. He stood up as she looked at him quizzically.

He knelt down behind her, brushing her hair aside as he laced the beaded string around her neck. His fingers grazed against her skin, smooth and refined, as though it had never been worn or broken. He wondered if this was a trait shared by all Roberts women, or reserved exclusively for her. He caught a waft of her relaxing, airy scent as he tied off the ends of the necklace together.

He returned to his seat, keeping his focus and maintaining his bearings. She looked down, taking only a moment to recognize what she now wore.

"Kody...thank you." He felt her sincere gratitude.

"Heh, it's a little charm. It isn't much, but it's helped me through some hard times."

"What's it mean?"

"Reminds me of an old book I read once. I like to think of it as something like, 'the path of self-reliance is something you should know well.' Until I found Alma, I was always alone. I mean, I guess everyone is, but I dunno...I needed something to hold on to. I could never find anything fitting or that really worked for me, so I made something of my own instead. I came up with this."

He pulled his own necklace out from underneath the collar of his shirt.

"It reminds me not to depend too much on anything and to always be able to take care of myself. Course, I'm not perfect. Still learning," he smirked, his devious grin having returned to form. "Anyway, I made one for you, too. It's like you said: it isn't okay for me to just be hanging around pretending I can be there for you when I can't. But this thing can. And maybe it can help you find a little strength if you're feeling down."

"Kody...I can't believe you..." Cris dropped her head only for a moment.

"Geez...you're kidding, right? There's no way I pissed you off this time!"

"No, silly. This is amazing...I..."

She swelled with pride as a serene, fuzzy warmth overcame her. She began to feel the budding blossom of passion. She looked at his lips: soft, simple, sweet. She wanted them badly. She needed to vent. Her breathing became shallow. She stood up and walked over to the river's edge, taking a seat on the bank and gazing out, watching the current. She needed a distraction.

Kody stood, watching Cris and the sights around her. A cool summer breeze signaled the end of the day and the beginning of night—the sun on the horizon. A flock of ducks drifted further on down the river. The cat gloated in his callow victory. This is exactly what he had hoped for. This is what he wished to share with his friends. But Alma wasn't here. None of them were. None, save one. He could still share it with her.

He knew, before he moved, that of course she must be cold. She was always cold, for some reason or another. He unbuttoned his dress shirt, looking down at it and examining the dark stripes that illustrated it. He meandered quiet and indirectly up to the riverbank, stopping just behind her. He draped his dress shirt over her shoulders as he took a seat next to her.

"Ever the gentleman, huh?" She looked over to him, a few stray hairs in her face.

"I dunno about that. Just do what I can."

"Mr. Lehane." She blew them out of the way.

"Present!"

She chuckled.

"Of course. Just a few minutes late, right?"

"Hey, I prefer to think of it as effective time management."

"Effective time management?" She tried to contain her amusement.

"Oh yeah. 'Cause see, at first you get all the boring intro stuff. Never was much for that. But right after that is when all the good action comes in! I'm all about being thrown into the fray and figuring it out as I go, ya know?"

"Hmm…bet that leaves you pretty confused sometimes, though."

He tapped the side of his head. "Quick learner."

She smiled. "Better be. You'll never be able to keep up with Alma otherwise."

"You ain't kiddin'."

"How long have we been friends now?"

"Hmm, dunno. Awhile, I guess?"

"Yeah…I wonder how come we never really took the time to get to know each other or hang out before now."

"Probably 'cause you and Alma always did your thing. Plus, I led a very rich and varied social life."

She looked at him, cracking a disbelieving smile.

"Hey, the Internet definitely constitutes a social life."

"I bet. Meet all sorts of exciting people, huh?"

"Ye of little faith! You have no idea! Carl the night elf priestess, for example…"

"Carl?" she raised an eyebrow.

"Heh…never mind. But, anyway, I guess we just led different lives."

"Pretty much."

He leaned back, falling to the ground as the sun dipped lower into the evening sky. He scratched his ruffled head, his cookie rumblings finally dying down.

"Do you think we'll still be friends when we get back?" Cris looked down to him.

"Definitely. We'll hang out and stuff. I'll invite all of you over for dinner or something. My mom's a mean cook. Or maybe we'll have a barbeque."

"I'd like that."

He flopped back up, wiggling his toes around in his shoe. The insatiable cat seemed to be frustrated at his lack of success with the river and perched himself quietly in front of it, watching and waiting. Cris leaned over, resting her head on Kody's shoulder.

"Um...Cris?"

"Yes?"

"Nothing."

They sat there, watching the sun disappear underneath the skyline and counting another day gone by. Cris felt at peace. Her heart was content. She was here with her best friend, resting quietly on his shoulder, where everything was as it should be. She was safe. This was how it should be. She was grateful for this moment.

"I wish I could stay here forever, just like this," Cris thought aloud, staring out onto the river, feeling the now warm breeze blowing through the air. She watched a flock of ducks floating by, catching the interest of the aggressive mini cougar—though, he let them go—and she caught the fragrance of various different flowers that were spread across the park. She let herself drift through thought, and experience everything as it came.

"Just keep this memory in your heart, and you'll have it forever. That way, if you ever go through hard times, or anything else, you can remember you had this, and you'll be able to make it through," Kody told her softly, as not to break her daydream.

"I feel like I've heard that before," Cris continued, though not paying any attention to her own words.

"It's something Alma told me once."

"Always Alma, even when it's just us. It's always Alma..."

Cris remained too lost in her daydream to be aware of what she was saying, or even that she was speaking. Almost as if she was just responding to a prompt in a dream.

"Cris...?"

"Hm…?"

She was taken aback a bit by not having something to respond to, but her daydream gripped her tightly.

"Hmm…nothing."

"Okay…"

Kody wrapped his arm around her, drawing her in closer as she lost herself completely. Her eyes became heavy with the comfort of being so close to him. She could smell the enchanting musk once more, this time greater than ever, and she was pleased to be overwhelmed. She lost focus of everything as she began to drift off. He sat on, vigilant, as he watched the cat yawn and finally decide to give his hunting a rest.

31. Not for the World

Decisions, decisions... why don't they make fortune cookies for these kinds of things? I'm sure love-triangle cookies would make a fortune...no pun intended.

– Cris's Journal

Kody watched, quietly but not alone, as the sun relinquished its hold on the day. Artemis, the goddess of the hunt, took charge and began illuminating the night sky. In his heart, Kody knew he was loyal to Alma; of that there was no question. But sitting on the riverside with Cris... She felt like the part of his life that had been missing, that he wasn't even aware was vacant. To keep her close, to keep her safe: it may have been the reason he was born. Despite all this, he was still concerned that Alma and Glenn hadn't returned yet.

Cris had been drifting in and out of consciousness for the better part of an hour as he held her closely, brushing his fingers through her hair before realizing what he was doing. He thought about it. He stopped. He looked down at her. Even sitting on the cold ground near the edge of a river, she slept better at his side than most infants do in their mother's arms. He had become important, necessary, essential.

Kody stopped to think about how everything had gone so far. How Alma had come back to him. How Cris had always been there for him. How the two of them got along. He remembered her singing and thought about how much he'd like to hear one of her songs. But he wouldn't wake her up for anything.

"Maybe it's just this place…" He thought aloud.

"What about this place?" She rubbed her eyes as she looked up at him. She stretched and readjusted herself, getting closer and more comfortable.

"Nothing. Just thinking."

He kept his arm around her as she shifted around, wondering if he should be holding her. It felt wrong, yet right, and he couldn't tell which was stronger. Worse, it was becoming more difficult to break away. The chirping of Cris's phone resting on the now ant-covered picnic blanket resolved the matter for the time being.

"Hey, you should probably—"

"Get that? Yeah. I'm going." She got up and placed his shirt back around his shoulders.

"No one says I can't look out for you, too."

She stuck her tongue out at him as she went to get her phone. She picked it up, taking it with her as she headed toward the run-down bathrooms. His gaze lingered on her as she went. She disappeared into the facility, and he turned his head back to the riverbed, to the hunter-cat rolling around in his sleep. Kody nudged the kitten with his foot, playing with him. The cat was reluctant to stir, but Kody's incessant intervention awoke the cat, vicious.

Loathing the stupid leather that had awaken him, his highness, with a raging roar of a meow-hiss, declared his nemesis the new public enemy of the fur ball kingdom. He slashed at it with relentless claws, throwing furry swipes maliciously. The foolish shoe cloth seemed too stupid to care. Such an unworthy opponent appeared to be a waste of his time, and his royal catness disassociated himself from such brigandry. Chicanery of this fashion would surely be dealt with in due time, on his terms.

Kody laughed as he kept chasing the annoyed cat with his foot until the meow-meow got out of his reach. Kody stood up, his pulse quickening with the realization Alma and Glenn were gone too long. He walked back to the picnic blanket, cleaning up whatever wasn't covered in ants, and tossing the rest. He packed everything up as he heard the rickety-rockety van finally come tumbling through the clearing of the woods and into the parking lot. He breathed a deep sigh of relief. He grabbed everything up and took it over to the parking lot.

Alma turned off the engine and hopped out, running up to Kody and giving him a strong hug. She held him close and buried her head in his chest.

"I missed you, baby!"

"Hey, Alm, missed you, too." He smiled, holding her closely and brushing his fingers through her hair. It wasn't the same.

"What took you guys so long?"

"That boy is seriously messed up. He's got some bigger issues than we can deal with. I think we might need to take him back." She looked up into his eyes.

"Seriously? He seemed like he was doing a lot better. If anything, I figured all this getting out and traveling might be good for him."

"I dunno...I guess we can wait and see, but you're gonna need to keep a close eye on him."

"Can do."

She leaned into him, pulling his head close and kissing him. She tasted him only for a moment before she let go and broke away. She canted her head, examining him.

"Hey honey bunny...what's wrong?"

Cris came out of the bathroom, now seeing the van and the others and ran up to join them.

"Hey, welcome back! Everything good with Glenn?" Cris asked.

"Yeah, fine." Alma answered her, looking them both over.

"Good! Let's get this show on the road!"

"Sounds good. Just lemme find—Ow, damn it!"

The harsh sting of narrow feline daggers dug into Kody's skin as Bixby clawed his way up Kody's back. The feline bit at his neck, restitution achieved. Kody grabbed the cat and pulled him off, glaring at the fur ball.

"Hey, be nice to the pussens!"

"He freakin' bit me!"

"He wouldn't bite you if you were nice to him, now would he?"

Alma stepped up as his personal savior, taking the cat from Kody and piling into the van behind the driver's seat. She could see Glenn still sound asleep in the passenger seat. She kept her attention elsewhere. Cris, invigorated and full of energy, jumped into the driver's seat as she waited for everyone else to get settled. Kody loaded up all the picnic stuff in the back as he climbed in next to Alma, keeping a distance from the devil cat.

Cris started up the van and carefully navigated her way through the dense forest road with little trouble. She found her way back to the Interstate 30, and they resumed their travels.

"So, lookie what I happened to save…" Alma knew it wouldn't take much to get Kody's attention.

"Hmm?"

She set the furry whiskers aside and pulled out a small white bag. She recognized the feral lust in her boy's eyes as he craved the chocolaty goodness.

"Uh-uh-uh. Not so fast. These cookies don't come cheap."

"Wha…what?" A hint of desperation escaped his voice.

"These are looooove cookies!"

He looked at her, clearly baffled and unconcerned with anything other than putting those cookies in his belly. She pulled one out, and he forcefully restrained himself. He winced in pain as he watched her take a giant bite out of one of them. She watched the expression on his face, drawing it out to ensure she had his full attention. Satisfied, she leaned forward and kissed him, sharing her cookie with her lover.

"Cookie kiss!"

Alma giggled and handed him a small bottle of milk. His eyes lit up and he chugged it with his cookie, choking while forcing it down. She handed him the rest of the bag, and he forcefully injected the contents into his mouth, in need of an immediate reprieve after. He lay in her lap and gurgled himself into a cookie-coma slumber as Cris watched from the rearview mirror. She plugged in her mp3 player and left it playing on low. She put on the Juliana Theory and kept driving.

Alma played with Kody's hair, tufting it back and forth, seeing if she could make funny shapes with it. She became bored with this, and started rubbing his belly instead. Eventually, he served as a glorified armrest. She looked up front, listening to the music and Cris singing along quietly.

"Hey, girly, you seem awfully chipper."

"Yep, good day." Cris smiled to herself.

"I can see that. Have a good time this afternoon?"

"The best."

"Uh huh…hey, can we stop by a gas station?" Alma examined Cris surreptitiously, not sure what she was looking for.

"Sure, what's up?"

"Need snacks."

Cris got off at the next exit and found a small gas station just inside of Texas. She grabbed a change of clothes before she and Alma walked inside, exchanging few words in the process.

"Hey, Almy, I'm gonna go get changed. Kinda weird wearing a dress late at night like this."

"Yeah, okay."

Alma looked around, wandering through the aisles, trying to figure out what was going on with Cris and Kody. She grabbed some cat food for Bixby and some snacks for the night ahead. She paid for her stuff and walked back out to the van, noticing a pay phone. She tried it, finding it dead; she wondered what the point of having one around was if it didn't work. She could ask to borrow Cris's phone, but she didn't feel like it. She didn't want to owe her any favors.

She made her way back to the van, finding Glenn asleep, or at least pretending to be—she could never tell with him—in the far back seat behind them and took her place as her cookie monster's pillow. A few minutes later she saw Cris emerge from the gas station decked out in blue jeans with faded-star outlines and a pink lace-trimmed camisole decorated with a butterfly pattern, complete with butterfly clips in her hair. Alma became unsettled by a building irritation inside, but couldn't tell why.

She kept a keen eye on Cris, who was outside refueling the van. As Cris leaned over to replace the gas cap, a small tribal necklace dangled from her neck. Cris paid at the pump and got back in the van with her Splash sodas as she started it up and got back on the highway.

"Hey, nice necklace," Alma started.

"Oh, thanks. I—" Cris stopped mid-sentence, the two exchanging a glance in the rearview mirror.

"Where'd you get it?" Alma continued.

"It was a gift."

"From Kody?"

"Yes."

"So, Cris, I'm curious…do tell why my boyfriend is giving you handmade gifts behind my back."

"It's not like that, Alm. He felt bad because you two were all couple-y and I was by myself all the time. That's all."

"Uh…what? I'm pretty much always with you. What do you mean by yourself?"

"Um…"

"You mean, as in, without a boyfriend? What, is he your boyfriend now?" Alma began to raise her voice.

"Alm, you know I would never do that to you! I love you, honey!"

Alma stopped to consider this. She looked down at her slumbering honey bunny and then back up at her bestie. The two most important people in her life. She stopped, and took a deep breath.

"Ugh…maybe you're right. I'm probably just overreacting…I haven't gotten any sleep and it's been a really weird day for me as it is. I need to talk to you about it later, actually."

"Of course, Almy."

"Yeah…hey, Cris?"

"Hmm?"

"I love this boy." She rubbed his head. "I love him more than anything. He's my everything. Do you know that?"

"What? Y-yes." Cris's voice wavered.

"Good. 'Cause I love you, too. And as my bestie I know you would never do anything to hurt me, so I'm gonna trust you. You know how hard things have been for us lately so please don't do anything to mess this up for me, 'kay?"

"I won't, Alm." Cris felt the guilt quickly rising inside of her.

Alma knew she could trust her best friend, but for some reason…she didn't. She lifted Kody's head off her as she moved next to the window, looking out of it. She sat thinking as she watched the road.

Cris continued driving. She genuinely believed she had done nothing wrong…but she had wanted to, and wasn't that enough? Given the chance, she would've betrayed Alma, and it made her sick. As much as she cared about Alma, when Kody was around her, Cris just couldn't think straight. She changed the album as she took a swig of her Splash cola and continued driving.

Several hours of Jimmy Eat World and quiet reflection on the open road provided a much-needed distraction. She saw Alma snoring heavily as her drool ran along the windowpane. She turned the radio up as one of her favorite songs came on. She sang along to "A Praise Chorus."

Midway through the song, she heard that all-too-familiar voice join in. She smelled stinky cookie breath as a boyishly charming face appeared next to hers. Even the Fates mocked her situation.

"Morning. Or evening, I guess." Kody said.

"Hey. Sleep well?"

"Dunno if I'd call it sleep. More like a rest break. Although come sunrise, all the cookies in the Great Plains will know and fear my name," Kody said, rubbing his belly, "but I could use a change of pace for a bit."

He looked next to Cris, noticing the open seat.

"This one taken?"

"Not so much."

He climbed up front and occupied the seat. About two songs later, he looked her over.

"You're quiet."

"Not much to say."

"Sure there is! See any good road kill lately?"

"Not really. Lots of road, few trees, some bushes…I think a cactus. Might've been a sign, though."

She glanced over at him, and couldn't help but want his arms around her. She loved the look of his soft lips. She grew queasy at the thought, but she still wanted him. She needed to come up with some kind of plan to either keep herself away from him, or at least not focus on him so much. If only she could go back to the time when she saw him as just another guy.

"Now, see, that's where you lose me."

"What?" She was completely lost in thought and didn't understand what he was talking about.

"You go from smiling to depressed just like that. What's going on, *chica*?"

"I don't know. Just got a lot on my mind."

"Care to share?"

"Sorry. Can't."

"Since when?" he cocked an eyebrow.

"I don't know…I just can't."

He turned to face her. "Can't, or won't?"

"Both?"

"It's gotta be one or the other; if it's can't, then that means you want to but something is stopping you, whereas if it's won't, it means you can but you feel you shouldn't. So…"

"I don't know…won't, I guess?" she shrugged.

"Okay, I can respect that. But if you change your mind or find that circumstances suddenly… shift, I'm here."

"I know." She smiled again.

"Heh, that's what I'm talkin' about. Just keep that up and you'll be all right."

She laughed, with the realization she might be royally screwed in this endeavor. If she was going to have any measure of success, she'd need help.

She changed the album, putting on Owl City. Kody tried to keep up the conversation, but Cris stayed focused on her music and Kody eventually returned to his writing. Cris found it odd that he wrote in a new notebook when there had been so much free space left in his old one. Knowing Alma as well as she did, she felt badly and wondered if he had ever gotten it back.

"Shouldn't you get some rest? We'll probably need you to drive later."

"Nah, I'm all right. I'll stay up with you. Besides, it's a good night for writing."

She continued driving through the early hours of the morning, having finished both of her Splash sodas and using up the small high she had gotten from her nap earlier in the evening. Fatigue began to set in, and she started looking for a rest stop to take a break. She found a small one off I-20, and stopped for a few minutes to take a break.

She got out, walking around and stretching her legs. Kody followed suit, opening the side door to let the fur ball out. Glenn awoke at this clamor and decided to stride along with Cris.

"Good morning, C-charisma. How've you b-been?"

"I don't even know. Good, I guess? I think I'm going to need your help, though."

"Oh?"

"It's getting bad, Glenn. I can't keep away from him. He made this necklace for me, and he's all nice and sweet and good smelling and cozy…"

"When did you find him 'c-cozy'?"

"Not the point!" Cris shrilly tried to cover up her tracks. "The point is…keep him away from me? Please? Alma thinks something's up and, if I'm not seriously careful, something might be. I mean, I don't want to hurt her or anything, but I don't know if I trust myself around him anymore."

"Ah, I know what you m-mean. And I take it the young man has recciprocated your affections?"

"Um…I don't think it's like that, but he's not exactly running away from me. And besides, I can be surprisingly forceful when I want to be." She smiled, showing teeth and determination.

"I've no d-doubt. So you want me to k-keep Kody away from you. Is that wh-what you're saying?"

"Yes, please!"

"You're c-certain about this."

"I don't really have a choice at this point."

"You're more mature than I realized, C-charisma…I'm proud of you."

"Not so mature that I'm gonna let you get away with calling me that again."

"Right…C-cris."

"Much better, thanks. How's everything with you? Are you doing all right? Seemed kinda intense back at the park yesterday."

"Ah. I j-just…it's nothing important. It's been resolved."

"So you're doing okay?"

"P-peachy, even. I'd like to continue d-driving this stretch if you don't mind."

"Sure, I could use a nap anyway."

"R-right then."

Glenn escorted Cris back to the van, both of them watching Kody in the passenger seat with the demonic kitten ball. Glenn took his place in the driver's seat. Alma, peeking an eye open and catching this, quietly made her way to the very back seat. Glenn was the only one who seemed to pay any attention to her as Cris took the middle seat.

"So, what's the game plan?" Kody asked.

"I'm going to d-drive for a bit; C-cris is rather tired."

"Heh, long night, right? I'm actually pretty wiped, too. Think I might crash for a bit."

Kody got up to climb into the back, but Cris stopped him.

"Kody, what're you doing?"

"Uh…climbing in back to take a nap?"

Cris tried to come up with an excuse. "There isn't a whole lot of room back here. Wouldn't you be more comfortable up front?"

"What're you talking about? There's plenty of—"

"K-kody, I may actually need some help u-up here, if you don't mind."

"What…?"

Glenn redirected his attention and pulled out a map, showing it to Kody. Glenn glanced briefly at the rearview mirror, catching Cris mouth a thank you as she leaned against the window to take a nap. Glenn waited a few minutes before he quit feigning with the map and continued on the road.

"Glenn, I'm flattered you asked for my help and all, but I really don't think you need me to read a map."

"You're right, K-kody, I don't."

"Oh, hey, look at that: there goes my manly pride!"

304

Kody pretended to watch his pride fly right out the window. He even made gestures with his hands, much like hand puppets. He waved goodbye.

"I d-didn't mean to insult you, but t-take a look in the back seat. What d-do you see?"

Kody looked back as Glenn watched him.

"And I don't mean the girl."

Kody shifted his attentive focus to the remainder of the seat. He saw a few James & Jonathan's wrappers, and clothes littered about.

"Just a bunch of crap, pretty much."

"And yet C-charisma told you there was no room. C-can you imagine why?"

"'Cause she was too lazy to clean off the seat?"

"Does that sound like C-charisma to you?"

"Not really, but I mean we all get lazy from time to time."

Glenn sighed. "K-kody, did it ever cross your mind that p-perhaps she doesn't want you sitting b-back there?"

Kody shook his head. "What? Why wouldn't she want me back there?"

"You really have n-no idea?"

"Nah, did I piss her off again or something? I feel like I would've remembered that, or at least noticed it." He lifted his arms, smelling his pits. "Don't smell bad," he paused for a moment, "well, *that* bad."

"Get some rest," Glenn sighed.

"Uh, 'kay."

Kody skipped the mind games and decided to follow Glenn's advice. He curled up in his seat, digging his head into the seat cushion, using his shirt for a pillow. He smelled light perfume on it. He stared without interest at the oft-repeating stripes in the road that bored him to sleep. He sniffed his shirt again.

32. Hustle Rose

"Trust, love… I suppose those things are useful enough when the time calls for them, but the only thing one can ever be sure of is herself."

– Matier's Memoirs

Somewhere near the Mojave Desert

Lexy sighed, catching a glimpse of herself as she stared out the window. Her skin was torn, bruised, but physical conditions meant nothing to her. Her body was worth only as much as she happened to be carrying on it. She knew not whose arm was sprawled across her chest, nor did she care. She heard the knock at the door, and shoved the man out of the bed. She crawled to her feet, stumbling along as the hangover set in. She didn't bother getting dressed. She threw on a robe as she opened the door, the delivery boy standing shocked and disturbed at her apparent lack of clothing.

"Uh, um…excuse me," the boy stammered self-conscious.

"What?" She asked.

"Heh, ma'am, shouldn't you put some clothes on?"

"You'd better have an outstanding reason for waking me up, *petit garçon*."

She wiped the haze from her eyes, the dust-shrouded sun burning far too bright for her so early in the afternoon.

"Um…I'm looking for Alexandria Matier?"

She looked up.

"You've a package for me?"

"Miss Matier?"

"Yes?"

"Just one. Overnighted. Could you sign this?"

She signed for the package and took it in, slamming the door on the poor kid outside. The random man she had found in bed with her earlier made his way into the kitchen, only now coming to.

"Mornin'." He had a sly, sick smile.

"Get out."

"Huh? What, you don't want another go?"

She set the envelope down in the kitchen and went to the junk drawer, pulling out a small well-sharpened knife. She left it on the counter, meeting his eyes.

"I loathe repeating myself."

"Crazy bitch…fine, just lemme get my stuff."

"Now." She picked up the knife, pointing it toward the door.

"At least lemme get my clothes!"

She grabbed the knife and walked around the side of the counter, holding it up and examining the blade as she drew near the man. She found no resistance forcing him out, slovenly and naked into the harsh light of day, covered only in the rough sand that blew through the air. She locked the door behind him. His problems were not her own—she had far greater issues at hand.

She returned to the kitchen and used the knife to open the envelope. She read the contents, needing only a small amount of time to find what she needed. She picked up her phone, making the call but getting no response. She left a voicemail.

"Hey, it's me. I called in a favor and got it expedited. Confirmed—he's a match for your boy. Let me know when you get this. *Au revoir.*"

A hollowness grew at having accomplished her mission. Another bittersweet success. She'd be paid, but it meant finding another new life. This one wasn't great, but it wasn't the worst. She heard keys jingling in the door and stuffed the envelope into the drawer, sliding the knife up her sleeve. She waited as the door opened.

"Lexy," Mr. Agramonte scoffed.

"Hey, honey, long night at the office?"

"If you're gonna stay here, at least make yourself useful. Make some damn food or somethin'."

He looked at her, more disappointed than anything else. He kicked off his shoes and closed the door behind him, taking a seat on the couch. She stuffed the knife back into the drawer.

"Sure. What'cha want?"

"Like I fuckin' care."

She pulled out one of the cans in the cupboard and tried to open it with the pull-tab. The tab broke off before she had any luck. At least she didn't break a nail. She resorted to her knife of choice, cutting the can open by force and pouring its contents into a bowl. She watched him watching TV as she listened to the hum of the microwave slowly spin-warm his food to perfection. It dinged its ornery ding, and she pulled the bowl from the microwave as she grabbed a bottle of vodka and sat on the couch next to him.

"Give it here." Mr. Agramonte demanded.

"No. You come over here."

"Lexy, knock the shit off."

"C'mon, sugar; gotta learn to play nice sometime."

"Hey, I show my appreciation in other ways."

"It's a bit early for that still; I just got up. Let's at least spend a little time out of the bedroom for a change."

She realized she hadn't cleaned the bed off from the slovenly jerk the night before.

"Fine, fuck it, whatever."

He resigned himself and scooted over. She held him in her arms, slowly blowing off the hot food in the spoon as she fed it to him. She knew she'd never have children: she wasn't the mothering kind. She wasn't capable of things like love or affection, at least not in the traditional sense. But she found ways to work out those unseemly maternal whims that passed through from time to time. He lay in her arms, uncomfortably relaxed, and ate the food with reluctance.

"I ain't no damn baby."

"We both know you like it. You can be a hard ass all you want everywhere else, but you aren't hiding anything from me. Now shut up and eat it."

They lay on the couch, watching TV as she fed him the rest of the food. He finished the bowl, and she set it aside; she took a swig of vodka before handing it to him. He started chugging it, and she pulled the bottle away from him, spilling it all over him.

"Goddamnit, Lexy!"

"You know better! Gotta take it slow."

"Fuckin'…"

"It's fine baby. Here, take your shirt off."

Rather than wait for him to do it himself, she lifted him up, pulling his shirt off. She licked her lips at the sight of his hairy, bare chest. She moved around and licked the vodka off him. His displeasure with her was clearly starting to fade. She knew how to play her cards well. She made her way back to the bedroom as her robe flapped around carelessly.

"Where're ya goin'?"

"I'm gonna draw us a bath."

"Hurry it up." He was always inpatient.

She got back into the bedroom and pulled the dirty sheets off the bed, throwing them into a corner. She took the clothes from the creep she'd kicked out earlier and threw them out the window. She went into the bathroom and turned on the warm water, letting the tub fill slowly. She took a sip from the whiskey bottle sitting on the back of the toilet.

She waited, sitting on the toilet seat and watching the water level rise as she stared into it. She had always liked the sound. It was a constant. No matter where you were, what you were doing, what you had done, the bath water always sounded the same. It never made her clean, but at least it washed away the dirt. She was grateful for that. No one could ever call her dirty.

She was surprised her consort hadn't called her back. This was his prerogative after all; she had just gotten swept up into the financially pleasing mix. But she had found something else as well. A kindred bastard spirit. No one else would ever understand. Few people were as disgusting as her. This made her world exclusive. They, the *those* outside of her, could never impose. She'd bring *him* around soon enough.

The door slammed and she looked back to see him standing in the bedroom. He dropped his pants as he made his way into the bathroom.

"You could've waited. I would've gotten you when it was ready."

"Makes you think I give a shit about that?"

He closed the door and picked her up, pinning her against it. He slid his hand under her robe as he forced his tongue into her mouth. She reciprocated in kind, strength of his muscle holding her back from everything but herself. She pushed against him, creating friction and causing him to push back harder, creating fierce animosity between them. He grabbed her wrists and it hurt. The right kind of pain. She fought back only enough to make sure he would win. She could feel the water flowing underneath her toes. She bit his lip.

"Fuckin'…"

"Tub's overflowing."

"Let it."

"Yeah, until I'm the one cleaning it up. Get your ass in there."

She pushed him off and dropped her robe, making him get in the tub. She followed him in shortly after. As they climbed in, the water splashed out, soaking the bathroom floor and creating a mess everywhere. Small bubbly suds lined the tile. She watched her robe become ruined in the filthy water. It was just stuff. She could always buy more stuff. She looked across at the dirty, rough, rugged face staring back at her. She wanted to bite him.

"God knows how I put up with you, Lexy."

He seemed equally interested and disinterested in everything about her. Even she herself wasn't entirely sure what drew him to her. But she didn't care.

"Love comes in all shapes and sizes, big guy."

"I ain't loved nothin', least of all you."

His harsh words were a sloppy kiss on the cheek.

"S'all right. We all have our own ways, Jake."

She lifted her leg up, rubbing her foot in his face and lightly tapping him on the nose with her big toe as she felt his roam around below. She barely remembered to turn the water off as she sank back and relaxed into the blissful run-down tub drawn for two.

33. On the Rocks

"Ever have that sick feeling in your gut, when you know something's up but you just can't figure it out? I'm not saying it's always right, but it's definitely there for a reason."

– Alma's Diary

Just outside Sierra Blanca, Texas

The van was quiet and had been for some time. They weren't far from El Paso, and driving along I-10 through the mountains became more than a little tedious.

Glenn watched his beloved kitten attempt in vain to clean his heavy coat of the dirt and mud that stained it. Glenn, too, wished for a shower, and a chance to stop and reassess his situation. His mission was of course the first priority, but Cris's request could not be taken lightly; and, while it might conflict with his own interests, he would support her as much as he was able. She had been a good friend to him, and he owed it to her sister. Though, if he failed...

He began searching for a place to rest. It didn't matter where. He thought he saw a sign for a bed and breakfast, but the dust outside began to pick up and obscured the better part of his vision. The fact that his glasses were dirty didn't help either. He'd need to pick up some lens cleaning solution, as soon as they found a place less sandy.

He drove on for another half hour until the weather had cleared a bit and he could discern the outlines of the signs. He found a cheap no-name motel only a few miles away and set his destination. The furrlicious fur ball curled up next to Glenn's leg with a pleading look in his eyes at his failure to clean himself. He pitied the kitten and hurried.

He pulled into the surprisingly crowded middle-of-nowhere motel. He parked the van and shut off the engine, listening to the clunking sound that was only getting worse. The van might need to be serviced soon. He made his way into the office. He spoke to the clerk at the front desk.

"Excuse me…d-do you have two rooms?"

"¿Que?"

It had been awhile, but Glenn hadn't forgotten his studies entirely.

"Hmm… ¿Tiene d-dos habitaciones?"

"Sí, sí. Los últimos dos."

"Los t-tomo."

"Si tú lo dices."

Glenn nodded, pleased with himself and his apparent success; He handed over his credit card and waited for the keys. He looked around the lobby, noting the rustic décor and old-fashioned themes. He was surprised at how much he appreciated the place. He had found a small gem in the middle of a barren region. Perhaps his luck was turning around. The man called him out and handed him his card and the keys. Glenn made his way back outside. He got back to the van and opened his door.

"We have rooms. With b-beds waiting!"

He waited. They hardly stirred. His phone rang, and he saw the name of the caller. It was time for business. They'd have to take care of themselves.

"V-very well, I'll leave your k-keys on the seat."

He reached over the seat, grabbing his bag in one hand and his cat in the other as he hustled over to his room. The keys dangled in the lock as he managed to get the door open. His voicemail chimed as he closed the door behind him.

* * *

Alma tried to roll over but found nothing other than seat cushion. She yawned and stretched as she sat up. She didn't know what time it was and, as usual, didn't really care. She straightened out her skirt as she looked around the van. She didn't see anyone. She got up to see where everyone went, or at least what was going on. She didn't see anyone and vaguely recalled hearing something about Glenn and his seat. She made her way up to the passenger seat and was delighted to find her cookie-bear-monster-belly-guy still passed out up front. She saw two sets of keys on the seat and grabbed them as she woke him up.

"Hey, snuffy-wuffles, get up."

"Uh…? Noooo."

He rolled over.

"I'm not asking, sweetie."

"Umph."

He buried his face deeper into his shirt, starting to rouse at the scent.

"Fine, don't want my nice, delicious cookies…"

"Uh…what?"

He looked up and turned around, seeing a deceitfully cheerful smile.

"You don't have cookies, do you?"

"Oh, I have cookies, just not the kind you're thinking of." She brandished a lusty grin as she got out and opened his door, helping him out.

"C'mon, snookums, mama wants some sugar."

Alma dragged him half-conscious down the walkway, trying to find the room identified on the key. She realized now that she had no idea if Cris or Glenn would be in the room.

"Please be empty, please be empty…"

She unlocked the door and opened it cautiously, finding no one in sight. She kicked off her sandals as she got inside.

"Oh, sweet! Jackpot!"

She dragged her sweetie bear inside and closed the door behind him.

"So, look at this, Mr. Lehane: you and me, all alone…haven't gotten any for days…I wonder how this'll end?"

She leaned up to kiss him, though she found his effort lacking. Deciding he needed more incentive, she dragged him toward the bathroom, dropping her skirt along the way. He followed only as much as she dragged him. As they got to the door, she became a little annoyed with the lack of effort on his part and stopped.

"Hey, I'm not doing all the work. Get naked already!"

"Alm, I'm kinda tired."

"You're tired." She stared at him blankly, waiting for some sort of explanation.

"Yeah, the van isn't the most comfortable place to sleep."

"You're telling me you're too tired to get in the shower with me?"

"Sorry, I'm just out of it."

"Huh." Alma propped her hands on her hips. "Okay, that's fine. It's not a problem, actually. C'mon."

She grabbed his hand and led him to the bed.

"Alm, I just told you—"

"I know. It's fine. We're gonna take a little nap then. That's all. Unless it's not," she smirked.

She laid herself down, waiting for him to come to her. Though a bit sluggish, he took his shoes off and lay beside her. She wasn't going to accept his lackadaisical manner and lack of initiative.

"Geez Kody, it hasn't been that long since we've been in a bed. Have you forgotten everything?"

She grabbed his wrist, wrapping his arm around her. They began to spoon, she rubbing herself against him waiting for a reaction. Though it took some work, she finally began to feel one.

"C'mon, baby…this isn't like you at all. Talk to me, what's going on with you?" She looked at him over her shoulder.

"I dunno…I just…haven't felt like myself, I guess."

"Is there something wrong? Is something the matter?"

"I don't think so…I don't really know what it is."

"If you did, would you tell me?"

"Yeah."

"Good. 'Cause I love you, my sweet boy. I love you sooo much."

"I know."

She turned to him.

"That's it?"

"I…" he yawned, "I love you, too, Alm."

"You better." She looked into his eyes. The warmth she had come to expect from them was nowhere to be found. "Hey, gimme some sugar."

He leaned forward and gave her a kiss.

"Don't be stingy! Think Cheerios! I need lots and lots of sugar!"

He leaned forward again, licking her lips before kissing her and pulling her close. She became immersed, feeling the passion from her boy of old.

"Mmm…there's what I'm talkin' about! Only my baby knows how to do it best."

She slid her hand down his back, hooking her thumb on his pants as she tried to slide them off. She couldn't get them around his waist, and settled for copping a feel of his firm but surprisingly spongy butt. Something didn't feel right. She slid her hand into his back pocket and pulled out some kind of cloth. She gently pushed him off as she stopped to figure out what it was.

"Kody, what do you…?" as it unfurled before her, she recognized Cris's bandana.

She looked at him, seeing an unfamiliar recognition in his eyes as he too saw it and accepted it as an admission of guilt.

"What the fuck is this?"

"Alm, it's nothing! She dropped it while we were in the woods and—"

"Oh, so you two are exchanging clothing now?"

She shoved him off the bed and stomped over to the bathroom, putting her skirt back on and fixing it before sliding on her sandals and heading out the door. As she opened it, she ran into Cris, who was just about to make her way inside.

"Oh, hey, Alm—"

"Get out of my face, you lying bitch!"

Alma shoved Cris aside as she stormed off. Cris called after her, but was completely disregarded by Alma as she disappeared behind the motel.

"What the hell…?"

Cris trudged inside and closed the door. She leaned her back against the door, trying to figure out what had just happened. She saw her bandana on the ground and walked over to examine it.

"What is this doing here?"

Kody slowly climbed up from behind the side of the bed, having hurt his back landing on some trinket left behind by a previous guest.

"Need…new…spine." He moaned.

"Kody! What're you doing here? What's going on?"

"Dunno. Kinda wish I did…kinda wish I didn't."

She helped him up and checked him over, making sure he was okay.

"What happened?"

He looked over at her bandana.

"I dunno…we were fine, and then she found that in my pocket and flipped out."

"Oh, God…"

"What?"

"She thinks we slept together!"

"What? Why would she think that?" he asked as he rubbed his back.

"Crap... that's the last thing we need."

"We?"

She chuckled nervously. He straightened up, making his way for the door. "Sorry, I gotta go make sure she's okay. We'll talk later though?"

"Yeah, sure."

"Kody, I'm really sorry about this."

"Not your fault."

He slid on his shoes and rushed outside after her.

* * *

Glenn put his phone down. He couldn't contain his excitement. The one thing he had hoped for had finally been confirmed. The one wish he'd had his entire life had just come true. This was a day faithfully unlike all the rest. He kicked it off by bathing his dirty cat.

He went into the bathroom and drew a small bath. He wasn't sure what his little prince's preference was, but he kept the water at about room temperature to be safe. He searched all over the room, but was unable to find the cat. He wondered if despite the consistent impression otherwise, if the little furry devil secretly had fears of his own. Surely, there would be no infirmity in the cat. But like everything else, he couldn't be perfect.

"Mew, mew, mew!"

Bixby reluctantly climbed out from under the bed, oddly compelled by the strange man-friend's funny sounds. Glenn picked him up, and carried him into the bathroom. The tiny kitten sensed danger, though he had no idea what it might be. Heredity told him that trouble was to follow.

Glenn carefully set him into the bath and latent animalistic instinct took hold. Bixby tried to fight his way out of the fur-soaking water. However, Glenn was determined and, once the cat was drenched, he was defeated. He accepted his benefactor's desire, and his fur was washed clean. Glenn toweled off the cat and freed him, the restless kitty finding a resting place underneath a vent, trying to expedite the drying process.

Glenn unpacked his bags, finding an old bottle of scotch among the mix. He no longer remembered why he had carried it, though he suspected it was for this very day, and the one soon to come. He opened it with relish.

"If ever there was a d-day..."

He poured himself a glass, pulling some ice from the mini fridge. He began work on his laptop, confirming the details and enjoying his bittersweet delight. He hummed a little ditty to himself as he heard a knock at his door. He married his way over as he opened it, welcoming and greeting Charisma with a smile.

"Welcome! P-please, come in!"

She accepted his invitation, still disturbed by the events that had only recently transpired.

"What's wrong, m-milady? You seem unusually…u-unusual." He snickered.

"Uh, yeah…you, too. I need to talk to you. Something's up with Alma."

"Oh?"

He poured himself another glass of scotch and offered Cris one as she realized why he seemed so off.

"Glenn, should you really be drinking right now? Or at all?"

"Eh, I s-suppose we'll see. Now, you h-had an issue?"

"Um…maybe now isn't the best time. Just come find me when you sober up, okay?"

"I d-doubt I'll be able to find you b-before then."

"It's okay. Just make sure you check in with me. I don't want anything happening to you."

"Of c-course."

Cris excused herself, heading back outside. She was concerned, though happy to see Glenn in such a good mood. It had been far too long since she had seen a real smile on his face.

She walked back over to her room, stopping outside the door. She didn't want to go back inside. It was a lovely day and it seemed wasteful to spend it indoors and idle. She leaned against the railing, watching the people go by. She watched them: how they talked, how they walked, preening themselves when they thought no one was looking, trying to hide the flaws they thought mattered. As if anyone else even noticed.

She imagined what it would be like to be one of those people, any one of them. She saw a woman in a suit, and wondered just how stressful it could really be not meeting a project deadline or being late for a board meeting. She saw a woman in a tank top and surf shorts and wondered if she ever felt stressed about anything. A man sleeping on a bench in the parking lot caused her to wonder how he could sleep in such heat, though she herself was only modestly warm. She couldn't understand how people lived so…casually. As if each day was as meaningless as the next. As if each day didn't contain heartache and heartbreaks and blissfully gratifying moments. Every day was different in some way, either great or bad, but nothing casual.

She fell in love, hurt her friend, closed her heart, and repeated the cycle within a matter of hours. It kept happening no matter what she did, no matter how hard she tried. It was driving her insane. She realized she had just left Glenn's room. Maybe not insane. But close.

She was proud that she could at least say that, even though she had wanted to give in, she was able to hold herself back. Her friend was pissed at her, but she knew Alma would come around. She had to. She would see the goodness in Cris's heart; she would see the suffering her friend endured trying to do the right thing. It wasn't as though she had done what Alma was thinking anyway. And she wasn't going to. She couldn't even imagine it. She could imagine it a little. Her thighs warmed. She needed to stop.

Though they were fighting, her friends were happy. They fought because they cared. Because of that, everything would be all right. She was doing the right thing, even if it hurt like hell. Because it did, it hurt like hell.

She had lived a long, insightful life for a girl just shy of eighteen. She had seen many things and learned many more. And what she herself couldn't find, she was taught by her friends and family. If love was truly not to be one of these things, at least she had everything else. It could be all right. She could still live a full, accomplished life with her friends and family at her side. It could be complete without love. Or close enough. Maybe she'd get a dog.

* * *

Footsteps approached from behind as Alma sat near a small, abandoned quarry not far behind the motel. She chucked rocks into the ravine below, ignoring the man standing behind her.

"Ya' know, you never know what's living down there. Might hit something and piss it off so bad it'll throw the rock right back up."

"Believe me; I'd like to see it try. It'll need a hell of a lot more than rocks to stop me."

Kody made his way over to her slowly, taking a seat next to her.

"What do you want, Kody? Kinda looking for some alone time right now."

"Alm, Cris and I never did anything."

"Yeah? Wanna explain to me why you two have been so weird lately? Maybe I'm not the smartest girl in the world, Kody, but I'm not stupid."

"Alm, no one ever said—"

"You stayed up with her all night, just to keep her company?"

"What?"

"Last night."

"You were awake?"

"I was waiting for you to come in back with me. But of course, you never did. You were too busy schmoozing it up." She exhaled, refusing to look at him.

"Alm, I wasn't…it wasn't like that. I couldn't sleep, and I needed to write."

"Uh huh. And conveniently that required you to pass the night up front with Cris instead of me. And why do you have her bandana, anyway?"

"It blew off in the storm. I was just carrying it for her."

"The storm?"

"Back in the woods."

"Hmph."

She turned away.

"Nothing happened, Alm. I'm here, right now, looking out for you. If it was all about Cris, wouldn't I be there right now?"

"I know you wanna be."

"No, I don't. I'm here because this is where I choose to be."

"Whatever." She shrugged him off.

She picked up another rock and threw it into the quarry. She watched as it bounced off the sidewall and slid the rest of the way down.

"C'mon, Kody, no secrets anymore. Let's just be completely honest." She turned to him.

"Yeah, of course."

"You wanna fuck her. We both know it. 'Cause she's in love with you and, oh, how awesome it'd be for you to pop that cherry just 'cause you can. Hell of a bragging right, I'm sure. I bet G would just love it."

"Alm, what in the hell are you talking about?"

His face contorted in such a way that even she couldn't mistake his genuine surprise at her remarks.

"You mean to tell me that you really don't know? You have no idea that Cris is in love with you?"

"Alm, that's insane!"

"God you're such a boy…fine, I'll play along. Say you didn't know and you aren't trying to get in her pants. Why the necklace? I know what those things mean to you. You don't give them away to just anyone."

"Is that what this is about? I made the necklace for her because I felt bad about her always being alone. I felt guilty for keeping you all to myself, and I was worried that if she started getting too down she'd just get jealous and start blaming you. I didn't want you to lose your best friend!"

"So, it was all for me?"

She looked at him with her bullshit detector in overdrive mode, eager to pick up a signal. She looked down into the quarry waiting for some kind of answer. She saw nothing but dirt.

"Of course! Alm, I…"

She took a deep breath.

"Glenn tried to kiss me."

"What?"

"He tried to kiss me, back in the woods. And again in the van."

She waited for his response, listening to the silence of the wind drifting through the quarry in the interim.

"Did you?"

"Of course not!" She whipped her head around.

"What happened?"

"I told him I'm in love with you, dummy! What do you think?"

She could see a seething bitterness cross Kody's face. He actually looked a little pissed off. She hated that Kody would ever question her fidelity, but it meant he still cared. She took his hand.

"Hey, sweetie, forget about it, okay? He's got his own stuff, and we've got ours. Let's just take a break from all this craziness for a while and enjoy ourselves."

"Yeah."

She stood up, taking his hand as the two of them started walking along the side of the road. They brushed against each other like an old married couple, forever entwined and always in accord—symbiotic. They wandered along until Alma caught sight of a balloon floating away in the sky. She looked ahead and saw a small carnival. She looked up at Kody; he could see the excitement in her eyes.

"Wanna go?" He asked.

"Yes, please!"

She began rushing and tugging at his arm as she caught sight of a strip mall ahead.

Alma came up with a better idea. "Wait, no."

"Huh?"

"Not yet."

She walked ahead of him, stopping and facing him.

"Tonight."

"Tonight?"

"Yeah, let's go on a date! We haven't had a real one since we got back together! I wanna go on a date!"

"Okay, but why tonight?"

"'Cause I gotta get all pretty and dressed up first, duh! A girl lives for this kind of stuff, you know. Geez, pookie, you need to brush up."

"Yeah, I guess…"

She pointed to a small beauty salon over on the corner of the strip mall.

"I'm gonna go over there and get started, okay? You go get pretty, too! Go shower; you stink."

"Hey!"

"Not my fault you smell," she teased as she headed off.

"So tonight then?"

"Definitely! Oh, and hey: I know this is gonna sound all crazy-jealous-girlfriend-y of me, but try and stay away from Cris for a while, 'kay?"

"Alm."

"Promise me, please…? Make me feel better?" She put on her pouty face.

"Well, when you put it like that, how can I say no?"

"Dunno, and you better not even try to figure it out!"

She started skipping off, her skirt flipping up in the back as she made her way off, knowing it's what her boy liked best. She grinned to herself, finally able to breathe with the warm wave of relief that came down upon her. She couldn't keep it to herself: she was excited. She had a big night ahead to prepare for, and it was going to be the best!

* * *

His fur stood on end. He didn't know why. There was nothing about to perturb him, yet his regal senses picked up something no other seemed to feel. It made him anxious, uncomfortable. For the first time in his relatively short life, the royal cat detected a situation greater than himself. He had enjoyed his time here; this place was better than the one he had found before. But his preternatural senses told him that it was time.

He stepped out from under the heater and watched his man-friend move into strange fashions in accord with the sounds that were much like music coming from his machine. The tinted water he drank made the man more unusual than what his felineness would expect. He might miss this one. He might. This stupid man-creature was kinder to his regalness that most. Kind. But the kitten was a child of the wild and heeded its call. With the door creaked open, he crept unnoticed through the crack.

His tailed wagged, and he acknowledged it. Narrow eyes looking back, seeing. He saw. He had had a name. The dancing fool behind him had given it to him, as if he had known all along. Allister Theodore Bixby the third, Esquire. He would not soon forget it. But that was unimportant. This time, it wasn't about him. His divine cat blood echoed and twitched in his veins; his whiskers twinged as the evening clouds came rolling in. It was time to go.

34. The Interregnum of Skeptics and True Believers

"The most important thing about my life is that I enjoy it. Because when that last day comes, it won't matter how rich, famous, or important I was... I'll still be dead."

– Glenn's Chronicles

Kody returned to his room to find the door cracked open. He opened it a little more as a strong, wafting aroma of alcohol crashed into him, overwhelming his nostrils. Kody continued into the room, his friend dancing around and shaking his moneymaker to the sounds of Cobra Starship's "Good Girls Go Bad." He set his jacket on the bed as he pulled up a chair and took a seat in front of Glenn's bed. Glenn, now noticing his compatriot, took a brief intermission from his dance marathon to speak with him.

"Ah, Kody. T-top of the evening to you."

"Uh huh. I need to talk to you."

"Another consult so soon? I really must start ch-charging for my services…"

"Yeah, it's your services that I'm concerned with. You tried to kiss my girlfriend."

"That's what th-this is about?"

Glenn laughed to himself as he poured two more glasses, offering one to Kody.

"I'm not even old enough to drink."

"Do you care?"

Kody thought it over and took the glass. He took a sip. His body revolted as it rejected the strong bitter burn running down his throat. Watching Glenn toss his back so casually, Kody would not be outdone. He soldiered on.

"I must say, I'm rather su-surprised. I was quite certain you were here about C-charisma."

"Cris? Why her?"

"As if you really require an explanation."

"So you think she's in love with me, too?" Kody raised an eyebrow.

"It's a fact, k-kiddo. At least you finally caught on."

"So you knew."

"I know a great number of things."

"Doesn't help much if you don't share."

"In due time. So, which issue is the more p-pertinent to you, I wonder? The girl in love with you? Or my m-minor indiscretions?"

"Minor? I wouldn't exactly call trying to make out with my girlfriend minor, Glenn. That's pretty fucked up."

"Eh, I suppose. It's more a matter of p-perspective. What I tried to do most might say is wrong, though we must consider that you d-don't own her and she's a fully grown woman in her own right. But regardless, it's a small crime in the greater sch-scheme of things. B-besides, what does it matter if she doesn't k-kiss me back? If you're the one in her heart, then she can do no wrong, c-correct?"

"I guess, but that really isn't the point."

"Still indecisive. As ever, I suppose. Well, th-there's an easy way to be sure."

"Be sure of what?"

"D-don't worry about it." Glenn smiled. "Look in your heart; even if you k-kissed another girl, it would mean nothing to you because you're in love with Alma, right?"

Kody mulled it over. Glenn attempted to watch him intently, though he had trouble staying seated.

"Kody?"

"What?" he said, lost in thought.

"Even if you kissed another girl, say…C-charisma, it wouldn't matter at all, would it?"

"Of course it would matter!" He finished his glass and set it aside.

"And why is that?"

"Because it would be cheating on Alma!"

"Really?" Glenn slammed his glass down, excited. "Perhaps it's my differing vantage point of the world, but as I recall c-cheating is the act of giving your heart to another. If you define it only by your actions, then the feeling and intent you hold m-must be worth very little."

"Keep drinking it off, old man."

Glenn laughed to himself. He did indeed keep drinking as he sat up.

"It's okay to not know what to do, Kody. C-charisma is stuck in that very same boat. After all, if she gets close to you, she hurts her friend. But if she stays away from you, she breaks her own heart. It's the hedgehog's dilemma, to be sure. It's gotten so b-bad she's even asked that I keep you away from her."

"What?"

Kody began to speculate on just how much pain Cris had been in this whole time, and how hard she must have been trying to keep everyone happy. She bore her burden with a strong heart and always smiled. He never knew.

"It's funny…I mention C-cris and finally I find the first reaction I've gotten out of you all night. And this is of c-course after we discussed my trying to kiss your girlfriend."

"That's enough, Glenn."

"Is it? Will it ever be enough, Kody? You're the c-curious type. Always thinking things over, always c-considering the alternative. You have to get a grasp on every perspective. W-wouldn't that include C-charisma?"

"Shut up, Glenn!"

"S-so be it. Your truth holds little value for me, in any case. But, s-since I am your friend, allow me this if you will: decide for yourself. Don't c-continue to live in this madness and subject everyone around you to the chaos of your c-calamity. Find out once and for all wh-where your intention lies for the sake of everyone here. God knows for whatever reason b-both of those women seem infatuated with you."

"Hey! I'm totally obsession worthy! But that's not the point…what the hell are you talking about?"

"The feeling, of course. No d-doubt you've kissed Alma recently."

Kody briefly fell back to his uninspired attempt at a nap with Alma earlier in the afternoon.

"So now you explore the alternative. One way or another, C-charisma will be able to show you where you need to be, no?"

He looked back distrustfully at Glenn. Glenn shrugged at him.

"What? It's as I've said. If you don't c-care about her and truly love Alma, I'm sure one tiny kiss would mean nothing. A d-dedicated heart cannot be so easily swayed, can it? If anything, it should tell you exactly where you belong. And if C-charisma isn't interested, that resolves your situation just as well."

"And this has nothing to do with trying to hook up with my girlfriend, I'm sure."

Glenn leaned back, cackling as he spilled his drink. He leaned over, grabbing the chipped glass, and refilling it as he spoke.

"I'm not the one falling for every g-girl I see. Nor am I caught in this rather uncomfortable junction. Right or wrong, at least I've c-clearly made my choice. Can you say the same?"

Kody looked him over. Past the disheveled hair, Glenn's eyes were actually not brown, but a rare sort of deep dark blue with a dull sheen, as if filled with the waves of the ocean on their calmest day. His posture showed no concern or regard for anything at all. Though he might be out of his mind from time to time, Glenn seemed to be more aware than anyone else Kody had ever met. He grabbed Glenn's bottle off the counter and took a weak swig as he got up and made his way back outside. Glenn stopped him on his way out.

"Here. You never know."

"What?"

Glenn nodded, handing Kody an extra key to Cris's room. Kody's body recoiled from the scotch as he fumbled to put it in his pocket. He needed to think, quietly and alone.

He found a railing, as he was prone to do, and leaned on it. The dusty, starry, darkly clouded night sky rolled in overhead. He was always looking up, dreaming. Compositions filled his head. Head trapped in the clouds. Melodious exercises of escaping reality. That exact habit being how he ended up in this situation. If he had been more aware, if he had paid more attention to his surroundings and what went on around him, maybe he could've caught this sooner. Even if he had, what would he have done?

He remembered the first time he ever saw Alma: junior year. A clumsy girl running late for class. The strap on her backpack snapped and dropped to the ground, spilling everything out. Naturally, she tripped over herself trying to catch the few things still falling, and lay sprawled out on the floor. She scratched her knees. The fabric in the knees of her jeans tore open on impact. He felt badly for her. Of course, everyone laughed, some applauded, and she sat there embarrassed and alone. Aloofness he understood well.

He helped her up. She snubbed him, pushed him off. He wasn't detoured so easily. He tried again, and she looked him over, trying to figure out his angle. All he could do was offer her a virgin smile, and started helping her put everything back in her bag. She observed him. Maybe he wasn't as much of a jerk as he first appeared. He offered to carry her bag, and she accepted. They ended up skipping class for the rest of the day, and she dragged him off to the park instead.

It seemed like so long ago. She wasn't the same person she had been then. Yet, it was exactly her, just the same. Only she had become more…mature. In every respect. Even despite her occasionally clumsiness, she still beamed like the sun at daybreak, and contained its same inexhaustible energy. She still knew every inch of him like no one else ever could. How could this be such a difficult decision? He started heading toward the carnival.

He noticed movement out of the corner of his eye, but remained too caught up in his own stream of thought. When he realized he recognized the silhouette, he looked a bit more to his periphery to see Cris watching him, apparently deciding whether she should come up to him or avoid him.

Curiously, he watched on, though maintaining the appearance of indifference, as she walked off in the other direction. He breathed a sigh of relief. She stopped for a moment and looked back. She stopped again. He could see her talking to herself and shaking her head. She turned. His heart started its thump-thump routine against the wall of his chest as he waited. She approached. She sidled up next to him, finding a spot on the railing.

"You know, for someone so in love, you look pretty lonely. Deep thoughts?" She asked.

"Heh, you could say that."

"I just did." She stuck her tongue out, teasing him.

"Right."

"Hey, talk to me. What's up? How's Alma?"

"She's fine."

"She feeling better from earlier?"

"Yeah."

Petty conversation seemed so…petty when there were bigger issues at hand.

"O—kay then. I'm clearly interrupting, so I'll go."

She started moseying along.

"Hey, Cris…"

"Hmm?"

She turned her head, her hair flipping around with the motion of it. He could smell it faintly. Same as the scent that lingered on his jacket.

"I, um…I need to talk to you."

His breathing slowed with the tightness in his chest as his hands started to shake.

"Sure, what's up?"

She became attentive, trying to figure out what was wrong with him.

"I, uh…" he began, losing his words.

"Hey, it's me. No worries. Just relax."

Her hair dangled carelessly in front of her face. He wanted to see her, the light freckles that so softly decorated her nose; he wanted to look into her almond eyes. For something so dark, they were so very bright. He reached forward and, with his trembling hand, brushed her hair aside, behind her ear.

"Oh, hey. Um, thanks?"

He held his hand there, it slowly calming and falling comfortably into place. He brought it around to the side of her face, holding her cheek.

"Um…Kody…what're you doing?" she blushed, unsure of what was going on.

"You've got something, an eyelash."

She looked down at her cheek, trying to find it. He leaned in, looking first at her lips and then at her eyes as they met. He moved forward, meeting her lips with his own. Her eyes went wide, disbelieving. He couldn't let her go. She tasted of sweetness and liberation. The ethereal sweet fragrance of innocence he could smell from her hair, her soft simple hair. It reminded him of fresh rain in the bloom. Her supple, unbroken skin was more than he could stand. The guilt sank in, and he sunk with it. Their lips parted. Glenn was right. The feeling would tell all.

His line of sight dropped completely, rising again to look over each aspect of her body. He wanted to enjoy the sight of each curve, nook, and cranny. He wanted every piece. He wanted to devour her whole. He saw her eyes, and he knew she held no other thought but the same. Hesitation and discretion kept them apart, knowing if they came together again they wouldn't be able to part. She was the first to back away, trembling but unable to hide her glorious white teeth behind a nervously resplendent smile.

He felt like sin and wanted to cover the Earth whole. He found Adam's remorse was not for taking the apple, but for not finishing it.

"Kody, we can't…Alma…"

"Cris. Are you in love with me?"

She started to become lost in his eyes. She said nothing.

"Cris…"

"Kody, she's your girlfriend and my best friend. We can't do this!"

"Then tell me you don't want me."

She remained silent and couldn't stop herself from shaking. He stepped forward and pulled her close, their lips meeting once more. He held her up against the wall, embracing every breath and squirm of her body. He held her waist firmly, sliding his hand around her lower back as he pulled her closer. She couldn't stop. She wanted him more and more, more so than any pleasure her expanding mind could conceive. She remembered Alma's face only for a moment. She pushed him back.

"Kody."

"I know you want me. We both need this."

"I can't do it!"

"Then don't."

He reached for her again, but she slipped out from around him and ran back to her room, quickly slamming the door shut behind her. She tried to calm herself down, trying to figure out what to do as the dizziness from her rapid breaths subsided. She felt horrible and wonderful at the same time. Her mind was expanding to try and hold all of the thoughts and feeling in, but there wasn't enough space. She couldn't contain herself.

She sat on Alma's bed, trying to think of anything to help her concentrate and get her mind off what had just happened. But she couldn't. Her heart's only obsession was begging to be realized, and she was the sole gatekeeper. This was too much, even for her. She knew of only one person wise enough to guide her through. She called her sister.

"C'mon, Emmy…"

Her breathing was still shallow; the room was too hot. She wanted to run outside and pin him to the ground. She couldn't, she—

"Hello?"

"Emmy, Emmy, Emmy!"

"Cris honey, what's up?"

"I kissed Kody! I mean he kissed me!"

"What? Oh my God! My baby sister had her first kiss? Honey, that's wonderful!"

"Em, he's Alma's boyfriend!"

"Girly, I'm sorry to have to tell you this: but in the world of love that doesn't always matter."

"What?"

"We only get so many chances at happiness. I know it sounds harsh, but no one is gonna walk up and hand you love. It's kind of like war. If you see your chance to strike and don't take it, someone else will and you'll lose it forever. That a chance you're willing to take?"

"Emmy, what're you—"

She heard a key jingle in the lock as the door flew open. Kody entered, kicking it carelessly behind him. It drifted as it attempted to close. He sat down on the bed next to her, taking her for his own and closing the phone in her hand. He brought his head close and locked lips with hers, tongues fully intact. She had fought long and hard, and it had been a good campaign. But she was not an amazon. She knew when she had been defeated and raised the white flag. She wrapped her arms around him, giving herself over to her wanderlust.

If fantasy was to be hers only a moment in her life, if she was allowed to be flawed and horrible only once, she chose now; she closed her eyes to embrace the moment. They fell back. He rested on top of her, lips fully locked and unyielding. She could feel the weight of his body and welcomed it with overwrought anticipation. She could hardly breathe and would have it no other way. She held him closely, feeling the strong definition of his back through his clothes, and she wanted more. His hands were all over her body, unable to get enough. Her dreams could not be so generous. He reluctantly broke their embrace.

"Heh…" She was rendered speechless.

"So, Roberts, what's it gonna be?"

She couldn't contain herself. She couldn't stop blushing and tried to control her continually warming body. She stared at him, directly into his eyes, and wanted him in his entirety. She accepted her sin. She nodded.

She pulled him in, unwilling to be apart for a moment longer. She found her way around his back, tugging at the bottom of his shirt and pulling it off over his head. He leaned in to kiss her as he slowly worked his way down her neck. He lifted her up, pulling her shirt off as he continued his way down, planting little kisses along her chest and down to her navel. She shivered with anticipation, her chest heaving. Kody unbuttoned her pants. She instinctively raised her hips, allowing him to slide them off. She thought she heard her phone, but it was unimportant.

She quivered, nervous and anxious at the thought of Kody seeing her. She couldn't stop shaking. Kody covered her body with his own, and she could feel him. This was her perfect day. So many times she had imagined this, so many times she had wished for her chance. If ever there was something she wanted in life, it was this and nothing else. Her heart was content. She slid herself up a little to get more comfortable and found herself on Alma's Daffy Duck pillow. A small contingent of guilt found its way into her conscience. She began to tense up. He must have sensed this as he slid down along her body. The remainder of her clothing now decorated the floor.

She quaked with anticipation, letting out only the faintest of shallow gasps. His warm breath curled off her skin as his hands trailed along her thighs, gently and warmly parting them.

She thought of him, only of him. He was her definition of perfection and her sole wish. He was the only one who could touch her. And she would let him. She writhed back in ecstasy, closing her eyes as her feet arched and her toes slowly curled along the foot of the bed.

* * *

Alma walked along the sidewalk illuminated with the store signs as they were closing. She found a small bakery and snuck inside before the man running it could flip the closing sign.

"I'm sorry, *bonita*; we're closed."

"Aw…even for a sweet little girl like me?"

Alma offered up her puppy dog eyes and, as expected, became an exception to the policy. She made her way up to the counter.

"I'll be quick. Promise!" she winked. "Do you guys have any cookies? Preferably the chocolaty kind?"

"You came in this late for some cookies?"

"Hey! Don't judge." She flashed him a playfully stern look.

"I got these. That's about it."

He brought out a tray of a few relatively fresh chocolaty chip cookies.

"Ooh, those are wonderful! I'll take 'em!"

The man started bagging up the cookies as she saw a little trinket stand on the counter. She noticed some small handcrafted jewelry, mostly bracelets and earrings.

"Hey, did you make these?"

"What do I look like? Some kind of jewelry-making guy? No, I didn't make them! My daughter did. She likes this kind of stuff. Why, do you like them?"

"Yeah, they're beautiful."

"I'll tell you what. How about one for the lovely señorita?

"Seriously?"

"It's a special day around here: 'Respeto de la vida.' We recognize our hardships and those of our friends and brothers. And sisters, of course. We treat everyone as we would our own flesh and blood. Keeps us honest."

"Wow...sounds nice!"

He handed her a bracelet and the bag of cookies.

"It is. If you really like the brazalete, you should stop by the gathering grounds out behind here. They've got a bunch of crap over there, but my daughter is selling more of her jewelry, too. I'm sure she'd be glad to hear how much you like her work."

"Yeah, definitely! I will. How much for the cookies?"

"Didn't I make it clear? We're closed. Now get out of here so I can go home."

"Thanks."

She flashed a genuine smile as she made her way out the door. She skipped along the dark street, holding her bag of cookies. The bag was still lukewarm from the fresh cookies, and she enjoyed the chocolaty smell as she found her way back by following the light of the motel. She felt happy and pretty. She was all dolled up and ready to go. She couldn't wait to get back to her snuggy bear so they could go on their first official date since they got back together. She continued skipping along, singing a happy little song to herself. She thought about how terrible she had been to Cris earlier.

"Crap...I was pretty mean to her; I gotta make it up to her."

She thought about her new bracelet.

"Oh, I could totally give this to her! I mean, I know it was a gift and all, but it's about respecting hardships, right? I think making amends is about one of the hardest hardships there is. She'd love it! And maybe it's shiny enough to make her forget I called her a lying bitch!"

As she skipped, she tripped over a small rock and fell. She scratched her knee.

"Ow!"

She looked it over.

"Eh, no biggie."

She got back up and continued along, unable to wait to get back to her precious cookie fiend.

"La la la la la, la la la la la, la la la la la la laaaa...that's how we sing the Alma song, the Alma song, the Alma song; I'm gonna teach him how to sing the Alma song, alllll night looooong!"

She tra-la-la-la-la'ed through the dark streets back to the motel, smelling the corn dogs and carnival food in the air. She wanted to get there as soon as possible. The Ferris wheel sounded especially awesome. It was so romantic.

She got back to the motel and started walking slowly, not wanting to get sweaty or risk her hair falling any more out of place before she got to see her sweetie bear. She looked damn good, so at least someone that mattered had to see her. She walked along the causeway as she started to hear a commotion in one of the rooms.

"Tsk, tsk. I'm already behind the power curve."

As she made her way further along, she could hear the commotion getting louder.

"Wow...not bad. But I bet my snuggy wuggy could still do better."

She snickered as she planned to test her theory later that night, after the carnival. She heard the moaning get louder as she got closer to her room and realized that it sounded, as best she could tell, a lot like Cris.

"No way...she's finally getting some? Good for her! I never thought she'd come out of her shell here of all places...I didn't figure her the type to go for just some random guy."

Alma's womanly intuition kicked in, and she began to feel nauseous as she realized what she hoped above all else wasn't true. She walked very slowly, but directly and with purpose toward her room. She reached the door with no desire to open it. She listened, and heard Cris's moans get louder. She couldn't move, but she had to know.

She didn't even need to turn the knob; her trembling hand simply touched it, and the door arched quietly forward. It broke only a few inches, providing enough light for Alma to see Cris on her back, but not who was on top of her. She unfortunately got a glimpse of a butt she'd rather not see, and even more unfortunately recognized. She didn't need to hear what came next in order to confirm her suspicion.

"Oh, God...Kody...I love you..." was all that came from the room.

She watched on in disgusted horror, unable to look away. She watched, but saw nothing. Queasy, seething hatred pulsed and flowed through her as Cris's eyes fell upon the door, her gaze met with Cris's only for an instant. Cris turned her head and closed her eyes, living in the moment. Alma watched on only a moment longer; they were on her bed. She couldn't accept this betrayal any longer. She stormed down the breezeway to Kody's room.

"'No, Almy, it isn't what you think...,' 'Alm, I'm just worried about her because of you...,' 'Alm I swear I don't wanna get all up in her and pop that cherry!'

"Stupid lying bastard!"

She had to stop. She knelt, unable to hold it back any longer. She threw up on the edge of the sidewalk. She could manage only writhing breaths in between. She finished heaving and rinsed her mouth out with the nearby drinking fountain. She spit the water out as she reached the door. She violently kicked it, hurting her ankle. She didn't care. It creaked open as a disheveled face appeared from behind it.

"You know, kn-knocking is also an acceptable alternative."

She pushed Glenn and the door out of her way as she made her way inside. She threw the cookies against the wall as she turned around and pinned him up against the door, slamming it shut.

"A-alma, what..."

"Apparently my boyfriend—that shit bag isn't my boyfriend anymore—apparently that stupid asshole thought it'd be a funny idea to tell me he loved me while he fucked my ex-best friend. Fine. I can play that game, too!"

She spoke to no one but herself. No one else mattered. She started making out with Glenn, unable to control her own spite. She didn't feel a thing and didn't care. This was unadulterated revenge. She pushed him off.

"Tell me you love me."

"I-I love you, Alma."

"Bullshit! Say it like you mean it!"

She pushed him into the door.

"I d-do love you, Alma."

"Say it like you want me! Like you need me! Like I'm the only woman in the world for you!"

"Alma, you are m-my everything."

She ripped his shirt off, myriad scars stained the landscape of his skin. She didn't care. She grabbed his hands and felt herself up with them.

"Then screw me, goddamn it!"

She started forcing herself on him, still against the door. He held her while guiding her back toward the bed.

"P-perhaps this is a matter better saved for the bed?"

"What? This isn't good enough for you?"

"I'm simply s-suggesting that if this is what you want, I don't imagine much could happen with the door for very long. H-however, on a bed…"

"Fine, whatever!"

She pushed him off, tossing him once again into the door as she laid out on his bed, setting his laptop on the nightstand. He made his way around the bed, heading for the bathroom.

"What the hell, Glenn? I'm over here!"

"I n-need my medic-cation first."

"Ugh, whatever. Hurry up!"

She lay out on his bed, waiting impatiently as he made his way into the bathroom. She could still hear Cris's moaning, though whether it was actually her, or if it was just in her head she couldn't tell. She rolled over, staring at Glenn's laptop, getting even more impatient. She began to read.

"Laughlin, Nevada, POC information: Matier, A., phone… Blah blah blah, location project boring horseshit…identification of a Mr. Agramonte…? *Agramonte*? Cousin Lauren?"

Alma sat up, reading intently now.

"Who the fuck is Mr. Agramonte? There's no—"

She continued reading.

"Confirmed adopted surname for Jacob Grey…?"

She reread the screen with precision, memorizing it verbatim. She heard shuffling as Glenn came out of the bathroom. He had stripped himself completely as he made his way for the bed.

"Ah, are you ready th-then?"

He displayed difficulty maintaining his balance and trying not to slur, the scotch finally catching up to him.

"Jake is alive?"

"What? How d-did you—"

She tossed a pillow at him. "You son of a bitch! You knew about this and didn't tell me! This is what you were talking about earlier! This is what you tried to blackmail me with!"

She tore the lamp off the nightstand and threw it at him, narrowly missing him and shattering it against the wall. He fell to the ground in disarray.

"I'm done. I'm done with all of this. You sick lying bastards! Stay the hell away from me!"

She grabbed Kody's jacket off the bed and slammed the door as she left.

Glenn sat on the ground, unable to think or surmise anything. His elation grounded. He had finally accomplished one goal only to fail another. The alcohol distorted his already debilitated judgment. Shame, embarrassment, humiliation. Things he thought he had known, until now. He had never felt such a crushing pain as from the opposite sex. There was no solution.

He fell back. His head hit the floor, and it should've hurt. He felt nothing. His insides wretched, they struggled against him. They tried to break free from his skin. He couldn't see. He pulled himself up the counter next to him and stumbled back into the bathroom. He grabbed his pills and clutched the wall for support, barely making it back to his bed.

He toppled over, landing on the harsh mattress. He opened the bottle and fed himself the pills, unaware of how many there were or how many he could ingest. Much less caring. He needed to calm down, to remove the anxiety, and he had no other way. He gagged on some and coughed them out, the few survivors to escape his mad rampage.

He became sick, yet dizzy. He was perplexed that two such complicated and competing feelings could coexist. He felt around, lost and confused. He had a knife, didn't he? He pulled open the nightstand drawer, feeling for it and fumbling with the blade. He cut his hand grabbing it. Ah, he had found it.

He brought it back to his arm, but could no longer feel either of them. He thought he had made contact with flesh, it seemed like it. He thought he was cut. There was a river of red; he made it. The red rain.

"Crimson embers alight…," that was his favorite verse. He never liked poetry. "Fire isn't violent, it's graceful. It flows and dances in the kindling, it doesn't consume. Watch it, it flees. Trying to escape to find something better. There is no malice in its destruction, only an unfortunate byproduct of its existence." A point he was unable to discern if they shared. It fell from his hand, the knife, he thinks.

He looked up. They looked down. They saw him; they had followed him all the way here. The sneaky bastard monsters. They rode from ceiling to ceiling all the way across the country to come find him. Considerate, if not cruel. Perhaps they had become family. He was doing their work for them. The blood continued to flow. He thought it felt dumb. Life connected to condensed red water. Without it, no breath. Need air and blood. And food. And of course, water. Life so stupid.

Breath, not as much now. Not nearly as needed. Good. One less thing to worry about. Words so hard. Spinning not stopping will get sick, getting sick, got sick. Herald heaven hark ye the angels, hast thou comest for me? May angels lead me in? Just kidding. The sky he remembered was not open, was not beautifully expansive with glorious clouds of white. The demons glaring back: eager, hungry, and ready, and the strawberry blonde all faded from view. Of the utmost, he missed the furrlicious fur ball. At least the whiskers had had the guts to admit he didn't care. Blur, blur, blurry—his monsters faded from view as they encroached. He couldn't see them anymore, or was it they who lost sight of him?

* * *

Cris lay there, euphoric. There was no way she could sleep on a night like this. She rubbed Kody's sleepy head as he lay there, passed out and snoring. She needed some fresh air. She threw on her shirt and underwear, already too much, with the newfound comfort of a true beauty in her skin. For the first time she loved being naked. She slipped on some sandals and tiptoed quietly to the door, pulling it closed as she stepped outside in the briskly warm early morning summer air. Her life could get no better.

Shoved to the ground, she fell and scrapped her arm. She brushed it off as she looked up, seeing the vengeful remnants of her former best friend. Alma let loose her fury.

"Get up, bitch; it's time for round two."

"Almy—"

"Shut your mouth, slut! You don't get to call me that, ever!"

Alma grabbed Cris by her hair and pulled her up, pushing her against the railing. She went to slap Cris, but Cris grabbed her wrist.

"Alma. I don't want to fight you. And I'm so sorry it happened this way."

"Don't you tell me you're sorry! You don't even try to hide it, do you? Did you enjoy fucking my boyfriend? Was it good for you? Was he your one perfect night?"

"Yes." Cris replied, direct and honest.

Alma was taken aback.

"I can't believe you, Cris! You really are a stupid slut! You were my best friend...and you...with my boyfriend..."

"I'm not going to try and explain it to you, Alma. It's not okay: I know that. It was probably the wrong choice. It's probably the worst choice I could've made. But it was one I needed to make, and I made it."

"You're disgusting trash...and to think something as low and dirty as you ever passed judgment on me."

Cris said nothing. Alma's eyes watered..

"Do you really love him?"

"Yes."

"You make me sick."

Alma thought for a minute. She turned to walk away.

"Charisma...you stole him from me. I'll never forgive you for that. You stole my everything from me. You damn well better not waste it, you stupid cunt. Don't ever let me find out you stole my love for nothing."

Alma walked off onto the dark and lonely road.

"Alma, where're you going to go?" Cris called out after her.

"Fuck off!"

Alma flipped her the bird and kept going. Cris noticed Alma drop a jacket while doing this. A jacket she recognized well. Alma picked it up before continuing. Cris brushed herself off and leaned on the railing for a little while longer. She looked back periodically to see if maybe Alma was coming back, but she knew in her heart that she wasn't.

This was the consequence. This is what her choice had cost her: her best friend. She sniffled as a tear escaped her, but she wasn't the crying type. She wiped it away and held the rest back, keeping her game face on. She had no idea what to do; the sick pit in her stomach continued to grow. Yet, part of her was glad. Despite everything, Kody was hers. For keeps. Even if she had won in such a detestable manner. She inhaled the warm, dusty desert air. As the shaking in her body subsided, she headed back inside. She looked at the man she had given up her old life for. She couldn't allow herself to regret it.

She threw off her clothes and climbed back into bed, snuggling up to Kody. He sleepily shuffled around and wrapped his arm around her. She was safe, warm, welcomed. This was what she'd given up her friendship for. She took a deep breath, inhaling their musk. It was an essence they had created together. He was her and she was him. She had become one with him, and nothing would ever take that from her. Soon sleep came over her in the comfort of his arms.

* * *

She woke up a few hours later, still smothered by his warm and loving embrace. She smelled of sweat, stink, and so much more. She loved it. This was the first session of the next season of her life. She closed her eyes again, hoping sleep would find her so she could awaken once more, though it'd be fine if it didn't. There was no place her mind could take her that was better than here. She turned her head to watch him sleep. She loved every inch of him. She looked him over and couldn't help but want to be all over him again. She lifted her head and licked his bare chest. She kissed it, and started lovingly nibbling on it, amusing herself, completely infatuated with him. He started to stir.

"Mmm…hey, Cris? Um…what're you doing?"

"Tasting you. You're delicious, you know."

"Uh…I'm a treat now?"

"That you are." She giggled, sliding her hands along his naked body.

He looked around for a moment, compiling the situation and taking accountability of everything. He looked at her, past her, seeing the pillow on which she had rested; he realized where he was.

"Cris…where's Alma?"

"You're thinking about her at a time like this?"

Cris suddenly recalled her encounter with Alma last night. She knew she was screwed. Though not so much literally this time.

"Um…she's probably not around…"

"Why do you say that?"

"She, um…she knows."

"Shit."

Kody got out of bed and stopped to think for a minute.

"How?"

"We didn't exactly close the door the last night."

Kody tried to remember if he had actually closed the door. The whole night was kind of a blur, and any details about the door would be the last thing he paid any attention to.

"Ugh...we gotta find her and make this right."

"Yeah...but hey, um...what about us?"

He looked over at her, she now sitting up wrapped in a blanket.

"What about us?"

"You know...things are different now... you made love to me..."

"Yeah..." he half-acknowledged her.

She sat up, wide-eyed. "What is it...? Was it...was I not...good?"

"No, Cris, it's nothing like that. You were great, wonderful! I just don't like leaving things with Alma like this. If we're gonna be a thing or whatever, I have to square it with her first."

"You need her permission?"

"No, no. It's just...I can't just do that to her and then let it go, ya know? I have to at least apologize to her for hurting her like that."

"Kody, I don't think we can ever make it up to her." She paused before continuing. "But...I guess we should at least try. About us...are we together?"

"I dunno...yeah, I guess." He said off-handedly.

"Well, are you sure?" She nearly shouted.

"Yeah, sorry. I'm sure. Just a lot all at once."

He came back over to the bed, sitting down and holding her. He brushed his fingers through her hair. The feeling was right; this was the place for him.

"I love you, Konrad."

He hesitated. She sat up and looked at him. He kissed her forehead. She smiled, leaning forward to kiss him. She then broke it off and wrapped her arms around him, hugging him.

"I love you."

She repeated herself as she kissed him again and got out of bed. She picked her clothes off the floor and she pulled out some new ones from her bag to get dressed. She felt something in her back pocket and found an old hotel key card. She laughed to herself as she stuffed it back into her bag.

"What're you doing?"

"I'm going to get us breakfast!"

"Oh. 'Cause I don't like that thing you do where you get dressed."

"Me either." She scrunched her nose playfully. "Won't last long, promise."

"Good. I'll start getting packed up, make sure we're ready to go as soon as everything's straight here."

"Okay."

Cris slipped on some clothes and picked up her phone, checking it and finding that she had several missed calls from Emma as she headed outside.

"Oops."

She giggled to herself as she headed for the community building, hoping to see if maybe their breakfast was a little more continental. She shuffled on in through the crowd and found that while there had probably been a reasonably sized spread, all that was left was a tray with her precious orange juice and some blueberry muffins. She snagged two cups as she headed back to her room.

She looked around, not seeing any sign of Alma, though noticing that the van was still there. She got back to her room, but figured she'd make a quick stop to give Glenn the courtesy of a wake-up call. She made her way to his room, and found the door was cracked open.

"Glenn? Are you decent? I'm coming in."

She didn't hear a response, and figured he was still asleep. She made her way inside. She walked up to the bed but couldn't see well in the dimly lit room. She opened up the blinds and saw a small little smushed bag on the ground. As she looked around, she noticed the room in disarray. A lamp was crushed on the floor. Her eyes found their way to Glenn, lying naked on his bed.

"Did you get so drunk that you broke everything and passed out? Geez...! You're almost as bad as Emmy...so much for checking in with me! All right, time to get up, sleepy head! Got a lot of mess to start cleaning up. Not to mention getting dressed."

He was still unresponsive to her voice. She came in closer to get a good look at him. She noticed for the first time all the scars that decorated his body and couldn't tell if he was breathing.

"Oh my God...Glenn? Glenn?"

She ran up and set her orange juice on the nightstand as she tried to check for his pulse. As she shakily grabbed his wrist, her fingers became warmly moist and crusty. She looked at her hand and saw it covered in blood. She screamed and jumped back, knocking her cup to the ground. She stood there in shrill horror as the stream of orange juice seeped into the carpet and ran along the seams on its way to the ledge. It began to pool into a puddle as it rose over the edge of the doorway and flowed quietly onto the sidewalk.

35. Fallout: New Mexico

"I'll never understand how life can change so quickly. One second I'm chilling out and things are just fine, the next I can't breathe because everything just changed forever."

– Kody's Notebook

El Paso, Texas

"What happened?"

Kody splashed through the orangey puddle as he rushed in through the doorway, seeing Cris stand near Glenn's bedside in shock. She kept wiping her hand off. Kody noticed the blood smeared across her shirt.

"Cris, what happened?"

"Kody…where did you…?"

"You screamed! I was packing up the van…what happened?"

"Glenn! I think he's…"

Kody looked over, noticing Glenn for the first time. He looked at Glenn, and then the room. He approached Glenn slowly. His steps seemed so quiet; his movements automatic. He saw the dried blood on Glenn's arm and couldn't tell if he was even breathing. He tried to extend his arm, but fear forbade it from moving.

Cris looked around the room, trying to see if she could find any clues as to what happened. Other than it being trashed, she couldn't find much. As she watched Kody, Glenn's laptop made a beeping noise. She looked it over as the battery started to die. Kody worked up the nerve to get closer to Glenn.

"Kody…"

"I'm going to, Cris, I just need a minute."

"No, not that. Here."

He looked over.

"I think I know what Glenn's project was about; the thing he was working on this whole time."

"What? What is it?"

"He found Alma's brother. It looks like he's alive."

"Are you serious?"

"It's all right here. That's why he wanted to go to Nevada. But, is he…?"

"I don't know…"

Kody jumped back, startled as he heard a jingling chime. Glenn's cellphone started ringing. He picked it up, debating on whether to answer it. Cris turned around to a crowd gathering outside as the manager stepped into the room.

"Hey, we heard a scream. What're you kids doing in here?"

"What? We aren't doing anything! You need to call an ambulance, our friend is seriously hurt!"

"Hurt? He looks dead. What, you just come to take his stuff?"

"What? Of course not!"

"Well, we'll let the police sort this out. You two stay here until they get here."

"We can't just stay here with him like this? Are you kidding? He needs help! We need to get him to a hospital!" Cris shouted.

"You're gonna stay right here!" The manager was getting angry as the onlookers started to crowd around like a mob.

Sweat forming on his brow, Kody slowly made his way up to Cris, casually working his hand into hers. She looked at him, and he nodded. He slid his hand up, grabbing her wrist, and started running. They booked through the crowd and hopped the railing as they made a rush for the van. The manager started chasing after them, but his copious years of motel administration, and precious few minutes a day spent on physique management during the lunch commercial break, left him in little shape to catch them. Kody started the van and peeled out of the parking lot, heading back on the highway.

Neither of them had any words. They got a few miles down the road before Kody pulled off to the side behind a small hill to take a breather. They got out, and Kody began pacing in circles. He couldn't breathe.

"Breathe, Kody, breathe."

She started rubbing his back, but it did little good. He felt sick, but he couldn't express it. The tears wouldn't come. He sat on the ground, rocking back and forth, holding his knees. Cris took a seat next to him, calming him and holding him in her arms.

"Kody, you've got to relax."

"Cris…do you realize what just happened?"

"With Glenn…?"

"They're going to think we did it!"

"Did what? Killed him?"

"Yeah! They're going to be hunting us like fugitives!"

"I don't think so, Kody…"

"Of course they are! We were the only ones there. We found him, we didn't say anything, and we ran!"

"Then we'll go back and explain."

"No, no way! If we go back, they'll arrest us. I'm not letting them do that to you…or me."

She couldn't shake the feeling that something was missing, that she had forgotten something. She turned her attention to immediate concerns, and went back to the van to get a small bottle of water, bringing it back for Kody. He took small sips, but his stomach couldn't tolerate it.

"Kody, what we did wasn't right."

"There's nothing we can do for Glenn now." He was resolute.

"So you're saying we just leave him?"

"They said he was dead. You saw him, Cris. He looked…we can't go back. I'm not going to jail, and I'm sure as hell not letting them take you away." Kody shuddered at the thought.

"Then what, Kody? What do we do?"

Kody stopped for a moment.

"We go find Jake."

"What? Why?"

"That was what we were doing all along, right? Even if we didn't know it. And if we're looking for Alma…that's where she'll go if she knows anything about this."

"But she might not know anything, and should we really—Oh, God! Bixby!"

She finally realized what she had forgotten.

"Damn it! We forgot the cat!"

His stomach had had enough. Kody fell to the side and retched. There wasn't much, but what little he had he offered to the barren sands. He became pale as sweat continued dripping from his brow.

"It's too hot out here, Kody, and you're not looking so great. Let's get you back into the van, okay? I'll drive for a bit."

He was too weak to fight her. She helped carry him back to the van and helped him into the passenger seat as she took the helm.

"Just rest, okay?" She patted his knee. "I have an idea. Hand me Glenn's phone?"

Kody pulled it out of his pocket as he sat wearily in his seat, handing to Cris who made a call.

"Hello, 911? Our friend is seriously hurt. I think he got drunk and cut himself pretty badly. Please send someone out right away!"

Cris provided the location and then immediately hung up, not wanting to incriminate themselves or get into any more trouble.

"There…at least we did something for Glenn."

She rubbed his shoulder, Kody looking up to her with gratitude covering his face, and she got them back on the road. She followed the expressway while trying to figure out how to get to where they were going. She plugged in her mp3 player, hoping that Coheed and Cambria would help her clear her mind.

"Laughlin. It'll be a little while before the next junction."

Cris simply drove. Her mind was bogged down with so many thoughts, weighted with the confluence of events that seemed to surround her. Another challenge for her to overcome, but at least she wouldn't have to face it alone. She looked over, watching her very own cookie monster rest against the side of the door as he looked like he was contemplating a plan.

She kept flashing back to Glenn lying on his bed, naked, with his wrist covered in blood. He had looked dead, it's true, and she couldn't remember him breathing…but he was still warm. When she touched him, his wrist was warm. She hoped for the very best for her longtime benefactor and friend, and prayed that her phone call would be enough. She started wondering about their furry companion, and where he might've gone, but it was too much for her to consider all at once.

They crossed the state line into New Mexico as Cris began to take stock of the dark, stormy mountains lining the plains. She hadn't imagined that there might be mountains or storms in the desert. She even caught sight of a few trees. She wondered what else could be hiding in the desolate landscape. As she continued to drive, the transmission started to slip, though it eventually fell back into place.

Kody sat up. "This shouldn't have happened."

"What?"

"Glenn. This shouldn't have happened to him. Even if he was kind of messed up and trying to get with Alma behind my back, he shouldn't have gone down like that. Someone should've stopped it." Cris could see Kody trying to repress anger.

"You mean us?"

He looked up at her.

"We knew he was having issues Kody. We knew and we did nothing about it."

"We tried, Cris."

"Then we didn't try hard enough! We shouldn't have let this happen! We should've been there! We should've been able to help him!"

"We did help him, Cris. He got out, made some friends, and had some good times with the rest of us. And up until yesterday, he seemed to be doing fine. Maybe there is no winning with this. Whatever was wrong with him, maybe there was no fixing it. But at least we tried. At least we made things a little better for him."

"Yeah, I guess." Cris sighed, even though she couldn't fully accept Kody's theory.

"I'm glad you're here with me." Cris rested her hand on his knee.

"Hey, same here."

"Promise me you won't go anywhere."

"Where would I go?"

"Kody, we've already lost everyone else… just promise me."

"I'll be by your side until the stars collide." He couldn't help but flash her a boyishly charming smile.

"That was so lame. Dork."

They held each other's hands as Cris continued driving down the road, watching the sun slowly settle into its resting place behind the mountains. She turned on the headlights as night began to set in.

"So, what's the game plan then?"

"I know we've had a long day, but the sooner we get this behind us the better. If you're up for it, I say we drive on through the night."

"Yeah, that's fine. I don't think I could sleep anyway. I'm going to need a break soon, though. And we still don't know where we're going exactly."

"Huh, you're right. Let's fix that."

Kody had an unusual air of commanding authority as he pulled out Glenn's phone, going through the recent calls list. He found a contact that sounded strikingly familiar. He seemed to have a plan and was focused on what they both needed to accomplish. He pushed the call button, believing Glenn's contact would answer, with hopes she might be able to give them some direction as the moon ascended into dusty desert night sky.

36. Gone with the Sandy Wind

"Runnin' might not solve everything, but it works fine enough for now."

– Agramonte's Dirty Napkin

Somewhere near the Mojave Desert

The Red Hot Chili Peppers's "Californication" echoed loudly through the thin door.

Mr. Agramonte slowly cocked one eye open, trying to figure out who would be dumb enough to make noise while he was trying to sleep. He crawled out of bed, the light blanket falling off his naked body. He stumbled across the floor, leaning up against the frame of his door, fumbling around for the knob, until he finally managed to twist it open.

The bright light of the kitchen glared into his sleep-hazed eyes and irritation overtook him as he groggily continued toward the now-singing couch. He stared at it, trying to figure out what was going on until he realized where he had heard that song before.

"Lexy left her goddamn phone in the fuckin' couch? Great."

He began digging around in the couch cushions, and finally found the phone as it stopped ringing. He set it on the countertop as he turned back toward his room, stopping first to glance at the clock in the kitchen, seeing just how much more sleep he could get and how much more he would take, anyway. He placed his hand on the knob when he heard the phone's chime go off.

Still tired and irritable, he went back to find a way to turn the damned thing off. As he opened the phone, the words "New Voicemail" appeared on the screen. He investigated. He tried a few combinations but didn't have much luck accessing the voicemail. He thought back to a tattoo he had seen on Lexy's secret spot and it gave him an idea. He gave it another go. Success. He pushed play.

"Hello, Alex? My name is Kody. I'm calling on behalf of Glenn. We're on our way to meet you... we're trying to find Jake. Call me back."

"Who the fuck is Kody...? And who...wait, Glenn... Atty?"

Jake's survival instincts kicked in and he prepared to do what he did best. He rushed back into his room and pulled out a small duffel bag. He emptied out all the crap that had been sitting in it and hastily threw in some clothes as he looked around for anything else he would need.

"Guess it's time to head back south of the border. Hope Adelais ain't still mad," Jake muttered to himself as he stuffed his bag full. He went to reach for his jacket still lying on his bed when the phone rang again. He grabbed his bag and hurried back into the kitchen to see who might be calling this time. The phone displayed "Unknown." He opened one of the cabinets, taking a shot of whiskey as he waited for the next message. It popped up, and he listened. This one was completely different.

"Hello, Matier? You don't know me, but my name is Alma. I really need to talk to you, but I think it's better if we do it in person. I'm catching the next bus to where you are. If you see Jake, if he's there with you...tell him I'll be there soon."

"Alma... the hell is going on?"

Jake paused for just a moment, but he knew his course was now clear. He grabbed Lexy's phone and smashed it against the counter into several smaller pieces. He took the pieces and rearranged them until they formed the letters B-I-C-H. He chuckled to himself as he looked them over. He grabbed his bag and headed out the door, not even bothering to close it behind him.

37. Break the Sky

"Things are seldom easy. There is no gain without sacrifice. But so long as I can justify my actions to myself, I have little need for regret."
– Cris's Journal

Tempe, Arizona

Yawning, stale Splash cola unfurled from his breath as Kody continued driving. Cris slept uneasily in the seat next to him, resting more from exhaustion than any real desire to sleep. The dark, early-morning road lay covered in a light veil of sandy haze, though it did little to impede the young man on his mission. The only thing that caught his attention was the faint glimmer of light crawling along the edge of the mountainside, slowly racing the ridges, trying to break the sky. The sun rose, the day following soon thereafter. The dawning transition of light made him all the more aware he had driven through the night.

Kody scratched his nose, oblivious to the unusual silence that surrounded him. Driving along the vast expanse of Interstate 93 he moved along outside of Tempe, Arizona—moving because that's what he was doing. Moving because there was little keeping him grounded.

"Mm…hey."

Cris shuffled about, looking up at the steel-faced boy. He scarcely took notice.

"Kody?"

No response.

"He—y, Konrad!"

"Hmm?"

He glanced over, seeing Cris still adorably slouched over in her chair looking up at him with her timeless eyes.

"Oh, hey. Morning."

"Morning to you, too. What's it like where you're at?"

"What?" He was lost.

"Off in daydream land or wherever you've been? Got something on your mind?"

"Oh, just thinking."

"About what?"

Kody hesitated, not entirely aware of what might actually be on his mind. He remembered Glenn and the image of remorse that came with the thought of his presumably deceased friend. And then there was Alma. His unconscionable actions would not allow him to forgive himself for hurting her the way he did. Both of them lost because of his actions, because of he and Cris. It was hard to see her the same.

"I dunno."

"Don't play that game with me, buster. It's all over your face. Come on: talk to me."

Cris tugged on his sleeve to loosen him up and offered him her award-winning smile, expecting something in return. He did his best to fake one. Although it wasn't what she was hoping for, she accepted his effort.

"It's okay. It's kind of hard for me to talk about, too. A lot of stuff in a short period. Maybe we should take a little break to stretch our legs, get some air. How does that sound?"

"We should focus on getting there. We can sort everything out after." He kept his eyes forward, dedicated to his mission.

"Hey, look at me," she said, looking up at him.

He began to slow down and pulled the van over to the side of the abandoned two-lane highway, trying to placate her.

"I know you've got a lot on your plate. We're both hurting. But this isn't the way to make things better. We can't just charge through this and hope we'll come out fine. We need to take this slow and help each other. It's the only way we're going to make it through, okay? We're in this together."

She sat up and leaned in, placing loving lips against his cheek. She pressed them just enough for him to feel the warmth of their satiny-soft touch as she pulled them away and waited for her gypsy magic to take hold.

"You're right. You are. I'm sorry, Cris, I just—"

"Don't worry about it. Let's find a place to rest for a little bit."

"Yeah."

Kody pulled back onto the road, the heat of her kiss still fresh on his cheek. Try as he might to focus on matters otherwise, he couldn't deny the depth of her charm.

Cris, now fully awake, began to wonder if she should have chewed some gum first. She breathed into her hand, trying to catch a whiff and wondered if she had horrible morning breath; it had never been something she had a reason to concern herself with before.

The silence in the air was unsettling. Having plenty of music and finding this a more-than-appropriate opportunity, Cris dug through her bag until she found her mp3 player. She hooked it up to the radio and shuffled through her songs until she found one she really wanted to hear. She set it up and pushed play.

"Hopefully this'll cheer you up!" Cris remarked as "To Be Alone with You" began to play. Watching Kody, she saw him start to become more than a little tense and moved to her second choice, though unaware of why her first would disturb him so. Finley Quaye's "Dice" began to play and the two of them rode along quietly. Cris took Kody's hand; he jumped at her touch. She could feel his pulse through his wrist starting to slow as she held it. Their breathing slowed to match each other's rhythms. Gently breezing, the desert wind blew on.

As the van moved its hefty hustle-bustled pace down the partially cemented road, it came upon a small shanty of houses and rundown stores just outside the Phoenix city limits. Cris spotted a quaint taco stand and identified it as the ideal location for the two of them to stop and take a breather. Kody slowed down and found a small spot up the road to park the van as Cris already started unbuckling her seatbelt. The two of them got out of the van and made their way back down the road to the taco stand, Cris taking Kody's hand into her own.

Cris couldn't understand how they managed to seem so comfortable and happy; Kody couldn't seem to interest himself in the matter. Cris sent him to go find a place for them to sit and eat while she ordered the food. She walked up to a small taco stand labeled "Romero" and was aptly greeted by a large, dark man who seemed very much out of place.

"Hello, um...Romero? I'd like to order some tacos."

"It's Alejandro. Romero is the family name. We have burritos, churros, and enchiladas."

"Hmm, will two burritos be enough?"

"For you and your friend over there? Yes."

"Okay, can I get two then?"

The man nodded.

Cris stood around, waiting patiently. She noticed a large red-and-brown horse tied up on the side of one of the small houses and wondered if anyone ever actually rode him. Taking a second look, she noticed there weren't many vehicles at all and began to wonder how people survived on so little or even managed to get around. She admired their strength and questioned whether she would be able to do the same.

She watched the burrito man make his burritos and wondered about what he did when he wasn't here, doing this.

"Hey, excuse me."

"What?" he didn't bother to turn around. His abrupt manner quickly changed her mind.

"Um...I was just wondering if you knew how to get to Laughlin."

He turned, his gaze burning into her, before dismissing her and continuing to prepare their food. "Follow 93 all the way there."

"Oh, wow, have you been there?"

"Take your burritos."

Cris came back to reality and paid for the burritos. She found Kody sitting on a small brick wall that looked like it was supposed to have been built for something but was simply abandoned.

"Got you a burrito."

"Thanks."

"Yep."

She took a seat next to him as they started to eat. He watched and saw. A small woman with a sturdy frame sweeping her porch. Seemed futile, pointless. Two girls playing along the road, trying to catch bugs. They were children, but he just couldn't see them as innocent. They wouldn't always be kids. One with a small green ribbon in her hair, the other with a dirty sundress. One day they'll grow up and hurt people, maybe even each other. They might lose someone important to them.

An old man drank and conversed with other elders about the days of old. A man who knew hardship and who would know further hardship still. Kody was beginning to see that life was not as silver-lined as he once thought. But he did retain the hope that someday it could be. The grass is only greener because of all the shit that's over there... He couldn't shake the thought.

Cris began to choke on her burrito and coughed up a small piece less than gracefully, cheese covering her mouth. He couldn't help but find it endearing. In all these other people he could see heartache, deceit, betrayal. He glanced toward the taco stand and felt an ominous intensity about the burrito man. Even the burrito man. But in Cris, he could only see hope. She kept him trusting. She was his light.

Kody set his half-finished burrito down as he grazed his hand along Cris's cheesy cheek. She looked over to him, chewing on a smaller piece of burrito. "Hmm?" she managed, trying to figure out what he wanted. Kody leaned in and kissed her; she tried not to choke on the piece of burrito remaining in her mouth. He pulled back and continued eating. She managed to swallow the remains of her food.

"What was all that?"

"Burrito kiss," he said between bites.

"Burrito kiss, huh? Seems kind of gross, if you ask me."

"I didn't," he teased as he kept eating.

Cris stopped eating and watched him, waiting for her moment. He got a decent-sized bite in his mouth when she grabbed him and started macking on him hard. Kody tried his best to swallow the burrito without issue but found it to be a nearly impossible task. She pulled away and laughed at him.

"Cris! You almost killed me!"

"Aw, but I wanted another burrito kiss! It was fun! Besides, that was kind of tasty."

The two laughed, grossed out and oblivious to the scene they were making in what could barely pass for a small town. They finished eating and sat watching the people go about their day.

They started playing back and forth, nudging and poking each other and eventually laying down in the sand, surrendering themselves to the dirt for the sake of having fun. They lay back, sweating, while the sun beat down upon them. They laid, their skin baking and basting within their clothes.

Cris turned to him. "It's hot."

"Yeah it is."

"It's really hot."

"It really is."

They looked over at each other, both realizing how ridiculous they were. The heat, the sweating, the hard desert dirt against their backs: they were alive. For the first time in a while, they were free to live and relax, to enjoy the simple pleasures of life that they had earned. The desert sand started to pick up and tumbleweeds started brushing passed them. Having nearly gotten caught up in one, Cris jumped back up to her feet and pulled Kody up along with her.

"I think it's time to get back on the road."

She intertwined her arm with his as they walked back to the van. Being the more rested of the two, Cris, with her very lady-like manner, opened the passenger door for Kody and pushed him into his seat.

"Heh, and they say chivalry is dead." Kody laughed it off.

Cris smirked as she walked around to the driver's seat and got situated, setting up a new playlist before anything else. Although she had managed to lighten him up a little bit, she could tell Kody still had a lot on his mind and it would take more than a little playing around to put him at ease. She took a drink of water from her water bottle laying on the floor as she tried to figure out what she could do. She started up the van and continued down the highway.

Kody, desperate for some kind of outlet, dug around in the back of the van for his notebook. Unable to find it, he reached further back into the van until he found one of Alma's bags. He looked at it, holding the zipper in his hand but hesitant to open it. He let go of the zipper and nudged the bag back with his hand when he felt the impression of a suspiciously large object in the side. He opened the bag and found a notebook sitting just inside.

He pulled it out and opened it up, immediately recognizing it. *So that's where my missing notebook got off to.* He flipped through it, trying to find an empty page, all the while seeing Alma's various graffiti plastered along the pages. "Kody N Alm 4 Ever!" with little hearts littered along the pages.

Cris watched out of the corner of her eye. She couldn't think of any words to make what they did better. She kept her eyes on the road as the heat-blazing sun crossed its arch into the late-afternoon sky. She hoped it wouldn't be too much longer until they could finish this and put everything behind them.

Driving, however, didn't provide much of a distraction for her. A sinking apprehension grew as they drew closer to their destination. She missed the comforting purr of the dastardly fur ball. She kept one eye on the road and one eye on her boy as he took up his pen once more and continued to do what he did best.

38. Choices

"Between a rock and a hard place... sorry G, doesn't look like there's a top of the rock this time. I guess sometimes no matter which way you cut it, losing is the only option."

– Kody's Notebook

The sun passed its prime, ushering in nightfall. Cris continued driving, exhausted, but eager to finish. She caught sight of a signpost that prominently displayed "Laughlin - 20 Miles" and began to feel a small adrenaline rush as their destination drew near.

"Kody, where do we go once we get there?"

He looked up, still absorbed in his notebook but seemingly unfocused on anything. He pulled out Glenn's phone and wondered why it was on vibrate as he searched through its stored notes trying to find directions.

"C'mon, gotta be here somewhere...here! Once we get into town we're going to...follow the main road until we reach Navarre. It's right off of there."

Cris nodded to him as she hit a bump in the road and returned her attention forward. The van's shaking inadvertently knocked the phone out of Kody's hand and dropped it to floor.

"Hey!"

"Sorry."

Kody reached around for the phone but couldn't find it. He redirected his attention to his writing, trying to finish his latest endeavor before they arrived. He had tried so hard to think of something, anything to keep himself preoccupied, but only managed brief thoughts and nuances. Constantly letting his eye wander back over all of Alma's graffiti wasn't helping. His scribbles turned to doodles that meandered into a graphite mess.

They continued driving, indistinguishable music occupying the background space. The tension refused to dissipate, and only grew the closer they got to their destination. Buildings started to populate the landscape: an old bar on the left, a bright convenience store on the right. Even an old dilapidated house with a broken swing and rickety old fence, completely unashamed, lined the road. Finally, they noticed the Laughlin welcome sign and sat quietly as they waited for what would come next.

Startled, Cris jumped as she felt her pocket start vibrating. She dug into it trying to keep her eyes on the road when she recognized the ringtone. She passed the phone over to Kody.

"Oh, crap! I totally forgot about her! Hey, can you talk to her for me? I'm horrible at talking and driving. It's Emma."

He took the phone and answered it.

"Hello?"

"Finally! Hey, who's this?"

"Kody. Cris is driving."

"Ohh, the man of the hour, huh? You didn't impregnate my little sister, did you?"

"What? No! Where'd you—why would you even think that?"

Cris looked on with amused interest in her eyes as she watched Kody become flustered.

"No reason. Hey, I need to talk to you guys about something."

"What's up?"

"It's about Glenn…what happened?"

Kody's heart sank in his chest as he immediately felt the dreaded chill of fear creep along his spine. He approached the subject with caution.

"What're you talking about? Why're you asking me about him?"

"Why do you think I'm asking? I just got—"

He waited but found only silence. He looked at Cris's phone and saw nothing. He tried pressing the power button but had no luck.

"Emmy hang up on you?" Cris wanted to know what the ruckus was.

"Not so much. Your phone died."

"What? Aw, crap…I forgot to charge it."

"Yeah, well—hey, isn't that it?"

Kody pointed to the street sign that read Navarre as they came up on it. Cris slowed down and followed the short road until she reached the end at an old apartment complex. She pulled the rusty-crusty van into the parking lot and idled in a parking spot, unsure of what to do next.

"So," she said, trying to think of something.

"Ready?"

"Is it all right to say no?"

"Sure. But we're going in." Kody was prepared.

Cris laughed self-consciously as she parked the van. She sat in her seat, unsure if it was all right to move. Kody got out first and walked around, opening the door for her and taking her hand as the two made their way to the building.

They reached the first door as Kody tried to recall the right door number. They walked along the building until they reached a set of stairs, following them up until they found the door they were looking for. Kody had some trouble making it out with the diminishing light from the setting sun, but managed to accomplish the task. Their hands were sweaty and clenched tightly. Kody knocked briefly and stepped back, waiting. He let go of Cris's hand out of sheer reflex as the doorknob began to turn. They were both unpleasantly surprised.

"Who the hell are you?"

A rather unattractive redhead in her mid-to-late twenties wearing a tight dress opened the door, less than composed, and obviously irritated. She spoke with a mixed accent, a composite from indistinguishable regions. The only one even remotely discernable being closer to French than English. Kody tried to hold back his surprise.

"Hey wait…I know you."

"*Excusez-moi*? Just who are you exactly?" she asked.

"I mean I saw your picture…I'm Kody and this is Cris. You must be Alex?"

"Who I am only matters if I have a reason to care who you are."

"We're friends of Glenn. Some stuff came up and he wasn't able to make it, so he sent us in his place. You didn't get my message?"

"Ah. Would that be the same 'stuff' that got my pretty little phone all smashed to pieces?" she sighed. "In any case, come in. And I don't know you; don't call me Alex. You may call me Matier, I suppose."

She inattentively invited them in, checking to make sure no one was behind them before closing the door and scoping the two of them out.

"Where's Glenn?"

"Like I said, he wasn't able to make it." Kody was on the defensive.

"Well, I'm still getting paid, so I suppose it isn't all that important. I assume you're looking for Mr. Agramonte, yes?"

"Who?" Cris was confused.

"Jacob Grey."

"Yeah," Kody said.

"I hate to break it to you, sugar, but Mr. Agramonte has stepped out, and from the looks of it he doesn't plan on coming back any time soon."

"He's gone?"

"Unless you saw him outside. Made a mess of my phone and redecorated the counter doing it. Making an educated guess, I'd assume he's nowhere around here."

"Damn it!" Kody hit the counter, bruising his hand.

"I wouldn't cry in front of the lady if I were you. If you want to sit around and wait for him, that's up to you. I wouldn't hold my breath, though."

With that, she left. Kody and Cris looked at each other, now clearly at a loss. Kody sighed as he took a seat on the couch. He ignored the ripe smell of perfume and vodka creating an obscurely off-putting fragrance in the dingy apartment.

"What're we gonna do now?" He asked.

"What can we do?"

Cris tried to be supportive as she inspected the kitchen for anything useful, her stomach beginning to rumble. She found some bread along with a few other things and started working her novice culinary magic.

"She was supposed to be here! What was the point of all this?"

"Don't you mean *he*?" Cris remarked as she started working on some sandwiches.

"Yeah. I just…damn it."

Cris applied the peanut butter on one slice of bread with the jelly on the other, making sure the two became fast friends. She cut the crusts off and made little smiley faces with them as she brought a plate over to the couch and took a seat next to Kody.

"Made you a sammich." She smiled as she handed it to him.

"Heh, thanks."

He took it hesitantly as he began to eat more out of obligation than hunger. They enjoyed their sandwiches together as they reclined on the raggedy couch. Cris finished first and set her plate on the floor as she rested her head on his shoulder, waiting for him to finish. She sighed. At least everything was over. Kody burped as he finished his sandwich and set the plate on the floor.

She continued resting on his shoulder as he shifted around to hold her, the two of them lying quietly together on the couch in the middle of the dim living room. Cris laid her head on Kody's chest, listening to the thumpity thump of his heart as she watched the sun take its final reprieve of the day through the window. She listened as his lungs took each wisp of air and exhaled them as precious breaths, each with the solemn expectation of another. She became content as Kody started brushing her hair back and forth slowly with his hand. After a minute, he got up and wandered into the back room.

"Hey, where're you going?"

She waited, but she got no response. She sat up, keeping his spot warm. He came back shortly after with a loose, light blanket that he carefully laid on top of her. He climbed back into his spot and held her as he wrapped the blanket around her, the two of them snuggling closely together.

"Why the blanket?" she said, looking up at him curiously.

"Because you're cold."

"I never said I was—"

"You're always cold. Now hush, get some rest. We'll figure all of this out in the morning."

She smiled and lifted her head up, giving him a kiss before taking her place with her head resting on his chest once more. Kody turned on the television, catching an old rerun of *The Nightly Show* while waiting to see if Jake would come back.

"Ooh, I love this show," she whispered as she wrapped her arms around Kody, using him as a pillow. The two gazed into the solitary bright light as she began to drift off. Shortly after she began snoring, he turned the TV off.

He sat there and watched her dream, still rapt with amazement that such an amazing woman was enamored with him. He loved her cute little nose, the enduring, peaceful resolve that always seemed to enshroud her, the innocent little freckles that dotted her face. He never wanted to hurt her, in particular the way he had hurt Alma. He wanted to protect her always and ensure that she would never come to harm. He wanted to become the kind of man who would never do what he did.

He kissed her forehead as his eyes grew too heavy to maintain. He could no longer find a reason to fight it. Finally beginning to find a little solace, he let the warm wave of calmness overtake him as he closed his eyes to find repose in a secluded slumber for two.

* * *

He awoke with a start, coming out of a nondescript nightmare he could barely remember. He looked around his unfamiliar surroundings trying to figure out what was going on. He felt the weight of Cris's head resting on his chest and recalled where he was.

"Hmm, I was beginning to think you'd sleep through the night."

He turned his head to see Matier sitting in a chair, patiently waiting.

"How long have you been here?"

"Long enough. We need to talk. Come with me."

"Where?"

"I'll wait outside."

Matier stood up and walked outside. Kody started to get up before realizing he wouldn't be able to move without waking Cris. He carefully slid out from underneath her as she began to stir.

"Mm…Kody? Where're you going?"

"Shh, nowhere. Gonna move to the bedroom. It's more comfortable, okay?"

"M'kay."

Cris drowsily nodded along as Kody wrapped his arms around her and picked her up, carrying her to the bedroom still wrapped in the blanket. He carefully set her down on the bed. He laid her down next to an old leather duster jacket, and picked it up as he quietly made his way back outside the room. He threw on the jacket as he slowly walked outside, wondering if he should even bother. The bed looked far more appealing.

"What did you want to talk to me about?"

"Jacob." She was somewhat sly, but presented herself with more candor than her persona implied her capable of.

"What about him?"

"I believe I know where he went, and I want you to go find him for me."

"Forget it. I'm not playing this game. I came here for Alma, not Jake. He was just a means to an end. And neither of them are here, so I'm going home."

"Alma? The sister?" Matier's focus shifted slightly.

"You know her?"

"Not in the least. But from what Glenn spoke of, he wanted to get those two crazy kids back together again. I'm guessing if you want to find her then helping me might well help you."

"Yeah, well Glenn's dead, so whatever plans he had are long gone. And you don't know where they're at any more than I do, so what's the point?" Kody shrugged.

"Redcliffe is dead? Hmm. What a waste. He was a good resource. I should think as his friend it might be a point of interest to fulfill his last wish. And while it may be true that I don't know where Jacob is, I can tell you where he'll be."

"Wait. Stop. Why should we go any further with this? Cris and I are tired. We just want to go home."

"Glenn told me a number of fascinating things, Kody. He was a man who liked to gossip, if only when he could find a friendly ear. Like how you were dating Jacob's sister, and now suddenly you're here with someone else. Yet you're still looking for her. You've got reasons the same as I for wanting to find those two, I'm sure. And let me be clear about this matter so you don't get confused: I've only the resources to send you. Your friend will have to stay behind."

"What? There's no way I'm leaving Cris." Kody began to turn away. Matier grabbed his shoulder.

"Listen carefully. You're obsessed with that girl, Alma. It's painted all over your face with a fine-tipped brush. I've spoken to you for all of a couple minutes and I can see it. Do you really believe that that cute little pixie stick in the bedroom can't tell? Besides, provided you find them in time, it'll only be a few days. A week at the most. Hardly seems like much of a gamble, don't you think?"

"Why don't you go yourself? Seems to me like you can handle something like this just fine."

"Unfortunately, I'm under multiple contracts. By the time I'll be able to leave here he'll be long gone."

Kody watched Matier, trying to determine her angle while at the same time considering what she was saying.

"You care about that girl in there?"

"Of course."

"Do you love her?"

Kody hesitated.

"Hmph. Teenage love. Well, your everlasting devotion aside, we're running out of time. You have two choices here, Kody. You can turn your back on this and let Alma vanish from your life forever, knowing full well that you still care about her, and lose your one chance to make things right. Alternatively, you can track her down while there's still a good chance of finding her and resolve this whole situation once and for all. Then you can return home with whichever girl you choose to live out the life you've always dreamed, or whatever crap it is you kids fantasize about."

"How can you expect me to make a decision like that?"

"I don't expect you to do anything. I won't have to answer for the calls you make. I'm providing the options; whatever you choose to do with them is up to you. But you have a very small window to decide because Jacob is already on the move, and getting further away the more we banter on."

Kody took a deep breath, looking up at the city lights, and stars shrouded by dark heavy clouds. It was such a rare opportunity to see the lights of nature and the lights of man intertwined, but the place did it well.

"You're right; I will be the one who will have to explain whichever choice I make. And how could I ever justify leaving Cris behind to anyone? I won't do it."

"But you'll torment her. Your choice." Matier began to turn away.

"What?"

"I realize you're a boy, but try to keep up. Cris is a woman, and one thing every woman knows quite well is her mate. She knows you're still thinking about Alma. Have you ever considered the turmoil you inflict upon her with just a thought? The longer you wait, the more you'll regret giving up the one shot you had at squaring everything away, and you'll grow to resent Cris for it. The same girl who will grow to hate you for keeping a part of yourself from her. Your 'love' is already tainted, poisoned. Can you really live with that? Finish this now, while you still can, and come back to whatever it is you're waiting for once you're done."

"Maybe you're right," he said, conceding the simple facts, "but I'm not going to leave Cris behind."

"What more can you do for her with a divided heart? How could you ever love her always thinking of someone else? I don't have the means to send her with you, but I can assure you that I'll find a way to get her back home safely. Either way, you need to decide now. What's it going to be, Kody? Are you going let Alma simply disappear, or are you going to settle this like a man?"

He hesitated. Matier sighed, irritated, as she pulled out a cigarette and lit it up, glaring impatiently at Kody as she offered him one. He refused. She pulled her own from her lips and forced it in his mouth as she lit up another.

"Inhale deep, slowly. Then breathe it out. It'll help you relax."

Kody tried it once, coughing on the smoke before letting it go. Matier laughed as she paced slowly along the breezeway, waiting for his response.

"It's not that easy, Matier, I need a little more time."

"Don't ask for more time when you've already wasted the precious little you had. After all, aren't you the one responsible for this situation? Every person born has a number, and today, on this matter, yours is up."

He looked up at her, helpless. He couldn't let the situation go unresolved; it wasn't in him to leave things unfinished. He had to make amends, or risk living with his guilty burden forever. Besides, he wasn't a quitter.

"I'll do it. But you swear to me that Cris will be taken care of."

"You have my word."

"Fine."

"You'll be crossing into Mexico, so you'll want to travel lightly. Bring Cris's things up here and we'll get started."

"Mexico?"

"Quickly."

He hated being ordered around, but he wanted this done with as soon as possible. He ran down to the van and grabbed Cris's bags as he saw his old dress shirt from the park lying on the ground in the back. He could already feel the regret sinking in, but found the will to force it back in order to accomplish his mission.

"It'll help keep her warm… just until I get back."

He picked up his dress shirt along with everything else and hurried back upstairs. He set her things down in the living room as he searched for a pad of paper. He found one in the kitchen and scribbled down a note as he folded it and stuck it in his dress shirt pocket. He walked quietly into the bedroom and crept up to the bed, kneeling down to Cris's side. He watched; she even slept gracefully as he gently lifted her head up to place his dress shirt underneath her as a pillow. He leaned forward to kiss her forehead, a lone tear escaping his eye and sliding down his cheek, falling onto hers.

He faltered, trying to find the strength to stand back up. His legs finally cooperated, and he reluctantly rose as he headed to the door. He turned back to look at her once more, watching his seraphim slumber peacefully, ever unaware. He closed the door and left.

39. The Damage in Your Heart

"Sometimes there just aren't words for all the craziness the world throws your way. Sometimes you just gotta ride it out and wait until the storm has passed."

– Alma's Diary

Alma used the stolen jacket to keep her seat warm. Its smell made her sick. She was tired of staring out the window, seeing the same old nothing pass her by. Bush, shrub, tumbleweed, bush, cactus, shrub. She'd seen it all, more than she could count. She needed exactly one thing: to find her brother.

"For a pessimist, I'm pretty optimistic," she muttered to herself.

She yawned as she tried to stay awake, wondering if Greyhound buses intentionally moved so slow just to test the limits of human patience. This was both a concept and thought with which she was becoming reluctantly familiar. She tried to chat with people on the bus, but they couldn't divine any sort of subject that might interest her. Or rather perhaps she was simply uninterestable. In either case, she wasn't very interested.

She tried to think about what he must look like now, what sort of things he must like. What was his life like? What had he been doing all these years? He must have had a good reason for not finding her. For never coming home. Of this much she was certain. He had gone to her aunt's instead. He must have, if he was bearing the Agramonte name. Would he like her? Would they still get along? She could only hope. She was going to find her big brother.

She imagined fancies beyond her control; he would come back with her and they would rebuild their family. Her father would come home; her mother would finally get better. She could finally have her life back, have it just the way it always should have been. Or maybe she would stay out West with him. Maybe that would be better. There wasn't much left for her back East; she could start a whole new life with her brother. Did he have a girlfriend? Maybe he even had kids. She might be an aunt!

She wondered about what sort of names he had picked out for his kids. Would they be new-agey modern names or more traditional ones like the rest of the family? He probably has a dog. He always liked dogs. Never was much for cats. He was a rough and tough boy; a dog would suit him much better. He probably has a dog.

"Arriving at Flagstaff, Arizona. All passengers headed for Flagstaff please gather up all your belongings and make sure you don't leave anything on the bus," the bus driver announced overhead as the bus came to a stop.

"Just one more stop before home," she thought to herself.

Home. The word meant so little to her, and yet it was everything. She used it carelessly yet it was the most important thing in the world to her. There were a lot of places she had called home, though none ever really felt like it. But she was headed to the only person she had left, and today that made it home.

"I never called Maria...I probably should. She'd want to know," Alma debated with herself. Knowing that her brother was out there felt like her own personal secret, as if she had found the greatest unknown gold stash in all of Yuma. She was eager to keep it to herself for a while.

She tried to remember to keep a certain degree of skepticism just in case Glenn's information didn't play out, but she couldn't contain herself. She thought back to Glenn, how cruel she had been with him. She'd overreacted and handled herself poorly. She had a horrible night, but that wasn't his fault. He was the one that made everything possible. She would have to find a way to make it up to him after she found her brother. Maybe Glenn could come stay with them, too. All three of them would like that. She played housekeeper in her head, planning their perfect, happy, little family.

Even though she still felt disgusting and violated, there were things that were all right with the world. She could fix the things she didn't like about her life and forget the rest. Things weren't perfect, and she had a lot of work ahead of her, but it might just be possible that everything could be all right.

She couldn't wait to see her brother.

40. Waiting for My Real Life to Begin

"If today is the beginning of the rest of my life, if today is what I have to look forward to from now on... I'm not so sure I want a tomorrow."

– Cris's Journal

Laughlin, Nevada

Cris saw herself on a dock, gazing into the ocean. Seagulls crying out overhead, misty salt sea breeze hazing the air. Calliope music cyclically repeating for a Ferris wheel not far from the pier. Kids, with their parents, fighting over a bright red balloon that would escape and float away. And always the clouds.

Her childhood puppy's collar jingling in the distance. She couldn't see him but she knew he was there. She remembered the wet slobber of his insatiable tongue all over her face. She missed him.

The school bells rang out, and class was back in session. A class she never wanted to attend, for a lesson she desperately needed to learn. There seemed little point to homework when life was her best teacher.

Desert sands filling the ocean. Her wet feet would soon become dry, though she knew not where to find water. Her throat was parched, but she wasn't thirsty.

She heard that all-too-familiar laugh of the boy she called love.

"Kody?"

Cris woke up to the brilliant rays of sunshine that seemed to sneak into the room from all sides. She lay there for a minute, coming back to reality and taking a deep breath, before allowing the day to begin. She reached over, trying to find her comfy man-pillow, but had no luck. She looked around trying to remember where she was; she found herself minus one Kody. She sat up, trying to see if she could spot him in the living room, when she noticed she had been lying on his dress shirt. She picked it up and sniffed it, intoxicated by his scent as she held it closely. She went to set it back down as a piece of paper fell out of one of the pockets.

"What's this?"

She opened it up and read it slowly.

Cris,

I'm so sorry that I left you a note instead of a proper goodbye, but I wouldn't be able to leave your side any other way. I've already dragged you into this too much as it is, and I don't want anything worse to happen to you. I have to find Jake and Alma before it's too late. I need to settle all of this for good. I'll finish as soon as I can and come back to you, I promise. I arranged for Matier to get you home; hopefully by the time you get back I'll already be waiting. I understand if you can't forgive me, but please know I'm doing this for us, so that we can put everything behind us and move onto a brighter future.

"I was a man lost in life, with a path that could never find its way. There would be no place for me, and this way was mine alone, you see... But I had a feeling that I was not always solitary, and that near and soon I should know why.

"I found then love had happened upon me, and had just yet to announce its presence. Of course, love had no need to speak your name, when for the first time I saw you smile to me.

"In that moment, my heart knew, though my mind protested, it was only for you that it beat.

"So in this letter, I leave to you my heart, so that you know I will return to you once more. I cannot abandon my hope that once again I will hold you under the stars, and we will dream our sweet and silly dreams."

Konrad Owen Lehane

Cris's heart sank. She stared blankly at the page, rereading it as though it was a bad joke and she was missing the punch line. When her breath returned to her, she jumped out of bed and ran through the living room; she stopped as she hit the ledge of the breezeway. She scanned the parking lot for the van but couldn't find it anywhere. She slowly walked back inside, now seeing her bags near the couch, and dragged herself back into the bedroom.

She collapsed onto the bed as a welt of reserved passion burned deep in her chest. She couldn't hold back as the flood gates opened up and she burst out crying. There was nothing left. She began sobbing uncontrollably, clutching his shirt close to her heart. Her mind was blank and she wanted nothing more than for her boyfriend to come back, to be at her side, holding her closely and telling her everything would be all right like he always did. She couldn't control herself. The pain inside wouldn't stop.

"Looks like this is a bad time, but we've got to get moving if we're gonna get you back."

Matier callously walked in, possessing no empathy for Cris's plight, or much else.

"You! Are you behind this? Are you the reason he left? What did you say to him?"

"That's not really important right now. The matter is I promised to get you home and that's exactly what I intend to do. But in order for me to do so, we need to get moving."

"What the fuck is wrong with you? Get out!"

Matier sighed.

"I don't have time for this emotional teenage bullshit. There's a schedule to keep, and we need to get moving."

Cris grabbed a shoe lying near the bed and threw it at Matier, striking her hip.

"Ow! *Vous êtes une petite putain*! Fine, throw a tantrum. I'll wait outside. If you aren't out in ten minutes I'm leaving you here."

Cris reached for the other shoe as Matier slipped out of the doorway, slamming the door behind her. Cris sat back down with her head in her hands trying to figure out what to do.

"Shhh…calm down, Crissy, calm down… think. You're a smart girl. What can you do right now?"

She sat there, slowing her breathing and trying to focus enough to come up with some kind of plan...anything. She wiped her face off with her sleeve as one started coming to mind.

"Okay, Kody doesn't have a phone, but he has Glenn's phone, so I'll just call him!"

She reached in her pocket and pulled out her phone, trying to turn it on before remembering it had died the night before.

"Crap! It's okay, it's okay. This isn't a problem. Maybe there's a charger around here somewhere..."

Cris got up and recomposed herself as she headed into the living room.

"Are you ready to go?" Matier was like a hawk in her determination to get on the road as she waited by the front door.

"You're still here? I'm ready for you to go. Kinda nowish, actually."

"I made a deal with your boyfriend and—"

"I don't care what or who you've done. He's my boyfriend handling our issues. So back the hell off and leave me alone before I decide to start handling those issues on your face."

Matier scoffed.

"Listen closely, *petite fille*. I'm sure plenty of people find your attitude problem charming. Seems to me that you probably coast by on being everyone's little sweetheart, so no one's ever put you in your place. But if you think, little miss Cris—"

"Say my name again and I'll break those pretty heels off in that sad excuse of what's supposed to pass for an ass. Leave. Now."

Matier waved her hand in the air, clearly finding her efforts to be a waste of her precious time. She walked out the door, leaving it hanging open in the hot morning air. Cris found her bags in the living room, both touched and upset that Kody would leave her stuff there as she dug through them for a phone charger. She found it and plugged it in, giving her phone a minute to charge up before making the call.

She dialed Glenn's number and waited as each ring seemed to chime exponentially longer than the last. Finally, it cut to voicemail and she listened as she heard Glenn's voice request that she leave a message. She did.

"Hey...I miss you."

She stopped for a moment, feeling a small tinge of absolution at hearing Glenn's voice again. She took a minute to think about her old friend.

As she sat there, still holding onto Kody's shirt and fingering her necklace, her voicemail went off. She dialed it frantically hoping it was Kody and waited for the message to play.

"Cris, sweetie?" She held mixed feelings as she heard her sister's voice.

"Look, I don't know what's going on, but you need to call me back ASAP. I love you."

Without possessing any clear thoughts, she pressed her sister's number on speed dial and waited for it to ring. She listened to the ring once again, hearing each one last forever, though she suspected they were only a few seconds apart.

"Cris?"

"Em, hey…"

"Cris, honey, where are you. What's going on?"

Hearing the comfort of her sister's voice brought back the flood of emotions and she couldn't stop from gushing again.

"Em, I'm stuck in Nevada. Alma's gone and Kody was taken away from me."

"He was taken away from you? Like kidnapped?"

"Ugh, I don't even know…what do I do, Em?"

"Where in Nevada are you?"

"Um…Laughlin, I think?"

"Will you be there for the next few hours?"

"Yeah, I don't know—"

"Hey, stay there. I'm gonna come get you. I'm actually not that far."

"What do you mean you're not that—"

"Just hang tight Crissy. I'll be there as soon as I can, and I'll explain everything. Promise."

"All right, Em…thanks. I love you."

She started sobbing after saying the words she wished she could say to him. The first time she received them from him was the last time she saw him. She had heard how rough it could be to be heartbroken, but she couldn't understand it until now.

"I'm on my way, sis. Love you."

Emma hung up the phone and Cris sat there, staring at her phone screen as it started to charge. She tried Glenn's number again, but this time the phone cut straight to voicemail.

"…and his phone is dead…"

She drew the parallel, not intending to use that word regarding anything of Glenn's. She sat down on the couch, staring at the turned-off television. She stared into it and could marginally see her own reflection, though it didn't look like her at all. For the first time, she didn't recognize the sight of her own face. But she didn't care.

She received a text message from Emma asking her the address; she responded and fell over on the couch, laying there, waiting. She heard birds chirping and idle conversations of people passing by outside. A few people peeked into the apartment to see why a door had been just left open, but she had absolutely no concern for their presence.

She gazed into various different directions, but she couldn't tell which was which and didn't even try to pay attention. She cried infrequently, unsure of whether she was actually doing it, and lay there waiting for something to happen. She passed more than half the day in a fugue state.

* * *

Cris stared at the walls. The longer she looked at them the sicker she became. She couldn't stand them anymore. The apartment was starting to drive her crazy. She needed to get out.

She got up and made her way to the bathroom, cleaning herself up as much as she could. She was inconsolable and nothing she could do would help, but she tried. She walked over to the bed and picked up the note, stuffing it in Kody's shirt pocket as she picked the shirt up and put it on. She wandered out of the apartment and down the causeway, finding her way to the street.

She walked around aimlessly, experiencing true desert heat for the first time. She kicked rocks around as she scuffed the bottoms of her shoes along the sand-soaked sidewalk. She kept her head low, trying to avoid eye contact with anyone, and drifted along the streets with no thoughts in her mind or plans to speak of. She moved along, but she was empty.

She walked into a corner shop and looked at some snacks, but she couldn't really tell if she was hungry. She didn't think she was, though she figured she ought to be by now. But she didn't think she was. She meandered out just as aimlessly and walked along.

She tried to remember how she got here. Interstate to freeway, expressway to service road. Literal answer to a literal question. It was only about a week ago that she and her best friend were goofing around in class with the cute but awkward poet boy, cracking smiles and coy glances. Fighting legendary pasta bowls and rocking out to amateur bands seemed like it was so far behind her. Now she had become obsessed with love, and lost everything she cared about because of it.

Despite that, she had now found that it was love that was the only thing she had ever cared about; gaining it had enabled her to lose it. But it wasn't entirely lost. He wasn't gone for good. He said he loved her; he promised to return to her. So she'd go to him. And if he was unable to find her, then she would find him. After all, isn't that what lovers do?

She stumbled over a rock in front of an apparently defunct bus station. Looking through the fence, she was surprised to see a Greyhound bus leaving the station. The place didn't look like it was even capable of supporting business. She couldn't help but wonder what riding one of those buses was like. She watched as the people departed, trying to see what kinds of people had arrived, and what reasons they must have for coming to a place like this.

She saw a little kid with a backpack much too large for him run up to his mother, a soldier moving out for some unknown mission, a somewhat tanned blonde girl embracing a rugged cowboy wannabe, even small dogs being carried out in crates. She was curious about what sort of glamour filled the lives these people led. She continued down the road.

She quickly turned back around to try to see through the crowd. She stood on her toes, but the fence and dispersing people were not in any way trying to assist her. She looked for the strawberry blonde but couldn't find her. She started trying to find a way around the fence to get to the other side of the road as the sun began setting once again. Her phone went off. She answered.

"Hello?"

"Cris?"

"Oh, hey, Em. Hold on a sec…!"

The crowd finally thinned but there was no sign of her ex-best friend anywhere. She looked around for the van, hoping maybe Kody was nearby, but it became apparent that the area was as vacant as the rest of the town.

"Damn…"

"What? Is this a bad time?"

"No, I just thought I—never mind. Are you here?"

"Yeah, just found the place. Where are you?"

"Doesn't matter. I'll be there soon, okay?"

"Will do, see ya soon, little sis. Love ya."

"Bye."

Cris started making her way back to the apartment, jogging to make time. She hadn't realized how long she had been walking or how far away she was, but the running helped her clear her head. She couldn't be certain it was Alma, but that girl had looked very much like her. Even if it had been, she wouldn't know what to say. She doubted Alma would forgive her and, even so, she wasn't sorry. *But if Alma's here then where is Kody?* She thought. She ran faster.

After a good long jog, she finally arrived back at the apartment as night began to set in. Her sister popped up off the couch and welcomed her back with open arms. Cris's mind was elsewhere.

"Is he here?"

"Who? Kody?"

"Yeah! Is he?"

"No, sorry sis. No one but me."

The disappointment in Cris's voice was crushing. Emma pulled her closer and gave her sister a bear hug.

"Hey, don't worry about it. Grab up your things and we'll get some dinner on the way back, okay? You can tell me all about everything, and then we'll see about finding that runaway boyfriend of yours. He is your boyfriend, right?"

"Yup."

"And so does that mean...?" Emma looked at Cris with eager eyes.

"Huh?" She looked up, confused.

"Oh, don't give me that innocent look! I'm not Dad! And judging by the way you're all up in knots about a kid you've known for, like, a week, I'd say someone's lost her V-card."

"Emma!" She couldn't stop blushing.

"Are you serious? I was just kidding! Oh, I'm gonna find that little punk! Nobody messes around with my little sister and just disappears on her!"

"Em..."

"One thing at a time. Let's get you home, and we'll go from there."

Emma helped her sister grab up her bags as they headed down to the rental sports car waiting in the parking lot. Cris looked at the car, and then at Emma

"Em, really? How're you going to explain this one to Dad?"

"I'm not. I'd be surprised if he even notices the bills anymore, and I really don't care if he does."

They both loaded up the car and hopped in, getting back on the road and heading home.

"Emma, thanks. I don't know what I would've done if you weren't here for me."

"Hey, I'm just happy I finally get to be the big sister for once. I was getting a little tired of always being the one calling you to come bail me out at the last minute."

"Yeah…"

Cris sat back in her seat, gazing out the window trying to figure out what was going on. Her sister had arrived with a plan, but Cris was still uneasy. Though she had little reason to believe it, she hoped maybe Kody had somehow resolved everything and was already heading home. *He has to be,* she thought. She couldn't accept anything else. She needed to see him again.

Cris looked up, trying to be optimistic. It was at this point she finally realized Emma had driven to pick her up, as her fatigue showed. And she was unusually quiet. Something didn't add up.

"Hey, Em? How—" Cris suddenly felt a sharp pain in her ankle. "Ow! What—"

"Meeerow."

The feline prince clawed his way up her leg and back into her lap, upset that his regal presence wasn't acknowledged sooner.

"Bixby? Em, what's going on?"

Emma sighed as she looked over to her sister. Exhaustion, frustration, and a number of things beside became evident in her expression as she placed a hand on her sister's knee.

"Okay brat. No more putting this off—we need to talk about Glenn."

Damn… it's been a long time since I've thought about any of that stuff. Makes me all sorts of nostalgic. There's more to the story, of course, but that's about as much as I care to tell for now.

It's a little personal for me, ya know? Don't like to ruminate all at once. But I promise this is far from over. Hell, personally I think the best is yet to come. Well, guess that depends on what you define as best. But I'm wiped, so I gotta call it for now.

…Aw, hell, it'd be kinda cold for me to leave you with nothing. All right, all right…I'll give just a little somethin' about what's comin' up next, 'cause after all, every good performer oughta know a thing or two about encores and fan service.

Our fun group of ragtag misfits got a lot coming up ahead of them. The Alm'ster, for example, really should've gotten around to calling her mother. Could've gotten a heads up on an issue before it was way too late. Kod man? Well, let's just say he ain't waitin' at home for his lady lovely. And of course, our heroine of the hour? Well, she's got a long, messy road ahead, although I guess she really don't have anyone to blame but herself. And of course, yours truly still has plenty more to come.

Until then.

www.ingramcontent.com/pod-product-compliance
Lightning Source LLC
Chambersburg PA
CBHW020322180626
46812CB00001B/14